O9-ABF-466

Born in the Kingdom of Fife in 1960, Ian Rankin graduated from the University of Edinburgh in 1982, and then spent three years writing novels when he was supposed to be working towards a PhD in Scottish Literature. His first Rebus novel, *Knots & Crosses*, was published in 1987, and the Rebus books are now translated into over thirty languages and are bestsellers worldwide.

Ian Rankin has been elected a Hawthornden Fellow, and is also a past winner of the Chandler-Fulbright Award. He is the recipient of four Crime Writers' Association Dagger Awards including the prestigious Diamond Dagger in 2005 and in 2009 was inducted into the CWA Hall of Fame. In 2004, Ian won America's celebrated Edgar award for *Resurrection Men*. He has also been shortlisted for the Anthony Awards in the USA, and won Denmark's *Palle Rosenkrantz* Prize, the French *Grand Prix du Roman Noir* and the *Deutscher Krimipreis*. Ian Rankin is also the recipient of honorary degrees from the universities of Abertay, St Andrews, Edinburgh, Hull and the Open University.

A contributor to BBC2's *Newsnight Review*, he also presented his own TV series, *Ian Rankin's Evil Thoughts*. He has received the OBE for services to literature, opting to receive the prize in his home city of Edinburgh. He has also recently been appointed to the rank of Deputy Lieutenant of Edinburgh, where he lives with his partner and two sons. Visit his website at www.ianrankin.net.

By Ian Rankin

All Ian Rankin's titles are available on audio.
Also available: *Jackie Leven Said* by Ian Rankin and Jackie Leven.

Ian Rankin

Strip Jack

An Orion paperback

First published in Great Britain in 1992
by Orion
This paperback edition published in 1993
by Orion Books Ltd,
Orion House, 5 Upper St Martin's Lane,
London WC2H 9EA

An Hachette UK company

27 29 30 28 26

Reissued 2008

A CIP catalogue record for this book is available
from the British Library.

ISBN 978-0-7528-8356-4

Printed and bound in Great Britain by Clays Ltd, St Ives plc

The Orion Publishing Group's policy is to use papers that
are natural, renewable and recyclable products and
made from wood grown in sustainable forests. The logging
and manufacturing processes are expected to conform to
the environmental regulations of the country of origin.

www.orionbooks.co.uk

To the only Jack I've ever stripped

He knows nothing; and he thinks he knows everything. That points clearly to a political career.

Shaw, *Major Barbara*

The habit of friendship is matured by constant intercourse.

Libianus, 4th century AD, quoted in *Edinburgh*, by Charles McKean

Acknowledgements

The first thing to acknowledge is that the constituency of North and South Esk is the author's creation. However, you don't need to be Mungo Park to work out that there must be some correlation between North and South Esk and the real world, Edinburgh being a real place, and 'south and east of Edinburgh' being a vaguely definable geographical area.

In fact, North and South Esk bears *some* resemblance to the Midlothian parliamentary constituency – prior to 1983's Boundary Commission changes – but also bites a small southernmost chunk out of the present Edinburgh Pentlands constituency and a westerly chunk out of East Lothian constituency.

Gregor Jack, too, is fiction, and bears no resemblance to any MP.

Thanks are due to the following for their inestimable help: Alex Eadie, who was until his retirement the MP for Midlothian; John Home Robertson MP; Professor Busuttil, Regius Professor of Forensic Medicine, University of Edinburgh; Lothian and Borders Police; City of Edinburgh Police; the staff of the Edinburgh Room, Edinburgh Central Library; the staff of the National Library of Scotland; staff and customers of Sandy Bell's, the Oxford Bar, Mather's (West End), Clark's Bar and the Green Tree.

Contents

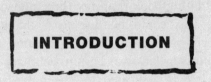

INTRODUCTION

Strip Jack was the first of the Rebus novels to be written entirely in the rundown French farmhouse which I'd moved to with my wife in 1990. Our first couple of years there, we put most of our effort into doing the place up: rewiring, putting up ceilings, and trying to cultivate the acre of brambled wilderness around us. The attic became my office. It was accessed by a rickety wooden ladder and a trapdoor. The floor was so badly warped that any pens placed on the desk would roll off with frightening speed. The decor consisted of bus maps of central Edinburgh, postcards of the city's monuments, and a list of police regions in Scotland.

Yet little of our French idyll seeped into the book. Quite the opposite: it's one of my most Scottish works, perhaps in reaction to the previous novel's London setting. Words such as 'brae', 'keech', 'birl', and 'haar' creep in. Whisky is referred to as 'the cratur', while 'ba-heid' is used as a term of insult. Many of the words, such as 'shoogly' and 'peching', were favourites of my father: it's possible I was thinking of him as I wrote. This was my first book since his funeral in 1990. Certainly, he was the only person I'd ever heard say, 'If shit was gold, ye'd have a tyke at yer erse,' words I would now give to Rebus's own father.

To reinforce the book's Scottishness, I suggested its original jacket design – a lion rampant flying cheekily from the Houses of Parliament. But as well as being very Scottish in its language, *Strip Jack* also seems to me a less savage and biting book than my three previous efforts in the series. This could be due to a change in family circumstances. My wife Miranda became pregnant in 1991, and our son Jack was born in February 1992. This is why *Strip Jack* is dedicated to 'the only Jack I've ever stripped' – something which now makes my teenage son cringe, of course.

The title came from a compendium of card games. I'd been looking for something which would reflect the playfulness of *Knots & Crosses* and *Hide & Seek*, and had compiled lists of children's and adults' games and pastimes. The card game 'Strip Jack Naked' appealed to me: I could give my chief suspect in the book the surname Jack. It seemed, after all, that someone was out to strip him of his standing, his good name – maybe even his life. The three-word title seemed clumsy, however, so I shortened it to two.

Curiously, it was only in leaving Scotland that I began really to become interested in my native country's history and politics. I started to devour books on these subjects, and would return to Edinburgh three or four times a year, usually begging a bed or sofa at a friend's place. I would take long walks around the city, using up rolls of film in my cheap camera, and spending hours in the various libraries. Now that I was a full-time writer, I felt a fresh obligation to get the details right. For *Strip Jack*, I wrote to the University of Edinburgh's Pathology Department, and was granted a meeting with Professor Anthony Busuttil. He became responsible for much of the forensic detail in the book (and in others in the series). When Dr Curt speaks of 'diatoms' and 'washerwoman's skin', it is really Professor Busuttil talking. That first meeting was memorable in that the Professor momentarily mistook me for a police officer and began discussing the case of a slashed throat. As he started to bring out the autopsy photos, my greying face told him he'd made a mistake . . .

Living and working so far from Edinburgh, I fell back on personal history and reminiscence for much of Rebus's inner life. When he recalls picnics and holiday destinations, they are my experiences rather than his. The MP Gregor Jack, however, comes from nowhere other than my imagination. I based him on no one I knew. His circle of friends, though, is another matter. I had made close friends in high school, and not many since. The story of how 'Suey' got his nickname comes from a real-life event which occurred during a school trip to Germany when I was sixteen. And the 'dyslexic bigotry' of 'Remember 1960' appeared on a friend's tenement stairwell in Easter Road.

Rebus also takes on some of my own characteristics. On one trip to Edinburgh, I'd consulted a doctor about the panic attacks I'd been suffering. Rather than medication, he'd prescribed self-hypnosis and relaxation techniques. In giving my problems to Rebus, I was using my writing as a form of therapy. Just as I had taken him to London in *Tooth & Nail*, so that he could dislike the place on my behalf, so I dumped my health problems on him too. However, I also did him the favour of placing him in a relationship with Dr Patience Aitken, who had a flat in Oxford Terrace next door to one of my high-school friends. (He would pop up in the book, actually, in the scene in the Horsehair Bar.) Patience would provide Rebus with some much-needed emotional stability . . . at least for a few books.

Reading the novel now, it seems to me that *Strip Jack* is partly a story of friendship, of ties formed at school and never loosed. But it's also another of my explorations of the theme of Scotland's Jekyll and Hyde character: people hide their true selves behind a veneer of respectability. By the end, the villain of the piece has been reduced to something ape-like, bringing to mind descriptions of Mr Hyde in Stevenson's story.

Up until the final moments of *Strip Jack*, Rebus had been based in a fictitious police station on a fictitious street. However, now that I was a full-time author, earning a living by writing about real professions, I felt I owed it to the real-life practitioners to make my books as authentic as possible. I would take Rebus out of my made-up Edinburgh and into the real one: he would work in a real cop-shop and drink in real bars.

My long apprenticeship was nearing its end.

April 2005

1
The Milking Shed

The wonder of it was that the neighbours hadn't complained, hadn't even – as many of them later told the newsmen – realized. Not until that night, the night their sleep was disturbed by sudden activity in the street. Cars, vans, policemen, the static chatter of radios. Not that the noise ever got out of hand. The whole operation was directed with such speed and, yes, even good humour that there were those who slept through the excitement.

'I want courtesy,' Chief Superintendent 'Farmer' Watson had explained to his men in the briefing room that evening. 'It may be a hoor-hoose, but it's on the right side of town, if you take my meaning. No telling who might be in there. We might even come across our own dear Chief Constable.'

Watson grinned, to let them know he was joking. But some of the officers in the room, knowing the CC better than Watson himself apparently did, exchanged glances and wry smiles.

'Right,' said Watson, 'let's go through the plan of attack one more time . . .'

Christ, he's loving this, thought Detective Inspector John Rebus. He's loving every minute. And why not? This was Watson's baby after all, and it was to be a home birth. Which was to say, Watson was going to be in charge all the way from immaculate conception to immaculate delivery.

Maybe it was a male menopause thing, this need to flex a bit of muscle. Most of the chief supers Rebus had known in his twenty years on the force had been content to push pens over paper and wait for retirement day. But not Watson. Watson was like Channel Four: full of independent programmes of minority interest. He didn't make waves exactly, but by Christ he splashed like hell.

And now he even seemed to have an informer, an invisible somebody who had whispered in his ear the word 'brothel'. Sin and debauchery! Watson's hard Presbyterian heart had been stirred to righteous indignation. He was the kind of Highland Christian who found sex within marriage just about acceptable – his son and daughter were proof – but who baulked at anything and everything else. If there was an active brothel in Edinburgh, Watson wanted it shut down with prejudice.

But then the informer had provided an address, and this caused a certain hesitation. The brothel was in one of the better streets of the New Town, quiet Georgian terraces, lined with trees and Saabs and Volvos, the houses filled with professional people: lawyers, surgeons, university professors. This was no seaman's bawdy-house, no series of damp, dark rooms above a dockside pub. This was, as Rebus himself had offered, an Establishment establishment. Watson hadn't seen the joke.

Watch had been kept for several days and nights, courtesy of unmarked cars and unremarkable plainclothes men. Until there could be little doubt: whatever was happening inside the shuttered rooms, it was happening after midnight and it was happening briskly. Interestingly, few of the many men arrived by car. But a watchful detective constable, taking a leak in the dead of night, discovered why. The men were parking their cars in side streets and walking the hundred yards or so to the front door of the four-storey house. Perhaps this was house policy: the slamming of after-hours car doors would arouse suspicion in the street. Or perhaps it was in the visitors' own interests not to leave their cars in broad street-light, where they might be recognized . . .

Registration numbers were taken and checked, as were photographs of visitors to the house. The owner of the house itself was traced. He owned half a French vineyard as well as several properties in Edinburgh, and lived in Bordeaux the year through. His solicitor had been responsible for letting the house to a Mrs Croft, a very genteel lady in her fifties. According to the solicitor, she paid her rent promptly and in cash. Was there any problem . . . ?

No problem, he was assured, but if he could keep the conversation to himself . . .

Meantime, the car owners had turned out to be business-men, some local, but the majority visiting the city from south of the border. Heartened by this, Watson had started planning the raid. With his usual blend of wit and acumen, he chose to call it Operation Creeper.

'Brothel creepers, you see, John.'

'Yes sir,' Rebus answered. 'I used to own a pair myself. I've often wondered how they got the name.'

Watson shrugged. He was not a man to be sidetracked. 'Never mind the creepers,' he said. 'Let's just get the creeps.'

The house, it was reckoned, would be doing good business by midnight. One o'clock Saturday morning was chosen as the time of the raid. The warrants were ready. Every man in the team knew his place. And the solicitor had even come up with plans of the house, which had been memorized by the officers.

'It's a bloody warren,' Watson had said.

'No problem, sir, so long as we've got enough ferrets.'

In truth, Rebus wasn't looking forward to this evening's work. Brothels might be illegal, but they fulfilled a need and if they veered towards respectability, as this one certainly did, then what was the problem? He could see some of this doubt reflected in Watson's eyes. But Watson had been enthusiastic from the first, and to pull back now was unthinkable, would seem a sign of weakness. So, with nobody really keen for it, Operation Creeper went ahead. While other, meaner streets went unpatrolled. While domestic violence took its toll. While the Water of Leith drowning still remained to be solved . . .

'Okay, in we go.'

They left their cars and vans and marched towards the

front door. Knocked quietly. The door was opened from within, and then things began to move like a video on double-speed. Other doors were opened ... how many doors could a house have? Knock first, then open. Yes, they were being courteous.

'If you wouldn't mind getting dressed, please ...'

'If you could just come downstairs now ...'

'You can put your trousers on first, sir, if you like ...'

Then: 'Christ, sir, come and take a look at this.' Rebus followed the flushed, youthful face of the detective constable. 'Here we are, sir. Feast your peepers on this lot.'

Ah yes, the punishment room. Chains and thongs and whips. A couple of full-length mirrors, a wardrobe full of gear.

'There's more leather here than in a bloody milking shed.'

'You seem to know a lot about cows, son,' Rebus said. He was just thankful the room wasn't in use. But there were more surprises to come.

In parts, the house resembled nothing more lewd than a fancy-dress party – nurses and matrons, wimples and high heels. Except that most of the costumes revealed more than they hid. One young woman seemed to be wearing a rubber diving suit with the nipples and crotch cut away. Another looked like a cross between Heidi and Eva Braun. Watson watched the parade, righteous fury filling him. He had no doubts now: it was absolutely proper that this sort of place be closed down. Then he turned back to the conversation he was having with Mrs Croft, while Chief Inspector Lauderdale lingered only a short distance away. He had insisted on coming along, knowing his superior and fearing some almighty cock-up. Well, thought Rebus with a smile, no cock-ups in sight yet.

Mrs Croft spoke in a kind of gentrified Cockney, which became less gentrified as time went on and more couples spilled down the stairs and into the large, sofa-crammed living room. A room smelling of expensive perfume and proprietary whisky. Mrs Croft was denying everything. She was even denying that they were standing in a brothel at all.

4

I am not my brothel's keeper, thought Rebus. All the same, he had to admire her performance. She was a business-woman, she kept saying, a taxpayer, she had rights . . . and where was her solicitor?

'I thought it was her that was doing the soliciting,' Lauderdale muttered to Rebus: a rare moment of humour from one of the dourest buggers Rebus had ever worked with. And as such, it deserved a smile.

'What are you grinning at? I didn't know there was an interval. Get back to work.'

'Yes, sir.' Rebus waited till Lauderdale had turned away from him, the better to hear what Watson was saying, and then flicked a quick v-sign at him. Mrs Croft, though, caught the gesture and, perhaps thinking it intended at her, returned it. Lauderdale and Watson both turned towards where Rebus was standing, but by then he was already on his way . . .

Officers who had been posted in the back garden now marched a few pale-faced souls back into the house. One man had leapt from a first-floor window, and was hobbling as a result. But he was insistent, too, that no doctor was necess-ary, that no ambulance be called. The women seemed to find the whole thing amusing, and appeared especially taken by the looks on their clients' faces, looks ranging from the ashamed and embarrassed to the furious and embarrassed. There was some short-lived bravado of the I-know-my-rights variety. But in the main, everybody did as they were told: that is, they shut up and tried to be patient.

Some of the shame and embarrassment started to lift when one of the men recalled that it wasn't illegal to visit a brothel; it was only illegal to run one or work in one. And this was true, though it didn't mean the men present were going to escape into the anonymous night. Give them a scare first, then send them away. Starve the brothels of clients, and you'd have no brothels. That was the logic. So the officers were prepared with their usual stories, the ones they used with kerb-crawlers and the like.

'Just a quiet word, sir, between you and me, like. If I were you, I'd have myself checked over for AIDS. I'm serious. Most of these women could well be carrying the disease, even if it doesn't show. Mostly, it doesn't show till it's too late anyway. Are you married, sir? Any girlfriends? Best tell them to have a test, too. Otherwise, you never know, do you . . .?'

It was cruel stuff, but necessary; and as with most cruel words, there was a truth to it. Mrs Croft seemed to use a small back room as an office. A cash-box was found. So was a credit-card machine. A receipt-book was headed Crofter Guest House. As far as Rebus could tell, the cost of a single room was seventy-five pounds. Dear for a B&B, but how many company accountants would take the trouble to check? It wouldn't surprise Rebus if the place was VAT registered to boot . . .

'Sir?' It was Detective Sergeant Brian Holmes, newly promoted and bristling with efficiency. He was halfway up one of the flights of stairs, and calling down to Rebus. 'I think you better come up here . . .'

Rebus wasn't keen. Holmes looked to be a long way up, and Rebus, who lived on the second floor of a tenement, had a natural antipathy to stairs. Edinburgh, of course, was full of them, just as it was full of hills, biting winds, and people who liked to girn about things like hills and stairs and the wind . . .

'Coming.'

Outside a bedroom door, a detective constable stood in quiet discussion with Holmes. When Holmes saw Rebus reaching the landing, he dismissed the DC.

'Well, Sergeant?'

'Take a look, sir.'

'Anything you want to tell me first?'

Holmes shook his head. 'You've seen the male member before, sir, haven't you?'

Rebus opened the bedroom door. What was he expecting to find? A mock-up dungeon, with someone stretched out naked on the rack? A farmyard scene with a few chickens and sheep? The male member. Maybe Mrs Croft had a collection of them displayed on her bedroom wall. *And here's*

*one I caught in '73. Put up a tough fight, but I had it in the
end . . .*

But no, it was worse than that. Much worse. It was an
ordinary bedroom, albeit with red lightbulbs in its several
lamps. And in an ordinary bed lay an ordinary enough
looking woman, her elbow pressed into the pillow, head
resting at an angle on her clenched fist. And on that bed,
dressed and staring at the floor, sat someone Rebus recognized: the Member of Parliament for North and South Esk.

'Jesus Christ,' said Rebus. Holmes put his head round the
door.

'I can't work in front of a fucking audience!' yelled the
woman. Her accent, Rebus noted, was English. Holmes
ignored her.

'This is a bit of a coincidence,' he said to Gregor Jack MP.
'Only, my girlfriend and me have just moved into your
constituency.'

The MP raised his eyes more in sorrow than in anger.

'This is a mistake,' he said. 'A terrible mistake.'

'Just doing a bit of canvassing, eh, sir?'

The woman had begun to laugh, head still resting on her
hand. The red lamplight seemed to fill her gaping mouth.
Gregor Jack looked for a moment as though he might be
about to throw a punch in her general direction. Instead he
tried a slap with his open hand, but succeeded only in
catching her arm, so that her head fell back on to the pillow.
She was still laughing, almost girl-like. She lifted her legs
high into the air, the bedcovers falling away. Her hands
thumped the mattress with glee. Jack had risen to his feet and
was scratching nervously at one finger.

'Jesus Christ,' Rebus said again. Then: 'Come on, let's get
you downstairs.'

Not the Farmer. The Farmer might go to pieces. Lauderdale
then. Rebus approached with as much humility as he could
muster.

'Sir, we've got a bit of a problem.'

'I know. It must have been that bugger Watson. Wanted

his moment of glory captured. He's always been keen on publicity, you should know that.' Was that a sneer on Lauderdale's face? With his gaunt figure and bloodless face, he reminded Rebus of a painting he'd once seen of some Calvinists or Seceders ... some grim bunch like that. Ready to burn anyone who came to hand. Rebus kept his distance, all the time shaking his head.

'I'm not sure I – '

'The bloody papers are here,' hissed Lauderdale. 'Quick off the mark, eh? Even for our friends in the press. Bloody Watson must have tipped them off. He's out there now. I tried to stop him.'

Rebus went to one of the windows and peeped out. Sure enough, there were three or four reporters gathered at the bottom of the steps up to the front door. Watson had finished his spiel and was answering a couple of questions, at the same time retreating slowly back up the steps.

'Oh dear,' Rebus said, admiring his own sense of understatement. 'That only makes it worse.'

'Makes what worse?'

So Rebus told him. And was rewarded with the biggest smile he'd ever seen flit across Lauderdale's face.

'Well, well, who's been a naughty boy then? But I still don't see the problem.'

Rebus shrugged. 'Well, sir, it's just that it doesn't do anyone any good.' Outside, the vans were arriving. Two to take the women to the station, two to take the men. The men would be asked a few questions, names and addresses taken, then released. The women ... well, that was another thing entirely. There would be charges. Rebus's colleague Gill Templer would call it another sign of the phallocentric society, something like that. She'd never been the same since she'd got her hands on those psychology books ...

'Nonsense,' Lauderdale was saying. 'He's only got himself to blame. What do you want us to do? Sneak him out the back door with a blanket over his head?'

'No, sir, it's just – '

8

'He gets treated the same as the rest of them, Inspector. You know the score.'

'Yes, sir, but –'

'But what?'

But what? Well, that was the question. What? Why was Rebus feeling so uncomfortable? The answer was complicatedly simple: because it *was* Gregor Jack. Most MPs, Rebus wouldn't have given the time of day. But Gregor Jack was … well, he was *Gregor Jack*.

'Vans are here, Inspector. Let's round 'em up and ship 'em out.'

Lauderdale's hand on his back was cold and firm.

'Yes, sir,' said Rebus.

So it was out into the cool dark night, lit by orange sodium lights, the glare of headlamps, and the dimmer light from open doors and twitching windows. The natives were restless. Some had come out on to their doorsteps, wrapped in paisley dressing gowns or wearing hastily found clothes, not quite hanging right.

Police, natives, and of course the reporters. Flash-guns. Christ, there were photographers too, of course. No camera crews, no video machines. That was something: Watson hadn't persuaded the TV companies to attend his little soirée.

'Into the van, quick as you can,' called Brian Holmes. Was that a new firmness, a new authority in his voice? Funny what promotion could do to the young. But by God they *were* quick. Not so much following Holmes' orders, Rebus knew, as keen to escape the cameras. One or two of the women posed, trying a lopsided glamour learned from page three, before being persuaded by WPCs that this was neither the time nor the place.

But the reporters were hanging back. Rebus wondered why. Indeed, he wondered what they were doing here at all. Was it such a big story? Would it provide Watson with useful publicity? One reporter even grabbed at a photographer's arm and seemed to warn him about shooting off too many pictures. But now they were keening, now they were shouting. And the flashbulbs were going off like flak. All because

9

they'd recognized a face. All because Gregor Jack was being escorted down the steps, across the narrow pavement, and into a van.

'Christ, it's Gregor Jack!'

'Mr Jack! A word!'

'Any comment to make?'

'What were you doing –'

'Any comment?'

The doors were closing. A thump with the constabulary hand on the side of the van, and it moved slowly away, the reporters jogging after it. Well, Rebus had to admit it: Jack had held his head high. No, that wasn't being accurate. He had, rather, held his head just low enough, suggesting penitence but not shame, humility but not embarrassment.

'Seven days he's been my MP,' Holmes was saying by Rebus's side. 'Seven days.'

'You must have been a bad influence on him, Brian.'

'Bit of a shock though, wasn't it?'

Rebus shrugged noncommitally. The woman from the bedroom was being brought out now, having pulled on jeans and a t-shirt. She saw the reporters and suddenly lifted the t-shirt high over her naked breasts.

'Get a load of this then!'

But the reporters were busy comparing notes, the photographers loading new film. They'd be off to the station next, ready to catch Gregor Jack as he left. Nobody paid her any attention, and eventually she let her t-shirt fall back down and climbed into the waiting van.

'He's not choosy, is he?' said Holmes.

'But then again, Brian,' answered Rebus, 'maybe he is.'

Watson was rubbing at his gleaming forehead. It was a lot of work for only one hand, since the forehead seemed to extend as far as Watson's crown.

'Mission accomplished,' he said. 'Well done.'

'Thank you, sir,' Holmes said smartly.

'No problems then?'

'Not at all, sir,' said Rebus casually. 'Unless you count Gregor Jack.'

10

Watson nodded, then frowned. 'Who?' he asked.

'Brian here can tell you all about him, sir,' said Rebus, patting Holmes' back. 'Brian's your man for anything smacking of politics.'

Watson, hovering now somewhere between elation and dread, turned to Holmes.

'Politics?' he asked. He was smiling. *Please be gentle with me.*

Holmes watched Rebus moving back inside the house. He felt like sobbing. Because, after all, that's what John Rebus was – an s.o.b.

2
Scratching the Surface

It is a truth universally acknowledged that some Members of Parliament have trouble keeping their trousers on. But Gregor Jack was not thought to be one of these. Indeed, he often eschewed troose altogether, opting for the kilt on election nights and at many a public function. In London, he took the jibes in good part, his responses matching the old questions with the accuracy of catechism.

'Tell us now, Gregor, what's worn beneath the kilt?'

'Oh nothing, nothing at all. It's all in perfect working order.'

Gregor Jack was not a member of the SNP, though he had flirted with the party in his youth. He *had* joined the Labour Party, but had resigned for never specified reasons. He was not a Liberal Democrat, nor was he that rare breed – a Scots Tory MP. Gregor Jack was an Independent, and as an Independent had held the seat of North and South Esk, south and east of Edinburgh, since his mildly surprising by-election win of 1985. 'Mild' was an adjective often used about Jack. So were 'honest', 'legal' and 'decent'.

All this John Rebus knew from memory, from old newspapers, magazines and radio interviews. There had to be something wrong with the man, some chink in his shining armour. Trust Operation Creeper to find the flaw. Rebus scanned the Saturday newsprint, seeking a story. He didn't find it. Curious that; the press had seemed keen enough last night. A story breaking at one thirty ... plenty of time, surely, to see it into print by the final morning edition. Unless, of course, the reporters hadn't been local. But they must have been, mustn't they? Having said which, he hadn't recognized any faces. Did Watson really have the front to get the London papers involved? Rebus smiled. The man had plenty of 'front' all right: his wife saw to that. Three meals a day, three courses each.

'Feed the body,' Watson was fond of saying, 'and you feed the spirit.' Something like that. Which was another thing: bible-basher or no, Watson was starting to put away a fair amount of spirits. A rosy glow to the cheeks and chins, and the unmistakable scent of extra-strong mints. When Lauderdale walked into his superior's room these days, he sniffed and sniffed, like a bloodhound. Only it wasn't blood he was sniffing, it was promotion.

Lose a Farmer, gain a Fart.

The nickname had perhaps been unavoidable. Word association. Lauderdale became Fort Lauderdale, and Fort quickly turned into Fart. Oh, but it was an apt name, too. For wherever Chief Inspector Lauderdale went, he left a bad smell. Take the Case of the Lifted Literature. Rebus had known the minute Lauderdale walked into his office that there would soon be a need to open the windows.

'I want you to stick close to this one, John. Professor Costello is highly thought of, an international figure in this field . . .'

'And?'

'And,' Lauderdale tried to look as though his next utterance meant nothing to him, 'he's a close personal friend of Chief Superintendent Watson.'

'Ah.'

'What is this – Monosyllable Week?'

'Monosyllable?' Rebus frowned. 'Sorry, sir, I'll have to ask DS Holmes what that means.'

'Don't try to be funny – '

'I'm not, sir, honest. It's just that DS Holmes has had the benefit of a university education. Well . . . five months' worth or thereabouts. He'd be the very man to coordinate the officers working on this highly sensitive case.'

Lauderdale stared at the seated figure for what seemed – to Rebus at least – a very long time. God, was the man really that stupid? Did no one appreciate irony these days?

'Look,' Lauderdale said at last, 'I need someone a bit more senior than a recently promoted DS. And I'm sorry to say that you, Inspector, God help us all, are that bit more senior.'

'You're flattering me, sir.'

A file landed with a dull thud on Rebus's desk. The chief inspector turned and left. Rebus rose from his chair and turned to his sash window, tugging at it with all his might. But the thing was stuck tight. There was no escape. With a sigh, he turned back and sat down at his desk. Then he opened the folder.

It was a straightforward case of theft. Professor James Aloysius Costello was Professor of Divinity at the University of Edinburgh. One day someone had walked into his office, then walked out again taking with them several rare books. Priceless, according to the Professor, though not to the city's various booksellers and auction rooms. The list seemed eclectic: an early edition of Knox's *Treatise on Predestination*, a couple of Sir Walter Scott first editions, Swedenborg's *Wisdom of Angels*, a signed early edition of *Tristram Shandy*, and editions of Montaigne and Voltaire.

None of which meant much to Rebus until he saw the estimates at auction, provided by one of the George Street auction houses. The question then was: what were they doing in an unlocked office in the first place?

'To be read,' answered Professor Costello blithely. 'To be enjoyed, admired. What good would they be locked up in a safe or in some old library display case?'

'Did anyone else know about them? I mean, about how valuable they are?'

The Professor shrugged. 'I had thought, Inspector, that I was amongst friends.'

He had a voice like a peat bog and eyes that gleamed like crystal. A Dublin education, but a life spent, as he put it, 'cloistered' in the likes of Cambridge, Oxford, St Andrews, and now Edinburgh. A life spent collecting books, too. Those left in his office – still kept unlocked – were worth at least as much as the stolen volumes, perhaps more.

'They say lightning never strikes twice,' he assured Rebus.

'Maybe not, but villains do. Try to lock your door when you step out, eh, sir? If nothing else.'

The Professor had shrugged. Was this, Rebus wondered, a kind of stoicism? He felt nervous sitting there in the office in Buccleuch Place. For one thing, he was a kind of Christian himself, and would have liked to be able to talk the subject through with this wise-seeming man. *Wise?* Well, perhaps not worldly-wise, not wise enough to know how snib locks and human minds worked, but wise in other ways. But Rebus was nervous, too, because he knew himself for a clever man who could have been cleverer, given the breaks. He had never gone to university, and never would. He wondered how different he would be if he had or could . . .

The Professor was staring out of his window, down on to the cobblestoned street. On one side of Buccleuch Place sat a row of neat tenements, owned by the university and used by various departments. The Professor called it Botany Bay. And across the road uglier shapes reared up, the modern stone mausoleums of the main university complex. If this side of the road was Botany Bay, Rebus was all for transportation.

He left the Professor to his muses and musings. Had the books been filched at random? Or was this designer theft, the thief stealing to order? There might well be unscrupulous collectors who would pay – no questions asked – for an early *Tristram Shandy*. Though the authors' names had rung bells, only that particular title had meant anything to Rebus. He owned a paperback copy of the book, bought at a car-boot sale on The Meadows for tenpence. Maybe the Professor would like to borrow it . . .

And so the Case of the Lifted Literature had, for Inspector John Rebus, begun. The ground had been covered before, as the case-notes showed, but it could be covered again. There were the auction houses, the bookshops, the private collectors . . . all to be talked to. And all to satisfy an unlikely friendship between a police chief superintendent and a professor of

Divinity. A waste of time, of course. The books had disappeared the previous Tuesday. It was now Saturday, and they would doubtless be under lock and key in some dark and secret corner.

What a way to spend a Saturday. Actually, if the time had been his own, this would have been a nice afternoon, which was perhaps why he hadn't balked at the task. Rebus collected books. Well, that was putting it strongly. He *bought* books. Bought more of them than he had time to read, attracted by this cover or that title or the fact that he'd heard good things about the author. No, on second thoughts it was just as well these were business calls he was making, otherwise he'd be bankrupting himself in record time.

In any case, he didn't have books on his mind. He kept thinking about a certain MP. Was Gregor Jack married? Rebus thought so. Hadn't there been some big society wedding several years previous? Well, married men were bread and butter to prostitutes. They just gobbled them up. Shame though, about Jack. Rebus had always respected the man – which was to say, now that he thought about it, that he'd been taken in by Jack's public image. But it wasn't all image, was it? Jack really had come from a working-class background, had clawed his way upwards, and *was* a good MP. North and South Esk was difficult territory, part mining villages, part country homes. Jack seemed to glide easily between the two hemispheres. He'd managed to get an ugly new road rerouted well away from his well-heeled constituents, but had also fought hard to bring new high-tech industry to the area, retraining the miners so that they could do the jobs.

Too good to be true. Too bloody good to be true . . .

Bookshops. He had to keep his mind on bookshops. There were only a few to check, the ones that had not been open earlier in the week. Footwork really, the stuff he should have been doling out to more junior men. But all that meant was that he'd feel bound to come round after them, double checking what they'd done. This way, he saved himself some grief.

Buccleuch Street was an odd mixture of grimy junk shops and bright vegetarian takeaways. Student turf. Not far from Rebus's own flat, yet he seldom ventured into this part of town. Only on business. Only ever on business.

Ah, this was it. Suey Books. And for once the shop looked to be open. Even in the spring sunshine there was a need for a light inside. It was a tiny shop, boasting an unenthusiastic window display of old hardbacks, mostly with a Scottish theme. An enormous black cat had made a home for itself in the centre of the display, and blinked slowly if malignly up at Rebus. The window itself needed washing. You couldn't make out the titles of the books without pressing your nose to the glass, and this was made difficult by the presence of an old black bicycle resting against the front of the shop. Rebus pushed open the door. If anything, the shop's interior was less pristine than its exterior. There was a bristle-mat just inside the door. Rebus made a note to wipe his feet before he went back into the street . . .

The shelves, a few of them glass-fronted, were crammed, and the smell was of old relatives' houses, of attics and the insides of school desks. The aisles were narrow. Hardly enough room to swing a . . . There was a thump somewhere behind him, and he feared one of the books had fallen, but when he turned he saw that it was the cat. It swerved past him and made for the desk situated to the rear of the shop, the desk with a bare lightbulb dangling above it.

'Anything in particular you're looking for?'

She was seated at the desk, a pile of books in front of her. She held a pencil in one hand and appeared to be writing prices on the inside leaves of the books. From a distance, it was a scene out of Dickens. Close up was a different story. Still in her teens, she had hennaed her short spiked hair. The eyes behind the circular tinted glasses were themselves round and dark, and she sported three earrings in either ear, with another curling from her left nostril. Rebus didn't doubt she'd have a pale boyfriend with lank dreadlocks and a whippet on a length of clothes-rope.

'I'm looking for the manager,' he said.

'He's not here. Can I help?'

Rebus shrugged, his eyes on the cat. It had leapt silently on to the desk and was now rubbing itself against the books. The girl held her pencil out towards it, and the cat brushed the tip with its jaw.

'Inspector Rebus,' said Rebus. 'I'm interested in some stolen books. I was wondering if anyone had been in trying to sell them.'

'Do you have a list?'

Rebus did. He drew it out of his pocket and handed it over. 'You can keep it,' he said. 'Just in case.'

She glanced down the typed list of titles and editions, her lips pursed.

'I don't think Ronald could afford them, even if he was tempted.'

'Ronald being the manager?'

'That's right. Where were they stolen from?'

'Round the corner in Buccleuch Place.'

'Round the corner? They'd hardly be likely to bring them here then, would they?'

Rebus smiled. 'True,' he said, 'but we have to check.'

'Well, I'll hang on to this anyway,' she said, folding the list. As she pushed it into a desk drawer, Rebus reached out a hand and stroked the cat. Like lightning, a paw flicked up and caught his wrist. He drew back his hand with a sharp intake of breath.

'Oh dear,' said the girl. 'Rasputin's not very good with strangers.'

'So I see.' Rebus studied his wrist. There were inch-long claw marks there, three of them. Whitened scratches, they were already rising, the skin swelling and breaking. Beads of blood appeared. 'Jesus,' he said, sucking on the damaged wrist. He glared at the cat. It glared back, then dropped from the desk and was gone.

'Are you all right?'

'Just about. You should keep that thing on a chain.'

She smiled. 'Do you know anything about that raid last night?'

Rebus blinked, still sucking. 'What raid?'

'I heard the police raided a brothel.'

'Oh?'

'I heard they caught an MP, Gregor Jack.'

'Oh?'

She smiled again. 'Word gets about.' Rebus thought, not for the first time, I don't live in a city, I live in a bloody village . . .

'I just wondered,' the girl was saying, 'if you knew anything about it. I mean, if it's true. I mean, if it is . . .' she sighed. 'Poor Beggar.'

Rebus frowned now.

'That's his nickname,' she explained. 'Beggar. That's what Ronald calls him.'

'Your boss knows Mr Jack then?'

'Oh yes, they were at school together. Beggar owns half of this. She waved a hand around her, as though she were proprietress of some Princes Street department store. She saw that the policeman didn't seem impressed. 'We do a lot of business behind the scenes,' she said defensively. 'A lot of buying and selling. It might not look much, but this place is a goldmine.'

Rebus nodded. 'Actually,' he said, 'now that you mention it, it *does* look a bit like a mine.' His wrist was crackling now, as though stung by nettles. Bloody cat. 'Right, keep an eye out for those books, won't you?'

She didn't answer. Hurt, he didn't doubt, by the 'mine' jibe. She was opening a book, ready to pencil in a price. Rebus nodded to himself, walked to the door, and rubbed his feet noisily on the mat before leaving the shop. The cat was back in the window, licking its tail.

'Fuck you too, pal,' muttered Rebus. Pets, after all, were his pet hate.

Dr Patience Aitken had pets. Too many pets. Tiny tropical fish . . . a tame hedgehog in the back garden . . . two budgies in a cage in the living room . . . and, yes, a cat. A stray which, to Rebus's relief, still liked to spend much of its time on the prowl. It was a tortoiseshell and it was called Lucky. It liked Rebus.

'It's funny,' Patience had said, 'how they always seem to go for the people who don't like them, don't want them, or are allergic to them. Don't ask me why.'

As she said this, Lucky was climbing across Rebus's shoulders. He snarled and shrugged it off. It fell to the floor, landing on its feet.

'You've got to have patience, John.'

Yes, she was right. If he did not have patience, he might lose Patience. So he'd been trying. He'd been trying. Which was perhaps why he'd been tricked into trying to stroke Rasputin. *Rasputin*! Why was it pets always seemed to be called either Lucky, Goldie, Beauty, Flossie, Spot, or else Rasputin, Beelzebub, Fang, Nirvana, Bodhisattva? Blame the breed of owner.

Rebus was in the Rutherford, nursing a half of eight-shilling and watching the full-time scores on TV, when he remembered that he was expected at Brian Holmes' new house this evening, expected for a meal with Holmes and Nell Stapleton. He groaned. Then remembered that his only clean suit was at Patience Aitken's flat. It was a worrying fact. Was he *really* moving in with Patience? He seemed to be spending an awful lot of time there these days. Well, he liked her, even if she did treat him like yet another pet. And he liked her flat. He even liked the fact that it was underground.

Well, not quite underground. In some parts of town, it might once have been described as the 'basement' flat, but in Oxford Terrace, well-appointed Oxford Terrace, Stockbridge's Oxford Terrace, it was a *garden* flat. And sure enough it had a garden, a narrow isosceles triangle of land. But the flat itself was what interested Rebus. It was like a shelter, like a children's encampment. You could stand in either of the front bedrooms and stare up out of the window to where feet and legs moved along the pavement above you. People seldom looked down. Rebus, whose own flat was on the second floor of a Marchmont tenement, enjoyed this new perspective. While other men his age were moving out of the city and into bungalows, Rebus found a sort of amused thrill from walking *downstairs* to the front door instead of walking *up*. More than novelty, it was a reversal, a major shift, and his life felt full of promise as a result.

Patience, too, was full of promise. She was keen for him to move more of his things in, to 'make himself at home'. And she had given him a key. So, beer finished, and car persuaded to make the five-minute trip, he was able to let himself in. His suit, newly cleaned, was lying on the bed in the spare bedroom. So was Lucky. In fact, Lucky was lying on the suit, was rolling on it, plucking at it with his claws, was shedding on it and marking it. Rebus saw Rasputin in his mind's eye as he swiped the cat off the bed. Then he picked up the suit and took it to the bathroom, where he locked the door behind him before running a bath.

The parliamentary constituency of North and South Esk was large but not populous. The population, however, was growing. New housing estates grew in tight clusters on the outskirts of the mining towns and villages. Commuter belt. Yes, the region was changing. New roads, new railway stations even. New kinds of people doing new kinds of jobs. Brian Holmes and Nell Stapleton, however, had chosen to buy an old terraced house in the heart of one of the smallest of the villages, Eskwell. Actually, it was all about Edinburgh in the end. The city was growing, spreading out. It was the city that swallowed villages and spawned new estates. People weren't moving *into* Edinburgh; the city was moving into *them* . . .

But by the time Rebus reached Eskwell he was in no mood to contemplate the changing face of country living. He'd had trouble starting the car. He was *always* having trouble starting the car. But wearing a suit and shirt and tie had made it that bit more difficult to tinker beneath the bonnet. One fine weekend he'd strip the engine down. Of course he would. Then he'd give up and phone for a tow truck.

The house was easy to find, Eskwell boasting one main street and only a few back roads. Rebus walked up the garden path and stood on the doorstep, a bottle of wine gripped in one hand. He clenched his free fist and rapped on the door. It opened almost at once.

'You're late,' said Brian Holmes.

'Perogative of rank, Brian. I'm allowed to be late.'

Holmes ushered him into the hall. 'I did say informal, didn't I?'

Rebus puzzled for a moment, then saw that this was a comment on his suit. He noticed now that Holmes himself was dressed in open-necked shirt and denims, with a pair of moccasins covering his bare feet.

'Ah,' said Rebus.

'Never mind, I'll nip upstairs and change.'

'Not on my account. This is your house, Brian. You do as you please.'

Holmes nodded to himself, suddenly looking pleased. Rebus was right: this *was* his house. Well, the mortgage was his . . . *half* the mortgage. 'Go on through,' he said, gesturing to a door at the end of the hall.

'I think I'll nip upstairs myself first,' Rebus said, handing over the bottle. He spread his hands out palms upwards, then turned them over. Even Holmes could see the traces of oil and dirt.

'Car trouble,' he said, nodding. 'The bathroom's to the right of the landing.'

'Right.'

'And those are nasty scratches, too. I'd see a doctor about them.' Holmes' tone told Rebus that the young man assumed a certain doctor had been responsible for them in the first place.

'A cat,' Rebus explained. 'A cat with eight lives left.'

Upstairs, he felt particularly clumsy. He rinsed the wash-hand-basin after him, then had to rinse the muck off the soap, then rinsed the basin again. A towel was hanging over the bath, but when he started to dry his hands he found he was drying them not on a towel but on a foot-mat. The real towel was on a hook behind the door. Relax, John, he told himself. But he couldn't. Socializing was just one more skill he'd never really mastered.

He peered round the door downstairs.

'Come in, come in.'

Holmes was holding out a glass of whisky towards him. 'Here you go, cheers.'

'Cheers.'

They drank, and Rebus felt the better for it.

'I'll give you the tour of the house later,' Holmes said. 'Sit down.'

Rebus did so, and looked around him. 'A real Holmes from home,' he commented. There were good smells in the air, and cooking and clattering noises from the kitchen, which seemed to be through another door off the living room. The living room was almost cuboid, with a table in one corner set with three places for dinner, a chair in another corner, a TV in the third, and a standard lamp in the fourth.

'Very nice,' commented Rebus. Holmes was sitting on a two-person sofa against one wall. Behind him was a decent-sized window looking on to the back garden. He shrugged modestly.

'It'll do us,' he said.

'I'm sure it will.'

Now Nell Stapleton strode into the room. As imposing as ever, she seemed almost too tall for her surroundings, Alice after the 'Eat Me' cake. She was wiping her hands on a dishcloth, and smiled at Rebus.

'Hello there.'

Rebus had risen to his feet. She came over and pecked him on his cheek.

'Hello, Nell.'

Now she was standing over Holmes, and had lifted the glass out of his hand. There was sweat on her forehead, and she too was dressed casually. She took a swallow of whisky, exhaled noisily, and handed the glass back.

'Ready in five minutes,' she announced. 'Shame your doctor friend couldn't make it, John.'

He shrugged. 'Prior engagement. A medical dinner party. I was glad of an excuse to get out of it.'

She gave him rather too fixed a smile. 'Well,' she said, 'I'll leave you two to talk about whatever it is boys talk about.'

And then she was gone, the room seeming suddenly empty. Shit, what had he said? Rebus had tried to find words to describe Nell when speaking about her to Patience Aitken. But somehow the words never told the story. Bossy, stroppy, lively, canny, big, bright, a handful . . . like another set of seven dwarves. Certainly, she didn't fit the stereotype of a university librarian. Which seemed to suit Brian Holmes just fine. He was smiling, studying what was left of his drink. He got up for a refill – Rebus refusing the offer – and came back with a manilla folder.

'Here,' he said.

Rebus accepted the folder. 'What is it?'

'Take a look.'

Newspaper cuttings mostly, magazine articles, press releases . . . all concerning Gregor Jack MP.

'Where did you . . . ?'

Holmes shrugged. 'Innate curiosity. When I knew I was moving into his constituency, I thought I'd like to know more.'

'The papers seem to have kept quiet about last night.'

'Maybe they've been warned off.' Holmes sounded sceptical. 'Or maybe they're just biding their time.' Having just reseated himself, he now leapt up again. 'I'll see if Nell needs a hand.'

Leaving Rebus with little to do but read. There wasn't much he didn't already know. Working-class background. Comprehensive school in Fife, then Edinburgh University. Degree in Economics and Accounting. Chartered accountant. Married Elizabeth Ferrie. They'd met at university. She, the daughter of Sir Hugh Ferrie the businessman. She was his only daughter, his only child. He doted on her, could refuse her nothing, all, it was said, because she reminded him of his wife, dead these past twenty-three years. Sir Hugh's most recent 'companion' was an ex-model less than half his age. Maybe she, too, reminded him of his wife . . .

Funny though. Elizabeth Jack was an attractive woman, beautiful even. Yet you never heard much about her. Since when was an attractive wife an asset not to be used by canny politicians? Maybe she wanted her own life. Skiing holidays and health resorts, rather than an MP's round of factory openings, tea parties, all that.

Rebus recalled now what it was that he liked about Gregor Jack. It was the background – so similar to his own. Born in Fife, and given a comprehensive education. Except that back then they'd been called secondary and high schools. Both Rebus and Gregor Jack had gone to a high school, Rebus because he passed his eleven-plus, the younger Jack because of good grades at his junior high. Rebus's school had been in Cowdenbeath, Jack's in Kirkcaldy. No distance at all, really.

The only muck that had ever been thrown at Jack seemed to be over the siting of a new electronics factory just inside his constituency. Rumours that his father-in-law had pulled a few strings . . . It had all died down quickly enough. No evidence, and a whiff of writs for libel. How old was Jack? Rebus studied a recent newspaper photograph. He looked younger on paper than he did in real life. People in the media always did. Thirty-seven, thirty-eight, something like that. Beautiful wife, plenty of money.

And he ends up caught on a tart's bed during a brothel raid. Rebus shook his head. It was a cruel world. Then he smiled: serve the bugger right for not sticking to his wife.

Holmes was coming back in. He nodded towards the file. 'Makes you wonder, doesn't it?'

Rebus shrugged. 'Not really, Brian. Not really.'

'Well, finish your whisky and sit at the table. I'm informed by the management that dinner is about to be served.'

It was a good dinner, too. Rebus insisted on making three toasts: one to the couple's happiness, one to their new home, and one to Holmes' promotion. By then, they were on to their second bottle of wine and the evening's main course – roast beef. After that there was cheese, and after the cheese, crannachan. And after all that there was coffee and Laphroaig and drowsiness in the armchair and on the sofa for all concerned. It hadn't taken long for Rebus to relax – the alcohol had seen to that. But it had been a nervous kind of relaxation, so that he felt he'd said too much, most of it rubbish.

There was some shop talk, of course, and Nell allowed it so long as it was interesting. She thought Farmer Watson's drinking habit was interesting. ('Maybe he doesn't drink at all. Maybe he's just addicted to strong mints.') She thought Chief Inspector Lauderdale's ambition was interesting. And she thought the brothel raid sounded interesting, too. She wanted to know where the fun was in being whipped, or dressed in nappies, or having sex with a scuba-diver. Rebus admitted he'd no answer. 'Suck it and see,' was Brian Holmes' contribution. It earned him a cushion over the head.

By quarter past eleven, Rebus knew two things. One was that he was too drunk to drive. The other was that even if he could drive (or be driven) he'd not know his destination – Oxford Terrace or his own flat in Marchmont? Where, these days, did he live? He imagined himself parking the car on Lothian Road, halfway between the two addresses, and kipping there. But the decision was made for him by Nell.

'The bed in the spare room's made up. We need someone to christen it so we can start calling it the guest bedroom. Might as well be you.'

Her quiet authority was not to be challenged. Rebus shrugged his acceptance. A little later, she went to bed herself. Holmes switched on the TV but found nothing there worth watching, so he turned on the hi-fi instead.

'I haven't got any jazz,' he admitted, knowing Rebus's tastes. 'But how about this . . .?'

It was *Sergeant Pepper*. Rebus nodded. 'If I can't get the Rolling Stones, I'll always settle for second best.'

So they argued 60s pop music, then talked football for a little while and shop for a bit longer still.

'How much more time do you think Doctor Curt will take?'

Holmes was referring to one of the pathologists regularly used by the police. A body had been fished out of the Water of Leith, just below Dean Bridge. Suicide, accident or murder? They were hoping Dr Curt's findings would point the way.

Rebus shrugged. 'Some of those tests take weeks, Brian. But actually, from what I hear, he won't be much longer. A day or two maybe.'

'And what will he say?'

'God knows.' They shared a smile; Curt was notorious for his fund of bad jokes and ill-timed levity.

'Should we stand by to repel puns?' asked Holmes. 'How about this: deceased was found near waterfall. However, study of eyes showed no signs of cataracts.'

Rebus laughed. 'That's not bad. Bit too clever maybe, but still not bad.'

They spent a quarter of an hour recalling some of Curt's true gems, before, somehow, turning the talk to politics. Rebus admitted that he'd voted only three times in his adult life.

'Once Labour, once SNP, and once Tory.'

Holmes seemed to find this funny. He asked what the chronological order had been, but Rebus couldn't remember. This, too, seemed worth a laugh.

'Maybe you should try an Independent next time.'

'Like Gregor Jack you mean?' Rebus shook his head. 'I don't think there's any such thing as an "Independent" in Scotland. It's like living in Ireland and trying not to take sides. Damned hard work. And speaking of work . . . some of us have been working today. If you don't mind, Brian, I think I'll join Nell . . .' More laughter. 'If you see what I mean.'

'Sure,' said Holmes, 'on you go. I don't feel so bad. I might watch a video or something. See you in the morning.'

'Mind you don't keep me awake,' said Rebus with a wink.

In fact, meltdown at the Torness reactor couldn't have kept him awake. His dreams were full of pastoral scenes, skin-divers, kittens, and last-minute goals. But when he opened his eyes there was a dark shadowy figure looming over him.

He pushed himself up on his elbows. It was Holmes, dressed and wearing a denim jacket. There was a jangle of car keys from one hand; the other hand held a selection of newspapers which he now threw down on to the bed.

'Sleep all right? Oh, by the way, I don't usually buy these rags but I thought you'd be interested. Breakfast'll be ready in ten minutes.'

Rebus managed to mumble a few syllables. He heaved himself upright and studied the front page of the tabloid in front of him. This was what he'd been waiting for, and he actually felt some of the tension leave his body and his brain. The headline was actually subtle – JACK THE LAD! – but the sub-head was blunt enough – MP NICKED IN SEX-DEN SWOOP. And there was the photograph, showing Gregor Jack on his way down the steps to the waiting van. More photos were promised inside. Rebus turned to the relevant pages. A pasty-faced Farmer Watson; a couple of the 'escorts' posing for the cameras; and another four shots of Jack, showing his progress all the way into the van. None from the cop-shop aftermath, so presumably he'd been spirited away. You couldn't hope to spirit this away though, photogenic or no. Ha! In the background of one of the photos Rebus could make out the cherubic features of Detective Sergeant Brian Holmes. One for the scrapbook and no mistake.

There were two more newspapers, both telling a similar tale graced by similar (sometimes even identical) photos. THE DISHONOURABLE MEMBER; MP'S VICE SHAME. Ah, the great British Sunday headline, coined by an elect of teetotal virgins boasting the combined wisdom of Solomon and the magnanimity of a zealot. Rebus could be as prurient as the next man, but this stuff was a class above. He prised himself out of bed and stood up. The alcohol inside him stood up too; then it began to pogostick its way around his head. Red wine and whisky. Bad news and a chaser. What was the phrase? Never mix the grain and the grape. Never mind, a couple of litres of orange juice would sort him out.

But first there was the little matter of the fry-up. Nell looked as though she'd spent all night in the kitchen. She had washed up the debris of the previous night, and now was providing a breakfast of hotel proportions. Cereal, toast, bacon, sausage and egg. With a pot of coffee taking pride of place on the dining table. Only one thing was missing.

'Any orange juice?' Rebus suggested.

'Sorry,' said Brian. 'I thought the paper shop would have some, but they'd run out. There's plenty of coffee though. Tuck in.' He was busy with another paper, a broadsheet this time. 'Didn't take them long to stick the knife in, did it?'

'You mean Gregor Jack? No, well, what can you expect?'

Holmes turned a page. 'Strange though,' he said, and let it lie at that, wondering whether Rebus would know . . .

'You mean,' Rebus replied, 'it's strange that the London Sunday's knew about Operation Creeper.'

Another page was turned. It didn't take long to read a newspaper these days, not unless you were interested in the adverts. Holmes folded the paper into four and laid it down on the table beside him.

'Yes,' he said, lifting a piece of toast. 'Like I say, it's strange.'

'Come on, Brian. Papers are always getting tip-offs to juicy stories. A copper looking for beer money, something like that. Chances are, you raid a posh brothel you're going to come out with some weel-kent faces.'

Hold on though . . . Even as he spoke, Rebus knew there was something more. That night, the reporters had been biding their time, hadn't they? Like they knew *exactly* who or what might be walking out of the door and down the steps. Holmes was staring at him now.

'What are you thinking?' Rebus asked.

'Nothing. No, nothing at all . . . yet. Not our business, is it? And besides, this is Sunday.'

'You're a sly bugger, Brian Holmes.'

'I've got a good tutor, haven't I?'

Nell came into the room carrying two plates, filled with glistening fried food. Rebus's stomach pleaded with its owner not to do anything rash, anything he would regret later on in the day.

29

'You're working too hard,' Rebus told Nell. 'Don't let him treat you like a skivvy.'

'Don't worry,' she said, 'I don't. But fair's fair. Brian did wash last night's dishes. And he'll wash this morning's too.'

Holmes groaned. Rebus opened one of the tabloids and tapped his finger against a photograph.

'Better not work him too hard, Nell, not now he's in pictures.'

Nell took the paper from him, studied it for a moment, then shrieked.

'My God, Brian! You look like something off the *Muppet Show*.'

Holmes was on his feet now, too, staring over her shoulder. 'And is that what Chief Superintendent Watson looks like? He could pass for an Aberdeen Angus.'

Rebus and Holmes shared a smile at that. He wasn't called Farmer for nothing . . .

Rebus wished the young couple well. They had made a commitment to living together. They had bought a house together and set up home. They seemed content. Yes, he wished them well with all his heart.

But his brain gave them two or three years at most.

A policeman's lot was not entirely a happy one. Striving towards inspectorship, Brian Holmes would find himself working still longer hours. If he could shut it all out when he got home of an evening or morning, fine. But Rebus doubted the young man would. Holmes was the type to get involved in a case, to let it rule his thinking hours whether on duty or off, and that was bad for a relationship.

Bad, and often terminal. Rebus knew more divorced and separated policemen (himself included) than happily married ones. It wasn't just the hours worked, it was the way police work itself gnawed into you like a worm, burrowing deep. Eating away from the inside. As protection against the worm, you wore armour plating – more of it, perhaps, than was necessary. And that armour set you apart from friends and family, from the 'civilians' . . .

Ach. Pleasant thoughts for a Sunday morning. After all, it wasn't *all* gloom. The car had started without a hitch (that is, without him having to hitch a ride to the nearest garage), and there was just enough blue in the sky to send hardy day-trippers off into the country. Rebus was going on a drive, too. An aimless tour, he told himself. A nice day for a drive. But he knew where he was headed. Knew where, if not exactly *why*.

Gregor Jack and his wife lived in a large, old, detached and walled residence on the outskirts of Rosebridge, a little further south than Eskwell, a little bit more rural. Gentry country. Fields and rolling hills and an apparent moratorium on new building work. Rebus had no excuse save curiosity for this detour, but he was not, it seemed, alone. The Jacks' house was recognizable by the half dozen cars parked outside its gates and by the posse of reporters who were lounging around, chatting to each other or instructing fed-up-looking photographers on how far they should go (morally rather than geographically) for that elusive picture. Clamber on to the wall? Climb that nearby tree? Try the back of the house? The photographers didn't seem keen. But just then something seemed to galvanize them.

By this time, Rebus had parked his own car further along the road. To one side of the road was a line of perhaps half a dozen houses, none of them spectacular in terms of design or size, but wonderfully isolated by those high walls, long driveways, and (doubtless) vast back gardens. The other side of the road was pasture. Bemused cows and fat-looking sheep. Some sizeable lambs, their voices not yet quite broken. The view ended at some steepish hills, three or so miles distant. It was nice. Even the troglodyte Rebus could appreciate that.

Which was perhaps why the reporters left a more bitter taste than usual beneath his tongue. He stood behind them, an observer. The house was dark-stoned, reddish from this distance. A two-storey construction, probably built in the early 1900s. Tacked on to it at one side was a large garage, and in front of the house at the top of the drive sat a white

Saab, one of the 9000 series. Sturdy and reliable, not cheap but not show-offish. Distinctive though: a car of distinction.

A youngish man, early thirties, a sneer creasing his face, was unlocking the gates just wide enough so that a younger woman, out of her teens but trying to look ten years older, could hand a silver tray to the reporters. She spoke louder than she needed to.

'Gregor thought you might like some tea. There may not be enough cups, you'll just have to share. There are biscuits in the tin. No ginger nuts, I'm afraid. We've run out.'

There were smiles at this, nods of appreciation. But throughout questions were being fired off.

'Any chance of a word with Mr Jack?'

'Can we expect a statement?'

'How's he taking it?'

'Is Mrs Jack in the house?'

'Any chance of a word?'

'Ian, is he going to be saying *anything*?'

This last question was directed at the sneering man, who now held up one hand for silence. He waited patiently, and the silence came. Then:

'No comment,' he said. And with that he began to close the gates. Rebus pushed through the good-natured crush until he was face to face with Mr Sneer.

'Inspector Rebus,' he said. 'Could I have a word with Mr Jack?'

Mr Sneer and Miss Teatray seemed highly suspicious, even when they accepted and examined Rebus's ID. Fair enough: he'd known of reporters who'd try a stunt just like this, fake ID and all. But eventually there was a curt nod, and the gates opened again wide enough to allow him to squeeze through. The gates were shut again, locked. With Rebus on the inside.

He had a sudden thought: What the hell am I doing? The answer was: He wasn't sure. Something about the scene at the gates had made him want to be on the other side of those gates. Well, here he was. Being led back up the gravel driveway, towards the large car, the larger house behind it,

32

and the garage off to the side. Being led towards Gregor Jack MP, with whom, apparently, he wanted a word.

I believe you want a word, Inspector?

No, sir, just being nosey.

It wasn't much of an opening line, was it? Watson had warned him before about this . . . this . . . was it a character flaw? This need to push his way into the centre of things, to become involved, to find out for himself rather than accepting somebody's word, no matter who that somebody was.

Just passing, thought I'd pay my respects. Jesus, and Jack would recognize him, wouldn't he? From the brothel. Sitting on the bed, while the woman in the bed kicked up her legs, screeching with laughter. No, maybe not. He'd had other things on his mind after all.

'I'm Ian Urquhart, Gregor's constituency agent.' Now that he had his back to the reporters, the sneer had left Urquhart's face. What was left was a mixture of worry and bewilderment. 'We got word last night of what was coming. I've been here ever since.'

Rebus nodded. Urquhart was compact, a bunching of well-kept muscles inside a tailored suit. A bit smaller than the MP, and a bit less good-looking. In other words, just right for an agent. He also looked efficient, which Rebus would say was a bonus.

'This is Helen Greig, Gregor's secretary.' Urquhart was nodding towards the young woman. She gave a quick smile towards Rebus. 'Helen came over this morning to see if there was anything she could do.'

'The tea was my idea actually,' she said.

Urquhart glanced towards her. 'Gregor's idea, Helen,' he warned.

'Oh yes,' she said, reddening.

Efficient and faithful, thought Rebus. Rare qualities indeed. Helen Greig, like Urquhart himself, spoke in an educated Scots accent which did not really betray county of origin. He would hazard at east coast for both of them, but couldn't narrow things down any further. Helen looked either like she'd been to an early Kirk service, or was planning to attend one later on. She was wearing a pale woollen two-piece with plain white blouse offset by a simple gold chain around her neck. Sensible black shoes on her feet and thick black tights. She was Urquhart's height, five feet six or seven, and shared something of his build. You wouldn't call her beautiful: you'd call her handsome, in the way Nell Stapleton was handsome, though the two women were dissimilar in many ways.

They were passing the Saab now, Urquhart leading. 'Was there anything in particular, Inspector? Only, I'm sure you can appreciate that Gregor's hardly in a state . . .'

'It won't take long, Mr Urquhart.'

'Well, in you come then.' The front door opened, and Urquhart ushered both Rebus and Helen Greig into the house before him. Rebus was immediately surprised by how modern the interior was. Polished pine flooring, scatter rugs, Mackintosh-style chairs and low-slung Italian-looking tables. They passed through the hall and into a large room boasting more modern furnishings still. Pride of place went to a long angular sofa constructed from leather and chrome. On which sat, in much the same position as when Rebus had first met him, Gregor Jack. The MP was scratching absent-mindedly at a finger and staring at the floor. Urquhart cleared his throat.

'We have a visitor, Gregor.'

The effect was that of a talented actor changing roles – tragedy to comedy. Gregor Jack stood up and fixed a smile on to his face. His eyes now sparkled, looking interested, his whole face speaking sincerity. Rebus marvelled at the ease of the transformation.

'Detective Inspector Rebus,' he said, taking the proffered hand.

'Inspector, what can we do for you? Here, sit down.' Jack gestured towards a squat black chair, matching the sofa in design. It was like sinking into marshmallow. 'Something to drink?' Now Jack seemed to remember something and turned to Helen Greig. 'Helen, you took the tea out to our friends?'

She nodded.

'Excellent. Can't have the gentlemen of the press going without their elevenses.' He smiled towards Rebus, then lowered himself on to the edge of the sofa, arms resting on his knees so that the hands remained mobile. 'Now, Inspector, what's the problem?'

'Well, sir, it's really just that I happened to be passing, and saw that gang at the gates, so I stopped.'

'You know why they're here though?'

Rebus was obliged to nod. Urquhart cleared his throat again.

'We're going to prepare a statement for them over lunch,' he said. 'It probably won't be enough to see them off, but it might help.'

'You know, of course,' said Rebus, aware that he had to tread carefully, 'that you've done nothing wrong, sir. I mean, nothing illegal.'

Jack smiled again and shrugged. 'It doesn't need to be illegal, Inspector. It just has to be news.' His hands kept fluttering, as did his eyes and head. It was as though his mind were elsewhere. Then something seemed to click. 'You didn't say, Inspector,' he said, 'tea or coffee? Something stronger perhaps?'

Rebus shook his head slowly. His hangover was a dull presence now. No point swaddling it. Jack raised his soulful eyes to Helen Greig.

'I'd love a cup of tea, Helen. Inspector, you're sure you won't . . .?'

'No, thank you.'

'Ian?'

Urquhart nodded towards Helen Greig.

'Would you, Helen?' said Gregor Jack. What woman, Rebus wondered, would refuse? Which reminded him . . .

'Your wife's not here then, Mr Jack?'

'On holiday,' Jack said quickly. 'We've a cottage in the Highlands. Not much of a place, but we like it. She's probably there.'

'Probably? Then you don't know for sure?'

'She didn't make out an itinerary, Inspector.'

'So does she know . . .?'

Jack shrugged. 'I've no idea, Inspector. Maybe she does.

She's an insatiable reader of newsprint. There's a village nearby stocks the Sundays.'

'But she hasn't been in touch?'

Urquhart didn't bother clearing his throat this time before interrupting. 'There's no phone at the lodge.'

'That's what we like about it,' Jack explained. 'Cut off from the world.'

'But if she knew,' Rebus persisted, 'surely she'd get in touch?'

Jack sighed, and began scratching at his finger again. He caught himself doing it and stopped. 'Eczema,' he explained. 'Just on the one finger, but it's annoying all the same.' He paused. 'Liz . . . my wife . . . she's very much a law unto herself, Inspector. Maybe she'd get in touch, maybe she wouldn't. She's just as likely not to want to talk about it. Do you see what I mean?' Another smile, a weaker one, seeking the sympathy vote. Jack ran his fingers through his thick dark hair. Rebus wondered idly whether the perfect teeth were capped. Maybe the thatch was capped, too. The open-necked shirt didn't look like chain-store stuff . . .

Urquhart was still standing. Or, rather, was on his feet but in constant movement. Over to the window to peer through the net curtains. Over to a glass-topped table to examine some papers lying there. Over to a smaller table where the telephone sat, disconnected at the wall. So that even if Mrs Jack *did* try to call . . . Neither Urquhart nor Jack seemed to have thought of that. Curious. The room, the taste it displayed, seemed to Rebus not Jack's but his wife's. Jack looked like a man for older established pieces of furniture, safe comfy armchairs and a chesterfield sofa. A conservative taste. Look at the car he chose to drive . . .

Yes, Jack's car: now there was an idea, or rather an excuse, an excuse for Rebus's presence.

'Maybe if we could get that statement out *by* lunchtime, Gregor,' Urquhart was saying. 'Sooner we dampen things down the better, really.'

Not very subtle, thought Rebus. The message was: state your business and leave. Rebus knew the question he wanted to ask: Do you think you were set up? Wanted to ask, but daren't. He wasn't here officially, was a tourist merely.

'About your car, Mr Jack,' he began. 'Only, I noticed when I stopped that it's sitting there in the drive, on full view so as to speak. And there are photographers out there. If any pictures of your car get into the papers . . .'

'Everyone will recognize it in future?' Jack nodded. 'I see what you're getting at, Inspector. Yes, thank you. We hadn't thought of that, had we, Ian?' Better put it in the garage. We don't want everyone who reads a newspaper to know what kind of car I drive.'

'And its registration,' Rebus added. 'There are all sorts of people out there . . . terrorists . . . people with a grudge . . . plain nutters. Doesn't do any good.'

'Thank you, Inspector.' The door swung open and Helen Greig entered, carrying two large mugs of tea. A far cry from the silver salver routine at the gates. She handed one to Urquhart and one to Gregor Jack, then removed a slim box from where it had been held between her arm and her side. It was a fresh box of ginger nuts. Rebus smiled.

'Lovely, Helen, thanks,' said Gregor Jack. He eased two biscuits from the packet.

Rebus rose to his feet. 'Well,' he said. 'I'd better be going. Like I say, I only dropped in . . .'

'I do appreciate it, Inspector.' Jack had placed mug and biscuits on the floor and was now standing, too, hand held out again towards Rebus. A warm, strong and unflawed hand. 'I meant to ask, do you live in the constituency?'

Rebus shook his head. 'One of my colleagues does. I was staying with him last night.'

Jack raised his head slowly before nodding. The gesture could have meant anything. 'I'll open the gates for you,' Ian Urquhart was saying.

'Stay here and drink your tea,' Helen Greig said. 'I'll see the Inspector out.'

'If you like, Helen,' Urquhart said slowly. Was there a warning in his voice? If there was, Helen Greig seemed not to sense it. He fished in his pocket for the keys and handed them to her.

'Right then,' Rebus said. 'Goodbye, Mr Jack ... Mr Urquhart.' He took Urquhart's hand for a moment and squeezed it. But his attention was on the man's left hand. Wedding ring on one finger, and a signet ring on another. Gregor Jack's left hand sported just the one thick band of gold. Not, however, on his wedding finger, but on the finger next to it. The wedding finger was the one with the eczema ...

And Helen Greig? A few trinket rings on both hands, but she was neither married nor engaged.

'Goodbye.'

Helen Greig was first out of the house, but waited for him beside the car, jangling the keys in her right hand.

'Have you worked for Mr Jack long?'

'Long enough.'

'Hard work, being an MP, isn't it? I expect he needs to unwind from time to time –'

She stopped and glared at him. 'Not you too! You're as bad as that lot!' She gestured with the keys towards the gates and the figures beyond. 'I won't hear a word said against Gregor.' She started walking again, more briskly now.

'He's a good employer then?'

'He's not *like* an employer at all. My mother's been ill. He gave me a bonus in the autumn so I could take her for a wee holiday down the coast. *That's* the sort of man he is.' There were tears in her eyes, but she forced them back. The reporters were passing cups between them, complaining about sugar or the lack of it. They didn't seem to expect much from the approach of the two figures.

'Talk to us, Helen.'

'A word with Gregor and we can all go home. We've got families to think of, you know.'

'I'm missing communion,' joked one of them.

'Yes, communion with your lunchtime pint,' returned another.

One of the local reporters – by the accents, there weren't many of them present – had recognized Rebus.

'Inspector, anything to tell us?' A few ears pricked up at that 'Inspector'.

'Yes,' said Rebus, causing Helen Greig to stiffen. 'Bugger off.'

There were smiles at this and a few groans. The gates opened and were about to close, leaving Rebus on the outside again. But he pressed his weight against the gate and leaned towards the young woman, his mouth close to her ear.

'I forgot, I'll have to go back in.'

'What?'

'I forgot, or rather Mr Jack did. He wanted me to check on his wife, in case she was taking the news badly . . .'

He waited for the notion of this to sink in. Helen Greig puckered her lips in a silent O. The notion had sunk in.

'Only,' Rebus went on, 'I forgot to get the address . . .'

She stood on her toes and, so the newsmen wouldn't hear, whispered into his ear: 'Deer Lodge. It's between Knockandhu and Tomnavoulin.'

Rebus nodded, and allowed her to close and lock the gates. His curiosity was not exactly dispelled. In fact, he was more curious now than when he'd gone in. Knockandhu and Tomnavoulin: the names of a couple of malt whiskies. His head told him never to drink again. His heart told him differently . . .

Damn, he'd meant to phone Patience from Holmes' house, just to let her know he was on his way. Not that she kept him to an itinerary or anything . . . but all the same. He made for the reporter he recognized, the local lad, Chris Kemp.

'Hello, Chris. Got a phone in your car? Mind if I make a call . . .?'

'So,' said Dr Patience Aitken, 'how was your *ménage à trois?*'

'Not bad,' said Rebus, before kissing her loudly on the lips. 'How was your orgy?'

She rolled her eyes. 'Shop talk and overcooked lasagne.

You didn't manage home then?' Rebus looked blank. 'I tried phoning Marchmont, and you weren't there either. Your suit looks like you slept in it.'

'Blame the bloody cat.'

'Lucky?'

'He was doing the twist all over the jacket till I rescued it.'

'The *twist*? Nothing shows a man's true age more than his choice of dance step.'

Rebus was shedding the suit now. 'You haven't got any orange juice, have you?'

'Bit of a sore head? Time to stop the drinking, John.'

'Time to settle down, you mean.' He pulled off his trousers. 'All right if I take a bath?'

She was studying him. 'You know you don't have to ask.'

'No, but all the same, I like to ask.'

'Permission granted . . . as always. Did Lucky do that, too?' She was pointing to the scratches on his wrist.

'He'd be in the microwave if he had.'

She smiled. 'I'll see about the orange juice.'

Rebus watched her make for the kitchen. He attempted a dry-mouthed wolf-whistle. From nearby, one of the budgies showed him how to do it properly. Patience turned towards the budgie and smiled.

He lay down in the foaming bath and closed his eyes, breathing deeply, the way his doctor had told him to. Relaxation technique, he'd called it. He wanted Rebus to relax a bit more. High blood pressure, nothing serious, but all the same . . . Of course, there were pills he could take, beta-blockers. But the doctor was in favour of self-help. Deep relaxation. Self-hypnosis. Rebus had had half a mind to tell the doctor that his own father had been a hypnotist, that his brother still might be a professional hypnotist somewhere . . .

Deep breathing . . . emptying the mind . . . relaxing the head, the forehead, the jaw, the neck muscles, the chest, the arms. Counting backwards down to zero . . . no stress, no strain . . .

At first, Rebus had accused the doctor of penny-pinching, of not wanting to give out costly drugs. But the damned thing seemed to work. He *could* help himself. He could help himself to Patience Aitken . . .

'Here you go,' she said, coming into the bathroom. She was holding a long thin glass of orange juice. 'As squeezed by Dr Aitken.'

Rebus slipped a sudsy arm around her buttocks. 'As squeezed by Inspector Rebus.'

She bent down and kissed him on his head. Then touched a finger to his hair. 'You need to start using a conditioner, John. All the life's going out of your follicles.'

'That's because it's headed somewhere else.'

She narrowed her eyes. 'Down, boy,' she said. Then, before he could make a grab for her again, she fled from the bathroom. Rebus, smiling, settled further into the bath.

Deep breathing . . . emptying the mind . . . *Had* Gregor Jack been set up. If so, who by? And to what purpose? A scandal, of course. A political scandal, a front-page scandal. But the atmosphere in the Jack household had been . . . well, *strange*. Strained, certainly, but also cold and edgy, as though the worst were still to happen.

The wife . . . Elizabeth . . . something didn't seem right there. Something seemed very odd indeed. Background, he needed more background. He needed to be *sure*. The lodge address was fixed in his mind, but from what he knew of Highland police stations little good would come of phoning on a Sunday. Background . . . He thought again of Chris Kemp, the reporter. Yes, why not? Wake up, arms, wake up, chest, neck and head. Sunday was no time to be resting. For some people, Sunday was a day of work.

Patience stuck her head round the door. 'Quiet night in this evening?' she suggested. 'I'll cook us a – '

'Quiet night be damned,' Rebus said, rising impressively from the water. 'Let's go out for a drink.'

'You know me, John. I don't *mind* a bit of sleaze, but this place is cheapskate sleaze. Don't you think I'm worth better?'

Rebus pecked Patience's cheek, placed their drinks on the table, and sat down beside her. 'I got you a double,' he said.

41

'So I see.' She picked up the glass. 'Not much room for the tonic, is there?'

They were seated in the back room of the Horsehair public house on Broughton Street. Through the doorway could be seen the bar itself, noisy as ever. People who wanted to have a conversation seemed to place themselves like duellists a good ten paces away from the person they wanted to talk with. The result was that a lot of shouting went on, producing much crossfire and more crossed wires. It was noisy, but it was fun. The back room was quieter. It was a U-shaped arrangement of squashy seating (around the walls) and rickety chairs. The narrow lozenge-shaped tables were fixed to the floor. Rumour had it that the squashy seating had been stuffed with horsehair in the 1920s and not restuffed since. Thus the Horsehair, whose real and prosaic name had long since been discarded.

Patience poured half a small bottle of tonic water into her gin, while Rebus supped on a pint of IPA.

'Cheers,' she said, without enthusiasm. Then: 'I know damned fine that there's got to be a reason for this. I mean, a reason why we're here. I *suppose* it's to do with your work?'

Rebus put down the glass. 'Yes,' he said.

She raised her eyes to the nicotine-coloured ceiling. 'Give me strength,' she said.

'It won't take long,' Rebus said. 'I thought afterwards we could go somewhere . . . a bit more your style.'

'Don't patronize me, you pig.'

Rebus stared into his drink, thinking about that statement's various meanings. Then he caught sight of a new customer in the bar, and waved through the doorway. A young man came forwards, smiling tiredly.

'Don't often see you in here, Inspector Rebus,' he said.

'Sit down,' said Rebus. 'It's my round. Patience, let me introduce you to one of Scotland's finest young reporters, Chris Kemp.'

Rebus got up and headed for the bar. Chris Kemp pulled over a chair and, having tested it first, eased himself on to it.

'He must want something,' he said to Patience, nodding towards the bar. 'He knows I'm a sucker for a bit of flattery.'

Not that it *was* flattery. Chris Kemp had won awards for his early work on an Aberdeen evening paper, and had then moved to Glasgow, there to be voted Young Journalist of the Year, before arriving in Edinburgh, where he had spent the past year and a half 'stirring it' (as he said himself). Everyone knew he'd one day head south. He knew it himself. It was inescapable. There didn't seem to be much left for him to stir in Scotland. The only problem was his student girlfriend, who wouldn't graduate for another year and wouldn't think of moving south before then, if ever . . .

By the time Rebus returned from the bar, Patience had been told all of this and more. There was a film over her eyes which Chris Kemp, for all his qualities, could not see. He talked, and as he talked she was thinking: Is John Rebus worth all this? Is he worth the effort I seem to have to make? She didn't love him: that was understood. 'Love' was something that had happened to her a few times in her teens and twenties and even, yes, in her thirties. Always with inconclusive or atrocious results. So that nowadays it seemed to her 'love' could as easily spell the end of a relationship as its beginning.

She saw it in her surgery. She saw men and women (but mostly women) made ill from love, from loving too much and not being loved enough in return. They were every bit as sick as the child with earache or the pensioner suffering angina. She had pity and words for them, but no medicines.

Time heals, she might say in an unguarded moment. Yes, heals into a callus over the wound, hard and protective. Just like she felt: hard and protective. But did John Rebus need her solidity, her protection?

'Here we are,' he said on his return. 'The barman's slow tonight, sorry.'

Chris Kemp accepted the drink with a thin smile. 'I've just been telling Patience . . .'

Oh God, Rebus thought as he sat down. She looks like a bucketful of ice. I shouldn't have brought her. But if I'd said I was popping out for the evening on my own . . . well, she'd have been the same. Get this over and done with, maybe the night can be rescued.

'So, Chris,' he said, interrupting the young man, 'what's the dirt on Gregor Jack?'

Chris Kemp seemed to think there was plenty, and the introduction of Gregor Jack into the conversation perked Patience up a bit, so that she forgot for a time that she wasn't enjoying herself.

Rebus was interested mostly in Elizabeth Jack, but Kemp started with the MP himself, and what he had to say was interesting. Here was a different Jack, different from the public image, the received opinion, but different too from Rebus's own ideas having met with the man. He would not, for example, have taken Jack for a drinker.

'Terrible one for the whisky,' Kemp was saying. 'Probably more than half a bottle a day, more when he's in London by all accounts.'

'He never looks drunk.'

'That's because he doesn't *get* drunk. But he drinks all the same.'

'What else?'

There was more, plenty more. 'He's a smooth operator, but cunning. Deep down cunning. I wouldn't trust him further than I can spit. I know someone who knew him at university. Says Gregor Jack never did anything in his life that wasn't premeditated. And that goes for capturing *Mrs* Gregor Jack.'

'How do you mean?'

'Story is, they met at university, at a party. Gregor had seen her around before, but hadn't paid much attention. Once he knew she was *rich* though, that was another matter. He went at it full throttle, charmed the pants off her.' He turned to Patience. 'Sorry, poor choice of words.'

Patience, on her second g and t, merely bowed her head a little.

'He's calculating, you see. Remember, he was trained as

an accountant, and he's got an accountant's mind all right. What are you having?'

But Rebus was rising. 'No, Chris, let me get them.'

But Kemp wouldn't hear of it. 'Don't think I'm telling you all this for the price of a couple of beers, Inspector . . .'

And when the drinks had been bought and brought to the table, it was this train of thought which seemed to occupy Kemp.

'Why do you want to know anyway?'

Rebus shrugged.

'Is there a story?'

'Could be. Early days.'

They were talking now as professionals: the meaning was all in what was left unsaid.

'But there might be a story?'

'If there is, Chris, as far as I'm concerned it's yours.'

Kemp gulped at his beer. 'I was out there all day, you know. And all we got was a statement. Plain and simple. No further comment to make, et cetera. The story ties in with Jack?'

Rebus shrugged again. 'Early days. That was interesting, what you were saying about Mrs Jack . . .'

But Kemp's eyes were cool. 'I get the story first?'

Rebus massaged his neck. 'As far as I'm concerned.'

Kemp seemed to size the offer up. As Rebus himself knew, there was almost no offer *there* for the sizing. Then Kemp placed his glass on the table. He was ready to say a little more.

'What Jack didn't know about Liz Ferrie was that she ran with a *very* fast crowd. A rich fast crowd. People like her. It took Gregor quite a while before he was able to insinuate his way into the group. A working-class kid, remember. Still gangly and a bit awkward. But it happened, he had Liz hooked. Where he went, she would et cetera. And Jack had his own gang. Still does.'

'I don't follow.'

'Old schoolfriends mostly, a few people he met at university. His circle, you could call it.'

'One of them runs a bookshop, doesn't he?'

Kemp nodded. 'That's Ronald Steele. Known to the gang as Suey. That's why his shop's called Suey Books.'

'Funny nickname,' said Patience.

'I don't know how he came by it,' admitted Kemp. 'I'd *like* to know, but I don't.'

'Who else is there?' asked Rebus.

'I'm not sure how many there are altogether. The interesting ones are Rab Kinnoul and Andrew Macmillan.'

'Rab Kinnoul the actor?'

'The very same.'

'That's funny, I've got to talk to him. Or rather, to his wife.'

'Oh?'

Kemp was sniffing his story, but Rebus shook his head. 'Nothing to do with Jack. Some stolen books. Mrs Kinnoul is a bit of a collector.'

'Not Prof Costello's missing hoard?'

'That's it.'

Kemp was nothing if not a newsman. 'Any progress?'

Rebus shrugged.

'Don't tell me,' said Kemp, 'it's early days yet.'

And he laughed, and Patience laughed with him. But something had just struck Rebus.

'Not *the* Andrew Macmillan, surely?'

Kemp nodded. 'They were at school together.'

'Christ.' Rebus stared at the plastic-topped table. Kemp was explaining to Patience who Andrew Macmillan was.

'A very successful something-or-other. Went off his head one day. Toddled off home and sawed off his wife's head.'

Patience gasped. 'I remember that,' she said. 'They never found the head, did they?'

Kemp shook his own firmly fixed head. 'He'd have done his daughter in, too, but the kid ran for her life. She's a bit dotty now herself, and no wonder.'

'Whatever happened to him?' Rebus wondered aloud. It had been several years ago, and in Glasgow not Edinburgh. Not his territory.

'Oh,' said Kemp, 'he's in that new psychiatric place, the one they've just built.'

'You mean Duthil?' said Patience.

'That's it. Up in the Highlands. Near Grantown, isn't it?'

Well, thought Rebus, curiouser and curiouser. His geography wasn't brilliant, but he didn't think Grantown was *too* far from Deer Lodge. 'Is Jack still in touch with him?'

It was Kemp's turn to shrug. 'No idea.'

'And they were at school together?'

'That's the story. To be honest, I think Liz Jack is the more interesting character by far. Jack's sidekicks are scrupulous in keeping her out of the way.'

'Yes, why is that?'

'Because she's still the proverbial wild child. Still runs around with her old crowd. Jamie Kilpatrick, Matilda Merriman, all that sort. Parties, booze, drugs, orgies ... God knows. The press never gets a sniff.' He turned again to Patience. 'If you'll pardon the phrase. Not a sniff do we get. And anything we *do* get is blue pencilled with a fair amount of prejudice.'

'Oh?'

'Well, editors are nervous at the best of times, aren't they? And you've got to remember that Sir Hugh Ferrie is never slow with a libel suit where his family's concerned.'

'You mean that electronics factory?'

'Case in point.'

'So what about this "old crowd" of Mrs Jack's?'

'Aristos, mostly old money, some new money.'

'What about the lady herself?'

'Well, she certainly spurred Jack on in the early days. I think he always wanted to go into politics, and MPs can hardly afford not to be married. People start to suspect a shirt-lifting tendency. My guess is he looked for someone pretty, with money, and with a father of influence. Found her and wasn't going to let go. And it's been a successful marriage, so far as the public's concerned. Liz gets wheeled out for the photo opportunities and looks just right, then she disappears again. Completely different to Gregor, you see.

47

Fire and ice. She's the fire, he's the ice, usually with whisky added . . .'

Kemp was in a talkative mood tonight. There was more, but it was speculation. Still, it was interesting to be given a different perspective, wasn't it? Rebus considered this as he excused himself and visited the gents'. The Horsehair's trough-like urinal was brimful of liquid, as had always, to Rebus's knowledge, been the case. The condensation on the overhead cistern dripped unerringly on to the heads of those unwise enough to get too close, and the graffiti was mostly the work of a dyslexic bigot: REMEMBER 1960. There was some new stuff though, written in biro. 'The Drunk as a Lord's Prayer,' Rebus read. 'Our Father which are in heavy, Alloa'd be they name . . .'

Rebus reckoned that if he didn't have all he needed, he had all Chris Kemp was able to give. No reason to linger then. No reason at all. He came out of the gents' briskly, and saw that a young man had stopped at the table to chat with Patience. He was moving away now, back to the main bar, while Patience smiled a farewell in his direction.

'Who was that?' Rebus asked, not sitting down.

'He lives next door in Oxford Terrace,' Patience said casually. 'Works in Trading Standards. I'm surprised you haven't met him.'

Rebus murmured something, then tapped his watch with his finger.

'Chris,' he said, 'this is all your fault. You're too interesting by half. We were supposed to be at the restaurant twenty minutes ago. Kevin and Myra will kill us. Come on, Patience. Listen, Chris, I'll be in touch. Meantime . . .' he leaned closer to the reporter, lowering his voice. 'See if you can find who tipped off the papers about the brothel raid. *That* might be the start of the story.' He straightened up again. 'See you soon, eh? Cheers.'

'Cheerio, Chris,' said Patience, sliding out of her seat.

'Oh, right, bye then. See you.' And Chris Kemp found himself alone, wondering if it was something that he'd said.

Outside, Patience turned to Rebus. 'Kevin and Myra?' she said.

'Our oldest friends,' explained Rebus. 'And as good a get-out clause as anything. Besides, I *did* promise you dinner. You can tell me all about our next-door neighbour.'

He took her arm in his and they walked back to the car – her car. Patience had never seen John Rebus jealous before, so it was hard to tell, but she could have sworn he was jealous now. Well well, wonders would never cease . . .

3
Treacherous Steps

Springtime in Edinburgh. A freezing wind, and near-horizontal rain. Ah, the Edinburgh wind, that joke of a wind, that black farce of a wind. Making everyone walk like mime artists, making eyes water and then drying the tears to a crust on red-nipped cheeks. And throughout it all, that slightly sour yeasty smell in the air, the smell of not-so-distant breweries. There had been a frost overnight. Even the prowling, fur-coated Lucky had yowled at the bedroom window, demanding entry. The birds had been chirping as Rebus let him in. He checked his watch: two thirty. Why the hell were the birds singing so early? When he next awoke, at six, they'd stopped. Maybe they were trying to avoid the rush hour...

This sub-zero morning, it had taken him a full five minutes to start his clown of a car. Maybe it was time to get one of those red noses for the radiator grille. And the frost had swollen the cracks in the steps up to Great London Road police station, swollen and then fissured, so that Rebus stepped warily over wafers of stone.

Treacherous steps. Nothing would be done about them. The rumours were still rife anyway; rumours that Great London Road was shagged out, wabbit, past its sell-by. Rumours that it would be shut down. A prime site, after all. Prime land for another hotel or office block. And the staff? Split up, so the rumours went. With most of them being transferred to St Leonard's, the Divisional HQ (Central). Much closer to Rebus's flat in Marchmont; but much further from

Oxford Terrace and Dr Patience Aitken. Rebus had made himself a little pact, a sort of contract in his head: if, within the next month or two, the rumours became fact, then it was a message from on high, a message that he should not move in with Patience. But if Great London Road remained a going concern, or if they were moved to Fettes HQ (five minutes from Oxford Terrace) ... what then? What then? The fine print on the contract was still being decided.

'Morning, John.'

'Hello, Arthur. Any messages?'

The duty desk sergeant shook his head. Rebus rubbed his hands over his ears and face, thawing them out, and climbed the stairs towards his room, where treacherous linoleum replaced treacherous stone. And then there was the treacherous telephone ...

'Rebus here.'

'John?' It was the voice of Chief Superintendent Watson. 'Can you spare a minute?'

Rebus made noisy show of rustling some papers on his desk, hoping Watson would think he'd been in the office for hours, hard at work.

'Well, sir ...'

'Don't piss about, John. I tried you five minutes ago.'

Rebus stopped shuffling papers. 'I'll be right along, sir.'

'That's right, you will.' And with that the phone went dead. Rebus shrugged off his weatherproof jacket, the one which always let water in at the shoulders. He felt the shoulders of his suit-jacket. Sure enough, they were damp, matching his enthusiasm for a Monday-morning meeting with the Farmer. He took a deep breath and spread his hands in front of him like an old-time song and dance man.

'It's showtime,' he told himself. Only five working days till the weekend. Then he made a quick phone call to Dufftown Police Station and asked them to check on Deer Lodge.

'Is that d-e-a-r?' asked the voice.

'D-double e-r,' corrected Rebus, thinking: But it probably *was* dear enough when they bought it.

'Anything we're looking for in particular?'

An MP's wife . . . leftovers from a sex orgy . . . flour bags full of cocaine . . . 'No,' said Rebus, 'nothing special. Just let me know what you find.'

'Right you are. It might take a while.'

'Soon as you can, eh?' And so saying, Rebus remembered that he should be elsewhere. 'Soon as you can.'

Chief Superintendent Watson was as blunt as a tramp's razor blade.

'What the hell were you doing at Gregor Jack's yesterday?'

Rebus was almost caught off guard. Almost. 'Who's been telling tales?'

'Never mind that. Just give me a bloody answer.' Pause. 'Coffee?'

'I wouldn't say no.'

Watson's wife had bought him the coffee-maker as a Christmas present. Maybe as a hint that he should cut down his consumption of Teacher's whisky. Maybe so that he'd stand a chance of being sober when he returned home of an evening. All it had done so far though was make Watson hyperactive of a morning. In the afternoon, however, after a few lunchtime nips, drowsiness would take over. Best, therefore, to avoid Watson in the mornings. Best to wait until afternoon to ask him about that leave you were thinking of taking or to tell him the news of the latest bodged operation. If you were lucky, you'd get off with a 'tut-tut'. But the mornings . . . the mornings were different.

Rebus accepted the mug of strong coffee. Half a packet of espresso looked as though it had been tipped into the generous filter. Now, it tipped itself into Rebus's bloodstream.

'Sounds stupid, sir, but I was just passing.'

'You're right,' said Watson, settling down behind his desk, 'it *does* sound stupid. Even supposing you *were* just passing . . .'

'Well, sir, to be honest, there was a little more to it than that.' Watson sat back in his chair, holding the mug in both hands, and waited for the story. Doubtless he was thinking: this'll be good. But Rebus had nothing to gain by lying. 'I like

Gregor Jack,' he said. 'I mean, I like him as an MP. He's always seemed to me to be a bloody good MP. I felt a bit . . . well, I thought it was bad timing, us happening to bust that brothel the same time he was there . . .' Bad timing? Did he really believe that was all there was to it? 'So, when I *did* happen to be passing – I'd stayed the night at Sergeant Holmes' new house . . . he lives in Jack's constituency – I thought I'd stop and take a look. There were a lot of reporters about the place. I don't know exactly why I stopped, but then I saw that Jack's car was sitting out on the drive in full view. I reckoned that was dangerous. I mean, if a photo of it got into the papers. Everybody'd know Jack's car, right down to its number plate. You can't be too safe, can you? So I went in and suggested the car be moved into the garage.'

Rebus stopped. That was all there was to it, wasn't it? Well, it was enough to be going on with. Watson was looking thoughtful. He took another injection of coffee before speaking.

'You're not alone, John. I feel guilty myself about Operation Creeper. Not that there's anything to feel guilty *about*, you understand, but all the same . . . and now the press are on to the story, they'll keep on it till the poor bugger's forced to resign.'

Rebus doubted this. Jack hadn't looked like a man ready or willing or about to resign.

'If we can help Jack . . .' Watson paused again, wanting to catch Rebus's eye. He was warning Rebus that this was all unofficial, all unwritten, but that it had already been *discussed*, at some level far above Rebus himself. Perhaps, even, above Watson. Had the Chief Super been rapped over the knuckles by the high heidyins themselves? 'If we can help him,' he was saying, 'I'd like him to get that help. If you see what I mean, John.'

'I think so, sir.' Sir Hugh Ferrie had powerful friends. Rebus was beginning to wonder just *how* powerful . . .

'Right then.'

'Just the one thing, sir. Who gave you the info about the brothel?'

Watson was shaking his head even before Rebus had finished the question. 'Can't tell you that, John. I know what you're thinking. You're wondering if Jack was set up. Well, if he was, it had nothing to do with my informant. I can promise you that. No, if Jack *was* set up, the question that needs answering is why *he* was there in the first place, not why *we* were there.'

'But the papers knew, too. I mean, they knew about Operation Creeper.'

Watson was nodding now. 'Again, nothing to do with my informant. But yes, I've been thinking about that. It had to be one of us, hadn't it? Someone on the team.'

'So nobody else knew when it was planned for?'

Watson seemed to hold his breath for a moment, then shook his head. He was lying, of course. Rebus could see that. No point probing further, not yet at any rate. There would be a reason behind the lie, and that reason would come out in good time. Right now, and for no reason he could put his finger on, Rebus was more worried about *Mrs* Jack. Worried? Well, maybe not quite worried. Maybe not even *concerned*. Call it . . . call it *interested*. Yes, that was it. He was interested in her.

'Any progress on those missing books?'

What missing books? Oh, *those* missing books. He shrugged. 'We've talked to all the booksellers. The list is doing the rounds. We might even get a mention in the trade magazines. I shouldn't think any bookseller is going to touch them. Meantime . . . well, there are the private collectors still to be interviewed. One of them's the wife of Rab Kinnoul.'

'The actor?'

'The very same. Lives out towards South Queensferry. His wife collects first editions.'

'Better try to get out there yourself, John. Don't want to send a constable out to see Rab Kinnoul.'

'Right, sir.' It was the answer he'd wanted. He drained his mug. His nerves were already sizzling like bacon in a pan. 'Anything else?'

But Watson had finished with him, and was rising to

replenish his own mug. 'This stuff's addictive,' he was saying as Rebus left the office. 'But by God, it makes me feel full of beans.'

Rebus didn't know whether to laugh or cry . . .

Rab Kinnoul was a professional hit man.

He had made his name initially through a series of roles on television: the Scottish immigrant in a London sitcom, the young village doctor in a farming serial, with the occasional guest spot on more substantial fare such as *The Sweeney* (playing a Glasgow runaway) or the drama series *Knife Ledge*, where he played a hired killer.

It was this last part which swung things for Kinnoul. Noticed by a London-based casting director, he was approached and screen-tested for the part of the assassin in a low-budget British thriller, which went on to do surprising business, picking up good notices in the USA as well as in Europe. The film's director was soon persuaded to move to Hollywood, and he in turn persuaded his producers that Rab Kinnoul would be ideal for the part of the gangster in an Elmore Leonard adaptation.

So, Kinnoul went to Hollywood, played minor roles in a series of major and minor murder flicks, and was again a success. He possessed a face and eyes into which could be read anything, simply anything. If you thought he should be evil, he *was* evil; if you thought he should be psychotic, he *was* psychotic. He was cast in these roles and he fitted them, but if things had taken a different turning in his career he might just as easily have ended up as the romantic lead, the sympathetic friend, the hero of the piece.

Now he'd settled back in Scotland. There was talk that he was reading scripts, was about to set up his own film company, was retiring. Rebus couldn't quite imagine retiring at thirty-nine. At fifty, maybe, but not at thirty-nine. What would you do all day? Driving towards Kinnoul's home just outside South Queensferry, the answer came to him. You could spend all day every day painting the exterior of your house; supposing, that is, it was the size of Rab Kinnoul's house. Like the Forth Rail Bridge, by the time you'd finished painting it, the first bit would be dirty again.

Which was to say that it was a very large house, even from a distance. It sat on a hillside, its surroundings fairly bleak. Long grass and a few blasted trees. A river ran nearby, discharging into the Firth of Forth. Since there was no sign of a fence separating house from surroundings, Rebus reckoned Kinnoul must own the lot.

The house was modern, if the 1960s could still be considered 'modern', styled like a bungalow but about five times the scale. It reminded Rebus mostly of those Swiss chalets you saw on postcards, except that the chalets were always finished in wood, whereas this house was finished in harling.

'I've seen better council houses,' he whispered to himself as he parked on the pebbled driveway. Getting out of the car he did, however, begin to see one of the house's attractions. The view. Both spectacular Forth Bridges not too far away at all, the firth itself sparkling and calm, and the sun shining on green and pleasant Fife across the water. You couldn't see Rosyth, but over to the east could just about be made out the seaside town of Kirkcaldy, where Gregor Jack and, presumably, Rab Kinnoul, had been schooled.

'No,' said Mrs Kinnoul – Cath Kinnoul – as she walked, a little later, into the sitting room. 'People are always making that mistake.'

She had come to the door while Rebus was still staring.

'Admiring the view?'

He grinned back at her. 'Is that Kirkcaldy over there?'

'I think so, yes.'

Rebus turned and started up the steps towards the front door. There were rockeries and neat borders to either side of them. Mrs Kinnoul looked the type to enjoy gardening. She wore homely clothes and a homely smile. Her hair had been permed into waves, but pulled back and held with a clasp at the back. There was something of the 1950s about her. He didn't know what he'd been expecting – some Hollywood blonde, perhaps – but certainly he'd not been expecting this.

'I'm Cath Kinnoul.' She held out a hand. 'I'm sorry, I've forgotten your name.'

He'd phoned, of course, to warn of his visit, to make sure someone would be at home. 'Detective Inspector Rebus,' he said.

'That's right,' she said. 'Well, come in.'

Of course, the whole thing could have been done by telephone. The following rare books have been stolen . . . has anyone approached you . . . ? If anyone should, please contact us immediately. But like any other policeman, Rebus liked to *see* who and what he was dealing with. People often gave something away when you were there in person. They were flustered, edgy. Not that Cath Kinnoul looked flustered. She came into the sitting room with a tray of tea things. Rebus had been staring out of the picture window, drinking in the scene.

'Your husband went to school in Kirkcaldy, didn't he?'

And then she'd said: 'No, people are always making that mistake. I think because of Gregor Jack. You know, the MP.' She placed the tray on a coffee table. Rebus had turned from the window and was studying the room. There were framed photographs of Rab Kinnoul on the walls, stills from his movies. There were also photos of actors and actresses Rebus supposed he should know. The photos were signed. The room seemed to be dominated by a thirty-eight-inch television, atop which sat a video recorder. To either side of the TV, piled high on the floor, were videotapes.

'Sit down, Inspector. Sugar?'

'Just milk, please. You were saying about your husband and Gregor Jack . . . ?'

'Oh yes. Well, I suppose because they're both in the media, on television I mean, people tend to think they must know one another.'

'And don't they?'

She laughed. 'Oh yes, yes, they know one another. But only through me. People get their stories mixed up, I suppose, so it started to appear in the papers and magazines that Rab and Gregor went to school together, which is nonsense. Rab went to school in Dundee. It was *me* that went to school with Gregor. And we went to university together, too.'

So not even the cream of young Scottish reporters always got it right. Rebus accepted the china cup and saucer with a nod of thanks.

'I was plain Catherine Gow then, of course. I met Rab later, when he was already working in television. He was doing a play in Edinburgh. I bumped into him in the bar after a performance.'

She was stirring her tea absent-mindedly. 'I'm Cath Kinnoul now, Rab Kinnoul's wife. Hardly anyone calls me Gowk any more.'

'Gowk?' Rebus thought he'd misheard. She looked up at him.

'That was my nickname. We all had nicknames. Gregor was Beggar . . .'

'And Ronald Steele was Suey.'

She stopped stirring, and looked at him as though seeing him for the first time. 'That's right. But how . . . ?'

'It's what his shop's called,' Rebus explained, this being the truth.

'Oh yes,' she said. 'Well, anyway, about these books . . .'

Three things struck Rebus. One was that there seemed precious few books around, for someone who was supposedly a collector. The second was that he'd rather talk some more about Gregor Jack. The third was that Cath Kinnoul was on drugs, tranquillizers of some kind. It was taking a second too long for her lips to form each word, and her eyelids had a droop to them. Valium? Moggies even?

'Yes,' he said, 'the books.' Then he looked around him. Any actor would have known it for a cheap effect. 'Mr Kinnoul's not at home just now?'

She smiled. 'Most people just call him Rab. They think if they've seen him on television, they know him, and knowing him gives them the right to call him Rab. Mr Kinnoul . . . I can see you're a policeman.' She almost wagged a finger at him, but thought better of it and drank her tea instead. She

58

held the delicate cup by its body rather than by the awkward handle, drained it absolutely dry, and exhaled.

'Thirsty this morning,' she said. 'I'm sorry, what were you saying?'

'You were telling me about Gregor Jack.'

She looked surprised. 'Was I?'

Rebus nodded.

'Yes, that's right, I read about it in the papers. Horrible things they were saying. About him and Liz.'

'Mrs Jack?'

'Liz, yes.'

'What's she like?'

Cath Kinnoul seemed to shiver. She got up slowly and placed her empty cup on the tray. 'More tea?' Rebus shook his head. She poured milk, lots of sugar, and then a trickle of tea into her cup. 'Thirsty,' she said, 'this morning.' She went to the window, holding the cup in both hands. 'Liz is her own woman. You've got to admire her for that. It can't be easy, living with a man who's in the public eye. He hardly sees her.'

'He's away a lot, you mean?'

'Well, yes. But she's away a lot, too. She has her own life, her own friends.'

'Do you know her well?'

'No, no, I wouldn't say that. You wouldn't believe what we got up to at school. Who'd have thought . . .' She touched the window. 'Do you like the house, Inspector?'

This was an unexpected turn in the conversation. 'It's . . . er, big, isn't it?' Rebus answered. 'Plenty of room.'

'Seven bedrooms,' she said. 'Rab bought it from some rock star. I don't think he'd have bothered if it hadn't been a *star*'s home. What do we need seven bedrooms for? There's only the two of us . . . Oh, here's Rab now.'

Rebus came to the window. A Land-Rover was bumping up the driveway. There was a heavy figure in the front, hands clenching the wheel. The Land-Rover gave a squeal as it stopped.

'About these books,' said Rebus, suddenly an efficient official. 'You collect books, I believe?'

'Rare books, yes. First editions, mostly.' Cath Kinnoul, too, was starting to play another part, this time the woman who's helping police with their . . .

The front door opened and closed. 'Cath? Whose car's that in the drive?'

Rab Kinnoul came massively into the room. He was six feet two tall, and probably weighed fifteen stone. His chest was huge, a predominantly red tartan shirt stretched across it. He wore baggy brown corduroys tied at the waist with a thin, straining belt. He'd started growing a reddish beard, and his brown hair was longer than Rebus remembered, curling over his ears. He looked expectantly at Rebus, who came towards him.

'Inspector Rebus, sir.'

Kinnoul looked surprised, then relieved, then, Rebus thought, worried. The problem was those eyes; they didn't seem to change, did they? So that Rebus began to wonder whether the surprise, relief and worry were in Kinnoul's mind or in his own.

'Inspector, what's . . . I mean, is there something wrong?'

'No, no, sir. It's just that some books have been stolen, rare books, and we're going around talking to private collectors.'

'Oh.' Now Kinnoul broke into a grin. Rebus didn't think he'd seen him grin in any of his TV or film roles. He could see why. The grin changed Kinnoul from ominous heavy into overgrown teenager, lighting his face, making it innocent and benign. 'So it's Cath you want then?' He looked over Rebus's shoulder at his wife. 'All right, Cath?'

'Fine, Rab.'

Kinnoul looked at Rebus again. The grin had disappeared. 'Maybe you'd like to see the library, Inspector? Cath and you can have a chat in there.'

'Thank you, sir.'

Rebus took the back roads on his way into Edinburgh. They were nicer, certainly quieter. He'd learned very little in the

Kinnoul's library, except that Kinnoul felt protective towards his wife, so protective that he'd felt unable to leave Rebus alone with her. What was he afraid of? He had stalked the library, had pretended to browse, and sat down with a book, all the time listening as Rebus asked his simple questions and left the simple list and asked Cath Kinnoul to be on the lookout. And she'd nodded, fingering the xeroxed sheet of paper.

The 'library' in fact was an upper room of the house, probably intended at one time as a bedroom. Two walls had been fitted with shelves, most of them sheeted with sliding glass doors. And behind these sheets of glass sat a dull collection of books – dull to Rebus's eyes, but they seemed enough to bring Cath Kinnoul out of her daydreams. She pointed out some of the exhibits to Rebus.

'Fine first edition . . . rebound in calfskin . . . some pages still uncut. Just think, that book was printed in 1789, but if I cut open those pages I'd be the first person ever to read them. Oh, and that's a Creech edition of Burns . . . first time Burns was published in Edinburgh. And I've some modern books, too. There's Muriel Spark . . . *Midnight's Children* . . . George Orwell . . .'

'Have you read them all?'

She looked at Rebus as though he'd asked her about her sexual preferences. Kinnoul interrupted.

'Cath's a collector, Inspector.' He came over and put his arm around her. 'It could have been stamps or porcelain or old china dolls, couldn't it, love? But it's books. She collects books.' He gave her a squeeze. 'She doesn't read them. She collects them.'

Rebus shook his head now, tapping his fingers against the steering wheel. He'd shoved a Rolling Stones tape into the car's cassette player. An aid to constructive thought. On the one hand, you had Professor Costello, with his marvellous library, the books read and reread, worth a fortune but still there for the borrowing . . . for the *reading*. And on the other hand there was Cath Kinnoul. He didn't quite know why he felt so sorry for her. It couldn't be easy being married to . . .

well, she'd said it herself, hadn't she? Except that she'd been talking about Elizabeth Jack. Rebus was intrigued by Mrs Jack. More, he was becoming *fascinated* by her. He hoped he would meet her soon . . .

The call from Dufftown came just as he got into the office. On the stairs, he'd been told of another rumour. By the middle of next week, there would be official notification that Great London Road was to close. Then back I go to Marchmont, Rebus thought.

The telephone was ringing. It was always ringing either just as he was coming in, or else just as he was about to go out. He could sit in his chair for hours and never once . . .

'Hello, Rebus here.'

There was a pause, and enough snap-crackle over the line for the call to be trans-Siberian.

'Is that Inspector Rebus?'

Rebus sighed and fell into his chair. 'Speaking.'

'Hello, sir. This is a terrible line. It's Constable Moffat. You wanted someone to go to Deer Lodge.'

Rebus perked up. 'That's right.'

'Well, sir, I've just been over there and – ' And there was a noise like an excited geiger counter. Rebus held the receiver away from his ear. When the noise had stopped, the constable was still speaking. 'I don't know what more I can tell you, sir.'

'You can tell me the whole bloody lot again for a start,' Rebus said. 'The line went supernova for a minute there.'

Constable Moffat began again, articulating his words as though in conversation with a retard. 'I was saying, sir, that I went over to Deer Lodge, but there's no one at home. No car outside. I had a look through the windows. I'd say someone *had* been there at some time. Looked like there'd been a bit of a party. Wine bottles and glasses and stuff. But there's no one there at the minute.'

'Did you ask any of the neighbours . . .?' As he said it, Rebus knew this to be a stupid question. The constable was already laughing.

'There *aren't* any neighbours, sir. The nearest would be Mr and Mrs Kennoway, but they're a mile hike the other side of the hills.'

'I see. And there's nothing else you can tell me?'

'Not that I can think of. If there was anything in particular ...? I mean, I know the lodge is owned by that MP, and I saw in the papers ...'

'No,' Rebus was quick to say, 'nothing to do with that.' He didn't want *more* rumours being tossed around like so many cabers at a Highland games. 'Just wanted a word with Mrs Jack. We thought she might be up there.'

'Aye, she's up this way occasionally, so I hear.'

'Well, if you hear anything else, let me know, won't you?'

'Goes without saying, sir.' Which, Rebus supposed, it did. The constable sounded a bit hurt.

'And thanks for your help,' Rebus added, but received only a curt 'Aye' before the phone went dead.

'Fuck you too, pal,' he said to himself, before going off in search of Gregor Jack's home telephone number.

Of course, there was an almighty chance that the phone would still be unplugged. Still, it was worth a try. The number itself would be on computer, but Rebus reckoned he'd be quicker looking for it in the filing cabinet. And sure enough, he found a sheet of paper headed 'Parliamentary Constituencies in Edinburgh and Lothians' on which were given the home addresses and telephone numbers of the area's eleven MPs. He punched in the ten numbers, waited, and was rewarded with the ringing tone. Not that that meant –

'Hello?'

'Is that Mr Urquhart?'

'I'm sorry, Mr Urquhart's not here right at the moment – '

But of course by now Rebus recognized the voice. 'Is that you, Mr Jack? It's Inspector Rebus here. We met yester – '

'Why yes, hello, Inspector. You're in luck. We plugged the phone back in this morning, and Ian's spent all day taking calls. He's just taken a break. He thought we should unplug the thing again, but I plugged it back in myself when he'd gone. I hate to think I'm completely cut off. My constituents, after all, might need to get – '

'What about Miss Greig?'

'She's working. Work must go on, Inspector. There's an office to the back of the house where she does the typing and so on. Helen's really been a – '

'And Mrs Jack? Any news?'

Now the flow seemed to have dried up. There was a parched cough. Rebus could visualize a readjustment of facial features, maybe even a scratching of finger, a running of fingers through hair . . .

'Why . . . yes, funny you should mention it. She phoned this morning.'

'Oh?'

'Yes, poor love. Said she'd been trying for hours, but of course the phone was disconnected all day Sunday and busy most of today – '

'She's at your cottage then?'

'That's right, yes. Spending a week there. I told her to stay put. No point in her getting dragged into all this rubbish, is there? It'll soon blow over. My solicitor – '

'We've checked Deer Lodge, Mr Jack.'

Another pause. Then: 'Oh?'

'She doesn't seem to be there. No sign of life.'

There was sweat beneath the collar of Rebus's shirt. He could blame it on the heating of course. But he knew the heating wasn't *all* to blame. Where was this leading? What was he wandering into?

'Oh.' A statement this time, a deflated sound. 'I see.'

'Mr Jack, is there anything you'd like to tell me?'

'Yes, Inspector, there is, I suppose.'

Carefully: 'Would you like me to come over?'

'Yes.'

'All right, I'll be there as soon as I can. Just sit tight, all right?'

No answer.

'All right, Mr Jack?'

'Yes.'

But Gregor Jack didn't sound it.

Of course, Rebus's car wouldn't start. The sound it made was more and more like an emphysema patient's last hacking laugh. Herka-herka-her-ka-ka. Herka-herka-her.

'Having trouble?' This was yelled from across the car park by Brian Holmes, waving and about to get into his own car. Rebus slammed his car door shut and walked briskly over to where Holmes was just – with a first-time turn of the ignition – starting his Metro.

'Off home?'

'Yes.' A nod towards Rebus's doomed car. 'Doesn't sound as if you are. Want a lift?'

'As it happens, Brian, yes. And you can come along for the ride if you like.'

'I don't get it.'

Rebus was trying to open the passenger-side door, without success. Holmes hesitated a moment before unlocking it.

'It's my turn to cook tonight,' he said. 'Nell'll be up to high doh if I'm late . . .'

Rebus settled into the passenger seat and pulled the seatbelt down across his chest.

'I'll tell you all about it on the way.'

'The way where?'

'Not far from where you live. You won't be late, honest. I'll get a car to bring me back into town. But I'd quite like your attendance.'

Holmes wasn't slow; careful – yes, but never slow. 'You mean the male member,' he said. 'What's he done this time?'

'I shudder to think, Brian. Believe me, I shudder to think.'

There were no pressmen patrolling the gates, and the gates themselves were unlocked. The car had been put away in the garage, leaving the driveway clear. They left Holmes' car sitting on the main road outside.

'Quite a place,' Holmes commented.

'Wait till you see inside. It's like a film set, Ingmar Bergman or something.'

Holmes shook his head. 'I still can't believe it,' he said. 'You, coming out here yesterday, barging your way in – '

'Hardly barging, Brian. Now listen, I'm going to have a word with Jack. You sniff around, see if anything smells rotten.'

'You mean literally rotten?'

'I'm not expecting to find decomposing bodies in the flower beds, if that's what you're thinking. No, just keep your eyes open and your ears keen.'

'And my nose wet?'

'If you haven't got a handkerchief on you, yes.'

They separated, Rebus to the front door, Holmes around to the side of the house, towards the garage. Rebus rang the doorbell. It was nearly six. No doubt Helen Greig would be on her way home . . .

But it was Helen Greig who answered the door.

'Hello,' she said. 'Come in. Gregor's in the living room. You know the way.'

'Indeed I do. Keeping you busy, is he?' He laid a finger on the face of his wristwatch.

'Oh yes,' she said smiling, 'he's a real slavemaster.'

An unkind image came to Rebus then, of Jack in leather gear and Helen Greig on a leash . . . He blinked it away. 'Does he seem all right?'

'Who? Gregor?' She gave a quiet laugh. 'He seems fine, under the circumstances. Why?'

'Just wondering, that's all.'

She thought for a moment, seemed about to say something, then remembered her place. 'Can I get you anything?'

'No, thanks.'

'Right, see you later then.' And off she went, back past the curving staircase, back to her office to the rear of the house. Damn, he hadn't told Holmes about her. If Holmes peered in through the office window . . . Oh well. If he heard a scream, he'd know what had happened. He opened the living room door.

Gregor Jack was alone. Alone and listening to his hi-fi. The volume was low, but Rebus recognized the Rolling Stones. It was the album he'd been listening to earlier, *Let It Bleed*.

Jack rose from his leather sofa, a glass of whisky in one hand. 'Inspector, you didn't take long. You've caught me indulging in my secret vice. Well, we all have *one* secret vice, don't we?'

Rebus thought again of the scene at the brothel. And Jack seemed to read his mind, for he gave an embarrassed smile. Rebus shook the proffered hand. He noticed that a plaster had been stuck on the left hand's offending finger. One secret vice, and one tiny flaw . . .

Jack saw him noticing. 'Eczema,' he explained, and seemed about to say more.

'Yes, you said.'

'Did I?'

'Yesterday.'

'You'll have to forgive me, Inspector. I don't usually repeat myself. But what with yesterday and everything . . .'

'Understood.' Past Jack, Rebus noticed a card standing on the mantelpiece. It hadn't been there yesterday.

Jack realized he had a glass in his hand. 'Can I offer you a drink?'

'You can, sir, and I accept.'

'Whisky all right? I don't think there's much else . . .'

'Whatever you're having, Mr Jack.' And for some reason he added: 'I like the Rolling Stones myself, their earlier stuff.'

'Agreed,' said Jack. 'The music scene these days, it's all rubbish, isn't it?' He'd gone over to the wall to the left of the fireplace, where glass shelves held a series of bottles and glasses. As he poured, Rebus walked over to the table where yesterday Urquhart had been fussing with some papers. There were letters, waiting to be signed (all with the House of Commons portcullis at the head), and some notes relating to parliamentary business.

'This job,' Jack was saying, approaching with Rebus's drink, 'really is what you make of it. There are some MPs who do the minimum necessary, and believe me that's still plenty. Cheers.'

'Cheers.' They both drank.

'Then there are those,' said Jack, 'who go for the maximum. They do their constituency work, and they become involved in the parliamentary process, the wider world. They debate, they write, they attend . . .'

'And which camp do you belong to, sir?' He talks too much, Rebus was thinking, and yet he says so little . . .

'Straight down the middle,' said Jack, steering a course with his flattened hand. 'Here, sit down.'

'Thank you, sir.' They both sat, Rebus on the chair, Jack on the sofa. Rebus had noticed straight away that the whisky was watered, and he wondered by whom? And did Jack know about it? 'Now then,' said Rebus, 'you said on the phone that there was something – '

Jack used a remote control to switch off the music. He aimed the remote at the wall, it seemed to Rebus. There was no hi-fi system in sight. 'I want to get things straight about my wife, Inspector,' he said. 'About Liz. I *am* worried about her, I admit it. I didn't want to say anything before . . .'

'Why not, sir?' So far, the speech sounded well prepared. But then he'd had over an hour in which to prepare it. Soon enough, it would run out. Rebus could be patient. He wondered where Urquhart was . . .

'Publicity, Inspector. Ian calls Liz my liability. I happen to think he's going a bit far, but Liz is . . . well, not quite temperamental . . .'

'You think she saw the newspapers?'

'Almost certainly. She always buys the tabloids. It's the gossip she likes.'

'But she hasn't been in touch?'

'No, no, she hasn't.'

'And that's a bit strange, wouldn't you say?'

Jack creased his face. 'Yes and no, Inspector. I mean, I don't know what to think. She's capable of just laughing the whole thing off. But then again . . .'

'You think she might harm herself, sir?'

'Harm herself?' Jack was slow to understand. 'You mean suicide? No, I don't think so, no, not that. But if she felt embarrassed, she might simply disappear. Or something could have happened to her, an accident ... God knows what. If she got angry enough ... it's just possible ...' He bowed his head again, elbows resting on his knees.

'Do you think it's police business, sir?'

Jack looked up with glinting eyes. 'That's the crux, isn't it? If I report her missing ... I mean report her *officially* ... and she's found, and it turns out she was simply keeping out of things ...'

'Does she seem the type who *would* stay out of things, sir?' Rebus's thoughts were spinning now. Someone had set Jack up ... but not his wife, surely? Sunday newspaper thoughts, but still they worried him.

Jack shrugged. 'Not really. It's hard to tell with Liz. She's changeable.'

'Well, sir, we could make a few discreet inquiries up north. Check hotels, guest houses – '

'It would have to be hotels, Inspector, where Liz is concerned. *Expensive* hotels.'

'Okay then, we check hotels, ask around. Any friends she might visit?'

'Not many.'

Rebus waited, wondering if Jack would change his mind. After all, there was always Andrew Macmillan, the murderer. Someone she probably knew, someone nearby. But Jack merely shrugged and repeated, 'Not many.'

'Well, a list would help, sir. You might even contact them yourself. You know, just phoning for a chat. If Mrs Jack was there, they'd be bound to tell you.'

'Unless she'd told them not to.'

Well, that was true.

'But then,' Jack was saying, 'if it turned out she'd been off to one of the islands and hadn't heard a thing ...'

Politics, it was all about politics in the end. Rebus was coming to respect Gregor Jack less, but, in a strange way, like him more. He rose and walked over towards the shelf unit, ostensibly to put his glass there. At the mantelpiece, he stopped by the card and picked it up. The front was a cartoon showing a young man in an open-topped sports car, champagne in an ice bucket on the passenger seat. The message above read GOOD LUCK! Inside was another message, written in felt pen: 'Never fear, The Pack is with you'. There were six signatures.

'Schoolfriends,' Jack was saying. He came over to stand beside Rebus. 'And a couple from university days. We've stuck pretty close over the years.'

A few of the names Rebus recognized, but he was happy to look puzzled and let Jack provide the information.

'Gowk, that's Cathy Gow. She's Cath Kinnoul now, Kinnoul as in Rab, the actor.' His finger drifted to the next signature. 'Tampon is Tom Pond. He's an architect in Edinburgh. Bilbo, that's Bill Fisher, works in London for some magazine. He was always daft on Tolkien.' Jack's voice had become soft with sentiment. Rebus was thinking of the schoolfriends *he'd* kept up with – a grand total of none. 'Suey is Ronnie Steele . . .'

'Why Suey?'

Jack smiled. 'I'm not sure I should tell you. Ronnie would kill me.' He considered for a moment, gave a mellow shrug. 'Well, we were on a school trip to Switzerland, and a girl went into Ronnie's room and found him . . . doing something. She went and told everyone about it, and Ronnie was so embarrassed that he ran outside and lay down in the road. He said he was going to kill himself, only no cars came past, so eventually he got up.'

'And suicide abbreviates to Suey?'

'That's right.' Jack studied the card again. 'Sexton, that's Alice Blake. Sexton Blake, you see. A detective like yourself.' Jack smiled. 'Alice works in London, too. Something to do with PR.'

'And what about . . .?' Rebus was pointing to the last secret name, Mack. Jack's face changed.

'Oh, that's . . . Andy Macmillan.'

'And what does Mr Macmillan do these days?' Mack, Rebus was thinking. As in Mack the Knife, grimly apt . . .

Jack was aloof. 'He's in prison, I believe. Tragic story, tragic.'

'In prison?' Rebus was keen to pursue the subject, but Jack had other ideas. He pointed to the names on the card.

'Notice anything, Inspector?'

Yes, Rebus had, though he hadn't been going to mention it. Now he did. 'The names are all written by the same person.'

Jack gave a quick smile. 'Bravo.'

'Well, Mr Macmillan's in prison, and Mr Fisher and Miss Blake could hardly have signed, could they, living in London? The story only broke yesterday . . .'

'Ah yes, good point.'

'So who . . .?'

'Cathy. She used to be an expert forger, though you might not think it to look at her. She used to have all our signatures off by heart.'

'But Mr Pond lives in Edinburgh . . . couldn't he have signed his own?'

'I think he's in the States on business.'

'And Mr Steele . . .?' Rebus tapped the 'Suey' scrawl.

'Well, Suey's a hard man to catch, Inspector.'

'Is that so,' mused Rebus, 'is that so.'

There was a knock at the door.

'Come in, Helen.'

Helen Greig put her head round the door. She was dressed in a raincoat, the belt of which she was tying. 'I'm just off, Gregor. Ian not back yet?'

'Not yet. Catching up on his sleep, I expect.'

Rebus was replacing the card on the mantelpiece. He was wondering, too, whether Gregor Jack was surrounded by friends or by something else entirely . . .

'Oh,' said Helen Greig, 'and there's another policeman here. He was at the back door . . .'

The door opened to its full extent, and Brian Holmes walked into the room. Awkwardly, it seemed to Rebus. It struck him that Holmes was awkward in the presence of Gregor Jack MP.

'Thank you, Helen. See you tomorrow.'

'You're at Westminster tomorrow, Gregor.'

'God, so I am. Right, see you the day after.'

Helen Greig left, and Rebus introduced Jack to Brian Holmes. Holmes still seemed unnaturally awkward. What the hell was the matter? It couldn't just be Jack could it? Then Holmes cleared his throat. He was looking at his superior, avoiding eye contact with the MP altogether.

'Sir, er . . . there's something maybe you should see. Round the back. In the dustbin. I had some rubbish in my pockets and I thought I'd get rid of it, and I happened to lift the lid off the bin . . .'

Gregor Jack's face turned stark white.

'Right,' said Rebus briskly, 'lead the way, Brian.' He made a sweeping motion with his arm. 'After you, Mr Jack.'

The back of the house was well lit. Two sturdy black plastic bins sat beside a bushy rhododendron. Each bin had attached inside it a black plastic refuse bag. Holmes lifted the lid off the left-hand bin and held it open so that Rebus could peer inside. He was staring at a flattened cornflake packet and the wrapping from some biscuits.

'Beneath,' Holmes stated simply. Rebus lifted the cornflake packet. It had been concealing a little treasure chest. Two video cassettes, their casings broken, tape spewing from them . . . a packet of photographs . . . two small gold-coloured vibrators . . . two pairs of flimsy-looking handcuffs . . . and clothing, body-stockings, knickers with zips. Rebus couldn't help wondering what the hacks would have done if they'd found this lot first . . .

'I can explain,' said Jack brokenly.

'You don't have to, sir. It's none of our business.' Rebus said this in such a way that his meaning was clear: it might not be our business, but you'd better tell us anyway.

'I . . . I panicked. No, not really a panic. It's just, what with that story about the brothel, and now Liz is off somewhere

... and I knew you were on your way ... I just wanted rid of the lot of it.' He was perspiring. 'I mean, I know it must look strange, that's precisely why I wanted rid of it all. Not my stuff, you see, it's Liz's. Her friends ... the parties they have ... well, I didn't want you to get the wrong impression.'

Or the right impression, thought Rebus. He picked up the packet of photographs, which just happened to burst open. 'Sorry,' he said, making a show of gathering them up. They were polaroids, taken at a party it was true. Quite a party, by the look of it. And who was this?

Rebus held the photograph up so that Jack could see it. It showed Gregor Jack having his shirt removed by two women. Everyone's eyes were red.

'The first and last party I ever went to,' Jack stated.

'Yes, sir,' said Rebus.

'Look, Inspector, my wife's life is her *own*. What she chooses to get up to ... well, it's out of my hands.' Anger was replacing embarrassment. 'I might not *like* it, I might not like her *friends*, but it's *her* choice.'

'Right, sir.' Rebus threw the photographs back into the bin. 'Well, maybe your wife's ... friends will know where she is, eh? Meantime, I wouldn't leave that lot in there, not unless you want to see yourself on the front pages again. The bins are the first place some journalists look. It's not called "getting the dirt" for nothing. And as I say, Mr Jack, it's none of *our* business ... not yet.'

But it would be soon enough; Rebus felt it in his gut, which tumbled at the thought.

It would be soon enough.

Back inside the house, Rebus tried to concentrate on one thing at a time. Not easy, not at all easy. Jack wrote down the names and addresses of a few of his wife's friends. If not quite high society, they were certainly more than a few rungs above the Horsehair. Then Rebus asked about Liz Jack's car.

'A black BMW,' said Jack. 'The 3-series. My birthday present to her last year.'

Rebus thought of his own car. 'Very nice too, sir. And the

registration?' Jack reeled it off. Rebus looked a little surprised, but Jack smiled weakly.

'I'm an accountant by training,' he explained. 'I never forget figures.'

'Of course, sir. Well, we'd better be – '

There was a sound, the sound of the front door opening and closing. Voices in the hall. Had the prodigal wife returned? All three men turned towards the living room door, which now swung open.

'Gregor? Look who I found coming up the drive . . .'

Ian Urquhart saw that Gregor Jack had visitors. He paused, startled. Behind him, a tired-looking man was shuffling into the room. He was tall and skinny, with lank black hair and round NHS-style spectacles.

'Gregor,' the man said. He walked up to Gregor Jack and they shook hands. Then Jack placed a hand on the man's shoulder.

'Meant to look in before now,' the man was saying, 'but you know how it is.' He really did look exhausted, with dark-ringed eyes and a stoop to his posture. His speech and movements were slow. 'I think I've clinched a nice collection of Italian art books . . .'

He now seemed ready to acknowledge the visitors' presence. Rebus had been given Urquhart's hand and was shaking it. The visitor nodded towards Rebus's right hand.

'You,' he said, 'must be Inspector Rebus.'

'That's right.'

'How do you know that?' said Gregor Jack, suitably impressed.

'Scratch marks on the wrist,' the visitor explained. 'Vanessa told me an Inspector Rebus had been in, and that Rasputin had made his mark . . . his considerable mark, by the look of things.'

'You must be Mr Steele,' said Rebus, shaking hands.

'The very same,' said Steele. 'Sorry I wasn't in when you called. As Gregor here will tell you, I'm a hard man to – '

'Catch,' interrupted Jack. 'Yes, Ronnie, I've already told the Inspector.'

'No sign of those books then, sir?' Rebus asked Steele. He shrugged.

'Too hot to handle, Inspector. Do you have any idea how much that lot would fetch? My guess would be a private collector.'

'Stolen to order?'

'Maybe. A fairly broad range though ...' Steele seemed to tire quickly of the topic. He turned again to Gregor Jack and held his arms wide open, half shrugging. 'Gregor, what the hell are they trying to do to you?'

'Obviously,' said Urquhart, who was helping himself unasked to a drink, 'someone somewhere is looking for a resignation.'

'But what were you doing there in the first place?'

Steele had asked *the* question. He asked it into a silence which lasted for a very long time. Urquhart had poured him a drink, and handed it over, while Gregor Jack seemed to study the four men in the room, as though one of them might have the answer. Rebus noticed that Brian Holmes was studying a painting on one wall, seemingly oblivious to the whole conversation. At last, Jack made an exasperated sound and shook his head.

'I think,' Rebus said, into the general silence, 'we'd better be off.'

'Remember to empty your dustbin, sir,' was his final message to Jack, before he led Holmes down the driveway towards the main road. Holmes agreed to give him a lift into Bonnyrigg, from where Rebus could pick up a ride back into town, but otherwise reached, opened and started the car without comment. As he moved up into second gear, however, Holmes finally said: 'Nice guy. Do you think maybe he'd give us an invite to one of those parties?'

'Brian,' Rebus said warningly. Then: 'Not *his* parties, parties attended by his wife. It didn't look like their house in those photos.'

'Really? I didn't get that good a look. All I saw was my MP

being stripped by a couple of eager ladies.' Holmes gave a sudden chuckle.

'What?'

'Strip Jack Naked,' he said.

'Pardon?'

'It's a card game,' Holmes explained. 'Strip Jack Naked. You might know it as Beggar My Neighbour.'

'Really?' Rebus said, trying not to sound interested. But was that precisely what someone was trying to do, strip Jack of his constituency, his clean-cut image, perhaps even his marriage? Were they trying to beggar the man whose nickname also was Beggar?

Or was Jack not quite as innocent as he seemed? No, hell, be honest: he didn't *seem* all that innocent anyway. Fact: he had visited a brothel. Fact: he had tried to get rid of evidence that he himself had attended at least one fairly 'high-spirited' party. Fact: his wife hadn't been in touch. Big deal. Rebus's money was still on the man. In religion, he might be more Pessimisterian than Presbyterian, but in some things John Rebus still clung to faith.

Faith and hope. It was charity he usually lacked.

4
Tips

'We've got to keep this away from the papers,' said Chief Superintendent Watson. 'For as long as we can.'

'Right, sir,' said Lauderdale, while Rebus stayed silent. They were not talking about Gregor Jack, they were discussing a suspect in the Water of Leith drowning. He was in an interview room now with two officers and a tape recorder. He was helping with inquiries. Apparently, he was saying little.

'Could be nothing, after all.'

'Yes, sir.'

There was an afternoon smell of strong mints in the room, and perhaps this was why Chief Inspector Lauderdale sounded and looked more starched than ever. His nose twitched whenever Watson wasn't looking at him. Rebus all of a sudden felt sorry for his Chief Superintendent, in the way that he felt sorry for the Scotland squad whenever it was facing defeat at the hands of third-world part-timers. There but for the grace of complete inability go I . . .

'Just a bit of bragging, perhaps, overheard in a pub. The man was drunk. You know how it is.'

'Quite so, sir.'

'All the same . . .'

All the same, they had a man in the interview room, a man who had told anyone who'd listen in a packed Leith pub that he had dumped that body under Dean Bridge.

'It wis me! Eh? How 'bout that, eh? Me! Me! I did it. She deserved worse. They all do.'

And more of the same, all of it reported to the police by a fearful barmaid, nineteen next month and this was her first bar job.

Deserved worse, she did . . . they *all* do . . . Only when the police had come into the pub, he'd quietened down, gone all sulky in a corner, standing there with head bent under the weight of a cigarette. The pint glass seemed heavy, too, so that his wrist sagged beneath it, beer dripping down on to his shoes and the wooden floor.

'Now then, sir, what's all this you've been telling these people, eh? Mind telling us about it? Down at the station, eh? We've got seats down there. You can have a seat while you tell us all about it . . .'

He was sitting, but he wasn't telling. No name, no address, nobody in the pub seemed to know anything about him. Rebus had taken a look at him, as had most of the CID and uniformed men in the building, but the face meant nothing. A sad, weak example of the species. In his late thirties, his hair was already grey and thin, the face lined, bristly with stubble, and the knuckles had grazes and scabs on them.

'How did you get them then? Been in a fight? Hit her a few times before you chucked her in?'

Nothing. He looked scared, but he was resilient. Their chances of keeping him in were, to put it mildly, not good. He didn't need a solicitor; he knew he just had to keep his mouth shut.

'Been in trouble before, eh? You know the score, don't you? That's why you're keeping quiet. Much good will it do you, pal. Much good.'

Indeed. The pathologist, Dr Curt, was now being harried. They needed to know: accident, suicide, or murder? They desperately needed to know. But before any news arrived, the man began to talk.

'I was drunk,' he told them, 'didn't know what I was saying. I don't know what made me say it.' This was the story he stuck to, repeating it and refining it. They pressed for his name and address. 'I was drunk,' he said. 'That's all there is to it. I'm sober now, and I'd like to go. I'm sorry I said what I did. Can I go now?'

Nobody at the pub had been keen to press charges, not once the offending body was removed from the premises. Unpaid bouncers, thought Rebus, that's all we are. Was the man going to walk? Were they going to lose him? Not without a fight.

'We need a name and address before we can let you go.'

'I was drunk. Can I go now, please?'

'Your name!'

'Please, can I go?'

Curt still wasn't ready to pronounce. An hour or two. Some results he was waiting for . . .

'Just give us a name, eh? Stop pissing about.'

'My name's William Glass. I live at 48 Semple Street in Granton.'

There was silence, then sighs. 'Check that, will you?' one officer asked the other. Then: 'Now that wasn't so painful, was it, Mr Glass?'

The other officer grinned, then had to explain why. 'Painful . . . Glass . . . pane of glass, see?'

'Just do that check, eh?' said his colleague, rubbing at a headache which, these days, never seemed to leave him.

'They've let him go,' Holmes informed Rebus.

'About time. A wild haggis chase and no mistake.'

Holmes came into the office and made himself comfortable on the spare chair.

'Don't stand on ceremony,' said Rebus from his desk, 'just because I'm the senior officer. Why not take a seat, Sergeant?'

'Thank you, sir,' said Holmes from the chair. 'I don't mind if I do. He gave his address as Semple Street, Granton.'

'Off Granton Road?'

'That's the one.' Holmes looked around. 'It's like an oven in here. Can't you open a window?'

'Jammed shut, and the heating's – '

'I know, either on full blast or nothing. This place ...'
Holmes shook his head.

'Nothing a bit of maintenance wouldn't fix.'

'Funny,' said Holmes, 'I've never seen you as the sentimental sort ...'

'Sentimental?'

'About this place. Give me St Leonard's or Fettes any day.'
Rebus wrinkled his nose. 'No character,' he said.

'Speaking of which, what news of the male member?'

'That joke's worn as thin as my hair, Brian. Why not part-ex it against a new one?' Rebus breathed out noisily through his nose and threw down the pen he'd been playing with. 'What you mean,' he said, 'is what news of *Mrs* Jack, and the answer is none, nada, zero. I've put out the description of her car, and all the posh hotels are being checked. But so far, nothing.'

'From which we infer ...?'

'Same answer: nothing. She could still be off at some Iona spiritual retreat, or shacked up with a Gaelic crofter, or doing the Munros. She could be pissed-off at her hubby, or not know a thing about any of it.'

'And all that kit I found, the sex-shop stock clearance?'

'What about it?'

'Well ...' Holmes seemed stuck for an answer. 'Nothing really.'

'And there you've put your finger on it, Sergeant. Nothing really. Meantime, I've got work enough to be getting on with.' Rebus laid a solemn hand on the pile of reports and case-notes in front of him. 'How about you?'

Holmes was out of his chair now. 'Oh, I've plenty keeping me busy, sir. Please, don't worry yourself about me.'

'It's natural for me to worry, Brian. You're like a son to me.'

'And you're like a father to me,' Holmes replied, heading for the door. 'The fa-ther I get from you, the easier my life seems to be.'

Rebus screwed a piece of paper into a ball, but the door closed before he had time to take aim. Ach, some days the job could be a laugh. Well, okay, a grin at least. If he forgot all about Gregor Jack, the load would be lighter still. Where would Jack be now? At the House of Commons? Sitting on some committee? Being fêted by businesses and lobbyists? It all seemed a long way from Rebus's office, and from his life.

William Glass . . . no, the name meant nothing to him. Bill Glass, Billy Glass, Willie Glass, Will Glass . . . nothing. Living at 48 Semple Street. Hold on . . . Semple Street in Granton. He went to his filing cabinet and pulled out the file. Yes, just last month. Stabbing incident in Granton. A serious wounding, but not fatal. The victim had lived at 48 Semple Street. Rebus remembered it now. Bedsits carved from a house, all of them rented. A rented bedsit. If William Glass was living at 48 Semple Street, then he was staying in a rented bedsit. Rebus reached for his telephone and called Lauderdale, to whom he told his story.

'Well, someone there vouched for him when the patrol car dropped him off. The officers were told to be sure he did live there, and apparently he does. Name's William Glass, like he said.'

'Yes, but those bedsits are short-let. Tenants get their social security cheque, hand half the cash over to the landlord, maybe more than half for all I know. What I'm saying is, it's not much of an address. He could disappear from there any time he liked.'

'Why so suspicious all of a sudden, John? I thought you were of the opinion we were wasting our time in the first place?'

Oh, but Lauderdale always knew the question to ask, the question to which, as a rule, Rebus did not have an answer.

'True, sir,' he said. 'Just thought I'd let you know.'

'I appreciate it, John. It's nice to be kept informed.' There was a slight pause there, an invitation for Rebus to join Lauderdale's 'camp'. And after the pause: 'Any progress on Professor Costello's books?'

Rebus sighed. 'No, sir.'

'Oh well. Mustn't keep you chatting then. Bye, John.'

'Goodbye, sir.' Rebus wiped his palm across his forehead. It *was* hot in here, like a dress rehearsal for the Calvinist hell.

The fan had been installed and turned on, and an hour or so later Doctor Curt provided the shit to toss at it.

'Murder, yes,' he said. 'Almost definitely murder. I've discussed my findings with my colleagues, and we're of a mind.' And he went on to explain about froth and unclenched hands and diatoms. About problems of differentiating immersion from drowning. The deceased, a woman in her late twenties or early thirties, had imbibed a good deal of drink prior to death. But she had been dead before she'd hit the water, and the cause of death was probably a blow to the back of the head, carried out by a right-handed attacker (the blow itself having come from the right of the head).

But who was she? They had a photograph of the dead woman's face, but it wasn't exactly breakfast-time viewing. And though her description and a description of her clothes had been given out, nobody had been able to identify her. No identification on the body, no handbag or purse, nothing in her pockets . . .

'Better search the area again, see if we can come up with a bag or a purse. She must have had *some*thing.'

'And search the river, sir?'

'A bit late for that probably, but yes, better give it a shot.'

'The alcohol,' Dr Curt was telling anyone who would listen, had 'muddied the water, you see', after which he smiled his slow smile. 'And the fish had eaten their fill: fish fingers, fish feet, fish stomach . . .'

'Yes, sir. I see, sir.'

All of which Rebus mercifully avoided. He had once made the mistake of making a sicker pun than Dr Curt, and as a result found himself in the doctor's favour. One day, he knew, Holmes would make a better pun yet, and then Curt would have himself a new pupil and confidant . . . So, skirting around the doctor, Rebus made for Lauderdale's office.

Lauderdale himself was just getting off the phone. When he saw Rebus, he turned stony. Rebus could guess why.

'I just sent someone round to Glass's bedsit.'

'And he's gone,' Rebus added.

'Yes,' Lauderdale said, his hand still on the receiver. 'Leaving little or nothing behind him.'

'Should be easy enough to pick him up, sir.'

'Get on to it, will you, John? He must still be in the city. What is it? – an hour since he left here. Probably somewhere in the Granton area.'

'We'll get out there right away, sir,' said Rebus, glad of this excuse for a little action.

'Oh, and John . . .?'

'Sir?'

'No need to look so smug, okay?'

So the day filled itself, evening coming upon him with surprising speed. But still they had not found William Glass. Not in Granton, Pilmuir, Newhaven, Inverleith, Canonmills, Leith, Davidson's Mains . . . Not on buses or in pubs, not by the shore, not in the Botanic Gardens, not in chip shops or wandering on playing fields. They had found no friends, no family, just bare details so far from the DHSS. And at the end of it all, Rebus knew, the man might be innocent. But for now he was their straw, to be clutched at. Not the most tasteful metaphor under the circumstances, but then, as Dr Curt himself might have said, it was all water under the bridge so far as the victim was concerned.

'Nothing, sir,' Rebus reported to Lauderdale at the end of play. It had been one of those days. Nothing was the sum total of Rebus's endeavours, yet he felt weary, bone and brain weary. So that he turned down Holmes' kindly offer of a drink, and didn't even debate over his destination. He headed for Oxford Terrace and the ministrations of Dr Patience Aitken, not forgetting Lucky the cat, the wolf-whistling budgies, the tropical fish, and the tame hedgehog he'd yet to see.

*

Rebus telephoned Gregor Jack's home first thing Wednesday morning. Jack sounded tired, having spent yesterday in Parliament and the evening at some 'grotesque function, and you can quote me on that'. There was a new and altogether fake heartiness about him, occasioned, Rebus didn't doubt, by the shared knowledge of the contents of that dustbin.

Well, Rebus was tired, too. The real difference between them was a question of pay scales . . .

'Have you heard anything from your wife yet, Mr Jack?'

'Nothing.'

There was that word again. Nothing.

'What about you, Inspector? Any news?'

'No, sir.'

'Well, no news is better than bad news, so they say. Speaking of which, I read this morning that that poor woman at Dean Bridge was murder.'

'I'm afraid so.'

'Puts my own troubles into perspective, doesn't it? Mind you, there's a constituency meeting this morning, so my troubles may just be starting. Let me know, won't you? If you hear anything, I mean.'

'Of course, Mr Jack.'

'Thank you, Inspector. Goodbye.'

'Goodbye, sir.'

All very formal and correct, as their relationship had to be. Not even room for a 'Good luck with the meeting'. He knew what the meeting would be about. People didn't like it when their MP got himself into a scandal. There would be questions. There would need to be answers . . .

Rebus opened his desk drawer and lifted out the list of Elizabeth Jack's friends, her 'circle'. Jamie Kilpatrick the antique dealer (and apparent black sheep of his titled family); the Hon. Matilda Merriman, notorious for her alleged night of non-stop rogering with a one-time cabinet member; Julian Kaymer, some sort of artist; Martin Inman, professional landowner; Louise Patterson-Scott, separated wife of the retail millionaire . . .

The 'names' just kept on coming, most of them, as Jack

84

himself had put it while making out the list, 'seasoned dissolutes and hangers-on'. Mainly old money, as Chris Kemp had said, and a long way away from Gregor Jack's own 'pack'. But there was one curio among them, one seeming exception. Even Rebus had recognized it as Gregor Jack scratched it on to the list.

'What? *The* Barney Byars? The original dirty trucker?'

'The haulier, yes.'

'A bit out of place in that sort of company, isn't he?'

Jack had owned up. 'Actually, Barney's an old school-pal of mine. But as time's gone on, he's grown friendlier with Liz. It happens sometimes.'

'Still, somehow I can't see him fitting in with that lot – '

'You'd be surprised, Inspector Rebus. Believe me, you would be surprised.' Jack gave each word equal weight, leaving Rebus in no doubt that he meant what he said. Still ... Byars was another fly Fifer, another famous son. While at school, he'd made his name as a hitchhiker, often claiming he'd spent the weekend in London without paying a penny to get there. After school, he made the news again by hitching his way across France, Italy, Germany, Spain. He'd fallen in love with the lorries themselves, with the whole business of them, so he'd saved, got his HGV licence, bought himself a lorry ... and now was the largest independent haulier that Rebus could think of. Even on last year's trip to London, Rebus had been confronted by a Byars Haulage artic trying to steer its way through Piccadilly Circus.

Well, it was Rebus's job to ask if anyone had seen hide or hair of Liz Jack. He'd gladly let others do the hard work with the likes of Jamie Kilpatrick and the grim-sounding Julian Kaymer; but he was keeping Barney Byars for himself. Another week or two of this, he thought, and I'll have to buy an autograph book.

As it happened, Byars was in Edinburgh, 'drumming up custom', as the girl in his office put it. Rebus gave her his telephone number, and an hour later Byars himself called back. He would be busy all afternoon, and he'd to go to dinner that evening 'with a few fat bastards', but he could see Rebus for a drink at six if that was convenient. Rebus wondered which luxury hotel would be the base for their drink, and was stunned, perhaps even disappointed, when Byars named the Sutherland Bar, one of Rebus's own watering holes.

'Right you are,' he said. 'Six o'clock.'

Which meant that the day stretched ahead of him. There was the Case of the Lifted Literature, of course. Well, he wasn't going to hold his breath waiting for a result there. They would turn up or they would not. His bet would be that by now they'd be on the other side of the Atlantic. Then there was William Glass, suspect in a murder inquiry, somewhere out there in a back close or a cobbled side street. Well, he'd turn up come giro day. If, that is, he was more stupid than so far he'd proved to be. No, maybe he was full of cunning. In which case he wouldn't go near a DHSS office or back to his digs. In which case he would have to get money from somewhere.

So – go talk to the tramps, the city's dispossessed. Glass would steal, or else he would resort to begging. And where he begged, there would be others begging, too. Put his description about, maybe with a tenner as a reward, and let others do your work for you. Yes, it was definitely worth mentioning to Lauderdale. Except that Rebus didn't want to do the Chief Inspector *too* many good turns, otherwise Lauderdale would think he was currying favour.

'I'd rather curry an alsatian,' he said to himself.

With a nice sense of timing, Brian Holmes came into the office carrying a white paper bag and a polystyrene beaker.

'What've you got there?' Rebus asked, suddenly hungry.

'You're the policeman, you tell me.' Holmes produced a sandwich from the bag and held it in front of Rebus.

'Corned chuck?' Rebus guessed.

'Wrong. Pastrami on rye bread.'

'What?'

'And decaffeinated filter coffee.' Holmes prised the lid from the beaker and sniffed the contents with a contented smile. 'From that new delicatessen next to the traffic lights.'

'Doesn't Nell make you up a sandwich?'

'Women have equal rights these days.'

Rebus believed it. He thought of Inspector Gill Templer and her psychology books and her feminism. He thought of the demanding Dr Patience Aitken. He even thought of the free-living Elizabeth Jack. Strong women to a man ... But then he remembered Cath Kinnoul. There were still casualties out there.

'What's it like?' he asked.

Holmes had taken a bite from the sandwich and was studying what was left. 'Okay,' he said. 'Interesting.'

Pastrami – now there was a sandwich filling that would be a long time coming to the Sutherland Bar.

Barney Byars, too, was a long time coming to the Sutherland. Rebus arrived at five minutes to six, Byars at twenty-five past. But he was well worth waiting for.

'Inspector, sorry I'm late. Some cunt was trying to knock me down five per cent on a four-grand contract, *and* he wanted sixty days to pay. Know what that does to a cash flow? I told him I ran a lorry firm, not fuckin' rickshaws.'

All of which was delivered in a thick Fife tongue and at a volume appreciably above that of the bar's early evening rumble of TV and conversation. Rebus was seated at one of the bar stools, but stood and suggested they take a table. Byars, however, was already making himself comfortable on the stool next to the policeman, laying his brawny arms along the bar-top and examining the array of taps. He pointed to Rebus's glass.

'That any good?'

'Not bad.'

'I'll have a pint of that then.' Whether from awe, fear, or just good management of his customers, the barman was on hand to pour the requested pint.

'Another yourself, Inspector?'

'I'm okay, thanks.'

'And a whisky, too,' ordered Byars. 'A double, mind, not the usual smear-test.'

Byars handed a fifty-pound note to the barman. 'Keep the change,' he said. Then he roared with laughter. 'Only joking, son, only joking.'

The barman was new and young. He held the note as though it were likely to ignite. 'Ehh ... you haven't got anything smaller on you?' His accent was effeminate west coast. Rebus wondered how long he'd last in the Sutherland.

Byars exasperated but rejecting Rebus's offer of help, dug into his pockets and found two crumpled one-pound notes and some change. He accepted his fifty back and pushed the coins towards the barman, then he winked at Rebus.

'I'll tell you a secret, Inspector, if I had to choose between having five tenners or one fifty, I'd go for the one fifty every time. Want to know why? Tenners in your pocket, people think nothing of it. But whip a fifty out, and they think you're Crœsus.' He turned to the barman, who was counting the coins out into the open till. 'Hey, son, got anything for eating?' The barman jerked round as though hit by a pellet.

'Ehh ... I think there's some Scotch broth left over from lunch.' His vowels turned broth into 'braw-wrath'. The braw wrath of the Scots, Rebus thought to himself. Byars was shaking his head. 'A pie or a sandwich,' he demanded.

The barman proffered the last lonely sandwich in the place. It looked unnervingly like pastrami, but turned out to be, as Byars put it, 'the guid roast beef'.

'One pound ten,' the barman said. Byars got out the fifty-pound note again, snorted, and produced a fiver instead. He turned back to Rebus and lifted his glass.

'Cheers.' Both men drank.

'Not bad at all,' Byars said of the beer.

Rebus gestured towards the sandwich. 'I thought you were going to dinner later on?'

'I am, but more importantly, *I'm* paying. This way, I won't eat as much and won't cost myself so much.' He winked again. 'Maybe I should write a book, eh? Business tips for sole traders, that sort of thing. Heh, speaking of tips, I once asked a waiter what "tips" meant. Know what he said?'

Rebus hazarded a wild guess. 'To insure prompt service?'

'No, to insure I don't piss in the soup!' Byars' voice was back to the level of megaphone diplomacy. He laughed, then took a bite of sandwich, still chortling as he chomped. He was not a tall man, five seven or thereabouts. And he was stocky. He wore newish denims and a black leather jacket, beneath which he sported a white polo-shirt. In a bar like this, you'd take him for . . . well, just about anybody. Rebus could imagine him ruffling feathers in plush hotels and business bars. Image, he told himself. It's just another image: the hard man, the no-nonsense man, a man who worked hard and who expected others to work hard, too – always in his favour.

He had finished the sandwich, and was brushing crumbs from his lap. 'You're from Fife,' he said casually, sniffing the whisky.

'Yes,' Rebus admitted.

'I could tell. Gregor Jack's from Fife too, you know. You said you wanted to talk about him. Is it to do with that brothel story? I found that a bit hard to swallow.' He nodded towards the empty plate in front of him. 'Not as hard as that sandwich though.'

'No, it's not really to do with the . . . with Mr Jack's . . .no, it's more to do with Mrs Jack.'

'Lizzie? What about her?'

'We're not sure where she is. Any ideas?'

Byars looked blank. 'Knowing Lizzie, you'd better get Interpol on the case. She's as likely to be in Istanbul as Inverness.'

'What makes you say Inverness?'

Byars looked stuck for an answer. 'It was the first place that came to mind.' Then he nodded. 'I see what you mean though. You were thinking she might be at Deer Lodge, it being up that way. Have you looked?'

Rebus nodded. 'When did you last see Mrs Jack?'

'A couple of weeks ago. Maybe three weekends ago, I can

check. Funnily enough, it was at the lodge. A weekend party. The Pack mostly.' He looked up from his drink. 'I better explain that . . .'

'It's all right, I know who The Pack are. Three weekends ago, you say?'

'Aye, but I can check if you like.'

'A weekend party . . . you mean a party lasting the whole weekend?'

'Well, just a few friends . . . all very civilized.' A light came on behind his eyes. 'Ah-ha, I know what you're getting at. You know about Liz's parties then? No, no, this was tame stuff, dinner and a few drinks and a brisk country walk on the Sunday. Not really my mug of gin, but Liz had invited me, so . . .'

'You prefer her other kinds of party?'

Byars laughed. 'Of course! You're only young once, Inspector. I mean, it's all above board . . . isn't it?'

He seemed genuinely curious, not without reason. Why should a policeman know about 'those' parties? Who could have told him if not Gregor, and what exactly *would* Gregor have said?

'As far as I know, sir. So you don't know any reason why Mrs Jack might want to disappear?'

'I can think of a few.' Byars had finished both drinks, but didn't look like he was hanging around for another. He kept shifting on the stool, as if unable to get comfortable. 'That newspaper story for a start. I think I'd want to be well away from it, wouldn't you? I mean, I can see how it's bad for Gregor's image, not having his wife beside him, but at the same time . . .'

'Any other reasons?'

Byars was half standing now. 'A lover,' he suggested. 'Maybe he's whisked her off to Tenerife for a bit of pash under the sun.' He winked again, then his face became serious, as though he'd just remembered something. 'There were those phone calls,' he said.

'Phone calls?'

Now he was standing. 'Anonymous phone calls. Lizzie told

me about them. Not to her, to Gregor. Bound to happen, the game he's in. Caller would phone up and say he was Sir Somebody-Somebody or Lord This 'n' That, and Gregor would be fetched to the phone. Soon as he got to it, the line would go dead. That's what she told me.'

'Did these calls worry her?'

'Oh yes, you could see she was upset. She tried to hide it, but you could see. Gregor just laughed it off, of course. Can't afford to let something like that rattle him. She might even have mentioned letters. Something about Gregor getting these letters, but tearing them up before anyone could see them. But you'd have to ask Lizzie about that.' He paused. 'Or Gregor, of course.'

'Of course.'

'Right ...' Byars stuck out his hand. 'You've got my number if you need me, Inspector.'

'Yes.' Rebus shook hands. 'Thanks for your help, Mr Byars.'

'Any time, Inspector. Oh, and if you ever need a lift to London, I've got lorries make that trip four times a week. Won't cost you a penny, and you can still claim the journey on expenses.'

He gave another wink, smiled generally around the bar, and marched back out as noticeably as he'd marched in. The barman came to clear away plate and glass. Rebus saw that the tie the young man was wearing was a clip-on, standard issue in the Sutherland. If a punter tried to grab you, the tie came away in his hand ...

'Was he talking about me?'

Rebus blinked. 'Eh? What makes you think that?'

'I thought I heard him mention my name.'

Rebus poured the dregs from his glass into his mouth and swallowed. Don't say the kid was called Gregor ... Lizzie maybe ... 'What name is that then?'

'Lawrie.'

Rebus was more than halfway there before he realized he was headed not for Stockbridge comforts and Patience

91

Aitken, but for Marchmont and his own neglected flat. So be it. Inside the flat, the atmosphere managed to be both chill and stale. A coffee mug beside the telephone resembled Glasgow insofar as it, too, was a city of culture, an interesting green and white culture.

But if the living room was growing mould, surely the kitchen would be worse. Rebus sat himself down in his favourite chair, stretched for the answering machine, and settled to listen to his calls. There weren't many. Gill Templer, wondering where he was keeping himself these days . . . as if she didn't know. His daughter Samantha, phoning from her new flat in London, giving him her address and telephone number. Then a couple of calls where the speaker had decided not to say anything.

'Be like that then.' Rebus turned off the machine, drew a notebook from his pocket, and, reading the number from it, telephoned Gregor Jack. He wanted to know why Jack hadn't said anything about his own anonymous calls. Strip Jack . . . beggar my neighbour . . . Well, if someone *were* out to beggar Gregor Jack, Jack himself didn't seem overly concerned. He didn't exactly seem resigned, but he did seem unbothered. Unless he was playing a game with Rebus . . . And what about Rab Kinnoul, on-screen assassin? What was he up to all the time he was away from his wife? And Ronald Steele, too, a 'hard man to catch'. Were they *all* up to something? It wasn't that Rebus distrusted the human race . . . wasn't just that he was brought up a Pessimisterian. He was sure there was something happening here; he just didn't know what it was.

There was nobody home. Or nobody was answering. Or the apparatus had been unplugged. Or . . .

'Hello?'

Rebus glanced at his watch. Just after quarter past seven. 'Miss Greig?' he said. 'Inspector Rebus here. He does keep you working late, doesn't he?'

'You seem to work fairly late hours yourself, Inspector. What is it this time?'

Impatience in her voice. Perhaps Urquhart had warned her

against being friendly. Perhaps it had been discovered that she'd given Rebus the address of Deer Lodge . . .

'A word with Mr Jack, if possible.'

'Not possible, I'm afraid.' She didn't sound afraid; she sounded if anything a bit smug. 'He's speaking at a function this evening.'

'Oh. How did his meeting go this morning?'

'Meeting?'

'I thought he had some meeting in his constituency . . .?'

'Oh, that. I think it went very well.'

'So he's not for the chop then?'

She attempted a laugh. 'North and South Esk would be mad to get rid of him.'

'All the same, he must be relieved.'

'I wouldn't know. He was on the golf course all afternoon.'

'Nice.'

'I *think* an MP is allowed one afternoon off a week, don't you, Inspector?'

'Oh yes, absolutely. That's what I meant.' Rebus paused. He had nothing to say, really; he was just hoping that if he kept her talking Helen Greig herself might tell him something, something he didn't know . . . 'Oh,' he said, 'about those telephone calls . . .'

'What calls?'

'The ones Mr Jack was getting. The anonymous ones.'

'I don't know what you're talking about. Sorry, I've got to go now. My mum's expecting me home at quarter to eight.'

'Right you are then, Miss Gr – ' But she had already put the phone down.

Golf? This afternoon? Jack must be keen. The rain had been falling steadily in Edinburgh since midday. He looked out of his unwashed window. It wasn't falling now, but the streets were glistening. The flat felt suddenly empty, and colder than ever. Rebus picked up the phone and made one more call. To Patience Aitken. To say he was on his way. She asked him where he was.

'I'm at home.'

'Oh? Picking up some more of your stuff?'

'That's right.'

'You could do with bringing a spare suit if you've got one.'

'Right.'

'And some of your precious books, since you don't seem to approve of my taste.'

'Romances were never my thing, Patience.' In fiction as in life, he thought to himself. On the floor around him were strewn some of his 'precious books'. He picked one up, tried to remember buying it, couldn't.

'Well, bring whatever you like, John, and as much as you like. You know how much room we've got here.'

We. We've got.

'Okay, Patience. See you later.' He replaced the receiver with a sigh and took a look around him. After all these years, there were *still* gaps on the wall-shelves from where his wife Rhona had removed her things. Still gaps in the kitchen, too, where the tumble-drier had sat, and her precious dishwasher. Still clean rectangular spaces on the walls where her posters and prints had been hung. The flat had last been redecorated–when?–in '81 or '82. Ach, it still didn't look too bad though. Who was he kidding? It looked like a squat.

'What have you done with your life, John Rebus?' The answer was: Not much. Gregor Jack was younger than him, and more successful. Barney Byars was younger than him, and more successful. Who did he know who was *older* than him and *less* successful? Not a single soul, discounting the beggars in the city centre, the ones he'd spent the afternoon with – without a result, but with a certain uncomfortable sense of belonging...

What was he thinking about? 'You're becoming a morbid old bugger.' Self-pity wasn't the answer. Moving in with Patience was the answer ... so why didn't it feel like one? Why did it feel like just another problem?

He rested his head against the back of the chair. I'm caught, he thought, between a cushion and a soft place. He sat there for a long time, staring up at the ceiling. It was dark outside, and foggy, too, a haar drifting in across the city from the North Sea. In a haar, Edinburgh seemed to shift backwards through time. You half expected to see press-gangs on the streets of Leith, hear coaches clattering over cobblestones and cries of gardy-loo in the High Street.

If he sold the flat, he could buy himself a new car, send some money to Samantha. If he sold the flat ... if he moved in with Patience ...

'If shit was gold,' his father used to say, 'you'd have a tyke at yer erse.' The old bugger had never explained exactly what a tyke was ...

Jesus, what made him think of that?

It was no good. He couldn't think straight, not here. Perhaps it was that his flat held too many memories, good and bad. Perhaps it was just the mood of the evening.

Or perhaps it was that the image of Gill Templer's face kept appearing unbidden (he told himself unbidden) in his mind ...

5
Up the River

Burglary with violent assault: just the thing for a dreich Thursday morning. The victim was in hospital, head bandaged and face bruised. Rebus had been to talk with her, and was at the house in Jock's Lodge, overseeing the dusting for prints and the taking of statements, when word reached him from Great London Road. The call came from Brian Holmes.

'Yes, Brian?'

'There's been another drowning.'

'Drowning?'

'Another body in the river.'

'Oh Christ. Whereabouts this time?'

'Out of town, up towards Queensferry. Another woman. She was found this morning by someone out for a walk.' He paused while someone handed him something. Rebus heard a muted 'thanks' as the person moved away. 'It could be our Mr Glass, couldn't it?' Holmes said now, pausing again to slurp coffee. 'We expected him to stick around the city, but he could as easily have headed north. Queensferry's an easy walk, and mostly across open land, well away from roads where he might be spotted. If I was on the run, that's the way I'd do it . . .'

Yes, Rebus knew that country. Hadn't he been out there just the other day? Quiet back roads, no traffic, nobody to notice . . . Hang on, there was a stream – no, more a river – running past the Kinnouls' house.

'Brian . . .' he started.

'And that's another thing,' Holmes interrupted. 'The woman who found the body . . . guess who it was?'

'Cathy Gow,' Rebus said casually.

Holmes seemed puzzled, 'Who? Anyway, no, it was Rab Kinnoul's wife. You know, Rab Kinnoul . . . the actor. Who's this Cathy Gow . . . ?'

It was uphill from the Kinnoul house, and along the side of the hill, too. Not too far a walk, but the country grew if anything bleaker still. Fifty yards from the fast-flowing river there was a narrow road, leading eventually to a wider road which meandered down to the coast. For someone to get here, they either had to walk past the Kinnoul house, or else walk down from the road.

'No sign of a car?' Rebus asked Holmes. Both men had zippered their jackets against the snell wind and the occasional smirr.

'Any car in particular?' Holmes asked. 'The road's tarmac. I've had a look for myself. No tyre tracks.'

'Where does it lead?'

'It peters out into a farm track, then, surprise surprise, a farm.' Holmes was moving his weight from one foot to the other, trying in vain to keep warm.

'Better check at the farm and see – '

'Someone's up there doing precisely that.'

Rebus nodded. Holmes knew this routine well enough by now: he would do something, and Rebus would double check that it had been done.

'And Mrs Kinnoul?'

'She's in the house with a WPC, drinking sweet tea.'

'Don't let her take too many downers. We'll need a statement.'

Holmes was lost, until Rebus explained about his previous visit here. 'What about Mr Kinnoul?'

'He went off somewhere this morning early. That's why Mrs Kinnoul went for a walk. She said she always went for a walk in the morning when she was on her own.'

'Do we know where he's gone?'

Holmes shrugged. 'Just on business, that's all she could tell us. Couldn't say where or how long he'd be. But he should be back this evening, according to Mrs Kinnoul.'

Rebus nodded again. They were standing above the river, near the roadway. The others were down by the river itself. It was in spate after the recent rain. Just about wide enough and deep enough to be classed a river rather than a stream. The 'others' included police officers, dressed in waders and plunging their arms into the icy water, feeling for evidence which would long have been flushed away, forensics men, hovering above the body, the Identification Unit, similarly hovering but armed with cameras and video equipment, and Dr Curt, dressed in a long flapping raincoat, its collar turned up. He trudged towards Rebus and Holmes, reciting as he came.

'When shall we three meet again ... blasted heath et cetera. Good morning, Inspector.'

'Morning, Doctor Curt. What have you got for us?'

Curt removed his glasses and wiped spots of water from them. 'Double pneumonia, I shouldn't wonder,' he answered, replacing them.

'Accident, suicide, or murder?' asked Rebus.

Curt tut-tutted him, shaking his head sadly. 'You know I can't make snap decisions, Inspector. Granted, this poor woman hasn't been in the water as long as the previous one, but all the same ...'

'How long?'

'A day at most. But with the weight of water and all ... debris and so on ... she's taken a bit of a battering. Lucky she was found at all, really.'

'How do you mean?'

'Didn't the sergeant say? Her wrist caught in a dead branch. Otherwise, she'd almost certainly have been swept down into the river and out into the sea.'

Rebus thought about the direction the river would take, bypassing the only settlements ... yes, a body falling into the stream here might well have disappeared without trace ...

'Any idea who she is?'

'No identification on the body. Plenty of rings on her

fingers though, and she's wearing quite a nice dress, too. Care to take a look?'

'Why not, eh? Come on, Brian.'

But Holmes stood his ground. 'I had a look earlier, sir. Don't let me stop you though . . .'

So Rebus followed the pathologist down the slope. He was thinking: difficult to bring a body down here . . . but you could always roll it from the top . . . yes, roll it . . . hear the splash and assume it had fallen into the river . . . you might not know the wrist had caught in a branch. But to get a body up here in the first place – dead *or* alive – surely you'd need a car. Was William Glass capable of stealing a car? Why not, everyone else seemed to know how to do it these days. Kids in primary school could show you how to do it . . .

'Like I say,' Curt was saying, 'she's been bashed about a bit . . . can't tell yet whether post- or ante-mortem. Oh, about that other drowning at Dean Bridge . . .'

'Yes?'

'Recent sexual intercourse. Traces of semen in the vagina. We should be able to get a DNA profile. Ah, here we go . . .'

The body had been laid out on a plastic sheet. Yes, it was a nice dress, distinctive, summery, though torn now and smeared with mud. The face was muddy, too . . . and cut . . . and swollen . . . the hair drawn back and part of the skull exposed. Rebus swallowed hard. Had he been expecting this? He wasn't sure. But the photographs he'd seen made him sure in his mind.

'I know her,' he said.

'What?' Even the forensics men looked up at him in disbelief. The tableau must have alerted Brian Holmes, for he came stumbling down the slope to join them.

'I said I know her. At least, I think I do. No, I'm *sure* I do. Her name is Elizabeth Jack. Her friends call her Liz or Lizzie. She's . . . she *was* married to Gregor Jack MP.'

'Good God,' said Dr Curt. Rebus looked at Holmes, and Holmes stared back at him, and neither seemed to know what to say.

*

99

There was more to identification than that, of course. Much more. Death was certainly suspicious, but this had to be decided *officially* by the gentleman from the Procurator Fiscal's office, the gentleman who now stood talking with Dr Curt, nodding his head gravely while Curt made hand gestures which would not have disgraced an excited Italian. He was explaining – explaining tirelessly, explaining for the thousandth time – about the movement of diatoms within the body, while his listener grew paler still.

The Identification Unit was still busy shooting off photographs and some video film, wiping their camera lenses every thirty seconds or so. The rain had, if anything, grown heavier, the sky an unbroken shading of grey-black. An autopsy was needed, agreed the Procurator Fiscal. The body would be transported to the mortuary in Edinburgh's Cowgate, and there formal identification would take place, involving two people who knew the deceased in life, and two police officers who had known her in death. If it turned out *not* to be Elizabeth Jack, Rebus was in a dung-pile of trouble. Watching the body being taken away, Rebus allowed himself a muffled sneeze. Perhaps Dr Curt's diagnosis of pneumonia was right. He knew where he was headed: the Kinnoul house. With luck, he might find hot tea there. The forensics team squeezed wetly into their car and headed back to police headquarters at Fettes.

'Come on, Brian,' said Rebus, 'let's see how Mrs Kinnoul's getting on.'

Cath Kinnoul seemed in a state of shock. A doctor had been to the house, but had left by the time Rebus and Holmes reached the scene. They shed their sodden jackets in the hall, while Rebus had a quiet word with the WPC.

'No sign of the husband?'

'No, sir.'

'How is she?'

'Comfortably numb.'

Rebus tried to look bedraggled and pathetic. It wasn't difficult. The WPC read his mind and smiled.

'I'll make some tea, shall I?'

'Anything hot would hit the spot, believe me.'

Cath Kinnoul was sitting in one of the living room's huge armchairs. The chair itself looked like it was in the process of consuming her, while she looked about half the size and a quarter of the age she'd been when Rebus had last seen her.

'Hello again,' he said, mock-cheerily.

'Inspector . . . Rebus?'

'That's it. And this is Sergeant Holmes. No jokes, please, he's heard them all before, haven't you, Sergeant?'

Holmes saw that they were playing the comedy duo, trying to bring some life back into Mrs Kinnoul. He nodded encouragingly. In fact, he was glancing around wistfully, hoping to find a roaring log or coal fire. But there wasn't even a roaring gas fire for him to stand in front of. Instead, there was a one-bar electric job, just about glowing with warmth, and there were two radiators. He went and stood in front of one of these, separating his trousers from his legs. He pretended to be admiring the pictures on the wall in front of him. Rab Kinnoul with a TV actor . . . with a TV comedian . . . with a gameshow host . . .

'My husband,' Mrs Kinnoul explained. 'He works in television.'

Rebus spoke. 'No idea what he's up to today though, Mrs Kinnoul?'

'No,' she said quietly, 'no idea.'

Two witnesses who had known the deceased in life . . . Well, thought Rebus, you can scrub Cath Kinnoul. She'd fall apart if she *knew* it was Liz Jack out there, never mind having to identify the body. Even now, someone was trying to get in touch with Gregor Jack, and Jack would probably arrive at the mortuary with Ian Urquhart or Helen Greig, either of whom would do as the second nod of the head. No need to bother Cath Kinnoul

'You look soaked,' she was saying. 'Something to drink?'

'The WPC's making some tea . . .' But as he spoke, Rebus knew this was not what she was suggesting. 'A drop of the cratur wouldn't go amiss though, if it's not too much trouble.'

She nodded towards a sideboard. 'Right-hand cupboard,' she said. 'Please help yourself.'

Rebus thought of suggesting that she join them. But what pills had the doctor given her? And what pills had she taken of her own? He poured Glenmorangie into two long slim glasses and handed one to Holmes, who had taken up a canny position in front of a radiator.

'Mind you don't get steaming,' Rebus said in a murmur. Just then, the WPC appeared, carrying a tray of tea things. She saw the alcohol and almost frowned.

'Here's tae us,' said Rebus, downing the drink in one.

At the mortuary, Gregor Jack seemed hardly to recognize Rebus at all. Jack had been holding his weekly constituency surgery, Ian Urquhart explained to Rebus in a conspiratorial whisper. This was usually held on a Friday, but there was a Private Member's Bill in the Commons this Friday, and Gregor Jack wanted to be part of the debate. So, Gregor having been in the area on Wednesday anyway, they'd decided to hold the surgery on Thursday, leaving Friday free.

Listening to all this in silence, Rebus thought: Why are you telling me? But Urquhart was clearly nervous and felt the need to talk. Well, mortuaries could have that effect, never mind the fact that your employer was about to see scandal heaped upon scandal. Never mind the fact that your job was about to be made more difficult than ever.

'How did the golf game go?' Rebus asked back.

'What golf game?'

'Yesterday.'

'Oh.' Urquhart nodded. 'You mean Gregor's game. I don't know. I haven't asked him yet.'

So Urquhart himself hadn't been involved. He paused for so long that Rebus thought a dead end had been reached, but the need to speak was too great.

'That's a regular date,' Urquhart went on. 'Gregor and Ronnie Steele. Most Wednesday afternoons.'

Ah, Suey, Mr would-be teenage suicide . . .

Rebus tried to make his next question sound like a joke. 'Doesn't Gregor *ever* do any work?'

Urquhart looked stunned. 'He's always working. That game of golf . . . it's about the only free time I've ever known him have.'

'But he doesn't seem to be in London very often.'

'Ah well, the constituency comes first, that's Gregor's way.'

'Look after the folk who voted you in, and they'll look after you?'

'Something like that,' Urquhart allowed. There was no more time for talk. The identification was about to take place. And if Gregor Jack looked bad before he saw the body, he looked like a half-filled rag doll afterwards.

'Oh Christ, that dress . . .' He seemed about to collapse, but Ian Urquhart had a firm grip on him.

'If you'll look at the face,' someone was saying. 'We need to be definite . . .'

They all looked at the face. Yes, thought Rebus, that's the person I saw beside the stream.

'Yes,' said Gregor Jack, his voice wavering, 'that's my . . . that's Liz.'

Rebus actually breathed a sigh of relief.

What nobody had expected, what nobody had really considered, was Sir Hugh Ferrie.

'Let's just say,' said Chief Superintendent Watson, 'that a certain amount of . . . pressure . . . is being applied.'

As ever, Rebus couldn't hold his tongue. 'There's nothing to apply pressure *to*! What are we supposed to do that we're not already doing?'

'Sir Hugh considers that we should have caught William Glass by now.'

'But we don't even know – '

'Now, we all know Sir Hugh can be a bit hot-headed. But he's got a point . . .'

Meaning, thought Rebus, he's got friends in high places.

'He's got a point, and we can do without the media interest that's bound to erupt. All I'm saying is that we should give the investigation an extra *push* whenever and wherever we can. Let's get Glass in custody, let's make sure we keep everyone informed, and let's get that autopsy report as soon as humanly possible.'

'Not so easy with a drowning.'

'John, you know Dr Curt fairly well, don't you?'

'We're on second-name terms.'

'How about giving him that extra little nudge?'

'What happens if he nudges me back, sir?'

Watson looked like a kindly uncle suddenly tiring of a precocious nephew. 'Nudge him harder. I *know* he's busy. I *know* he's got lectures to give, university work to do, God knows what else. But the longer we have to wait, the more the media are going to fill the gaps with speculation. Go have a word, John, eh? Just make sure he gets the message.'

Message? What message? Dr Curt told Rebus what he'd always told him. I can't be rushed ... delicate business, deciding an actual drowning from mere immersion ... professional reputation ... daren't make mistakes ... more haste, less speed ... patience is a virtue ... many a mickle maks a muckle ...

All of this delivered between appointments in the doctor's Teviot Place office. The Department of Pathology's Forensic Medicine Unit, divided in loyalties between the Faculty of Medicine and the Faculty of Law, had its offices within the University Medical School in Teviot Place. Which seemed, to Rebus, natural enough. You didn't want your Commercial Law students mixing with people who keened over cadavers ...

'Diatoms ...' Dr Curt was saying. 'Washerwoman's skin ... blood-tinged froth ... distended lungs ...' Almost a litany now, and none of it got them any further. Tests on tissue ... examination ... diatoms ..., toxicology ... fractures ... diatoms. Curt really did have a thing about those tiny algae.

'Unicellular algae,' he corrected.

Rebus bowed his head to the correction. 'Well,' he said, rising to his feet, 'fast as you can, eh, Doctor? If you can't catch me in the office, you can always try me by unicellular phone.'

'Fast as I can,' agreed Doctor Curt, chuckling. He too got to his feet. 'Oh, one thing I can tell you straight away.' He opened his office door for Rebus.

'Yes?'

'Mrs Jack was depilated. There'd be no getting *her* by the short-and-curlies . . .'

Because Teviot Place wasn't far from Buccleuch Street, Rebus thought he'd wander along to Suey Books. Not that he was expecting to catch Ronald Steele, for Ronald Steele was a hard man to catch. Busy behind the scenes, busy out of sight. The shop itself was open, the rickety bicycle chained up outside. Rebus pushed the door open warily.

'It's okay,' called a voice from the back of the shop. 'Rasputin's gone out for a wander.'

Rebus closed the door and approached the desk. The same girl was sitting there, and her duties still seemed to entail the pricing of books. There wasn't any room for any more books on the shelves. Rebus wondered where these new titles were headed . . .

'How did you know it was me?' he asked.

'That window.' She nodded towards the front-of-shop. 'It might look filthy from the outside, but you can see out of it all right. Like one of those two-way mirrors.'

Rebus looked. Yes, because the shop's interior was darker than the street, you could see out all right, you just couldn't see in.

'No sign of your books, if that's what you're wondering.'

Rebus nodded slowly. It was *not* what he was wondering . . .

'And Ronald's not here.' She checked the oversized face of her wristwatch. 'Should have been in half an hour ago. Must have got held up.'

Rebus kept on nodding. Steele had told him this girl's name. What was it again . . .? 'Was he in yesterday?'

She shook her head. 'We were shut. All day. I was a bit off

105

colour, couldn't come in. At the start of the university year, we do okay business on a Wednesday, Wednesday being a half-teaching day, but not just now . . .'

Rebus thought of Vaseline . . . vanishing cream . . . Vanessa! That was it.

'Well, thanks anyway. Keep an eye out for those books . . .'

'Oh! Here's Ronald now.'

Rebus turned round, just as the door rattled open. Ronald Steele closed it heavily behind him, started up the central aisle of books, but then almost lost balance and had to rest against a bookcase. His eyes caught a particular spine, and he levered the book out from the others around it.

'*Fish out of Water*,' he said. 'Out of water . . .' He threw the book as far as he could – a matter of a yard or so. It crashed into a bookcase and fell open on to the floor. Then he began picking books out at random and throwing them with force, his eyes red with tears.

Vanessa screamed at him and came round from her desk, making towards him, but Steele pushed past her and stumbled past Rebus, past the desk, and through a doorway at the very back of the shop. There was the sound of another door closing.

'What's back there?'

'The loo,' said Vanessa, stooping to recover a few of the books. 'What the hell's the matter with him?'

'Maybe he's had a bit of bad news,' Rebus speculated. He was helping her retrieve books. He stood up and examined the blurb on the back jacket of *Fish out of Water*. The front cover illustration showed a woman seated more or less demurely on a chaise longue, while a rugged suitor leant over her from behind, his lips just short of her bared shoulder. 'I think I might buy this,' he said. 'Looks like just my sort of thing.'

Vanessa accepted the book, then stared up from it to him, her disbelief not quite showing through the shock of the scene she'd just witnessed. 'Fifty pence,' she told him quietly.

'Fifty pence it is,' said Rebus.

*

And after the formal identification, while the autopsy took its defined and painstaking course, there were the questions. There were an awful lot of questions.

Cath Kinnoul had to be questioned. Gently questioned, with her husband by her side and a bloodstream dulled by tranqs. No, she hadn't really taken a close look at the body. She'd known from a good way off what it was. She could see the dress, could see that it *was* a dress. She'd run back to the house and telephoned for the police. Nine-nine-nine, the way they told you to in emergencies. No, she hadn't gone back out to the river. She doubted she'd ever go there again.

And, turning to Mr Kinnoul, where had *he* been this morning? Business meetings, he said. Meetings with potential partners and potential backers. He was trying to set up an independent television company, though he'd be grateful if the information went no further. And the previous evening? He'd spent it at home with his wife. And they hadn't seen or heard anything? Not a thing. They'd been watching TV all night, not current TV but old stuff kept on video, stuff featuring Mr Kinnoul himself . . . *Knife Ledge*. The on-screen assassin.

'You must have learned a few tricks of the trade in your time, Mr Kinnoul.'

'You mean acting?'

'No, I mean about how to kill . . .'

And then there was Gregor Jack . . . Rebus kept out of that altogether. He'd look at any notes and transcripts later. He didn't want to get involved. There was too much he already knew, too much prejudgement, which was another way of saying potential prejudice. He let other CID men deal with Mr Jack, and with Ian Urquhart, and with Helen Greig, and with *all* Elizabeth Jack's cronies and cohorts. For this wasn't merely a case of the lady vanishing; this was a matter of death. Jamie Kilpatrick, the Hon. Matilda Merriman, Julian Kaymer, Martin Inman, Louise Patterson-Scott, even Barney Byars. They'd all either been questioned, or were about to be. Perhaps they'd all be questioned again at a later date. There were missing days to be filled. Huge gaps in Liz Jack's life, the whole final week of her life. Where had she been? Who had she seen? When had she died? (Hurry up, please, Dr Curt. Chop-chop.) *How* had she died? (Ditto.) Where was her car?

But Rebus read all the transcripts, all the notes. He read through the interview with Gregor Jack, and the interview with Ronald Steele. A Detective Constable was sent to Braidwater Golf Course to check the story of the Wednesday afternoon game. The interview with Steele, Rebus read very carefully indeed. Asked about Elizabeth Jack, Steele admitted that 'she always accused me of not being enough fun. She was right, I suppose. I'm not exactly what you'd call a "party animal". And I never had enough money. She liked people with money to throw around, or who threw it around even if they couldn't afford it.'

A touch of bitterness there? Or just the bitter truth?

To all of which Rebus added one other question – had Elizabeth Jack ever left Edinburgh in the first place?

Then there was the separate hunt, the hunt for William Glass. If he *had* gone to Queensferry, where would be next? West, towards Bathgate, Linlithgow, or Bo'ness? Or north, across the Forth to Fife? Police forces were mobilized. Descriptions were issued. *Had* Liz Jack spent any time at all at Deer Lodge? How could William Glass simply disappear? Was there any connection between Mrs Jack's death and her husband's 'night out' at an Edinburgh brothel?

This last line was the one pursued most eagerly by the newspapers. They seemed to be favouring a verdict of suicide in the case of Elizabeth Jack. Husband's shame . . . discovered after she's been on retreat . . . on her way home she decides she can't face things . . . sets off perhaps to visit her friend the actor Rab Kinnoul . . . but grows more desperate and, having read the details of the Dean Bridge murder, decides to end it all. Throws herself into the river above Rab Kinnoul's house. End of story.

Except that it wasn't the end of the story. As far as the papers were concerned, it was just the beginning. After all, this one had it all – a TV actor, an MP, a sex scandal, a death. The headline writers were boggled, trying to decide which order to put things in. Sex Scandal MP's Wife Drowns in TV Star's Stream? Or TV Star's Agony at MP Friend's Wife's Suicide Act? You could see the problem ... All those possessives ...

And the grieving husband? Kept well away from the media by protective friends and colleagues. But he was always available for interview by the police, when clarification of some point was required. While his father-in-law gave the media as many interviews as they needed, but kept his comments to the police succinct and scathing.

'What do you want to talk to me for? Find the bugger who did it, then you can talk all you want. I want the animal who did this put behind bars! Better make them bloody strong bars, too, otherwise I might just pull them apart and strangle the life out of the bugger myself!'

'We're doing what we can, believe me, Sir Hugh.'

'Is it enough though, that's what I want to know!'

'Everything we can ...'

Yes, everything. Leaving just the one final question: Did *any*one do it? Only Dr Curt could answer that.

6
Highland Games

Rebus packed an overnight bag. It was a large sports holdall,
bought for him by Patience Aitken when she'd decided he
should get fit. They'd enrolled together in a health club,
bought all the gear, and had attended the club four or five
times together. They'd played squash, been massaged, had
saunas, encountered the plunge pool, gone swimming, sur-
vived the expensively equipped gymnasium, tried jogging ...
but ended up spending more and more time in the health
club bar, which was stupid, the drinks being double the price
they were at the pleasant-enough pub round the corner.

No longer a sports bag then, but these days an overnight
bag. Not that Rebus was taking much this trip. He packed a
change of shirt, socks and underwear, toothbrush, camera,
notebook, a kagoul. Would he require a phrase book?
Probably, but he doubted if one existed. Something to read
though ... bedtime reading. He found the copy of *Fish out of
Water* and threw it in on top of everything else. The phone
was ringing. But he was in Patience's flat, and she had her
own answering machine. All the same ...

He went through to the living room and listened as the
message played. Then the caller's voice. 'This is Brian Holmes,
trying to get in touch with -'

Rebus picked up the receiver. 'Brian, what's up?'

'Ah, caught you. Thought maybe you'd already headed for
the hills.'

'I was just leaving.'

'Sure you don't want to drop by the station first?'

'Why should I?'

'Because Dr Curt is about to pronounce . . .'

The problem with drowning was that drowning and immersion were two entirely different things. A body (conscious or unconscious) might fall (or be pushed) into water and drown. Or an already dead body might be dumped into water as a means of concealment or to lead the police astray. Cause of death became problematical, as did time of death. Rigor mortis might or might not be present. Bruising on and damage to the body might be the result of rocks or other objects in the water itself.

However, froth from mouth and nose when the chest was pumped down on was a sign that the body was alive when it entered the water. So was the presence in the brain, marrow, kidney and so forth of diatoms. Diatoms, Dr Curt never tired of explaining, were micro-organisms which penetrated the lung membrane and would be pumped around the bloodstream by a still-beating heart.

But there were other signs, too. Silted matter in the bronchial tubes provided evidence of inhalation of water. A living person falling into water made attempts to grip something (a true-life 'clutching at straws') and so the hands of the corpse would be clenched. Washerwoman's skin, the shedding of nails and hair, the swelling of the body – all these could lead to an estimate of the amount of time the corpse had spent in the water.

As Curt pointed out, not all the relevant tests had been completed yet. It would be a few more days before the toxicology tests would yield results, so they couldn't be sure yet whether the deceased had taken any drink or drugs prior to death. No semen had been found in the vagina, but then the deceased's husband had provided information that the deceased 'had trouble' with the pill, and that her preferred method of contraception had always been the sheath . . .

Christ, thought Rebus, imagine poor old Jack being asked about that. Still, there might be even less pleasant questions to answer . . .

'What we have so far,' Curt said, while everyone begged him silently to get on with it, 'is a series of negatives. No froth from the mouth and nose ... no silted matter ... no clenched hands. What's more, rigor mortis would suggest that the body was dead prior to immersion, and that it had been kept in a confined space. You'll see from the photographs that the legs are bent quite unnaturally.'

At that moment, they knew ... but still he hadn't said it.

'I'd say the body was in the water not less than eight hours and not more than twenty-four. As to when death occurred, well, some time before that, obviously, but not too long, a matter of hours ...'

'And cause of death?'

Dr Curt smiled. 'The photographs of the skull show a clear fracture to the right-hand side of the head. She was hit very hard from behind, gentlemen. I'd say death was almost instantaneous ...'

There was more, but not much more. And much mumbling between officers. Rebus knew what they were thinking and saying: it was the same M.O. as the Dean Bridge killing. But it wasn't. The woman found at Dean Bridge had been murdered at that spot, not transported there, and she had been murdered on a riverside path in the middle of a city, not ... well, where *had* Liz Jack died? Anywhere. It could be anywhere. While people were muttering that William Glass had to be found, Rebus was thinking in a different direction: Mrs Jack's BMW had to be found, and found quickly. Well, he was already packed, and he'd okayed the trip with Lauderdale. Constable Moffat would be there to meet him, and Gregor Jack had provided the keys.

'So there it is, ladies and gentlemen.' Curt was saying. 'Murder would be my opinion. Yes, murder. The rest is down to your forensic scientists and yourselves.'

'Off are you?' Lauderdale commented, seeing Rebus toting his bag.

'That's right, sir.'

112

'Good hunting, Inspector.' Lauderdale paused. 'What's the name of the place again?'

'Where is it expensive to be a Mason, sir?'

'I don't follow . . . ah, right, a dear lodge.'

Rebus winked at his superior and made his way out towards his car.

It was very pleasing the way Scotland changed every thirty miles or so – changed in landscape, in character, and in dialect. Mind you, stick in a car and you'd hardly guess. The roads all seemed much the same. So did the roadside petrol stations. Even the towns, long, straight main streets with their supermarkets and shoe shops and wool shops and chip shops . . . even these seemed to blur one into the other. But it was possible to look beyond them; possible, too, to look further *into* them. A small country, thought Rebus, yet so various. At school, his geography teacher had taught that Scotland could be divided into three distinct regions: Southern Uplands, Lowlands, and Highlands . . . something like that. Geography didn't begin to tell the story. Well, maybe it did actually. He was heading due north, towards a people very different to those found in the southern cities or the coastal towns.

He stopped in Perth and bought some supplies – apples, chocolate, a half bottle of whisky, chewing gum, a box of dates, a pint of milk . . . You never knew what might not be available further north. It was all very well on the tourist trail, but if he stepped off that trail . . .

In Blairgowrie he stopped for fish and chips, which he ate at a Formica-topped table in the chip shop. Lashings of salt, vinegar and brown sauce on the chips. Two slices of white pan bread thinly spread with margarine. And a cup of dark-brown tea. The haddock was covered in batter, which Rebus picked off, eating it first before starting on the fish.

'You look as if you enjoyed that,' the frier's wife said, wiping down the table next to him. He had enjoyed it. All the more so since Patience wouldn't be smelling his breath this evening, checking for cholesterol and sodium and starch . . .

He looked at the list of delights printed above the counter. Red, white and black puddings, haggis, smoked sausage, sausage in batter, steak pie, mince pie, chicken ... with pickled onions or pickled eggs on the side. Rebus couldn't resist. He bought another bag of chips to eat while he drove ...

Today was Tuesday. Five days since Elizabeth Jack's body was found, probably six days since she died. Memories were short, Rebus knew. Her photograph had been in all the newspapers, had appeared on television and on several hundred police posters. And still no one had come forward with information. He'd worked through the weekend, seeing little of Patience, and he'd come up with this notion, this latest straw to be clutched at.

The scenery deepened around him, growing wilder and quieter. He was in Glenshee. In it and through it as quickly as he could. There was something sinister and empty about the place, a louring sense of dis-ease. The Devil's Elbow wasn't the treacherous spot it had seemed in his youth; the road had somehow been levelled, or the corner straightened. Braemar ... Balmoral ... turning off just before Ballater towards Cockbridge and Tomintoul, that stretch of road which always seemed to be the first of the winter to close for snow. Bleak? Yes, he'd call it bleak. But it was impressive, too. It just went on and on and on. Deep valleys hewn by glaciers, collections of scree. Rebus's geography teacher had been an enthusiast.

He was close now, close to his destination. He turned to the directions which he had scribbled down, an amalgam of notes from Sergeant Moffat and Gregor Jack. Gregor Jack ...

Jack had wanted to talk with him about something, but Rebus hadn't given him the chance. Too dangerous to get involved. Not that Rebus believed for one second that Jack had anything to hide. All the same ... The others though, the Rab Kinnouls and Ronald Steeles and Ian Urquharts ... there was definitely ... well, maybe not definitely ... but there was ... ach, no, he couldn't put it into words. He didn't really want to think about it even. Thinking about it, about all those permutations and possibilities, all those what ifs . . . well, they just made his head birl.

'Left and then right . . . along the track beside a fir plantation . . . up to the top of the rise . . . through a gateway. It's like *Treasure Hunt*.' The car was behaving impeccably (touch wood). Touch wood? He only had to stop the car and stretch his arm out of the window. No plantation now, but a wild wood. The track was heavily rutted, with grass growing high along a strip between the ruts. Some of the larger potholes had been filled in with gravel, and Rebus's speed was down to five miles an hour or less, but that didn't seem to stop his bones being shaken, his head snapped from side to side. It didn't seem possible that there could be a habitation ahead. Maybe he'd taken a wrong turning. But the tyre tracks he was following were fresh enough, and besides, he didn't fancy reversing all the way back along the trail, and there was no spot wide enough for a three-point turn.

At last, the surface improved, and he was driving on gravel. As he turned a long, high-cambered bend, he found himself suddenly in front of a house. On the grass outside was parked a police Mini Metro. A narrow stream trickled past the front entrance. There was no garden to speak of, just meadow and then forest, and a smell of wet pine in the air. In the distance, beyond the back of the house, the land climbed and climbed. Rebus got out of the car, feeling his nerves jangle back into position. The door of the Metro had already opened, and out stepped a farm labourer in police uniform.

It was like some sort of Guinness challenge: how large a man can you get in the front of a Mini Metro? He was also young, late teens or early twenties. He gave a big rubicund smile.

'Inspector Rebus? Constable Moffat.' The hand Rebus shook was as large as a coal shovel but surprisingly smooth, almost delicate. 'Detective Sergeant Knox was going to be here, but something came up. He sends his apologies and hopes I'll do instead, this being my neck of the woods, so to speak.'

Rebus, who was rubbing his neck at this point, smiled at the joke. Then he pressed a thumb either side of his spine and straightened up, exhaling noisily. Vertebrae clicked and crunched.

'Long drive, eh?' Constable Moffat commented. 'But you've made not bad time. I've only been here five minutes myself.'

'Have you had another look round?'

'Not yet, no. Thought I'd best wait.'

Rebus nodded. 'Let's start with the outside. Big place, isn't it? I mean, after that road up to it I was expecting something a bit more basic.'

'Well, the house was here first, that's the point. Used to have a fine garden, well-kept drive, and that forest was hardly there at all. Before my time, of course. I think the place was built in the 1920s. Part of the Kelman estate. The estate got sold off bit by bit. There used to be estate workers to keep the place in check. Not these days, and this is what happens.'

'Still, the house looks in good nick.'

'Oh, aye, but you'll see there's a few slates missing, and the gutters could do with patching up.'

Moffat spoke with the confidence of the DIYer. They were circling the house. It was a two-storey affair of solid-looking stone. To Rebus's mind, it wouldn't have been out of place on the outskirts of Edinburgh; it was just a bit odd to find it in a clearing in the wilderness. There was a back door, beside which sat a solitary dustbin.

'Do the bins get emptied around here?'

'They do if you can get them down to the roadside.'

Rebus lifted the lid. The smell was truly awful. A rotting side of salmon, by the shape of it, and some chicken or duck bones. .

'I'm surprised the animals haven't been at those,' Moffat said. 'The deer or the wildcats . . .'

'Looks as though it's been in the bin long enough, doesn't it?'

'I wouldn't say they were last week's leavings, sir, if that's what you're getting at.'

Rebus looked at Moffat. 'That's what I'm getting at,' he agreed. 'The whole of last week, and for a few days before that, Mrs Jack was away from home. Driving a black BMW. Supposedly staying here.'

'Well, if she did, nobody I've spoken to saw her.'

Rebus held up a door key. 'Let's see if the inside of the house tells a different story, eh?' But first he returned to his car and produced two pairs of clear polythene gloves. He handed one pair to the constable. 'I'm not even sure these'll fit you,' he told him. But they did. 'Right, try not to touch anything, even though you're wearing gloves. It might be you could smear or wipe a fingerprint. Remember, this is murder we're talking about, not joyriding or cattle rustling. Okay?'

'Yes, sir.' Moffat sniffed the air. 'Did you enjoy your chips? I can smell the vinegar from here.'

Rebus slammed shut the car door. 'Let's go.'

The house smelt damp. At least, the narrow hallway did. The doors off this hallway were wide open, and Rebus stepped through the first, into a room which stretched from the front of the house to the back. The room had been decorated with comfort in mind. There were three sofas, a couple of armchairs, and beanbags and scatter cushions. There were TV and video, and a hi-fi system sitting on the floor, one of its speakers lying side on. There was also mess.

Mugs, cups and glasses for a start. Rebus sniffed one of the mugs. Wine. Well, the vinegary stuff left in it had once been wine. Empty bottles of burgundy, champagne, armagnac. And stains – on the carpet, on the scatter cushions, and on one wall, where a glass had landed with some force, shattering on impact. Ashtrays overflowed, and there was a small hand-mirror half hidden under one of the floor cushions. Rebus bent down over it. Traces of white powder around its rim. Cocaine. He left it where it was and approached the hi-fi, examining the choice of music. Cassettes, mostly. Fleetwood Mac, Eric Clapton, Simple Minds ... and opera. *Don Giovanni* and *The Marriage of Figaro*.

'A party, sir?'

'Yes, but how recent?' Rebus got the feeling that this wasn't all the result of a single evening. A load of bottles looked to have been pushed to one side, making a little oasis of space on the floor, in the midst of which sat a solitary bottle – still upright – and two mugs, one with lipstick on its rim.

'And how many people, do you reckon?'

'Half a dozen, sir.'

'You could be right. A lot of booze for six people.'

'Maybe they don't bother clearing up between parties.'

Just what Rebus was thinking. 'Let's have a look around.'

Across the hall there was a front room which had probably once been dining room or lounge, but now served as a makeshift bedroom. A mattress took up half the floor space, sleeping bags covering the other half. There were a couple of empty bottles in here, too, but nothing to drink out of. A few art prints had been pinned to the walls. On the mattress sat a pair of shoes, men's, size nine, into one of which had been stuffed a blue sock.

The only room left was the kitchen. Pride of place seemed to go to a microwave oven, beside which sat empty tins, and packets of something called Microwave Popcorn. The tins had contained lobster bisque and venison stew. The double sink was filled with dishes and grey, speckled water. On a foldaway table sat unopened bottles of lemonade, packs of orange juice, and a bottle of cider. There was a larger pine breakfast table, its surface dotted with soup droppings but free from dishes and other detritus. On the floor around it, however, lay empty crisp packets, a knocked-over ashtray, bread-sticks, cutlery, a plastic apron and some serviettes.

'Quick way of clearing a table,' said Moffat.

'Yes,' said Rebus. 'Have you ever seen *The Postman Always Rings Twice*? The later version, with Jack Nicholson?'

Moffat shook his head. 'I saw him in *The Shining* though.'

'Not the same thing at all, Constable. Only, there's a bit in the film where ... you must have heard about it ... where

Jack Nicholson and the boss's wife clear the kitchen table so they can have a spot of you-know-what on it.'

Moffat looked at the table suspiciously. 'No,' he said. Clearly, this idea was new to him. 'What did you say the film was called . . .?'

'It's only an idea,' said Rebus.

Then there was upstairs. A bathroom, the cleanest room in the house. Beside the toilet sat a pile of magazines, but they were old, too old to yield any clue. And two more bedrooms, one a makeshift attempt like the one downstairs, the other altogether more serious, with a newish-looking wooden four-poster, wardrobe, chest of drawers and dressing table. Improbably, above the bed had been mounted the head of a Highland cow. Rebus stared at the stuff on the dressing table: powders, lipsticks, scents and paints. There were clothes in the wardrobe – mostly women's clothes, but also men's denims and cords. Gregor Jack could give no description of what clothing his wife had taken with her when she left. He couldn't even be sure that she'd taken any until he noticed that her small green suitcase was missing.

The green suitcase jutting out from beneath the bed. Rebus pulled it out and opened it. It was empty. So were most of the drawers.

'We keep a change of clothes up there,' Jack had told detectives. 'Enough for emergencies, that's all.'

Rebus stared at the bed. Its pillows had been fluffed up, and the duvet lay straight and smooth across it. A sign of recent habitation? God knows. This was it, the last room in the house. What had he learned at the end of his hundred-odd-mile drive? He'd learned that Mrs Jack's suitcase – the one Mr Jack *said* she'd taken with her – was here. Anything else? Nothing. He sat down on the bed. It crackled beneath him. He stood up again and pulled back the duvet. The bed was covered in newspapers, Sunday newspapers, all of them open at the same story.

MP Found in Sex Den Raid.

So she'd been here, and she knew. Knew about the raid,

about Operation Creeper. Unless someone else had been here and planted this stuff . . . No, keep to the obvious. His eye caught something else. He moved aside one of the pillows. Tied to the post behind it was a pair of black tights. Another pair had been tied to the opposite post. Moffat was staring quizzically, but Rebus thought the young man had learned enough for one day. It was an interesting scenario all the same. Tied to her bed and left there. Moffat could have come, looked the house over, and gone, without ever being aware of her presence upstairs. But it wouldn't work. If you were *really* going to restrain someone, you wouldn't use tights. Too easy to escape. Tights were for sex-games. For restraint, you'd use something stronger, twine or handcuffs . . . Like the handcuffs in Gregor Jack's dustbin?

At least now Rebus knew that she'd known. So why hadn't she got in touch with her husband? There was no telephone at the lodge.

'Where's the nearest call-box?' he asked Moffat, who still seemed interested in the tights.

'About a mile and a half away, on the road outside Cragstone Farm.'

Rebus checked his watch. It was four o'clock. 'Okay, I'd like to take a look at it, then we'll call it a day. But I want this place gone over for fingerprints. Christ knows, there should be enough of them. Then we need to check and double check the shops, petrol stations, pubs, hotels. Say, within a twenty-mile radius.'

Moffat looked doubtful. 'That's an awful lot of places.'

Rebus ignored him. 'A black BMW. I think some more handouts are being printed today. There's a photo of Mrs Jack, and the car description and registration. If she was up this way – and she *was* – *some*body must have seen her.'

'Well . . . folk keep to themselves, you know.'

'Yes, but they're not blind, are they? And if we're lucky, they won't be suffering from amnesia either. Come on, sooner we look at that phone-box, the sooner I can get to my digs.'

*

Actually, Rebus's original plan had been to sleep in the car and claim the price of a B&B, pocketing the money. But the weather looked uninviting, and the thought of spending a night cramped in his car like a half-shut knife ... So, on the way to the phone-box, he signalled to a stop outside a roadside cottage advertising bed & breakfast and knocked on the door. The elderly woman seemed suspicious at first, but finally agreed that she had a vacancy. Rebus told her he'd be back in an hour, giving her time to 'air' the room. Then he returned to his car and followed Moffat's careful driving all the way to Cragstone Farm.

It wasn't much of a farm actually. A short track led from the main road to a cluster of buildings: house, byre, some sheds and a barn. The phone-box was by the side of the main road, fifty yards along from the farm and on the other side of the road, next to a lay-by big enough to allow them to park their two cars. It was one of the original red boxes.

'They daren't change it,' said Moffat. 'Mrs Corbie up at the farm would have a fit.' Rebus didn't understand this at first, but then he opened the door to the phone-box – and he understood. For one thing, it had a carpet – a good carpet, too, a thick-piled offcut. There was a smell of air freshener, and a posy of field flowers had been placed in a small glass jar on the shelf beside the apparatus.

'It's better kept than my flat,' Rebus said. 'When can I move in?'

'It's Mrs Corbie,' Moffat said with a grin. 'She reckons a dirty phone-box would reflect badly on her, seeing her house is closest. She's been keeping it spick and span since God knows when.'

A pity though. Rebus had been hoping for something, some hint or clue. But supposing there had been anything, it must certainly have been tidied away ...

'I'd like to talk to Mrs Corbie.'

'It's a Tuesday,' said Moffat. 'She's at her sister's on a Tuesday.' Rebus pointed back along the road to where a car was braking hard, signalling to pull into the farm's driveway. 'What about him?'

Moffat looked, then smiled coldly. 'Her son, Alec. A bit of a tearaway. He won't tell us anything.'

'Gets into trouble, does he?'

'Speeding mostly. He's one of the local boy racers. Can't say I blame him. There's not much to occupy the teenagers round here.'

'You can't be much more than a teenager yourself, Constable. *You* didn't get into trouble.'

'I had the Church, sir. Believe me, the fear of God is something to reckon with . . .'

Rebus's landlady, Mrs Wilkie, was something to reckon with, too. It started when he was changing in his bedroom. It was a nice bedroom, a bit overdone on the frills and finery, but with a comfortable bed and a twelve-inch black and white television. Mrs Wilkie had shown him the kitchen, and told him he should feel free to make himself tea and coffee whenever he felt like it. Then she had shown him the bathroom, and told him the water was hot if he felt like a bath. Then she had led him back to the kitchen and told him that he could make himself a cup of tea or coffee whenever he felt like it.

Rebus didn't have the heart to tell her he'd heard it all before. She was tiny, with a tiny voice. Between his first visit and his second, she had dressed in her best B&B-keeper's clothes and tied some pearls around her neck. He reckoned her to be in her late seventies. She was a widow, her husband Andrew having died in 1982, and she did the B&B 'as much for the company as the money'. She always seemed to get nice guests, interesting people like the German jam-buyer who had stayed for a few nights last autumn . . .

'And here's your bedroom. I've given it a bit of an airing and – '

'It's very nice, thank you.' Rebus put his bag on the bed, saw her ominous look, and shifted it off the bed and on to the floor.

'I made the bedspread myself,' she said with a smile. 'I was once advised to go professional, selling my bedspreads. But at my age . . .' She gave a chuckle. 'It was a German gentleman told me that. He was in Scotland to buy jam. Would you credit it? He stayed here a few nights . . .'

Eventually, she recalled her duties. She'd just go and make them a spot of supper. Supper. Rebus glanced at his watch. Unless it had stopped, it was not yet five thirty. But then, he'd booked bed and breakfast, and any hot meal tonight would be a bonus. Moffat had given him directions to the closest pub – 'tourist place, tourist prices' – before leaving him for the undoubted delights of Dufftown. The fear of God . . .

He had just slipped off his trousers when the door opened and Mrs Wilkie stood there.

'Is that you, Andrew? I thought I heard a noise.' Her eyes had a glassy, faraway look. Rebus stood there, frozen, then swallowed.

'Go and make us some supper,' he said quietly.

'Oh yes,' Mrs Wilkie said. 'You must be hungry. You've been gone such a long time . . .'

Then, the idea of a quick bath appealed. He looked into the kitchen first, and saw that Mrs Wilkie was busy at the stove, humming to herself. So he headed for the bathroom. There was no lock on the door. Or rather, there was a lock, but half of it was hanging loose. He looked around him, but saw nothing he could wedge against the door. He decided to take his chance and started both taps running. There was a furious pressure to the water, and the bath filled quickly and hotly. Rebus undressed and sank beneath the surface. His shoulders were stiff from the drive, and he massaged them as best he could. Then he lifted his knees so that his shoulders, neck and head slid into the water. Immersion. He thought of Dr Curt, of drowning and immersion. Skin wrinkling . . . hair and nails shedding . . . silt in the bronchial . . .

A noise brought him to the surface. He cleared his eyes, blinked, and saw that Mrs Wilkie was staring down at him, a dish towel in her hands.

'Oh!' she said. 'Oh dear, I'm sorry.' And she retreated behind the door, calling through it: 'I quite forgot you were here! I was just going to . . . well . . . never mind, it can wait.'

123

Rebus screwed shut his eyes and sank beneath the waves . . .

The meal was, to his surprise, good, if a bit odd. Cheese pudding, boiled potatoes, and carrots. Followed by tinned steamed pudding and packet custard.

'So convenient,' as Mrs Wilkie commented. The shock of seeing a naked man in her bathtub seemed to have brought her into the here and now, and they talked about the weather, the tourists and the government until the meal was over. Rebus asked if he could wash the dishes, and was told he could not – much to his relief. Instead, he asked Mrs Wilkie for a front-door key, then set off, stomach full, clean of body and underwear, for the Heather Hoose.

Not a name he would have chosen for his own pub. He entered by the lounge door, but, the place being dead, pushed through another door into the public bar. Two men and a woman stood at the bar and shared a joke, while a barman studiously filled glasses from a whisky optic. The group looked round at Rebus as he came and stood not too far from them.

'Evening.'

They nodded back, almost without seeing him, and the barman returned the greeting, setting down three double measures of whisky on the bar.

'And one for yourself,' said one of the customers, handing across a ten-pound note.

'Thanks,' said the barman, 'I'll have a nip myself for later on.'

Behind the array of optics, bottles and glasses, the wall was mirrored, so Rebus was able to study the group without seeming to. The man who had spoken sounded English. There had been only two cars in the pub's courtyard, a beaten-up Renault 5 and a Daimler. Rebus reckoned he knew who owned which . . .

'Yes, sir?' asked the barman and Renault 5 owner.

'Pint of export, please.'

'Certainly.'

The wonder of it was that three well-off English tourists would drink in the public bar. Maybe they just hadn't noticed that the Heather Hoose possessed such an amenity as a lounge. All three looked a bit the worse for wear, mostly from drink. The woman had a formidable face, framed by dyed platinum hair. Her cheeks were too red and her eyelashes too black. When she sucked on her cigarette, she arched her head up to blow the smoke ceilingwards. Rebus tried counting the lines on her neck. Maybe it worked the way it did with tree-rings . . .

'There you are.' The pint glass was placed on a mat in front of him. He handed over a fiver.

'Quiet tonight.'

'Midweek and not quite the season,' recited the barman, who had obviously just said the same thing to the other group. 'It'll get busier later on.' Then he retreated to the till.

'Another round here when you're ready,' said the Englishman, the only one of the three to have finished his whisky. He was in his late thirties, younger than the woman. He looked fit, prosperous, but somehow faintly disreputable. It had something to do with the way he stood, slightly slouched and looming, as though he might be about either to fall down or else pounce. And his head swayed a little from side to side in time with his sleepy eyelids.

The third member of the group was younger still, mid-thirties. He was smoking French cigarettes and staring at the bottles above the bar. Either that, thought Rebus, or he's looking at *me* in the mirror, the way I'm looking at *him*. Certainly, it was a possibility. The man had an affected way of tapping the ash from his affected cigarette. Rebus noticed that he smoked without inhaling, holding the smoke in his mouth and releasing it in a single belch. While his companions stood, he rested on one of the high bar stools.

Rebus had to admit, he was intrigued. An unlikely little threesome. And about to become more unlikely still . . .

A couple of people had entered the lounge bar, and looked like staying there. The barman slipped through a doorway between rooms to serve these new customers, and this seemed to start off a conversation between the two men and the woman.

'God, the nerve. He hasn't served *us* yet.'

'Well, Jamie, we're not exactly gasping, are we?'

'Speak for yourself. I hardly felt that first one slip down. Should have asked for quadruples in the first place.'

'Have mine,' said the woman, 'if you're going to become ratty.'

'I am not becoming ratty,' said the slouching pouncer, becoming very ratty indeed.

'Well fuck you then.'

Rebus had to stifle a grin. The woman had said this as though it were part of any polite conversation.

'And fuck you, too, Louise.'

'Ssh,' the French-smoker warned. 'Remember, we're not alone.'

The other man and woman looked towards Rebus, who sat staring straight ahead, glass to lips.

'Yes we are,' said the man. 'We're all alone.'

This utterance seemed to signal the end of the conversation. The barman reappeared.

'Same again, barman, if you'll be so kind . . .'

The evening hotted up quickly. Three locals appeared and started to play dominoes at a nearby table. Rebus wondered if they were paid to come in and add the requisite local colour. There was probably more colour in a Meadowbank Thistle–Raith Rovers friendly. Two other drinkers appeared, wedging themselves in between Rebus and the threesome. They seemed to take it as an insult that there were other drinkers in the bar before them, and that some of those drinkers were standing next to *their* space at the bar. So they drank in dour silence, merely exchanging looks whenever the Englishman or his two friends said anything.

'Look,' said the woman, 'are we heading back tonight? If not, we'd better think about accommodation.'

'We could sleep at the lodge.'

Rebus put down his glass.

'Don't be so sick,' the woman retorted.

126

'I thought that was why we came.'

'I wouldn't be able to sleep.'

'Maybe that's why they call it a wake.'

The Englishman's laughter filled the silent bar, then died. A domino clacked on to a table. Another chapped. Rebus left his glass where it was and approached the group.

'Did I hear you mention a lodge?'

The Englishman blinked slowly. 'What's it to you?'

'I'm a police officer.' Rebus brought out his ID. The two dour regulars finished their drinks and left the bar. Funny how an ID had that effect sometimes . . .

'Detective Inspector Rebus. Which lodge did you mean?'

All three looked sober now. It was an act, but a good act, years in the learning.

'Well, officer,' said the Englishman, 'now what business is that of yours?'

'Depends which lodge you were talking about, sir. There's a nice police station at Dufftown if you'd prefer to go there . . .'

'Deer Lodge,' said the French-smoker. 'A friend of ours owns it.'

'Owned it,' corrected the woman.

'You were friends of Mrs Jack then?'

They were. Introductions were made. The Englishman was actually a Scot, Jamie Kilpatrick the antique dealer. The woman was Louise Patterson-Scott, wife (separated) of the retail tycoon. The other man was Julian Kaymer, the painter.

'I've already spoken with the police,' Julian Kaymer said. 'They telephoned me yesterday.'

Yes, they had *all* been questioned, asked if they knew Mrs Jack's movements. But they hadn't seen her for weeks.

'I spoke to her on the telephone,' Mrs Patterson-Scott announced, 'a few days before she went off on holiday. She didn't say where she was going, just that she fancied a few days away by herself.'

'So what are you all doing here?' Rebus asked.

'This is a wake,' said Kilpatrick. 'Our little token of

127

friendship, our time of mourning. So why don't you bugger off and let us get on with it.'

'Ignore him, Inspector,' said Julian Kaymer. 'He's a bit pissed.'

'What I am,' stated Kilpatrick, 'is a bit *upset*.'

'Emotional,' Rebus offered.

'Exactly, Inspector.'

Kaymer carried on the story. 'It was my idea. We'd all been on the phone to each other, none of us really able to take it in. Devastated. So I said why don't we take a run to the lodge? That was where we all met last.'

'At a party?' asked Rebus.

Kaymer nodded. 'A month back.'

'A great bloody big piss-up it was,' confirmed Kilpatrick.

'So,' said Kaymer, 'the plan was to drive here, have a few drinks in memory of Lizzie, and drive back. Not everybody could make it. Prior commitments and so on. But here we are.'

'Well,' said Rebus, 'I *would* like you to look inside the house. But there's no point going out there in the dark. What I *don't* want is the three of you going out there on your own. The place still has to be gone over for fingerprints.'

They looked a bit puzzled at this. 'You haven't heard?' Rebus said, recalling that Curt had only revealed his findings that morning. 'It's a murder hunt now. Mrs Jack was murdered.'

'Oh no!'

'Christ . . .'

'I'm going to be – '

And Louise Patterson-Scott, wife of the et cetera, threw up on to the carpeted floor. Julian Kaymer was weeping, and Jamie Kilpatrick was losing all the blood from his face. The barman stared in horror, while the domino players stopped their game. One of them had to restrain his dog from investigating further. It cowered under the table and licked its whiskery chops . . .

Local colour, as provided by John Rebus.

*

Finally, a hotel was found, not far out of Dufftown. It was arranged that the three would spend the night there. Rebus had considered asking Mrs Wilkie if she had any spare rooms, but thought better of it. They would stay at the hotel, and meet Rebus at the lodge in the morning. Bright and early: some of them had jobs to get back to.

When Rebus returned to the cottage, Mrs Wilkie was knitting by her gas fire and watching a film on the TV. He put his head round the living room door.

'I'll say goodnight, Mrs Wilkie.'

'Night-night, son. Mind, say your prayers. I'll be up to tuck you in a bit later on . . .'

Rebus made himself a mug of tea, went to his room, and wedged the chair against the door handle. He opened the window to let in some air, switched on his own little television, and fell on to the bed. There was something wrong with the picture on the TV, and he couldn't fix it. The vertical hold had gone. So he switched it off again and dug into his bag, coming up with *Fish out of Water*. Well, he'd nothing else to read, and he certainly didn't feel tired. He opened the book at chapter one.

Rebus woke up the next morning with a bad feeling. He half expected to turn and see Mrs Wilkie lying beside him, saying 'Come on, Andrew, time for the conjugals'. He turned. Mrs Wilkie was not lying beside him. She was outside his door and trying to get in.

'Mr Rebus, Mr Rebus.' A soft knock, then a hard. 'The door seems to be jammed, Mr Rebus! Are you awake? I've brought you a cup of tea.'

During which time Rebus was out of bed and half dressed. 'Coming, Mrs Wilkie.'

But the old lady was panicking. 'You're locked in, Mr Rebus. The door's stuck! Shall I call for a carpenter? Oh dear.'

'Hold on, Mrs Wilkie, I think I've got it.' His shirt still unbuttoned, Rebus put his weight to the door, keeping it shut, and at the same time lifted the chair away, stretching so as to place it nearer the bed. Then he made show of thumping the edges of the door before pulling it open.

'Are you all right, Mr Rebus? Oh dear, that's never happened before. Dear me no . . .'

Rebus lifted the cup and saucer from her hand and began pouring the tea back from saucer into cup. 'Thank you, Mrs Wilkie.' He made show of sniffing. 'Is something cooking?'

'Oh dear, yes. Breakast.' And off she toddled, back down the stairs. Rebus felt a bit guilty for having pulled the 'locked-door' stunt. He'd show her after breakfast that the door was all right really, that she didn't need to phone for cowboy carpenters to put it right. But for now he had to continue the process of waking up. It was seven thirty. The tea was cold but the day seemed unseasonally warm. He sat on the bed for a moment, collecting his thoughts. What day was it? It was Wednesday. What needed to be done today? What was the best order to do it in? He'd to return to the cottage with the Three Stooges. Then there was Mrs Corbie to speak to. And something else . . . something he'd been thinking about last night, in the melting moment between waking and sleep. Well, why not? He was in the area anyway. He'd telephone after breakfast. A fry-up by the smell of it, rather than Patience's usual choice of muesli or Bran Crunch. Ah, that was another thing. He'd meant to phone Patience last night. He'd do it today, just to say hello. He thought about her for a little while, Patience and her collection of pets. Then he finished dressing and made his way downstairs . . .

He was first to arrive at the lodge. He let himself in and wandered into the living room. Immediately, he knew something was different. The place was tidier. Tidier? Well, say then that there was less debris around than before. Half the bottles looked to have disappeared. He wondered what else had vanished. He lifted the scatter cushions, searching in vain for the hand-mirror. Damn. He fairly flew through to the kitchen. The back window was lying in shards in the sink and on the floor. Here, the mess was as bad as before. Except that the microwave had gone. He went upstairs . . . slowly.

The place seemed deserted, but you never could tell. The bathroom and small bedroom were as before. So was the main bedroom. No, hold on. The tights had been untied from their bedposts and were now lying innocently on the floor. Rebus crouched and picked one up. Then dropped it again. Thoughtfully, he made his way back downstairs.

A burglary, yes. Break in and steal the microwave. That was the way it was supposed to look. But no petty thief would take empty bottles and a mirror with him, no petty thief would have reason to untie pairs of tights from bedposts. That didn't matter though, did it? What mattered was that the evidence had to disappear. Now it would merely be Rebus's word.

'Yes, sir, I'm sure there was a mirror in the living room. Lying on the floor, a small mirror with traces of white powder on it . . .'

'And you're sure you're not merely *imagining* this, Inspector? You could be wrong, couldn't you?'

No, no, he couldn't. But it was too late for all that. Why take the bottles . . . and only some of them, not all? Obviously, because some bottles had certain prints on them. Why take the mirror? Maybe fingerprints again . . .

Should have thought of all this yesterday, John. Stupid, stupid, stupid.

'Stupid, stupid, stupid.'

And he'd done the damage himself. Hadn't he told the Three Stooges not to go near the lodge? Because it hadn't been fingerprinted. Then he'd let them wander off, with no guard left on the house. A constable should have been here all night.

'Stupid, stupid.'

It had to be one of them, didn't it? The woman, or one of the men. But why? Why had they done it? So it couldn't be proved they'd been there in the first place? Again, why? It didn't make much sense. Not much sense at all.

'Stupid.'

He heard a car approaching, pulling up outside, and went to meet it. It was the Daimler, Kilpatrick driving, Patterson-

131

Scott in the passenger seat, and Julian Kaymer emerging from the rear. Kilpatrick looked a lot breezier than before.

'Inspector, good morning to you.'

'Morning, sir. How was the hotel?'

'Fair, I'd say. Only fair.'

'Better than average,' added Kaymer.

Kilpatrick turned to him. 'Julian, when you're used to excellence as I am, you no longer recognize "average" and "better than".'

Kaymer stuck his tongue out.

'Children, children,' chided Louise Patterson-Scott. But they all seemed light of heart.

'You sound chirpy,' Rebus said.

'A decent night's sleep and a long breakfast,' said Kilpatrick, patting his stomach.

'You stayed at the hotel last night?'

They seemed not to understand his question.

'You didn't go for a drive or anything?'

'No,' Kilpatrick said, his tone wary.

'It's your car, isn't it, Mr Kilpatrick?'

'Yes . . .'

'And you kept the keys with you last night?'

'Look, Inspector . . .'

'Did you or didn't you?'

'I suppose I did. In my jacket pocket.'

'Hanging up in your bedroom?'

'Correct. Look, can we go ins – '

'Any visitors to your room?'

'Inspector,' interrupted Louise Patterson-Scott, 'perhaps if you'd tell us . . . ?'

'Someone broke into the lodge during the night, disturbing potential evidence. That's a serious crime, madam.'

'And you think one of us – ?'

'I don't think anything yet, madam. But whoever did it must have come by car. Mr Kilpatrick here has a car.'

'Both Julian and I are capable of driving, Inspector.'

'Yes,' said Kaymer, 'and besides, we all went to Jamie's room for a late-night brandy . . .'

'So any one of you could have taken the car?'

Kilpatrick shrugged mightily. 'I still don't see,' he said, 'why you think we should want – '

'As I say, Mr Kilpatrick, I don't think anything. All I know is that a murder inquiry is under way, Mrs Jack's last known whereabouts remain this lodge, and now someone's trying to tamper with evidence.' Rebus paused. 'That's all I know. You can come inside now, but, please, don't touch anything. I'd like to ask you all a few questions.'

Really, what he wanted to ask was: Is the house pretty much in the state you remember it from the last party here? But he was asking too much. Yes, they remembered drinking champagne and armagnac and a lot of wine. They remembered cooking popcorn in the microwave. Some people drove off – recklessly, no doubt – into the night, while others slept where they lay or staggered off into the various bedrooms. No, Gregor hadn't been present. He didn't enjoy parties. Not his wife's, at any rate.

'A bit of a bore, old Gregor,' commented Jamie Kilpatrick. 'At least, I thought he was till I saw that story about the brothel. Just goes to show . . .'

But there had been another party, hadn't there? A more recent party. Barney Byars had told Rebus about it that night in the pub. A party of Gregor's friends, of The Pack. Who else knew Rebus was on his way up here? Who else knew what he might find? Who else might want to stop him finding anything? Well, Gregor Jack knew. And what he knew, The Pack might know, too. Maybe not one of these three then; maybe someone entirely different.

'Seems funny,' said Louise Patterson-Scott, 'to think we won't be having parties here any more . . . to think Liz won't be here . . . to think she's gone . . .' She began to cry, loudly and tearfully. Jamie Kilpatrick put an arm around her, and she buried her face in his chest. She reached out a hand and found Julian Kaymer, pulling him to her so that he, too, could be embraced.

And that's pretty much how they were when Constable Moffat arrived . . .

Rebus, with a real sense of bolting the stable door, left Moffat to stand guard, much against the young man's will. But the forensics team would be arriving before lunchtime, and Detective Sergeant Knox with them.

'There are some magazines in the bathroom, if you need something to read,' Rebus told Moffat. 'Or, better still, here . . .' And he opened the car, reached into his bag, and took out *Fish out of Water*. 'Don't bother returning it. Think of it as a sort of present.'

Then, the Daimler having already left, Rebus got into his own car, waved back at Constable Moffat, and was off. He'd read *Fish out of Water* last night, every fraught sentence of it. It was a dreadful romantic tale of doomed love between a young Italian sculptor and a wealthy but bored married woman. The sculptor had come to England to work on a commission for the woman's husband. At first, she uses him like a plaything, but then falls in love. Meantime, the sculptor, bowled over by her at first, has moved his attentions to her niece. And so on.

It looked to Rebus as though the title alone had been what had made Ronald Steele pluck it from the shelf and throw it with such venom. Yes, just that title (the title, too, of the young sculptor's statue). The fish out of water was Liz Jack. But Rebus wondered whether she'd been out of water, or just out of her depth . . .

He drove to Cragstone Farm, parking in the yard to the rear of the farmhouse, scattering chickens and ducks before him. Mrs Corbie was at home, and took him into the kitchen, where there was a wondrous smell of baking. The large kitchen table was white with flour, but only a few globes of leftover pastry remained. Rebus couldn't help recalling that scene in *The Postman Always Rings Twice* . . .

'Sit yourself down,' she ordered. 'I've just made a pot . . .'

Rebus was given tea, and some of yesterday's batch of fruit scones, with fresh butter and thick strawberry jam.

'Ever thought about doing B&B, Mrs Corbie?'

'Me? I wouldn't have the patience.' She was wiping her hands on her white cotton apron. She seemed always to be wiping her hands. 'Mind you, it's not for shortage of space. My husband passed away last year, so now there's just Alec and me.'

'What? Running the whole farm?'

She made a face. 'Running it *down* would be more like it. Alec just isn't interested. It's a sin, but there you are. We've got a couple of workers, but when they see *he's* not interested, they can't see why *they* should be. We'd be as well selling up. That's what Alec would like. Maybe that's the only thing that stops me from doing it . . .' She was looking at her hands. Then she slapped them against her thighs. 'Goodness, would you listen to me! Now, Inspector, what was it you wanted?'

After all his years on the force, Rebus reckoned that at last he was in the presence of someone with a genuinely clear conscience. It didn't usually take so long for people to ask what a policeman was after. When it *did* take so long, the person either knew already what was wanted, or else had absolutely nothing to fear or to hide. So Rebus asked his question.

'I notice you keep the telephone kiosk sparkling, Mrs Corbie. I was wondering if you'd noticed anything suspicious recently? I mean, anything up at the box?'

'Oh, well, let me think.' She placed the flat of one hand against her cheek. 'I can't say . . . what sort of thing exactly, Inspector?'

Rebus couldn't look her in the eye – for he knew that she had started to lie to him.

'A woman perhaps. Making a telephone call. Something left in the box . . . a note or a telephone number . . . anything at all.'

'No, no, nothing in the box.'

His voice hardened a little. 'Well, outside the box then, Mrs

Corbie. I'm thinking specifically of a week ago, last Wednesday or maybe the Tuesday . . .?'

She was shaking her head. 'Have another scone, Inspector.'

He did, and chewed slowly, in silence. Mrs Corbie looked to be doing some thinking. She got up and checked in her oven. Then she poured the last of the tea from the pot, and returned to her seat, studying her hands again, laying them against her lap for inspection.

But she didn't say anything. So Rebus did.

'You *were* here last Wednesday?'

She nodded. 'But not the Tuesday. I go to my sister's on a Tuesday. I was here all day Wednesday though.'

'What about your son?'

She shrugged. 'He might have been here. Or maybe he was in Dufftown. He spends a lot of time off gallivanting . . .'

'He's not here just now?'

'No, he's gone to town.'

'Which town?'

'He didn't say. Just said he was off . . .'

Rebus stood up and went to the kitchen window. It faced on to the yard, where chickens now pecked at Rebus's tyres. One of them was sitting on the bonnet of the car.

'Is it possible to see the kiosk from the house, Mrs Corbie?'

'Eh . . . yes, from the sitting room. But we don't spend much time in there. That is, I don't. I prefer here in the kitchen.'

'Could I take a look?'

Well, it was clear enough who *did* spend time in the living room. There was a direct line between sofa, coffee table and television set. The coffee table was marked with rings made by too many hot mugs. On the floor by the sofa there was an ashtray and the remains of a huge bag of crisps. Three empty beer cans lay on their sides beneath the coffee table. Mrs Corbie tut-tutted and went to work, lifting the cans. Rebus went to the window and peered out.

He could make out the kiosk in the distance, but only just. It was possible Alec Corbie might have seen something. Possible, but doubtful. Not worth sticking around for. He'd let DS Knox come and ask Corbie the questions.

'Well,' he said, 'thanks for your help, Mrs Corbie.'

'Oh.' Her relief was palpable. 'Right you are, Inspector. I'll see you out.'

But Rebus knew he had one last bet worth laying. He stood with Mrs Corbie in the yard and looked around him.

'I used to love farms when I was a lad. A pal of mine lived on one,' he glibly lied. 'I used to go up there every evening after tea. It was great.' He turned his wide-eyed nostalgic smile towards her. 'Mind if I take a wander round?'

'Oh.' No relief now; rather, sheer terror. Which didn't stop Rebus. No, it pushed him on. So that before she knew it, he was walking up to the hutches and sties, looking in, moving on. On past the chickens and the roused ducks, into the barn. Straw underfoot and a strong smell of cattle. Concrete cubicles, coiled hosepipes, and a leaking tap. There were pools of water underfoot. One sick-looking cow blinked slowly at him from its enclosure. But the livestock wasn't his concern. The tarpaulin in the corner was.

'What's under here, Mrs Corbie?'

'That's Alec's property!' she shrieked. 'Don't touch it! It's nothing to do with – '

But he'd already yanked the tarpaulin off. What was he expecting to find? Something . . . nothing. What he *did* find was a black BMW 3-series bearing Elizabeth Jack's registration. It was Rebus's turn to tut-tut, but only after he'd sucked in his breath and held back a whoop of delight.

'Dear me, Mrs Corbie,' he said. 'This is just the very car I've been looking for.'

But Mrs Corbie wasn't listening. 'He's a good laddie, he doesn't mean any harm. I don't know what I'd do without him.' And so on. While Rebus circled the car, looking but not touching. Lucky the forensics team was on its way. They'd be kept busy . . .

Wait, what was that? On the back seat. A huddled shape. He peered in through the tinted glass.

'Expect the unexpected, John,' he muttered to himself.

It was a microwave.

7
Duthil

Rebus telephoned Edinburgh to make his report and request an extra day's stay up north. Lauderdale sounded so impressed that the car had been found that Rebus forgot to tell him about the break-in at the lodge. Then, once Alec Corbie had arrived home (drunk and in charge of a vehicle – but let that pass), he'd been arrested and taken to Dufftown. Rebus seemed to be stretching the local police like they'd never been stretched before, so that Detective Sergeant Knox had to be diverted from the lodge and brought to the farm instead. He looked like an older brother of Constable Moffat, or perhaps a close cousin.

'I want forensics to go over that car,' Rebus told him. 'Priority, the lodge can wait.'

Knox rubbed his chin. 'It'll take a tow-truck.'

'A trailer would be better.'

'I'll see what I can do. Where will you want it taken?'

'Anywhere secure and with a roof.'

'The police garage?'

'It'll do.'

'What exactly are we looking for?'

'Christ knows.'

Rebus went back into the kitchen, where Mrs Corbie was sitting at the table studying an array of burnt cakes. He opened his mouth to speak, but kept his silence. She was an accessory, of course. She'd lied to him to protect her son. Well, they had the son now, and *he* was the one that mattered. As quietly as he could, Rebus left the farmhouse and started his car, staring through the windscreen at his bonnet, where one of the chickens had left him a little gift . . .

He was able to avail himself of Dufftown police station for the interview with Alec Corbie.

'You're in keech up to your chin, son. Start at the beginning and leave nothing out.'

Rebus and Corbie, seated across the table from one another, were smoking, DS Knox, resting against the wall behind Rebus, was not. Corbie had prepared an extremely thin veneer of macho indifference, which Rebus was quick to wipe off.

'This is a murder investigation. The victim's car has been found in your barn. It'll be dusted for prints, and if we find yours I'm going to have to charge you with murder. Anything you think you know that might help your case, you'd better talk.'

Then, seeing the effect of these words: 'You're in keech up to your chin, son. Start at the beginning and leave nothing out.'

Corbie sang like his namesake: it didn't make for edifying listening, but it had an honest sound. First, though, he asked for some paracetamol.

'I've got a hell of a headache.'

'That's what daytime drinking does to you,' said Rebus, knowing it wasn't the drinking that was to blame – it was the stopping. The tablets were brought and swallowed, washed down with water. Corbie coughed a little, then lit another cigarette. Rebus had stubbed his out. He just couldn't deal with them any more.

'The car was in the lay-by,' Corbie began. 'It was there for hours, so I went and took a look. The keys were still in the ignition. I started her up and brought her back to the farm.'

'Why?'

He shrugged. 'Never refuse a gift horse.' He grinned. 'Or gift horse-power, eh?' The two detectives were not impressed. 'No, well, it was, you know, like with treasure. Finders keepers.'

'You didn't think the owner was coming back?'

He shrugged again. 'Never really thought about it. All I knew was that there were going to be some gey jealous looks if I turned up in town driving a BMW.'

'You planned to race it?' The question came from DS Knox.

'Sure.'

Knox explained to Rebus. 'They take cars out on to the back roads and race them one against one.'

Rebus remembered the phrase Moffat had used: boy racer. 'You didn't see the owner then?' he asked.

Corbie shrugged.

'What does that mean?'

'It means maybe. There was another car in the lay-by. Looked like a couple were in it, having an argument. I heard them from the yard.'

'What did you see?'

'Just that the BMW was parked, and this other car was in front of it.'

'You didn't get a look at the other car?'

'No. But I could hear the shouting, sounded like a man and a woman.'

'What were they arguing about?'

'No idea.'

'No?'

Corbie shook his head firmly.

'Okay,' said Rebus, 'and this was on . . .?'

'Wednesday. Wednesday morning. Maybe around lunchtime.'

Rebus nodded thoughtfully. Alibis would need re-checking . . . 'Where was your mother all this time?'

'In the kitchen, same as always.'

'Did you mention the argument to her?'

Corbie shook his head. 'No point.'

Rebus nodded again. Wednesday morning: Elizabeth Jack was killed that day. An argument in a lay-by . . .

'You're sure it was an argument?'

'I've been *in* enough in my time, it was an argument all right. The woman was screeching.'

140

'Anything else, Alec?'

Corbie seemed to relax at the use of his first name. Maybe he wouldn't be in trouble after all, so long as he told them . . .

'Well, the other car disappeared, but the BMW was still there. Couldn't tell if there was anyone in it, windows being tinted. But a radio was playing. Then in the afternoon – '

'So the car had been there all morning?'

'That's right. Then in the afternoon – '

'What time precisely?'

'No idea. I think there was horse-racing or something on the telly.'

'Go on.'

'Well, I looked out and there was *another* car had turned up. Or maybe it was the same one come back.'

'You still couldn't see?'

'I saw it better the second time. Don't know what make it was, but it was blue, light blue. I'm fairly sure of that.'

Cars would need checking . . . Jamie Kilpatrick's Daimler wasn't blue. Gregor Jack's Saab wasn't blue. Rab Kinnoul's Land-Rover wasn't blue.

'Anyway,' Corbie was saying, 'then there was *more* shouting the odds. I reckon it was coming from the BMW, because at one point the volume went right up on the radio.'

Rebus nodded appreciation of the observation.

'Then what?'

Corbie shrugged. 'It went quiet again. Next time I looked out, the other car was gone and the BMW was still there. Later on, I took a wander into the yard and through the field. Took a closer look. The passenger door was a bit open. Didn't look as though anyone was there, so I crossed the road. Keys were in the ignition . . .' He gave a final shrug. He had told his all.

And an interesting all it was. Two other cars? Or had the car from the morning returned in the afternoon? Who had Liz Jack been calling from the phone-box? What had she been arguing about? The volume rising on the radio . . . to mask an argument, or because, in the course of a struggle, the knob had been moved? His head was beginning to birl again. He suggested they have some coffee. Three plastic cups were brought, with sugar and a plate containing four digestive biscuits.

Corbie seemed relaxed in the hard-back chair, one leg slung over the other, and smoking yet another cigarette. So far Knox had eaten all the biscuits . . .

'Right,' said Rebus, 'now what about the microwave . . .?'

The microwave was easy. The microwave was more treasure, again found by the side of the road.

'You don't expect us to believe that?' Knox sneered. But Rebus could believe it.

'It's the truth,' Corbie said easily, 'whether you believe it or not, Sergeant Knox. I was out in the car this morning, and saw it lying in a ditch. I couldn't believe it. Someone had just dumped it there. Well, it looked good enough, so I thought I'd take it home.'

'But why did you hide it?'

Corbie shifted in his seat. 'I knew my mum would think I'd nicked it. Well, anyway, she'd never believe I just *found* it. So I decided to keep it out of her way till I could come up with a story . . .'

'There was a break-in last night,' Rebus said, 'at Deer Lodge. Do you know it?'

'That MP owns it, the one from the brothel.'

'You know it then. I think that microwave was stolen during the break-in.'

'Not by me it wasn't.'

'Well, we'll know soon enough. The place is being dusted for prints.'

'Lot of dusting going on,' Corbie commented. 'You lot are worse than my mum.'

'Believe it,' Rebus said, rising to his feet. 'One last thing, Alec. The car, what did you tell your mum about it?'

'Nothing much. Said I was storing it for a friend.'

Not that she'd have believed it. But if she lost her son, she lost her farm, too.

'All right, Alec.' said Rebus, 'it's time to get it all down on paper. Just what you've told us. Sergeant Knox will help

142

you.' He paused by the door. 'Then, if we're *still* not happy that you've told us the truth and nothing but, maybe it'll be time to talk about drunk driving, eh?'

It was a long drive back to Mrs Wilkie's, and Rebus regretted not having taken a room in Dufftown. Still, it gave him time to think. He had made a telephone call from the station, putting back a certain appointment until tomorrow morning. So the rest of today was free. Clouds had settled low over the hills. So much for the nice weather. This was how Rebus remembered the Highlands – louring and forbidding. Terrible things had happened here in the past, massacres and forced migrations, blood feuds as vicious as any. Cases of cannibalism, too, he seemed to recall. Terrible things.

Who had killed Liz Jack? And why? The husband was always the first to fall under suspicion. Well, others could do the suspecting. Rebus, for one, didn't believe it. Why not?

Why not?

Well, look at the evidence. That Wednesday morning, Jack had been at a constituency meeting, then a game of golf, and in the evening he'd attended some function . . . according to whom? According to Jack himself and to Helen Greig. Plus, his car was white. There could be no mistaking it for blue. Plus, someone was out to get Jack into terrible trouble. And *that* was the person Rebus needed to find . . . unless it had been Liz Jack herself. He'd thought about that, too. But then there were the anonymous phone calls . . . according to whom? Only Barney Byars. Helen Greig had been unable (or unwilling) to confirm their existence. Rebus realized now that he really did need to talk to Gregor Jack again. Did his wife have any lovers? Judging by what Rebus had learned of her, the question needed changing to: how many did she have? One? Two? More? Or was he guilty of judging what he did not know? After all, he knew next to nothing about Elizabeth Jack. He knew what her allies and her critics thought of her. But he knew nothing *of her*. Except that, judging by her tastes in friends and furnishings, she hadn't had much taste . . .

*

143

Thursday morning. A week since the body had been found.

He woke up early, but was in no hurry to rise, and this time he let Mrs Wilkie bring him his tea in bed. She'd had a good night, never once thinking him her long-dead husband or long-lost son, so he reckoned she deserved not to be kept out of the bedroom. Not only tea this morning, but ginger nuts, too. And the tea was hot. But the day was cool, still grey and drizzly. Well, never mind. He'd be heading back to civilization, just as soon as he'd paid his respects elsewhere.

He ate a hurried breakfast, and received a peck on the cheek from Mrs Wilkie before leaving.

'Come back again some time,' she called, waving to him from the door. 'And I hope the jam sells all right . . .'

The rain came on at its heaviest just as his windscreen wipers gave up. He stopped the car to study his map, then dashed outside to give the wipers a quick shake. It had happened before: they just stuck, and could be righted with a bit of force. Except this time they really had packed in. And not a garage in sight. So he drove slowly, and found after a while that the heavier the rain fell, the clearer his windscreen became. It was the slow fine rain that was the problem, blotting out all but the vaguest shapes and outlines. The heavy dollops of rain came and went so fast that they seemed to clear the windscreen rather than obscuring it.

Which was just as well, for the rain stayed heavy all the way to Duthil.

Duthil Special Hospital had been planned and built to act as a showpiece for treatment of the criminally insane. Like the other 'special hospitals' dotted around the British Isles, it was just that – a hospital. It wasn't a prison, and patients who arrived in its care were treated like patients, not prisoners. Treatment, not punishment, was its function, and with the brand new buildings came up-to-date methods and understandings.

All this the hospital's medical director, Dr Frank Forster, told Rebus in his pleasant but purposeful office. Rebus had spent a long time last night on the telephone with Patience, and she'd told him much the same thing. Fine, thought

Rebus. But it was still a place of detention. The people who came here came with no time limit attached, no 'sentence' that had to be served. The main gates were operated electronically and by guards, and everywhere Rebus had gone so far the doors had been locked again behind him. But now Dr Forster was talking about recreation facilities, staff/patient ratios, the weekly disco ... He was obviously proud. He was also obviously overdoing it. Rebus saw him for what he was: the front-man whose job it was to publicize the benefits of this particular special hospital, the caring attitude, the role of treatment. The likes of Broadmoor had come in for a lot of criticism in previous years. To avoid criticism, you needed good PR. And Dr Forster looked good PR. He was young for a start, a good few years younger than Rebus. And he had a healthy, scrupulous look to him, with a smile always just around the corner.

He reminded Rebus of Gregor Jack. That enthusiasm and energy, that public image. It used to be the sort of stuff Rebus associated with American presidential campaigns; now it was everywhere. Even in the asylums. The lunatics hadn't taken over; the image-men had.

'We have just over three hundred patients here,' Forster was saying, 'and we like the staff to get to know as many of them as possible, I don't just mean faces, I mean names. First names at that. This isn't Bedlam, Inspector Rebus. Those days are long past, thank God.'

'But you're a secure unit.'

'Yes.'

'You deal with the criminally insane.'

Forster smiled again. 'You wouldn't know it to look at most of our patients. Do you know, the majority of them – over sixty per cent, I believe – have above-average IQs? I think some of them are brighter than I am!' A laugh this time, then the serious face again, the caring face. 'A lot of our patients are confused, deluded. They're depressed, or schizophrenic. But they're not, I assure you, anything like the lunatics you see in the movies. Take Andrew Macmillan, for example.' The file had been on Forster's desk all along. He now opened it. 'He's been with us since the hospital opened. Before that, he was in much less ... savoury surroundings. He was making no progress at all before he came here. Now, he's becoming more talkative, and he seems about ready to participate in some of the available activities. I believe he plays a very good game of chess.'

'But is he still dangerous?'

Forster chose not to answer. 'He suffers occasional panic attacks ... hyperventilation, but nothing like the frenzies he went into before.' He closed the file. 'I would say, Inspector, that Andrew Macmillan is on his way to a complete recovery. Now, why do you want to talk to him?'

So Rebus explained about The Pack, about the friendship between 'Mack' Macmillan and Gregor Jack, about Elizabeth Jack's murder and the fact that she had been staying not forty miles from Duthil.

'I just wondered if she'd visited.'

'Well, we can check that for you.' Forster was flipping through the file again. 'Interesting, there's nothing in here about Mr Macmillan knowing Mr Jack, or about his having that nickname. Mack, did you say?' He reached for a pencil. 'I'll just make a note ...' He did so, then flicked through the file again. 'Apparently, Mr Macmillan has written to several MPs in the past ... and to other public figures. Mr Jack is mentioned ...' He read a little more in silence, then closed the file and picked up the telephone. 'Audrey, can you bring me the records of recent visitors ... say in the last month? Thanks.'

Duthil wasn't exactly a tourist attraction, and, out of sight being out of mind, there were few enough entries in the book. So it was the work of minutes to find what Rebus was looking for. The visit took place on Saturday, the day after Operation Creeper, but before the story became public knowledge.

'"Eliza Ferrie,"' he read. '"Patient visited: Andrew Macmillan. Relation to patient: friend." Signed in at three o'clock and out again at four thirty.'

'Our regular visiting hours,' Forster explained. 'Patients

can have visitors in the main recreation room. But I've arranged for you to see Andrew in his ward.'

'His ward?'

'Just a large room, really. Four beds to a room. But we call them wards to enforce . . . perhaps enhance would be a better word . . . to enhance the hospital atmosphere. Andrew's in the Kinnoul Ward.'

Rebus started. 'Why Kinnoul?'

'Pardon?'

'Why call the ward Kinnoul?'

Forster smiled. 'After the actor. You must have heard of Rab Kinnoul? He and his wife are among the hospital's patrons.'

Rebus decided not to say anything about Cath Kinnoul being one of The Pack, about her having known Macmillan at school . . . It was no business of his. But the Kinnouls went up in his estimation; well, Cath did. She had not, it seemed, forgotten her one-time friend. *Nobody calls me Gowk any more.* And Liz Jack, too, had visited, albeit under her maiden name and with a twist to her Christian name to boot. He could understand that: the papers would have had a field day. MP's Wife's Visits to Crazed Killer. All those possessives. She couldn't have known that the papers were about to have their story anyway . . .

'Perhaps at the end of your visit,' Dr Forster said, 'you'd like to see some of our facilities? Pool, gym, workshops . . .'

'Workshops?'

'Simple mechanics. Car maintenance, that sort of thing.'

'You mean you give the patients spanners and screwdrivers?'

Forster laughed. 'And we count them in again at the end of the session.'

Rebus had thought of something. 'Did you say *car* maintenance? I don't suppose somebody could take a look at my windscreen wipers?'

Forster started to laugh again, but Rebus shook his head.

'I'm serious,' he said.

'Then I'll see what we can do.' Forster rose to his feet. 'Ready when you are, Inspector.'

'I'm ready,' said Rebus, not at all sure that he was.

There was much passing through corridors, and the nurse who was to show Rebus to Kinnoul Ward had to unlock and relock countless doors. A heavy chain of keys swung from his waistband. Rebus attempted conversation, but the nurse replied with short measures. There was just the one incident. They were passing along a corridor when from an open doorway a hand appeared, grabbing at Rebus. A small, elderly man was trying to say something, eyes shining, mouth making tiny movements.

'Back into your room, Homer,' said the nurse, prising the fingers from Rebus's jacket. The man scuttled back inside. Rebus waited a moment for his heart rate to ease, then asked: 'Why do you call him Homer?'

The nurse looked at him. 'Because that's his name.' They walked on in silence.

Forster had been right. There were few moans or groans or sudden curdling shrieks, and few enough signs of movement, never mind *violent* movement. They passed through a large room where people were watching TV. Forster had explained that actual television wasn't allowed, since it couldn't be pre-determined. Instead, there was a daily diet of specially chosen video titles. *The Sound of Music* seemed to be a particular favourite. The patients watched in mute fascination.

'Are they on drugs?' Rebus hazarded.

The nurse suddenly became talkative. 'As many as we can stick down their throats. Keeps them out of mischief.'

So much for the caring face . . .

'Nothing wrong with it,' the nurse was saying, 'giving them drugs. It's all in the MHA.'

'MHA?'

'Mental Health Act. Allows for sedation as part of the treatment process.'

Rebus got the feeling the nurse was reciting a little defence he'd prepared to deal with visitors who asked. He was a big bugger: not tall, but broad, with bulging arms.

'Do any weight training?' Rebus asked.

'Who? That lot?'

Rebus smiled. 'I meant you.'

'Oh.' A grin. 'Yeah, I push some weights. Most of these places, the patients get all the facilities and there's nothing for the staff. But we've got a pretty good gym. Yeah, pretty good. In here . . .'

Another door was unlocked, another corridor beckoned, but off this corridor a sign pointed through yet another door – unlocked – to the Kinnoul Ward. 'In there,' the guard commanded, pushing open the door. His voice became firm. 'Okay, walk to the wall.'

Rebus thought for a moment the nurse was talking to *him*, but he saw that the object of the command was a tall, thin man, who now rose from his bed and walked to the far wall, where he turned to face them.

'Hands against the wall,' the nurse commanded. Andrew Macmillan placed the palms of his hands against the wall behind him.

'Look,' began Rebus, 'is this really – ?'

Macmillan smiled wryly. 'Don't worry,' the nurse told Rebus. 'He won't bite. Not after what we've pumped into him. You can sit there.' He was pointing to a table on which a board had been set for chess. There were two chairs. Rebus sat on the one which faced Andrew Macmillan. There were four beds, but they were all empty. The room was light, its walls painted lemon. There were three narrow barred windows, through which some rare sunshine poured. The nurse looked to be staying, and took up position behind Rebus, so that he was reminded of the scene in Dufftown interview room, with himself and Corbie and Knox.

'Good morning,' Macmillan said quietly. He was balding, and looked to have been doing so for some years. He had a long face, but it was not gaunt. Rebus would have called the face 'kindly'.

'Good morning, Mr Macmillan. My name's Inspector Rebus.'

This news seemed to excite Macmillan. He took half a step forward.

'Against the wall,' said the nurse. Macmillan paused, then retreated.

'Are you an Inspector of Hospitals?' he asked.

'No, sir, I'm a police inspector.'

'Oh.' His face dulled a little. 'I thought maybe you'd come to . . . they don't treat us well here, you know.' He paused. 'There, because I've told you that I'll probably be disciplined, maybe even put into solitary. Everything, any dissension, gets reported back. But I've got to keep telling people, or nothing will be done. I have some influential friends, Inspector.' Rebus thought this was for the nurse's ears more than his own. 'Friends in high places . . .'

Well, Dr Forster knew that now, thanks to Rebus.

'. . . friends I can trust. People need to be told, you see. They censor our mail. They decide what we can read. They won't even let me read *Das Kapital*. And they give us drugs. The mentally ill, you know, by whom I mean those who have been *judged* to be mentally ill, we have less rights than the most hardened mass murderer . . . hardened but *sane* mass murderer. Is that fair? Is that . . . humane?'

Rebus had no ready answer. Besides, he didn't want to be sidetracked.

'You had a visit from Elizabeth Jack.'

Macmillan seemed to think back, then nodded. 'So I did. But when she visits me she's Ferrie, not Jack. It's our secret.'

'What did you talk about?'

'Why are you interested?'

Rebus decided that Macmillan did not know of Liz Jack's murder. How could he know? There was no access to news in this place. Rebus's fingers toyed with the chessmen.

'It's to do with an investigation . . . to do with Mr Jack.'

'What has he done?'

Rebus shrugged. 'That's what I'm trying to find out, Mr Macmillan.'

Macmillan had turned his face towards the ray of sunshine. 'I miss the world,' he said, his voice dropping to a murmur. 'I had so many – friends.'

'Do you keep in touch with them?'

'Oh yes,' Macmillan said. 'They come and take me home with them for the weekend. We enjoy evenings out at the cinema, the theatre, drinking in bars. Oh, we have some wonderful times together.' He smiled ruefully, and tapped his head. 'But only in here.'

'Hands against the wall.'

'Why?' he spat. 'Why do I have to keep my hands against the wall? Why can't I just sit down and have a normal conversation like ... a ... normal ... person.' The angrier he got, the lower his voice dropped. There were flecks of saliva either side of his mouth, and a vein bulged above his right eye. He took a deep breath, then another, then bowed his head slightly. 'I'm sorry, Inspector. They give me drugs, you know. God knows what they are. They have this ... effect on me.'

'That's all right, Mr Macmillan,' Rebus said, but inside he was quivering. Was this madness or sanity? What happened to sanity when you chained it to a wall? Chained it, moreover, with chains that weren't real.

'You were asking,' Macmillan went on, breathless now, 'you were asking about ... Eliza ... Ferrie. You're right, she did come and visit. Quite a surprise. I know they have a home near here, yet they've never visited before. Lizzie ... Eliza ... did visit once, a long time ago. But Gregor ... Well, he's a busy man, isn't he? And she's a busy woman. I hear about these things ...'

From Cath Kinnoul, Rebus didn't doubt.

'Yes, she visited. A very pleasant hour we spent. We talked about the past, about ... friends. Friendship. Is their marriage in trouble?'

'Why do you say that?'

Another creased smile. 'She came alone, Inspector. She told me she was on holiday alone. Yet a man was waiting for her outside. Either it was Gregor, and he didn't want to see me, or else it was one of her . . . friends.'

'How do you know?'

'Nursie here told me. If you don't want to sleep tonight, Inspector, get him to show you the punishment block. I bet Doc Forster didn't mention the punishment block. Maybe that's where they'll throw me for talking like this.'

'Shut it, Macmillan.'

Rebus turned to the nurse. 'Is it true?' he asked. 'Was someone waiting outside for Mrs Jack?'

'Yeah, there was somebody in the car. Some guy. I only saw him from one of the windows. He'd got out of the car to stretch his legs.'

'What did he look like?'

But the nurse was shaking his head. 'He was getting back in when I saw him. I just saw his back.'

'What kind of car was it?'

'Black 3-series, no mistake about that.'

'Oh, he's very good at noticing things, Inspector, except when it suits him.'

'Shut it, Macmillan.'

'Ask yourself this, Inspector. If this is a *hospital*, why are all the so-called "nurses" members of the Prison Officers' Association? This isn't a hospital, it's a warehouse, but full of headcases rather than packing cases. The twist is, the headcases are the ones *in charge*!'

He was moving away from the wall now, walking on slow, doped legs, but his energy was unmistakable. Every nerve was blazing.

'Against the wall – '

'Headcases! I took her head off! God knows, I did – '

'Macmillan!' The nurse was moving too.

'But it was so long ago . . . a different – '

'Warning you – '

'And I want so much . . . so much to – '

'Right, that's it.' The nurse had him by the arms.

' – touch the earth.'

In the end, Macmillan offered little resistance, as the straps were attached to his arms and legs. The guard laid him out on the floor. 'If I leave him on the bed,' he told Rebus, 'he just rolls off and injures himself.'

'And you wouldn't want that,' said Macmillan, sounding almost peaceful now that he'd been restrained. 'No, nurse, you wouldn't want that.'

Rebus opened the door, making to leave.

'Inspector!'

He turned. 'Yes, Mr Macmillan?'

Macmillan had twisted his head so it was facing the door. 'Touch the earth for me . . . please.'

Rebus left the hospital on shakier legs than he'd entered it. He didn't want the tour of the pool and the gym. Instead, he'd asked the nurse to show him the punishment block, but the nurse had refused.

'Look,' he'd said, 'you might not like what goes on here, I might not like some of what goes on, but you've seen how it is. They're supposed to be "patients", but you can't turn your back on them, you can't leave them alone. They'll swallow lightbulbs, they'll be shitting pens and pencils and crayons, they'll try to put their head through the television. I mean, they might *not*, but you just can't ever be sure . . . ever. Try to keep an open mind, Inspector. I know it's not easy, but try.'

And Rebus had wished the young man luck with his weight training before making his exit. Into the courtyard. He stooped by a flowerbed and plunged his fingers deep into it, rubbing the soil between forefinger and thumb. It felt good. It felt good to be outside. Funny the things he took for granted, like earth and fresh air and free movement.

He looked up at the hospital windows, but couldn't be sure which, if any, belonged to Macmillan's ward. There were no faces staring at him, no signs of life at all. He rose to his feet, went to his car and got in, staring out through the windscreen. The brief sunshine had vanished. There was drizzle again, obscuring the view. Rebus pressed the button . . . and the windscreen wipers came on, came on and stayed on, their blades moving smoothly. He smiled, hands resting on the steering wheel, and asked himself a question.

'What happens to sanity when you chain it to a wall?'

He took a detour on his way back south, coming off the dual carriageway at Kinross. He passed Loch Leven (scene of many a family picnic when Rebus had been a kid), took a right at the next junction, and headed towards the tired mining villages of Fife. He knew this territory well. He'd been born and brought up here. He knew the grey housing schemes and the corner shops and the utilitarian pubs. The people cautious with strangers, and almost as cautious with friends and neighbours. Street-corner dialogues like bare-knuckle fights. His parents had taken his brother and him away from it at weekends, travelling to Kirkcaldy for shopping on the Saturday, and Loch Leven for those long Sunday picnics, sitting cramped in the back of the car with salmon-paste sandwiches and orange juice, flasks of tea smelling of hot plastic.

And for summer holidays there had been a caravan in St Andrews, or bed and breakfast in Blackpool, where Michael would always get into trouble and have to be hauled out by his older brother.

'And a lot of bloody thanks I got for it.'

Rebus kept driving.

Byars Haulage was sited halfway up a steep hill in one of the villages. Across the road was a school. The kids were on their way home, swinging satchels at each other and swearing choicely. Some things never changed. The yard of Byars Haulage contained a neat row of artics, a couple of nondescript cars, and a Porsche Carrera. None of the cars was blue. The offices were actually Portakabins. He went to the one marked 'Main Office' (below which someone had crayoned 'The Boss') and knocked.

Inside a secretary looked up from her word-processor. The room was stifling, a calor-gas heater roaring away by the side of the desk. There was another door behind the secretary. Rebus could hear Byars talking fast and loud and uproariously behind the door. Since no one answered him back, Rebus reckoned it was a phone call.

'Well tell Shite-for-brains to get off his arse and get over here.' (Pause.) 'Sick? *Sick?* Sick means he's shagging that missus of his. Can't blame him, mind . . .'

'Yes?' the secretary said to Rebus. 'Can I help you?'

'Well never mind what he says,' came Byars' voice, 'I've got a load here that's got to be in Liverpool yesterday.'

'I'd like to see Mr Byars, please,' said Rebus.

'If you'll take a seat, I'll see whether Mr Byars is available. What's the name, please?'

'Rebus, Detective Inspector Rebus.'

At that moment, the door of Byars' office opened and Byars himself came out. He was holding a portable phone in one hand and a sheet of paper in the other. He handed the paper to his secretary.

'That's right, wee man, and there's a load coming up from London the day after.' Byars' voice was louder than ever. Rebus noticed that, unseen by her, Byars was staring at his secretary's legs. He wondered if this whole performance was for her benefit . . .

But now Byars had spotted Rebus. It took Byars a second to place him, then he nodded a greeting in Rebus's direction. 'Aye, you give him big licks, wee man,' he said into the telephone. 'If he's got a sick-note, fine, if not tell him I'm looking out his cards, okay?' He terminated the call and shot out a hand.

'Inspector Rebus, what the hell brings you to this blighted neck of the bings?'

'Well,' said Rebus, 'I was passing, and – '

'Passing my arse! Plenty of people pass through, but nobody stops unless they want something. Even then, I'd advise them to keep on going. But you come from round here, don't you? Into the office then, I can spare you five minutes.' He turned to the secretary and rested a hand on her shoulder. 'Sheena, hen, get on to tadger-breath in Liverpool and tell him tomorrow morning definite.'

'Will do, Mr Byars. Will I make a cup of coffee?'

'No, don't bother, Sheena. I know what the polis like to drink.' He gave Rebus a wink. 'In you go, Inspector. In you go.'

Byars' office was like the back room of a dirty bookshop, its walls apparently held together by nude calendars and centrefolds. The calendars all seemed to be gifts donated by garages and suppliers. Byars saw Rebus looking.

'Goes with the image,' he said. 'A hairy-arsed truck driver with tattoos on his neck comes in here, he thinks he knows the sort of man he's dealing with.'

'And what if a woman comes in?'

Byars clucked. '*She*'d think she knew, too. I'm not saying she'd be all wrong either.' Byars didn't keep his whisky in the filing cabinet. He kept it inside a wellington boot. From the other boot he produced two glasses, which he sniffed. 'Fresh as the morning dew,' he said, pouring the drinks.

'Thanks,' said Rebus. 'Nice car.'

'Eh? Oh, outside you mean? Aye, it's no' bad. Nary a dent in it either. You should see the insurance payments though. Talk about steep. They make this brae look like a billiard table. Good health.' He sank the measure in one gulp, then noisily exhaled.

Rebus, having taken a sip, examined the glass, then the bottle. Byars chuckled.

'Think I'd give Glenlivet to the ba'-heids I get in here? I'm a businessman, not the Samaritans. They look at the bottle, think they know what they're getting, and they're impressed. Image again, like the scuddy pics on the wall. But it's really just cheap stuff I pour into the bottle. Not many folk notice.'

Rebus thought this was meant as a compliment. Image, that's what Byars was, all surface and appearance. Was he so different from MPs and actors? Or policemen come to that. All of them hiding their ulterior motives behind a set of gimmicks.

'So what is it you want to see me about?'

That was easily explained. He wanted to ask Byars a little more about the party at Deer Lodge, seemingly the last party to be held there.

'Not many of us there,' Byars told him. 'A few cried off pretty late. I don't think Tom Pond was there, though he was expected. That's right, he was off to the States by then. Suey was there.'

'Ronald Steele?'

'That's the man. And Liz and Gregor, of course. And me. Cathy Kinnoul was there, but her husband wasn't. Let's see ... who else? Oh, a couple who worked for Gregor. Urquhart...'

'Ian Urquhart?'

'Yes, and some young girl ...'

'Helen Greig?'

Byars laughed. 'Why bother to ask if you already know? I think that was about it.'

'You said a *couple* who worked for Gregor. Did you get the impression that they *were* a couple?'

'Christ, no. I think everybody *but* Urquhart tried to get the girl into the sack.'

'Did anyone succeed?'

'Not that I noticed, but after a couple of bottles of champagne I tend not to notice very much. It wasn't like one of Liz's parties. You know, not wild. I mean, everybody had plenty to drink, but that was all.'

'All?'

'Well, you know ... Liz's crowd was *wild*.' Byars stared towards one of the calendars, seemingly reminiscing. 'A real wild bunch and no mistake ...'

Rebus could imagine Barney Byars lapping it up, mixing with Patterson-Scott, Kilpatrick and the rest. And he could imagine them ... tolerating Byars, a bit of nouveau rough. No doubt Byars was the life and soul of the party, a laugh a minute. Only they were laughing *at* him rather than with him ...

'How was the lodge when you arrived?' Rebus asked.

Byars wrinkled his nose. 'Disgusting. It hadn't been cleaned since the last party a fortnight before. One of Liz's parties, not one of Gregor's. Gregor was going spare. Liz or somebody was supposed to have had it cleaned. It looked like a bloody sixties squat or something.' He smiled. 'Actually, I probably shouldn't be telling you this, you being a member of the constabulary and all, but I didn't bother staying the night. Drove back about four in the morning. Absolutely guttered, but there was nobody about on the roads for me to be a menace to. Wait till you hear this though. I thought my feet were cold when I stopped the car. Got out to open the garage ... and I didn't have any shoes on! Just the one sock and no fucking shoes! Christ knows how come I didn't notice ...'

8

Spite and Malice

Did John Rebus receive a hero's welcome? He did not. There were some who felt he'd merely added to the chaos of the case. Perhaps he had. Chief Superintendent Watson, for example, still felt William Glass was the man they were looking for. He sat and listened to Rebus's report, while Chief Inspector Lauderdale rocked to and fro on another chair, sometimes staring ruminatively at the ceiling, sometimes studying the one immaculate crease down either trouser-leg. It was Friday morning. There was coffee in the air. There was coffee, too, coursing through Rebus's nervous system as he spoke. Watson interrupted from time to time, asking questions in a voice as thin as an after-dinner mint. And at the end of it all, he asked the obvious question.

'What do you make of it, John?'

And Rebus gave the obvious, if only mostly truthful, answer.

'I don't know, sir.'

'Let's get this straight,' said Lauderdale, raising his eyes from a trouser-crease. 'She's at a telephone box. She meets a man in a car. They're arguing. The man drives off. She hangs around for some time. Another car, maybe the same car, arrives. Another argument. The car goes off, leaving her car still in the lay-by. And next thing we know of her, she's turning up dumped in a river next to the house owned by a friend of her husband's.' Lauderdale paused, as though inviting Rebus to contradict him. 'We still don't know when or where she died, only that she managed to end up in

Queensferry. Now, you say this actor's wife is an old friend of Gregor Jack's?'

'Yes.'

'Any hint that they were a bit *more* than friends?'

Rebus shrugged. 'Not that I know of.'

'What about the actor, Rab Kinnoul? Maybe he and Mrs Jack . . .?'

'Maybe.'

'Convenient, isn't it?' said the Chief Superintendent, rising to pour himself another cup of black death. 'I mean, if Mr Kinnoul *did* ever want to dispose of a body, what better place than his own fast-flowing river, discharging into the sea, body turning up weeks later, or perhaps never at all. *And* he's always played killers on the TV and in films. Maybe it's all gone to his head . . .'

'Except,' said Lauderdale, 'that Kinnoul was in a series of meetings all day that Wednesday.'

'And Wednesday night?'

'At home with his wife.'

Watson nodded. 'We come back to Mrs Kinnoul again. Could she be lying?'

'She's certainly under his thumb,' said Rebus. 'And she's on all sorts of anti-depressants. I'd be surprised if she could tell Wednesday night at home in Queensferry from the twelfth of July in Londonderry.'

Watson smiled. 'Nicely put, John, but let's *try* to stick to facts.'

'What precious few there are,' said Lauderdale. 'I mean, we all *know* who the obvious candidate is: Mrs Jack's husband. She finds out he's been caught trousers-down in a brothel, they have a row, he may not mean to kill her but he strikes her. Next thing, she's dead.'

'He was caught trousers-up,' Rebus reminded his superior.

'Besides,' added Watson, 'Mr Jack, too, has his alibis.' He read from a sheet of paper. 'Constituency meeting in the morning. Round of golf in the afternoon – corroborated by his playing partner and checked by Detective Constable Broome. Then a dinner appointment where he made a speech to eighty or so fine upstanding members of the business community in Central Edinburgh.'

'And he drives a white Saab,' Rebus stated. 'We need to check car colours for everyone involved in the case, all Mrs Jack's friends and all Mr Jack's.'

'I've already put DS Holmes on to it,' said Lauderdale. 'And forensics say they'll have a report on the BMW ready by morning. I've another question though.' He turned to Rebus. 'Mrs Jack was, apparently, up north for anything up to a week. Did she stay all that time at Deer Lodge?'

Rebus had to give Lauderdale credit, the bugger had his thinking cap on today. Watson was nodding as though he'd been about to ask the selfsame thing, but of course he hadn't. Rebus *had* thought about it though.

'I don't think so,' he said. 'I *do* think she spent some time there, otherwise where did the Sunday papers and the green suitcase come from? But a whole week ...? I doubt it. No signs of recent cooking. All the food and cartons and stuff I found were either from one party or another. There *had* been an attempt to clear a space on the living room floor, so one person or maybe two could sit and have a drink. But maybe that goes back to the last party, too. I suppose we could ask the guests while we're fingerprinting them ...'

'Fingerprinting them?' asked Watson.

Lauderdale sounded like an exasperated parent. 'Purposes of elimination, sir. To see if any prints are left that can't be identified.'

'What would that tell us?' Watson said.

'The point is, sir,' commented Lauderdale, 'if Mrs Jack didn't stay at Deer Lodge, then *who* was she with and where *did* she stay? Was she even up north all that time?'

'Ah ...' said Watson, nodding again as though understanding everything.

'She visited Andrew Macmillan on the Saturday,' added Rebus.

'Yes,' said Lauderdale, getting into his stride, 'but then she's next seen on the Wednesday by that yob at the farm. What about the days in between?'

'She was at Deer Lodge on the Sunday with her news-papers,' Rebus said. Then he realized the point Lauderdale was making. 'When she saw the story,' he continued, 'you think she may have headed south again?'

Lauderdale spread out his hands, examining the nails. 'It's a theory,' he said, merely.

'Well, we've plenty bloody theories,' said Watson, slapping one of his own much meatier hands down on the desk. 'We need something concrete. And let's not forget friend Glass. We still want to talk to him. About Dean Bridge if nothing else. Meanwhile . . .' he seemed to be trying to think of some path they might take, of some instructions or inspiration he might give. But he gave up and swigged back his coffee instead. 'Meanwhile,' he said at last, while Rebus and Lauder-dale waited for the imparted wisdom, 'let's be careful out there.'

The old man's really showing his age now, thought Rebus, as he waited to follow Lauderdale out of the office. *Hill Street Blues* was a long, long time ago. In the corridor, after the door was closed behind them, Lauderdale grasped Rebus's arm. His voice was an excited hiss.

'Looks like the Chief Super's on the way out, doesn't it? Can't be long before the high heidyins see what's going on and pension him off.' He was trying to control his glee. Yes, Rebus was thinking, one or two very public foul-ups, that's all it would take. And he wondered . . . he wondered if Lauderdale was capable of engineering a balls-up with this in mind. Someone had tipped off the papers about Operation Creeper. Christ, it seemed such a long time ago. But wasn't Chris Kemp supposed to be doing some digging into that? He'd have to remember to ask Kemp what he'd found. So much still needed to be done . . .

He was shrugging his arm free of Lauderdale when Wat-son's door opened again, and Watson stood there staring at the two of them. Rebus wondered if they looked as guilty and conspiratorial as he himself felt. Then Watson's eyes settled on him.

'John,' he said, 'telephone call. It's Mr Jack. He says he'd be grateful if you'd go and see him. Apparently, there's something he'd like to talk to you about . . .'

Rebus pressed the bell at the locked gate. The voice over the intercom was Urquhart's.

'Yes?'

'Inspector Rebus to see Mr Jack.'

'Yes, Inspector, be right with you.'

Rebus peered through the bars. The white Saab was parked outside the house. He shook his head slowly. Some people never learned. A reporter had been sent from one of the line of cars to ask who Rebus was. The other reporters and photographers took shelter in the cars themselves, listening to the radio, reading newspapers. Soup or coffee was poured from flasks. They were here for the duration. And they were bored. As he waited, the wind sliced against Rebus, squeezing through a gap between jacket and shirt collar, trickling down his neck like ice water. He watched Urquhart emerge from the house, apparently trying to sort out the tangle of keys in his hand. The reconnaissance reporter still stood beside Rebus, twitching, readying himself to ask Urquhart his questions.

'I shouldn't bother, son,' advised Rebus.

Urquhart was at the gate now.

'Mr Urquhart,' blurted the reporter, 'anything to add to your previous statement?'

'No,' said Urquhart coolly, opening the gate. 'But I'll repeat it for you if you like – bugger off!'

And with that, Rebus safely through the gate, he slammed it shut and locked it, giving the bars an extra shake to make sure they were secure. The reporter, smiling sourly, was heading back to one of the cars.

'You're under siege,' Rebus observed.

Urquhart looked like he'd done without sleep for a night or two too many. 'It's diabolical,' he confided as they walked towards the house. 'Day and night they're out there. God knows what they think they're going to get.'

'A confession?' Rebus hazarded. He was rewarded with a weak smile.

'That, Inspector, they'll never get.' The smile left his face. 'But I *am* worried about Gregor . . . what all this is doing to him. He's . . . well, you'll see for yourself.'

'Any idea what this meeting's all about?'

'He wouldn't say. Inspector . . .' Urquhart had stopped. 'He's very fragile. I mean, he might say *any*thing. I just hope you can tell truth from fantasy.' Then he started to walk again.

'Are you still diluting his whisky?' Rebus asked.

Urquhart gave him an appraising look, then nodded. 'That's not the answer, Inspector. That's not what he needs. He needs friends.'

Andrew Macmillan, too, had gone on about friends. Rebus wanted to talk to Jack about Andrew Macmillan. But he wasn't in a hurry. He had paused beside the Saab, causing Urquhart to pause too.

'What is it?'

'You know,' said Rebus, 'I've always liked Saabs, but I've never had the money around to buy one. Do you think Mr Jack would mind if I just sat in the driver's seat for a minute?'

Urquhart looked at a loss for an answer. He ended up making a gesture somewhere between a shrug and a shake of the head. Rebus tried the driver's door. It was unlocked. He slid into the seat and rested his hands on the steering wheel, leaving the door itself open so Urquhart could stand there and watch.

'Very comfortable,' Rebus said.

'So I believe.'

'You've never driven it yourself then?'

'No.'

'Oh.' Rebus stared out of the windscreen, then at the passenger seat and the floor. 'Yes, well designed, comfortable. Plenty of room, eh?' And he turned in his seat, twisting his whole body round to examine the rear seat . . . the rear floor. 'Heaps of room,' he commented. 'Lovely.'

'Maybe Gregor would let you take her for a spin?'

Rebus looked up keenly. 'Do you think so? I mean, when this has all blown over, of course.' He started to get out of the car. Urquhart snorted.

'Blown over? This sort of thing doesn't "blow over", not when you're an MP. The broth – . . . those allegations in the newspapers, they were bad enough, but now murder? No.' He shook his head. 'This won't just blow over, Inspector. It's not a raincloud, it's a mud bath, and mud sticks.'

Rebus closed the door. 'Nice solid clunk, too, when you shut it, isn't there? How well did you know Mrs Jack?'

'Pretty well. I used to see her most days.'

'But I believe Mr and Mrs Jack led fairly separate lives?'

'I wouldn't go that far. They *were* married.'

'And in love?'

Urquhart thought for a moment. 'I'd say so, yes.'

'Despite everything?' Rebus was walking around the car now, as though deciding whether or not to buy it.

'I'm not sure I understand.'

'Oh, you know, different sorts of friends, different lifestyles, separate holidays . . .'

'Gregor is an MP, Inspector. He can't always get away at the drop of a hat.'

'Whereas,' Rebus said, 'Mrs Jack was . . . what would you say? Spontaneous? Flighty, maybe even? The sort who'd say, let's just up and go?'

'Actually, yes, that's fairly accurate.'

Rebus nodded and tapped the boot. 'What about luggage room?'

Urquhart himself actually came forward and opened the boot.

'Goodness,' said Rebus, 'yes, there's plenty of room. Quite deep, isn't it?'

It was also immaculately clean. No mud or scuff marks, no crumbs of earth. It looked as though it had never been used. Inside were a small reserve petrol tank, a red warning triangle, and a half-set of golf clubs.

'He's keen on golf, isn't he?'

'Oh yes.'

Rebus closed the boot shut. 'I've never seen the attraction myself. The ball's too small and the pitch is too big. Shall we go in?'

Gregor Jack looked like he'd been to hell and back on an LRT bus. He'd probably combed his hair yesterday or the day before, and last changed his clothes then, too. He was shaven, but there were small patches of dark stubble the razor had missed. He didn't bother rising when Rebus entered the room. He just nodded a greeting and gestured with his glass to a vacant chair, one of the infamous marshmallow chairs. Rebus approached with care.

There was whisky in Jack's crystal tumbler, and a bottle of the stuff – three quarters empty – on the rug beside him. The room smelt unaired and unpolished. Jack took a gulp of liquid, then used the edge of the glass to scratch at his raw red finger.

'I want to talk to you, Inspector Rebus.'

Rebus sat down, sinking, sinking . . . 'Yes, sir?'

'I want to say a few things about me . . . and maybe about Liz, too, in a roundabout way.'

It was another prepared speech, another well-considered opening. There were just the two of them in the room. Urquhart had said he'd make a pot of coffee. Rebus, still jumpy from his meeting with Watson, had begged for tea. Helen Greig, it seemed, was at home, her mother having been taken ill – 'again', as Urquhart put it, before marching off kitchenwards. Faithful women: Helen Greig and Cath Kinnoul. Doggedly faithful. And Elizabeth Jack? Doggie-style faithful maybe . . . Christ, that was a terrible thing to think! And especially of the dead, especially of a woman he'd never met! A woman who liked to be tied to bedposts for a spot of . . .

'It's nothing to do with . . . well, I don't know, maybe it is.' Jack paused for thought. 'You see, Inspector, I can't help feeling that *if* Liz saw those stories about me, and *if* they upset her, then maybe she did something . . . or stayed away . . . and maybe . . .' He leapt to his feet and wandered over towards the window, looking out at nothing. 'What I'm trying to say is, what if I'm responsible?'

'Responsible, sir?'

'For Liz's ... murder. If we'd been together, if we'd been *here* together, it might never have happened. It *wouldn't* have happened. Do you see what I mean?'

'No good blaming yourself, sir – '

Jack whirled towards him. 'But that's just it, I *do* blame myself.'

'Why don't you sit down, Mr Jack – '

'Gregor, please.'

'All right ... Gregor. Now why don't you sit down and calm down.'

Jack did as he was told. Bereavement affected different people in different ways, the weak becoming strong and the strong becoming weak. Ronald Steele hurled books around, Gregor Jack became ... pathetic. He was scratching at the finger again. 'But it's all so ironic,' he spat.

'How's that?' Rebus wished the tea would hurry up. Maybe Jack would pull himself together in Urquhart's presence.

'That brothel,' Jack said, fixing Rebus's eyes with his own. 'That's what started it all. And the reason I was there ...'

Rebus sat forward. 'Why *were* you there, Gregor?'

Gregor Jack paused, swallowed, seemed to take a breath while he thought about whether to answer or not. Then he answered.

'To see my sister.'

There was silence in the room, so profound that Rebus could hear his watch ticking. Then the door flew open.

'Tea,' said Ian Urquhart, sidling into the room.

Rebus, who had been so eager for Urquhart's arrival, now couldn't wait for the man to leave. He rose from the chair and walked to the mantelpiece. The card from The Pack was still there, but it had been joined by over a dozen condolence cards – some from other MPs, some from family and friends, some from the public.

Urquhart seemed to sense the atmosphere in the room. He

left the tray on a table and, without a word, made his exit. The door had barely closed before Rebus said, 'What do you mean, your sister?'

'I mean just that. My sister was working in that brothel. Well, I suspected she was, I'd been *told* she was. I thought maybe it was a joke, a sick joke. Maybe a trap, to get me to a brothel. A trap and a trick. I thought long and hard before I went, but I still went. He'd sounded so confident.'

'Who had?'

'The caller. I'd been getting these calls ...' Ah yes, Rebus had meant to ask about those. 'By the time I got to the phone, the caller would have hung up. But one night, the caller got me straight away, and he told me: "Your sister's working in a brothel in the New Town." He gave me the address, and said if I went around midnight she'd just be starting her ... shift.' The words were like some food he didn't enjoy, but given him at a banquet so that he didn't dare spit it out, but had to go on chewing, trying hard not to swallow ... He swallowed. 'So along I went, and she *was* there. The caller had been telling the truth. I was trying to talk to her when the police came in. But it was a trap, too. The newsmen were there ...'

Rebus was remembering the woman in the bed, the way she kicked her legs in the air, the way she'd lifted her t-shirt for the photographers to see ...

'Why didn't you say anything at the time, Gregor?'

Jack laughed shrilly. 'It was bad enough as it was. Would it have been any better if I'd let everyone know my sister's a tart?'

'Well then, why tell me now?'

His voice was calm. 'It looks to me, Inspector, like I'm in deep water. I'm just jettisoning what I don't need.'

'You must know then, sir ... you must have known all along, that someone is setting you up to take a very big fall.'

Jack smiled. 'Oh yes.'

'Any idea who? I mean, any enemies?'

The smile again. 'I'm an MP, Inspector. The wonder is that I have any *friends*.'

'Ah yes, The Pack. Could one of them . . . ?'

'Inspector, I've racked my brain and I'm no nearer finding out.' He looked up at Rebus. 'Honest.'

'You didn't recognize the caller's voice?'

'It was heavily muffled. Gruff. A man probably, but to be honest it could have been a woman.'

'Okay then, what about your sister? Tell me about her.'

It was soon told. She'd left home young, and never been heard of. Vague rumours of London and marriage had drifted north over the years, but that was all. Then the phone call . . .

'How could the caller know? How might they have found out?'

'Now *that's* a mystery, because I've never told anybody about Gail.'

'But your schoolfriends would know of her?'

'Slightly, I suppose. I doubt any of them remember her. She was two years below us at school.'

'You think maybe she came back up here looking for revenge?'

Jack spread his palms. 'Revenge for what?'

'Well, jealousy then.'

'Why didn't she just get in touch?'

It was a point. Rebus made a mental note to get in touch with *her*, supposing she was still around. 'You haven't heard from her since?'

'Not before, not since.'

'Why *did* you want to see her, Gregor?'

'One, I really was interested.' He broke off.

'And two?'

'Two . . . I don't know, maybe to talk her out of what she was doing.'

'For her own good, or for yours?'

Jack smiled. 'You're right, of course, bad for the image having a sister on the game.'

'There are worse forms of prostitution than whoring.'

Jack nodded, impressed. 'Very deep, Inspector. Can I use that in one of my speeches? Not that I'll be making many of *those* from now on. Whichever way you look at it, my career's down the Swanny.'

'Never give up, sir. Think of Robert the Bruce.'

'And the spider, you mean? I hate spiders. So does Liz.' He halted. '*Did* Liz.'

Rebus wanted to keep the conversation moving. The amount of whisky Jack had drunk, he might tip over any minute. 'Can I ask you about that last party up at Deer Lodge?'

'What about it?'

'For a start, who was present?'

Having to use his memory seemed to sober Jack up. Not that he could add much to what Barney Byars had already told Rebus. It was a boozy, sit-around-and-chat evening, followed by a morning hike up some nearby mountain, lunch – at the Heather Hoose – and then home. Jack's only regret was inviting Helen Greig to go.

'I'm not sure she saw any of us in a decent light. Barney Byars was doing elephant impressions, you know, where you pull out your trouser pockets and – '

'Yes, I know.'

'Well, Helen took it in good enough part, but all the same . . .'

'Nice girl, isn't she?'

'The sort my mum would have wanted me to marry.'

Mine too, thought Rebus. The whisky wasn't just loosening Jack's tongue, it was also loosening his accent. The polish was fading fast, leaving the raw wood of towns like Kirkcaldy, Leven, Methil.

'This party was a couple of weeks ago, wasn't it?'

'Three weeks ago. We were back here five days when Liz decided she needed a holiday. Packed a case and off she went. Never saw her again . . .' He raised a fist and punched the soft leather of the sofa, making hardly a sound and no discernible mark. 'Why are they doing this to me? I'm the best MP this constituency's ever had. Don't take my word for it. Go out and talk to them. Go to a mining village or a farm or a factory or a fucking afternoon tea party. They tell me the same thing: well done, Gregor, keep up the good work.' He was on his feet again now, feet holding their ground but the rest of the body in motion. 'Keep up the good work, the hard work. Hard work! It bloody is hard work, I can tell you.' His voice was rising steadily. 'Worked my balls off for them! Now somebody's trying to piss on my whole life from a very high place. Why me? Why me? Liz and me . . . Liz . . .'

Urquhart tapped twice before putting his head round the door. 'Everything all right?'

Jack put on a grotesque mask of a smile. 'Everything's fine, Ian. Listening behind the door, are you? Good, wouldn't want you to miss a word, would we?'

Urquhart glanced at Rebus. Rebus nodded: everything's okay in here, really it is. Urquhart retreated and closed the door. Gregor Jack collapsed into the sofa. 'I'm making such a mess of everything,' he said, rubbing his face with his hand. 'Ian's such a good friend . . .'

Ah yes, friends.

'I believe,' said Rebus, 'that you haven't just been receiving anonymous calls.'

'What?'

'Someone said something about letters, too.'

'Oh . . . oh yes, letters. Crank letters.'

'Do you still have them?'

Jack shook his head. 'Not worth keeping.'

'Did you let anyone see them?'

'Not worth reading.'

'What exactly was in them, Mr Jack?'

'Gregor,' Jack reminded him. 'Please, call me Gregor. What was in them? Rubbish. Garbled nonsense. Ravings . . .'

'I don't think so.'

'What?'

'Someone told me you'd refuse to let anyone open them. He thought they might be love letters.'

Jack hooted. 'Love letters!'

'I don't think they were either. But it strikes me, how could Ian Urquhart or anyone else *know* which letters they were to hand to you unopened? The handwriting? Difficult to tell

171

though, isn't it? No, it had to be the postmark. It had to be what was on the envelope. I'll tell you where those letters came from, Mr Jack. They came from Duthil. They came from your old friend Andrew Macmillan. And they weren't raving, were they? They weren't garbled or nonsense or rubbish. They were asking you to do something about the system in the special hospitals. Isn't that right?'

Jack sat and studied his glass, mouth set petulantly, a kid who's been caught out.

'Isn't that right?'

Jack gave a curt nod. Rebus nodded, too. Embarrassing to have a sister who's a prostitute. But how much *more* embarrassing to have an old friend who's a murderer? And mad, to boot. Gregor Jack had worked hard to form his public image, and harder still to preserve it. Rushing around with his vacuously sincere grin and strong-enough-for-the-occasion handshake. Working hard in his constituency, working hard in *public*. But his private life . . . well, Rebus wouldn't have wanted to swop. It was a mess. And what made it so messy was that Jack had tried to hide it. He didn't have skeletons in his closet; he had a crematorium.

'Wanted me to start a campaign,' Jack was muttering. 'Couldn't do that. Why did you start this crusade, Mr Jack? To help an old friend. Which old friend is that, Mr Jack? The one who cut his wife's head off. Now, if you'll excuse me. Oh, and please remember to vote for me next time round . . .' And he began a drunken, wailing laugh, near-manic, near-crying. Finally actually becoming crying, tears streaming down his cheeks, dripping into the glass he still held.

'Gregor,' Rebus said quietly. He repeated the name, and again, and again, always quietly. Jack sniffed back more tears and looked blurrily towards him. 'Gregor,' said Rebus, 'did you kill your wife?'

Jack wiped his eyes on his shirt-sleeve, sniffed, wiped again. He began to shake his head.

'No,' he said. 'No, I didn't kill my wife.'

*

172

No, because William Glass killed her. He killed the woman under Dean Bridge, and he killed Elizabeth Jack.

Rebus had missed all the excitement. He had driven back into town unaware of it. He had climbed the steps up to Great London Road station without knowing. And he had entered a place of jumpy, jittery clamour. Christ, what did it mean? Was the station definitely staying open? No move to St Leonard's? Which meant, if he remembered his bet, that he'd set up home with Patience Aitken. But no, it was nothing to do with the station staying open or being reduced to rubble. It was William Glass. A beat constable had come across him sleeping amidst the dustbins behind a supermarket in Barnton. He was in custody. He was talking. They were feeding him soup and giving him endless cups of tea and fresh cigarettes, and he was talking.

'But what's he saying?'

'He's saying he did them – both of them!'

'He's saying *what*?'

Rebus started calculating. Barnton ... not so far from Queensferry when you thought about it. They were thinking he'd have headed north or west, but in fact he'd started crawling back into town ... supposing he'd ever got as far as Queensferry in the first place.

'He's admitting both murders.'

'Who's with him?'

'Chief Inspector Lauderdale and Inspector Dick.'

Lauderdale! Christ, he'd be loving it. This would be the making of him, the final nail in the Chief Super's coffee-maker. But Rebus had other things to be doing. He wanted Jack's sister found, for a start. Gail Jack, but she wouldn't be calling herself that, would she? He went through the Operation Creeper case-notes. Gail Crawley. That was her. She'd been released, of course. And had given a London address. He found one of the officers who'd interviewed her.

'Yes, she said she was heading south. Couldn't keep her, could we? Didn't want to either. Just gave her a kick up the arse and told her not to come back up here again. Isn't it incredible? Catching Glass like that!'

'Incredible, yes,' said Rebus. He photocopied what notes there were, along with Gail Crawley's photograph, and scribbled some further notes of his own on to the copy. Then he telephoned an old friend, an old friend in London.

'Inspector Flight speaking.'

'Hello George. When's the retirement party then?'

There was laughter. 'You tell me, you were the one who persuaded me to stay on.'

'Can't afford to lose you.'

'Meaning you want a favour?'

'Official business, George, but speed is of the – '

'As usual. All right, what is it?'

'Give me your fax number and I'll send you the details. If she's at the address, I'd like you to talk to her. I've put down a couple of phone numbers. You can reach me anytime on one or the other.'

'Two numbers, eh? Got yourself in deep, have you?'

In deep . . . jettisoning what I don't need . . .

'You could say that, George.'

'What's she like?' By which he meant Patience, not Gail.

'She likes domesticity, George. Pets and nights in, candles and firelight.'

'Sounds perfect.' George Flight paused. 'I'll give it three months max.'

'Sod you,' said Rebus, grinning. Flight was laughing again.

'Four months then,' he said. 'But that's my final offer.'

That done, Rebus headed for the nerve centre, the one place he needed to station himself – the gents' toilets. Part of the ceiling had fallen down and had been replaced with a piece of brown cardboard on which some joker had drawn a huge eyeball. Rebus washed his hands, dried them, chatted to one of the other detectives, shared a cigarette. In a public toilet, he'd have been picked up for loitering. He *was* loitering, too, loitering with intent. The door opened. Bingo. It was Lauderdale, a frequent user of rest rooms when he was on an interrogation.

'All the time you're coming and going,' he'd told Rebus,

174

'the suspect's sweating that bit more, wondering what's up, what's happened that's new.'

'What's up?' Rebus asked now. Lauderdale smiled and went to splash water on his face, patting his temples and the back of his neck. He looked pleased with himself. More worrying, he didn't smell.

'Looks like our Chief Super may have got it right for once,' Lauderdale admitted. 'He said we should be concentrating on Glass.'

'He's confessed?'

'As good as. Looks as though he's sorting his defence out first.'

'What's that then?'

'The media,' said Lauderdale, drying himself. 'The media pushed him into doing it. I mean, killing again. He says it was *expected* of him.'

'Sounds to me like he's one domino shy of a set.'

'I'm not putting any words into his mouth, if that's what you're thinking. It's all on tape.'

Rebus shook his head. 'No, no, I mean, if he says he did it, then fair enough. That's fine. And by the way, it was me that shot JFK.'

Lauderdale was examining himself in the spattered mirror. He still looked triumphal, his neck rising from his shirt collar so that his head sat on it like a golf ball on its tee.

'A confession, John,' he was saying, 'it's a powerful thing is a confession.'

'Even when the guy's been sleeping rough for nights on end? Strung out on Brasso and hunted by Edinburgh's finest? Confession might be good for the soul, sir, but sometimes all it's worth is a bowl of soup and some hot tea.'

Lauderdale tidied himself, then turned towards Rebus. 'You're just a pessimist, John.'

'Think of all the questions Glass *can't* answer. Ask him some of them. How did Mrs Jack get to Queensferry? How come he dumped her *there*? Just ask him, sir. I'll be interested to read the transcript. I think you'll find the conversation's all one way.'

Exit the Inspector Rebus, leaving behind the Chief Inspector Lauderdale, brushing himself down like a statue examining itself for chips. He seems to find one, too, for he frowns suddenly, and spends longer in the washroom than intended ...

'I need just a little bit more, John.'

They were lying in bed together, just the three of them: Rebus, Patience, and Lucky the cat. Rebus affected an American accent.

'I gave ya everything I got, baby.'

Patience smiled, but wasn't to be placated. She thumped her pillows and sat up, drawing her knees up to her chin. 'I mean,' she said, 'I need to know what you're going to do ... what *we're* going to do. I can't decide whether you're moving in with me, or else moving out.'

'In and out,' he said, a final attempt at humour and escape. She punched him on the shoulder. Punched him hard. He sucked in his breath. 'I bruise easily,' he said.

'So do I!' There were almost tears in her eyes, but she wasn't going to give him the satisfaction. 'Is there anybody else?'

He looked surprised. 'No, what makes you think that?'

The cat had crawled up the bed to lie in Patience's lap, plucking at the duvet with its claws. As it settled, she started stroking its head. 'It's just that I keep thinking there's something you're about to tell me. You look as though you're gathering up the strength to say it, but then you never quite manage. I'd rather *know*, whatever it is.'

What was there to know? That he still hadn't made up his mind about moving in? That he still carried if not a flame then at least an unstruck Scottish Bluebell for Gill Templer? What was there to know?

'You know how it is, Patience. A policeman's lot is not a happy one, and all that.'

'Why do you have to get involved?'

'What?'

'In all these bloody cases, why do *you* have to get involved,

John? It's just a job like any other. I manage to forget about my patients for a few hours at a stretch, why can't you?'

He gave her just about his only honest answer of the evening. 'I don't know.'

The telephone rang. Patience picked the extension up off the floor and held it between them. 'Yours or mine?' she asked.

'Yours.'

She picked up the receiver. 'Hello? Yes, this is Doctor Aitken. Yes, hello, Mrs Laird. Is he now? Is that right? It isn't maybe just flu?'

Rebus checked his watch. Nine thirty. It was Patience's turn to do standby emergency for her group practice.

'A-ha,' she was saying, 'a-ha,' as the caller talked on. She held the receiver away from her for a second and hurled a silent scream towards the ceiling. 'Okay, Mrs Laird. No, just leave him be. I'll be there as soon as I can. What was your address again?'

At the end of the call, she stomped out of bed and started to dress. 'Mrs Laird's husband says he's on the way out this time,' she said. 'That's the third time in as many months, damn the man.'

'Do you want me to drive you?'

'No, it's all right, I'll go myself.' She paused, came over and pecked him on the cheek. 'But thanks for the offer.'

'You're welcome.' Lucky, disturbed from his rest, was now kneading Rebus's half of the duvet. Rebus made to stroke its head, but the cat shied away.

'See you later then,' said Patience, giving him another kiss. 'We'll have a talk, eh?'

'If you like.'

'I like.' And with that she was gone. He could hear her in the living room, getting together her stuff, then the front door opening and closing. The cat had left Rebus and was investigating the warm section of mattress from which Patience had lately risen. Rebus thought about getting up, then thought about not. The phone rang again. Another patient? Well, he wouldn't answer. It kept on ringing. He answered with a noncommittal 'Hello'.

'Took your time,' said George Flight. 'Haven't interrupted anything, have I?'

'What have you got, George?'

'Well, I've got the trots, since you ask. I blame it on that curry I had at Gunga's last night. I've also got the information you requested, Inspector.'

'Is that so, Inspector? Well would you mind passing it the hell on!'

Flight snorted. 'That's all the thanks I get, after a hard day's graft.'

'We all know the kind of graft the Met's interested in, George.'

Flight tut-tutted. 'Wires have ears, John. Anyway, the address was a no-show. Yes, a friend of Miss Crawley's lives there. But she hasn't seen her for weeks. Last she heard, Crawley was in Edinburgh.' He pronounced it head-in-burrow.

'Is that it?'

'I tried asking a couple of sleazebags connected with Croft.'

'Who's Croft?'

Flight sighed. 'The woman who ran the brothel.'

'Oh, right.'

'Only, we've had dealings with her before, you see. Maybe that's why she moved her operation north. So I talked to a couple of her "former associates".'

'And?'

'Nothing. Not even a trade discount on French with spanking.'

'Right. Well, thanks anyway, George.'

'Sorry, John. When are we going to see you down here?'

'When are we going to see you up *here*?'

'No offence, John, but it's all that square sausage and fizzy beer. It doesn't agree with me.'

'I'll let you get back to your smoked salmon and Scotch then. Night, George.'

He put the phone down, and considered for a moment.

Then he got out of bed and started to dress. The cat looked satisfied with this arrangement, and stretched himself out. Rebus searched for paper and a pen and scribbled a note to Patience. 'Lonely without you. Gone for a drive. John.' He thought about adding a few kisses. Yes, a few kisses were definitely in order.

'xxx'

Checking that he had car keys, flat keys and money, he let himself out, locking the door behind him.

If you didn't know, you wouldn't see.

It was a pleasant enough night for a drive, as it happened. The cloud cover kept the air mild, but there was no sign of rain or wind. It wasn't at all a bad night for a drive. Inverleith, then Granton, an easy descent to the coast. Past what had been William Glass's digs ... then Granton Road ... then Newhaven. The docks.

If you didn't know, you wouldn't see.

He was a lonely man, just out driving, just out driving slowly. They stepped out of shadowy doorways, or else crossed and recrossed at the traffic lights, like a sodium-lit fashion show. Crossed and recrossed. While drivers slowly drove, and slower yet, and slower. He saw nothing he wanted, so he took the car the length of Salamander Street, then turned it. Oh, he was a keen one. Shy, lonely, quiet and keen. Driving his beaten-up old car around the night-time streets, looking for ... well, maybe just looking *at*, unless he could be tempted ...

He stopped the car. She came walking smartly towards him. Not that her clothes were smart. Her clothes were cheap and cheerless, a pale raincoat, one size too big, and beneath it a bright red blouse and a mini-skirt. The mini-skirt, Rebus felt, was her big mistake, since her legs were bare and thinly unattractive. She looked cold; she looked as if she *had* a cold. But she tried him with a smile.

'Get in,' he said.

'Hand-job's fifteen, blow's twenty-five, thirty-five the other.'

Naïve. He could have arrested her on the spot. You never, *never* talked money till you were sure the punter was straight.

'Get in,' he repeated. She had a lot to learn. She got in. Rebus fished out his ID. 'Detective Inspector Rebus. I'd like a word, Gail.'

'You lot never give up, do you?' There was still Cockney in the accent, but she'd been back north long enough for her native Fife to start reasserting itself. A few more weeks, and that final 'you' would be a 'yiz': youse lot nivir gie up, dae yiz . . .?

She was a slow learner. 'How come you know my name?' she asked at last. 'Were you on that raid? After a freebie, are you, is that it?'

That wasn't it at all. 'I want to talk about Gregor.'

The colour drained from her face, leaving only eye make-up and slick red lipstick. 'Who's he when he's at home?'

'He's your brother. We can talk down the station, or we can talk at your flat, either suits me.' She made a perfunctory attempt at getting out of the car. It only needed a touch of his hand to restrain her.

'The flat then,' she said levelly. 'Just don't be all night about it, eh?'

It was a small room in a flat full of bed-sits. Rebus got the feeling she never brought men back here. There was too much of her about the place; it wasn't anonymous enough. For a start, there was a picture of a baby on the dressing table. Then there were newspaper cuttings pinned to the walls, all of them detailing the fall of Gregor Jack. He tried not to look at them, and instead picked up the photograph.

'Put that down!'

He did so. 'Who is it?'

'If you must know, it's me.' She was sitting on the bed, her two arms stretched out behind her, her mottled legs crossed. The room was cold, but there was no sign of any means of heating it. Clothes spilled from an open chest of drawers, and the floor was littered with bits and pieces of make-up. 'Get on with it then,' she said.

There being nowhere to sit, he stood, keeping his hands in his jacket pockets. 'You know that the only reason your brother was in that brothel was so he could talk to you?'

'Yeah?'

'And that if you'd told this to anyone –'

'Why should I?' she spat. 'Why the fuck should I? I don't owe him no favours!'

'Why not?'

'Why not? Because he's an oily git's why not. Always was. He's got it made, hasn't he? Mum and Dad always liked him better than me . . .' Her voice trailed off into silence.

'Is that why you left home?'

'None of your business why I left home.'

'Ever see any old friends?'

'I don't have any "old friends".'

'You came back north. You must have known there was a chance you'd bump into your brother.'

She snorted. 'We don't exactly move in the same circles.'

'No? I thought prostitutes always reckoned MPs and judges were their best clients?'

'They're just johns to me, that's all.'

'How long have you been on the game?'

She folded her arms tight. 'Just sod off, will you?' And there they were again, the not-quite-tears. Twice tonight he'd just failed to reduce a woman to tears. He wanted to go home and have a bath. But where was home?

'Just one more question, Gail.'

'Ms Crawley to you.'

'Just one more question, *Ms* Crawley.'

'Yeah?'

'Someone knew you were working in that brothel. Some-one who then told your brother. Any idea who it might be?'

There was a moment's thought. 'Not a clue.'

She was lying, obviously. Rebus nodded towards the clippings. 'Still, you're interested in him, aren't you? You know he came to see you that night because he cares –'

'Don't give me that crap!'

Rebus shrugged. It *was* crap, too. But if he didn't get this woman on to Gregor Jack's side, then he might never find out who was behind this whole ugly thing.

'Suit yourself, Gail. Listen, if you want to talk, I'm at Great London Road police station.' He fished out a card with his name and phone number on it.

'That'll be the day.'

'Well . . .' He headed for the door, a matter of two and a half strides.

'The more trouble that piss-pot's in, the better I'll like it.' But her words had lost their force. It wasn't quite indecision, but perhaps it was a start . . .

9
Within Range

On Monday morning, first findings started filtering down from Dufftown, where the forensic tests of Elizabeth Jack's BMW were under way. Specks of blood found on the driver's-side carpet matched Mrs Jack's type, and there were signs of what might have been a struggle: marks on the dashboard, scuff-marks on the interiors of both front doors, and damage to the radio-cassette, as though it had been hit with the heel of a shoe.

Rebus read the notes in Chief Inspector Lauderdale's office, then handed them back across the desk.

'What do you think?' Lauderdale asked, stifling a Monday morning yawn.

'You know what I think,' said Rebus. 'I think Mrs Jack was murdered in that lay-by, inside her car or outside it. Maybe she tried to run away and was hit from behind. Or maybe her assailant knocked her unconscious first, *then* hit her from behind to make it look like the work of the Dean Bridge murderer. However it happened, I don't think William Glass did it.'

Lauderdale shrugged and rubbed his chin, checking the closeness of the shave. 'He still says he did. You can read the transcripts any time you like. He says he was lying low, knowing we were after him. He needed money for food. He came upon Mrs Jack and hit her over the head.'

'What with?'

'A rock.'

'And what did he do with all her stuff?'

'Threw it into the river.'

'Come on, sir . . .'

'She didn't have any money. That's what made him so angry.'

'He's making it up.'

'Sounds plausible to me – '

'No! With respect, sir, what it sounds like is a quick solution, one that'll please Sir Hugh Ferrie. Doesn't it matter to you that it isn't the truth?'

'Now look here . . .' Lauderdale's face was reddening with anger. 'Look here, Inspector, all I've had from you so far is . . . well, what is it? It's nothing really, is it? Nothing solid or concrete. Nothing you could hang a shirt on, never mind a case in a court of law. Nothing.'

'How did she get to Queensferry? Who drove her there? What sort of state was she in?'

'For Christ's sake, I *know* it's not cut and dried. There are still gaps – '

'Gaps! You could fit Hampden into them three times over!'

Lauderdale smiled. 'There you go again, John, exaggerating. Why can't you just accept there's less to this than meets your eye?'

'Look, sir . . . fine, charge Glass with the Dean Bridge murder, that's okay by me. But let's keep an open mind on Mrs Jack, eh? At least until forensics are finished with the car.'

Lauderdale thought about it.

'Just till they finish the car,' Rebus pressed. He wasn't about to give up: Monday mornings were hell for Lauderdale, and the man would agree to just about anything if it meant getting Rebus out of his office.

'All right, John,' Lauderdale said, 'have it your way. But don't get bogged down in it. Remember, *I'll* keep an open mind if *you* will. Okay?'

'Okay.'

Lauderdale seemed to relax a little. 'Have you seen the Chief Superintendent this morning?' Rebus had not. 'I'm not even sure he's in yet. Maybe he had a heavy weekend, eh?'

'None of our business really, sir.'

Lauderdale stared at him. 'Of course, none of our business. But if the Chief Super's *personal* problems start interfering with his – '

The phone rang. Lauderdale picked up the receiver. 'Yes?' He straightened suddenly in his chair. 'Yes, sir. Was I, sir?' He flipped open his desk diary. 'Oh yes, ten.' He checked his watch. 'Well, I'll be there right away. Yes, sir, sorry about that.' He had the good grace to blush as he put down the receiver.

'The Chief Super?' guessed Rebus. Lauderdale nodded.

'I was supposed to be in a meeting with him five minutes ago. Forgot all about the bloody thing.' Lauderdale got to his feet. 'Plenty to keep you occupied, John?'

'Plenty. I believe DS Holmes has some cars for me to look at.'

'Oh? Thinking of getting rid of that wreck of yours? About time, eh?'

And, this being his idea of wit, Lauderdale actually laughed.

Brian Holmes had cars for him, cars aplenty. Well actually, a Detective Constable seemed to have done the work. Holmes, it appeared, was already learning to delegate. A list of the cars owned and run by friends of the Jacks. Make, registration, and colour. Rebus glanced down it quickly. Oh great, the only possessor of a colour blue was Alice Blake (The Pack's Sexton Blake), but she lived and worked in London. There were whites, reds, blacks, and a green. Yes, Ronald Steele drove a green Citroën BX. Rebus had seen it parked outside Gregor Jack's house the night Holmes had gone through the bins ... Green? Well, yes, green. He remembered it more as a greeny-blue, a bluey-green. *Keep an open mind.* Okay, it was green. But it was easier to mistake green for blue than, say, red for blue, or white, or black. Wasn't it?

Then there was the question of that particular Wednesday. Everyone had been asked: where were you that morning, that afternoon? Some of the answers were vaguer than others. In fact, Gregor Jack's alibis were more watertight than most. Steele, for example, had been uncertain about the morning. His assistant, Vanessa, had been off work that day, and Steele himself couldn't recall whether or not he'd gone into the shop. There was nothing in his diary to help him remember either. Jamie Kilpatrick had been sleeping off a hangover all day – no visitors, no phone calls – while Julian Kaymer had been 'creating' in his studio. Rab Kinnoul, too, was hesitant; he recalled meetings, but not necessarily the people he'd met. He could check, but it would take time . . .

Time, the one thing Rebus didn't have. He, too, needed all the friends he could get. So far, he'd ruled out two suspects: Tom Pond, who was abroad, and Andrew Macmillan, who was in Duthil. Pond was a nuisance. He wasn't back from the States yet. He had been questioned by telephone of course, and he knew all about the tragedy, but he had yet to be fingerprinted.

Anyone who might have been at Deer Lodge had been, or was being, or would be, fingerprinted. Just, so they were reassured, for processes of elimination. Just in case there were any fingerprints left in the lodge, any that couldn't be accounted for. It was painstaking work, this collection and collation of tiny facts and tiny figures. But it was how murder cases worked. Mind you, they worked more easily when there was a distinct scene of crime, a locus. Rebus wasn't in much doubt that Elizabeth Jack had been killed, or as good as, in the lay-by. Had Alec Corbie seen something, something he was holding back? Was there something he might know, without knowing he knew? Maybe something he didn't think was important. What if Liz Jack had said something to Andrew Macmillan, something he didn't realize might be a clue? Christ, Macmillan still didn't know she was *dead*. How would he react were Rebus to tell him? Maybe it would jog his memory. Then again, maybe it would have an altogether different effect. And besides, could anything he said be trusted? Wasn't it possible that he held a grudge against Gregor Jack, the way Gail Crawley did? The way others might, too . . .

Who, really, was Gregor Jack? Was he merely a tarnished saint, or was he a bastard? He'd ignored Macmillan's letters; he'd tried to keep his sister from disgracing him; he was embarrassed by his wife. Were his friends really friends? Or were they truly a 'pack'? Wolves ran in packs. Hounds ran in packs. And so did newshounds. Rebus remembered that he'd still to track down Chris Kemp. Maybe he was clutching at straws, but it felt more as if they were clutching at *him* . . .

And speaking of clutch, that was something else to be added to his car's list of woes. There was a worrying whirring and grinding as he pushed the gear-shift from neutral into first. But the car wasn't behaving badly (windscreen wipers aside – they'd begun sticking again). It had taken him north and back without so much as a splutter. All of which worried Rebus even more. It was like a terminal patient's final rally, that last gleam of life before the support machines took over.

Maybe next time he'd take the bus. After all, Chris Kemp's flat was only a quarter of an hour from Great London Road. The harassed-sounding woman on the news desk had given him the address as soon as he asked for it. And he had asked for it only when told that Kemp was on his day off. She'd given him the reporter's home phone number first, and, recognizing the first three digits as designating a local code, Rebus had asked for the address.

'You could just as easily have looked in the book,' she'd said before ringing off.

'Thank you, too,' he answered to the dead connection.

It was a second-floor flat. He pressed the intercom button beside the main door of the tenement, and waited. And waited. Should have phoned first, John. But then a crackle, and after the crackle: 'Yeah?' The voice groggy. Rebus glanced at his watch. Quarter to two.

'Didn't wake you, did I, Chris?'

'Who is that?'

'John Rebus. Get your breeks on and I'll buy you a pie and a pint.'

A groan. 'What time is it?'

'Nearly two.'

'Christ ... Never mind the alcohol, I need coffee. There's a shop at the corner. Fetch some milk, will you? I'll put the kettle on.'

'Back in two ticks.'

The intercom crackled into silence. Rebus went and fetched the milk, then buzzed the intercom again. There was a louder buzz from behind the door, and he pushed it open, entering the dim stairwell. By the time he reached the second floor, he was peching and remembering exactly why he liked living in Patience's basement. The door to Kemp's flat was ajar. Another name had been fixed to the door with Sellotape, just below Kemp's own. V. Christie. The girlfriend, Rebus supposed. A bicycle wheel, missing its tyre, rested against the hall wall. So did books, dozens of them, rickety, towering piles of them. He tiptoed past.

'Milkman!' he called.

'In here.'

The living room was at the end of the hall. It was large, but contained almost no space. Kemp, dressed in last week's t-shirt and the week before's denims, ran his fingers through his hair.

'Morning, Inspector. A timely alarm call. I'm supposed to be meeting someone at three o'clock.'

'Hint taken. I was just passing and – '

Kemp threw him a disbelieving glance, then busied himself at the sink, where he was trying his damnedest to get the stains off two mug-rims. The room served as living room and kitchen both. There was a fine old cooking range in the fireplace, but it had become a display case for pot plants and ornamental boxes. The actual cooker was a greasy-looking electrical device sited just next to the sink. On a dining table sat a word processor, boxes of paper, files, and next to the table stood a green metal filing cabinet, four drawers high, its bottom drawer open to show more files. Books, magazines, and newspapers were stacked on most of the available floor space, but there was room for a sofa, one armchair, TV and video, and a hi-fi.

'Cosy,' said Rebus. He actually thought he meant it. But Kemp looked around and made a face.

'I'm supposed to be cleaning this place up today.'

'Good luck.'

Coffee was spooned into the mugs, the milk splashed in after it. The kettle came to the boil and switched itself off, and Kemp poured.

'Sugar?'

'No thanks.' Rebus had settled on the arm of the sofa, as if to say: don't worry, I'm not about to linger. He accepted the mug with a nod. Kemp threw himself on to the armchair and gulped at the coffee, screwing up his face as it burned his mouth and throat.

'Christ,' he gasped.

'Heavy night?'

'Heavy week.'

Rebus wandered over in the direction of the dining table. 'It's a terrible thing, drink.'

'Maybe it is, but I was talking about *work.*'

'Oh. Sorry.' He turned from the table and headed over to the sink ... the cooker ... stopping beside the fridge. Kemp had left the carton of milk sitting on top of the fridge, next to the kettle. 'I'd better put this away,' he said, lifting the carton. He opened the fridge. 'Oh, look,' he said, pointing. 'There already *is* milk in the fridge. Looks fresh enough, doesn't it? I needn't have bothered going to the shop.'

He put the new carton of milk in beside the other, slammed shut the door, and returned to the arm of the sofa. Kemp was attempting something like a grin.

'You're sharp for a Monday.'

'But I can be blunt when I need to. What were you hiding from old Uncle Rebus, Chris? Or did you just need the time to check there was nothing *to* hide? A bit of blaw? That sort of thing. Or maybe something else, eh? Some story you're working on ... working on late into the night. Something *I* should know about. How about it?'

'Come on, Inspector. I'm the one who's doing *you* a favour, remember?'

'You'll have to refresh my memory.'

'You wanted me to see what I could find about the brothel story, about how the Sundays knew it was breaking.'

'But you never got back to me, Chris.'

'Well, I've been pressed for time.'

'You still are. Remember, you've got that meeting at three. Better tell me what you know, then I can be on my way.' Now Rebus slid off the arm and on to the sofa proper. He could feel the springs probing at him through what was left of the patterned covering.

'Well,' said Kemp, sitting forward in his chair, 'it looks like there was a kind of mass tip-off. All the papers thought they were getting an exclusive. Then, when they all turned up they knew they'd been had.'

'How do you mean?'

'Well, if there *was* a story, they had to publish. If they didn't, and their rivals did . . .'

'Editors would be asking questions about how come they got scooped?'

'Exactly. So whoever set the story up was guaranteed maximum exposure.'

'But who did set it up?'

Kemp shook his head. 'Nobody knows. It was anonymous. A telephone call on the Thursday to all the news desks. Police are going to raid a brothel in Edinburgh on Friday night . . . here's the address . . . if you're there around midnight, you're guaranteed to bag an MP.'

'The caller said that?'

'Apparently, his exact words were "at least one MP will be inside".'

'But he didn't name any names?'

'He didn't have to. Royalty, MPs, actors and singers – give those papers a sniff of any category and you've got them hooked. I'm probably mixing metaphors there, but you get the gist.'

'Oh yes, Chris, I get the gist. So what do you make of it?'

'Looks like Jack was set up to take a fall. But note, his name wasn't mentioned by the caller.'

'All the same . . .'

'Yes, all the same.'

Rebus was thinking furiously. If he hadn't been slouching on the sofa, he might have said he was thinking on his feet. Actually, he was debating with himself. About whether or not to do Gregor Jack a huge favour. Points against: he didn't owe Jack any favours; besides, he should try to remain objective – wasn't that what Lauderdale had been getting at? Points for: one really – he wouldn't just be doing Jack a favour, he might also flush out the rat who'd set Jack up. He made his decision.

'Chris, I want to tell you something . . .'

Kemp caught the whiff of a story. 'Attributable?'

But Rebus shook his head. 'Afraid not.'

'Accurate then?'

'Oh yes, I can guarantee it's accurate.'

'Go on, I'm listening.'

Last chance to bottle out. No, he wasn't going to bottle out. 'I can tell you why Gregor Jack was at that brothel.'

'Yes?'

'But I want to know something first – *are* you holding something back?'

Kemp shrugged. 'I don't think so.'

Rebus still didn't believe him. But then Kemp had no reason to tell Rebus anything. It wasn't as if Rebus was going to tell *him* anything that he didn't want him to know. They sat in silence for half a minute, neither friends nor enemies: more like trench soldiers on a Christmas Day kickabout. At any moment, the sirens might sound and shrapnel pierce the peace. Rebus recalled that he knew *one* thing Kemp wanted to know: how Ronald Steele got his nickname . . .

'So,' Kemp said, 'why *was* he there?'

'Because someone told him his sister was working there.'

Kemp pursed his lips.

'Working as a prostitute,' Rebus explained. 'Someone phoned him – anonymously – and told him. So he went along.'

'That was stupid.'

191

'Agreed.'

'And *was* she there?'

'Yes. She calls herself Gail Crawley.'

'How do you spell that?'

'C-r-a-w-l-e-y.'

'And you're sure of this?'

'I'm sure. I've spoken with her. She's still in Edinburgh, still working.'

Kemp kept his voice level, but his eyes were gleaming. 'You know this is a story?'

Rebus shrugged, saying nothing.

'You want me to place it?'

Another shrug.

'Why?'

Rebus stared at the empty mug in his hands. Why? Because once it was public knowledge, the caller would have failed, at least in his or her own terms. And, having failed, maybe they'd feel compelled to try something else. If they did, Rebus would be ready . . .

Kemp was nodding. 'Okay, thanks. I'll think it over.'

Rebus nodded too. He was already regretting the decision to tell Kemp. The man was a reporter, and one with a reputation to make. There was no way of knowing what he'd do with the story. It could be twisted to make Jack sound like samaritan or slime . . .

'Meantime,' Kemp was saying, rising from his chair, 'I better take a bath if I'm going to make that meeting . . .

'Right.' Rebus rose, too, and placed his mug in the sink. 'Thanks for the coffee.'

'Thanks for the milk.'

The bathroom was on the way to the front door. Rebus made show of looking at his watch. 'Go get into your bath,' he said. 'I'll let myself out.'

'Bye then.'

'See you, Chris.' He walked to the door, checking that his weight on the floorboards did not make them creak, then glanced round and saw that Kemp had disappeared into the bathroom. Water started splashing. Gently, Rebus turned the snib and locked it at the off position. Then he opened the door and slammed it noisily behind him. He stood in the stairwell, pulling the door by its handle so that it couldn't swing back open. There was a spy-hole, but he kept himself tucked in against the wall. Anyway, if Kemp came to the door he'd notice the snib was off ... A minute passed. Nobody came to the door. More fortuitously, perhaps, nobody came into the stairwell. He didn't fancy explaining what he was doing standing there holding on to a door handle ...

After two minutes, he crouched down and opened the letter box, peering in. The bathroom door was slightly ajar. The water was still running, but he could hear Kemp humming, then a-ha-hee-ha-ing as he got into the bath. The water continued to run, giving the noise-cover he needed. He opened the door quietly, slipped back indoors, and closed it, jamming it shut with a hardback book from the top of one of the stacks. The remaining books looked as though they might topple, but they steadied again. Rebus exhaled and crept along the corridor, past the door. Taps pouring ... Kemp still humming. This part was easy; getting back out would be the hard part, *if* he had nothing to show for the deception.

He crossed the living room and studied the desk. The files gave nothing away. No sign of the 'big story' Kemp was working on. The computer disks were marked numerically – no clues there. Nothing interesting in the open drawer of the filing cabinet. He turned back to the desk. No scribbled sheets of notes had been tucked beneath other, blank sheets. He flipped through the pile of LPs beside the stereo, but no sheets had been hidden there either. Under the sofa ... no. Cupboards ... drawers ... no. Bugger it. He went to the great iron range. Tucked away at the back, behind three or four pot plants, sat an ugly-looking trophy, Kemp's Young Journalist of the Year Prize. Along the front of the range sat the row of ornamental boxes. He opened one. It contained a CND badge and a pair of ANC earrings. In another box was a 'Free Nelson Mandela' badge and a ring which looked to be carved out of ivory. The girlfriend's stuff, obviously. And in the third box ... a tiny cellophane package of dope. He smiled. Hardly enough to run someone in for, half a quarter at most. Was this what Kemp had been so eager to conceal? Well, Rebus supposed a conviction wouldn't do the 'campaigning journalist' tag much good. Difficult to chastise public figures for their small vices when you'd been done for possession.

Bugger it. And on top of everything, he'd now to get out of the flat without being seen or heard. The taps had stopped running. No noise to cover his retreat . . . He crouched by the range and considered. The bold as brass approach might be best. Just go marching past saying something about having left behind your keys . . . Aye, sure, Kemp would fall for *that*. Might as well put five bar on Cowdenbeath for the league and cup double.

He found that, as he thought, he was staring at the range's small oven, or rather at the closed door of that oven. A spider-plant sat above it, with two of its fronds trapped in the door. Dear me, he couldn't have that, could he? So he pulled open the door, releasing the leaves. Sitting in the oven itself were some books. Old hardbacks. He lifted one and examined its spine.

John Knox on predestination. Well, wasn't *that* a coincidence.

The bathroom door flew in.

'Christ's sake!' Chris Kemp, who had been lying with his head floating on the surface of the water, now shot up. Rebus marched over to the toilet, lowered its lid, and made himself comfortable.

'Carry on, Chris. Don't mind me. Just thought I might borrow a few of your books.' He slapped the pile he was holding. They were resting on his knees, all seven of them. 'I like a good read.'

Kemp actually blushed. 'Where's your search warrant?'

Rebus looked stunned. 'Search warrant? Why should I need a search warrant? I'm just borrowing a few books, that's all. Thought I might show them to my old friend Professor Costello. You know Professor Costello, don't you?

Only this stuff's right up his street. No reason why you should mind me borrowing them . . . is there? If you like, I'll go get that search warrant and – '

'Fuck off.'

'Language, son,' Rebus reprimanded. 'Don't forget, you're a journalist. You're the protector of our language. Don't go cheapening it. You just cheapen yourself.'

'I thought you wanted me to do you a favour?'

'What? You mean the story about Jack and his sister?' Rebus shrugged. 'I thought *I* was doing *you* a favour. I know keen young reporters who'd give their eye teeth for – '

'What do you want?'

Now Rebus sat forward. 'Where did you get them, Chris?'

'The books?' Kemp ran his hands down his sleek hair. 'They're my girlfriend's. As far as I know, she borrowed them from her university library . . .'

Rebus nodded. 'It's a fair story. I doubt it would get you off the hook, but it's a fair story. For a start, it won't explain why you hid them when you knew I was on my way up to see you.'

'Hid them? I don't know what you're talking about.'

Rebus chuckled. 'Fine, Chris, fine. There I was, thinking I could do you a favour. *Another* favour, I should say . . .'

'What favour?'

Rebus slapped the books again 'Seeing these get back to their rightful owner without anyone needing to know where they've been in the interim.'

Kemp considered this. 'In exchange for what?'

'Whatever it is you're keeping from me. I *know* you know something, or you think you do. I just want to help you do your duty.'

'My duty?'

'Helping the police. It *is* your duty, Chris.'

'Like it's *your* duty to go creeping around people's flats without their permission.'

Rebus didn't bother replying. He didn't need to reply; he just needed to bide his time. Now that he had the books, he had the reporter in his pocket, too. Safe and snug for future use . . .

Kemp sighed. 'The water's getting cold. Mind if I get out?'

'Any time you like. I'll go wait next door.'

Kemp came into the living room wearing a blue towelling robe and using a matching towel to rub at his hair.

'Tell me about your girlfriend,' Rebus said. Kemp filled the kettle again. He had used the minute's solitary time to do a little thinking, and he was ready now to talk.

'Vanessa?' he said. 'She's a student.'

'A divinity student? With access to Professor Costello's room?'

'*Everybody*'s got access to Prof Costello's room. He told you that himself.'

'But not everyone knows a rare book when they see it . . .'

'Vanessa also works part time in Suey Books.'

'Ah.' Rebus nodded. Pencilling in her prices. Earrings and a bicycle . . .

'Old Costello's a customer, so Vanessa knows him fairly well,' Kemp added.

'Well enough to steal from him, at any rate.'

Chris Kemp sighed. 'Don't ask me why she did it. Was she planning to sell them? I don't know. Did she want to keep them for herself? I don't know. I've asked her, believe me. Maybe she just had a . . . a brainstorm.'

'Yes, maybe.'

'Whatever, she reckoned Costello might not even miss them. Books are books to him. Maybe she thought he'd be as happy with the latest paperback editions . . .'

'But she, presumably, wouldn't be?'

'Look, just take them back, okay? Or keep them for yourself. Anything.'

The kettle clicked off. Rebus refused the offer of more coffee. 'So,' he said, as Kemp made himself a mug, 'what have you got to tell me, Chris?'

'It's just something Vanessa told me about her employer.'

'Ronald Steele?'

'Yes.'

'What about him?'

'He's having an affair with Mrs Rab Kinnoul.'

'Really?'

'Yes. Not your business, you see, Inspector. Nothing to do with law and order.'

'But a juicy story nevertheless, eh?' Rebus found it hard to talk. His head was birling again. New possibilities, new configurations. 'So how did she come to this conclusion?'

'It started a while back. Our entertainment correspondent on the paper had gone to interview *Mr* Kinnoul. But there'd been a cock-up over the dates. He turned up on a Wednesday afternoon when it should have been Thursday. Anyway, Kinnoul wasn't there, but Mrs Kinnoul was, and she had a friend with her, a friend introduced as Ronald Steele.'

'One friend visits another . . . I don't see – '

'But then Vanessa told me something. A couple of Wednesdays back, there was an emergency at the shop. Well, not exactly an *emergency*. Some old dear wanted to sell some of her deceased husband's books. She brought a list to the shop. Vanessa could see there were a few gems in there, but she needed to talk to the boss first. He doesn't trust her when it comes to the buying. Now, Wednesday afternoons are sacrosanct . . .'

'The weekly round of golf – '

'With Gregor Jack. Yes, precisely. But Vanessa thought, he'll kill me if this lot get away. So she rang the golf club, out at Braidwater.'

'I know it.'

'And they told her that Messrs Steele and Jack had cancelled.'

'Yes?'

'Well, I started to put two and two together. Steele's supposed to be playing golf every Wednesday, yet one Wednesday my colleague finds him out at the Kinnoul house, and another Wednesday there's no sign of him on the golf course. Rab Kinnoul's known to have a temper, Inspector.

He's known as a very *possessive* man. Do you think he knows that Steele's visiting his wife when he's not there?'

Rebus's heart was racing. 'You might have a point, Chris. You might have a point.'

'But like I say, it's hardly police business, is it?'

Hardly! It was *absolutely* police business. Two alibis chipped into the same bunker. Was Rebus nearer the end of the course than he'd suspected? Was he playing nine holes rather than eighteen? He got up from the sofa.

'Chris, I've got to be going.' Like spokes on a bicycle wheel, turning in his head: Liz Jack, Gregor Jack, Rab Kinnoul, Cath Kinnoul, Ronald Steele, Ian Urquhart, Helen Greig, Andrew Macmillan, Barney Byars, Louise Patterson-Scott, Julian Kaymer, Jamie Kilpatrick, William Glass. Like spokes on a bicycle wheel.

'Inspector Rebus?'

He paused by the door. 'What?'

Kemp pointed to the sofa. 'Don't forget to take your books with you.'

Rebus stared at them as though seeing them for the first time. 'Right,' he said, heading back towards the sofa. 'By the way,' he said, picking up the bundle, 'I *know* why Steele's called Suey.' Then he winked. 'Remind me to tell you about it some time, when this is all over . . .'

He returned to the station, intending to share some of what he knew with his superiors. But Brian Holmes stopped him outside the Chief Superintendent's door.

'I wouldn't do that.'

Rebus, his fist raised high, ready to knock, paused. 'Why not?' he asked, every bit as quietly as Holmes himself had spoken.

'Mrs Jack's father's in there.'

Sir Hugh Ferrie! Rebus lowered his hand carefully, then began backing away from the door. The last thing he wanted was to be dragged into a discussion with Ferrie. Why haven't you found . . . what are you doing about . . . when will you . . . ? No, life was too short, and the hours too long.

'Thanks, Brian. I owe you one. Who else is in there?'

'Just the Farmer and the Fart.'

'Best leave them to it, eh?' They moved a safe distance from the door. 'That list of cars you made up was pretty comprehensive. Well done.'

'Thanks. Lauderdale never told me exactly what it was – '

'Anything else happening?'

'What? No, quiet as the grave. Oh, Nell thinks she might be pregnant.'

'What?'

Holmes gave a bemused smile. 'We're not sure yet . . .'

'Were you . . . you know, *expecting* it?'

The smiled stayed. 'Expect the unexpected, as they say.'

Rebus whistled. 'How does she feel about it?'

'I think she's holding back on the feelings till we know one way or the other.'

'What about you?'

'Me? If it's a boy he'll be called Stuart and grow up to be a doctor and a Scottish international.'

Rebus laughed. 'And if it's a girl?'

'Katherine, actress.'

'I'll keep my fingers crossed for you.'

'Thanks. Oh, and another bit of news – Pond's back.'

'Tom Pond?'

'The very one. Back from across the pond. We reached him this morning. I thought I'd go have a talk with him, unless you want to?'

Rebus shook his head. 'He's all yours, Brian, for what he's worth. Right now, he's about the only bugger I think is in the clear. Him and Macmillan and Mr Glass.'

'Have you seen the interview transcript?'

'No.'

'Well, I know you and Chief Inspector Lauderdale don't always get on, but I'll say this for him, he's sharp.'

'A Glass-cutter, you might say?'

Holmes sighed. 'I might, but you always seem to beat me to the pun.'

*

Edinburgh was surrounded by golf courses catering to every taste and presenting every possible degree of difficulty. There were links courses, where the wind was as likely to blow your ball backwards as forwards. And there were hilly courses, all slope and gully, with greens and flags positioned on this or that handkerchief-sized plateau. The Braidwater course belonged to the latter category. Players made the majority of their shots trusting either to instinct or fortune, since the flag would often be hidden from view behind a rise or the brow of a hill. A cruel course designer would have tucked sand traps just the other side of these obstacles, and indeed a cruel course designer had.

People who didn't know the course often started their round with high hopes of a spot of exercise and fresh air, but finished with high blood pressure and the dire need of a couple of drams. The club house comprised two contrasting sections. There was the original building, old and solid and grey, but to which had been added an oversized extension of breeze block and pebbledash. The old building housed committee rooms, offices and the like, but the bar was in the new building. The club secretary led Rebus into the bar, where he thought one of the committee members might be found.

The bar itself was on the first floor. One wall was all window, looking out over the eighteenth green and beyond to the rolling course itself. On another wall were framed photos, rolls of honour, mock-parchment scrolls and a pair of very old putters looking like emaciated crossbones. The club's trophies – the small trophies – were arrayed on a shelf above the bar. The larger, the more ancient, the more valuable trophies were kept in the committee room in the old building. Rebus knew this because some of them had been stolen three years before, and he'd been one of the investigating officers. They had been recovered, too, though utterly by accident, found lying in an open suitcase by officers called out to a domestic.

The club secretary remembered Rebus though. 'Can't recall the name,' he'd said, 'but I know the face.' He showed Rebus the new alarm system and the toughened glass case the trophies were kept in. Rebus hadn't the heart to tell him that even an amateur burglar could still be in and out of the place in two minutes flat.

'What will you have to drink, Inspector?'

'I'll have a small whisky, if it's no trouble.'

'No trouble at all.'

The bar wasn't exactly busy. A late-afternoon hiatus, as the secretary had explained. Those who played in the afternoon usually liked to get started before three, while those who came for an early evening round arrived around five thirty.

Two men in identical yellow V-neck pullovers sat at a table by the window and stared out in silence, sipping from time to time at identical bloody marys. Two more men sat at the bar, one with a flat-looking half pint of beer, the other with what looked suspiciously like a glass of milk. They were all in their forties, or slightly older; all my contemporaries, thought Rebus.

'Bill here could tell you a few stories, Inspector,' the club secretary said, nodding towards the barman. Bill nodded back, half in greeting, half in agreement. His own V-neck was cherry red, and did nothing to hide his bulging stomach. He didn't look like a professional barman, but took a slow, conspicuous pride in the job. Rebus reckoned him for just another member, doing his stint of duty.

Nobody had twitched at the secretary's mention of 'Inspector'. These men were law-abiding; or, if not, they were certainly law-*abetting*. They believed in law and order and that criminals should be punished. They just didn't think fiddling your tax was a criminal act. They looked ... secure. They thought of themselves as secure. But Rebus knew *he* held the skeleton keys.

'Water, Inspector?' The secretary pushed a jug towards him.

'Thank you.' Rebus adulterated the whisky. The secretary was looking around him, as though surrounded by bodies.

'Hector's not here. I thought he was.'

Bill the Barman chipped in: 'He'll be back in a sec.'

'Gone for the proverbial jimmy,' added the drinker of milk, while Rebus pondered which proverb he meant.

'Ah, here he comes.'

Rebus had imagined a large Hector, curly hair, distended gut, tangerine V-neck. But this man was small and had thinning, Brylcreemed black hair. He, too, was in his forties, and peered at the world through thick-lensed, thick-rimmed glasses. His mouth was set in a defiance at odds with his appearance, and he examined Rebus thoroughly while the introductions were made.

'How do you do?' he said, slipping a small, damp hand into Rebus's paw. It was like shaking hands with a well-brought-up child. His V-neck was camel-coloured but expensive-looking. Cashmere . . .?

'Inspector Rebus,' the secretary said, 'is wondering about a particular round which was either played or was not played a couple of Wednesdays ago.'

'Yes.'

'I told him you're the brains of the set-up, Hector.'

'Yes.'

The secretary seemed to be struggling. 'We thought maybe you'd – '

But Hector now had enough information, and had digested it. 'First thing to do,' he said, 'is look at the bookings. They may not tell us the whole story, but they're the place to start. Who was playing?'

The question was directed at Rebus. 'Two players, sir,' he replied. 'A Mr Ronald Steele and a Mr Gregor Jack.'

Hector glanced behind Rebus to where the two drinkers sat at the bar. The room hadn't exactly grown quieter, but there was a palpable change of atmosphere. The drinker of milk spoke first.

'Those two!'

Rebus turned to him. 'Yes, sir, those two. How do you mean?'

But it was Hector's place to answer. 'Messrs Jack and Steele have a regular booking. Mr Jack was an MP, you know.'

'He still is, sir, so far as I know.'

'Not for much longer,' muttered the milk-drinker's companion.

'I'm not aware that Mr Jack has committed any crime.'

'I should think not,' snapped Hector.

'He's still a royal pain in the arse,' commented the milk-drinker.

'How's that, sir?'

'Books and never shows. Him and his cronies.' Rebus became aware that this was a long-festering sore, and that the man's words were directed more towards the club secretary and Hector than towards him. 'Gets away with it, too. Just because he's an MP.'

'Mr Jack has been warned,' Hector said.

'Reprimanded,' corrected the club secretary. The milk-drinker just screwed up his face.

'You kissed his bloody arse and you know it.'

'Now then, Colin,' said Bill and the Barman, 'no need to – '

'It's about time *some*body said it out loud!'

'Hear hear,' said the beer-drinker. 'Colin's right.'

An argument wasn't much use to Rebus. 'Do I take it,' he said, 'that Mr Jack and Mr Steele had a regular booking, but then wouldn't turn up?'

'You take it absolutely right,' said Colin.

'Let's not exaggerate or misrepresent,' said Hector quietly. 'Let us deal in facts.'

'Well, sir,' said Rebus, 'while we're dealing in facts, it's a fact that a colleague of mine, Detective Constable Broome, came out here last week to check on whether that particular round of golf had been played. I believe he dealt with *you*, seeing how the club secretary here was ill that day.'

'Remember, Hector,' the secretary interrupted nervously, 'one of my migraines.'

Hector nodded curtly. 'I remember.'

'You weren't exactly honest with DC Broome, were you, sir?' said Rebus. Colin was licking his lips, enjoying the confrontation.

'On the contrary, Inspector,' said Hector. 'I was *scrupulously* honest in answering the detective constable's questions. He just didn't ask the right ones. In fact, he was very sloppy indeed. Took one look at the bookings and seemed satisfied. I recall he was in a hurry . . . he had to meet his wife.'

Right, thought Rebus, Broome was for a carpeting then. Even so . . .

'Even so, sir, it was your duty – '

'I answered his questions, Inspector. I did not lie.'

'Well then, let's say that you were "economical with the truth".'

Colin snorted. Hector gave him a cold look, but his words were for Rebus. 'He wasn't thorough enough, Inspector. It's as simple as that. I don't expect my patients to help me if I'm not thorough enough in my treatment of them. *You* shouldn't expect *me* to do your work for you.'

'This is a serious criminal case, sir.'

'Then why are we arguing? Ask your questions.'

The barman interrupted. 'Hold on, before you start, *I've* got a question.' He looked at each of them in turn. 'What are you having?'

Bill the Barman poured the drinks. The round was on him, and he totted up the amount and scribbled it into a small notebook kept beside the till. The bloody marys from the window came over to join in. The beer-drinker was introduced to Rebus as David Cassidy – 'No jokes, please. How were my parents supposed to know?' – and the man called Colin was indeed drinking milk – 'ulcer, doctor's orders'.

Hector accepted a thin, delicate glass filled to the lip with dry sherry. He toasted 'our general health'.

'But not the National Health, eh, Hector?' added Colin, going on to explain to Rebus that Hector was a dentist.

'Private,' Cassidy added.

'Which,' Hector retorted, 'is what this club is supposed to be. Private. Members' private business should be none of our concern.'

'Which is why,' Rebus speculated, 'you've been acting as alibi for Jack and Steele?'

Hector merely sighed. '"Alibi" is rather strong, Inspector.

As club members, they are allowed to book *and* to cancel at short notice.'

'And that's what happened?'

'Sometimes, yes.'

'But not all the time?'

'They played occasionally.'

'How occasionally?'

'I'd have to check.'

'About once a month,' Barman Bill said. He held on to the glass-towel as if it were a talisman.

'So,' said Rebus, 'three weeks out of four they'd cancel? How did they cancel?'

'By telephone,' said Hector. 'Usually Mr Jack. Always very apologetic. Constituency business ... or Mr Steele was ill ... or, well, there were a number of reasons.'

'Excuses you mean,' Cassidy said.

'Mind you,' said Bill, 'sometimes Gregor'd turn up anyway, wouldn't he?'

Colin conceded that this was so. 'I went a round with him myself one Wednesday when Steele hadn't shown up.'

'So,' said Rebus, 'Mr Jack came to the club more often than Mr Steele?'

There were nods at this. Sometimes he'd cancel, then turn up. He wouldn't play, just sit in the bar. Never the other way round: Steele never turned up without Jack. And on the Wednesday in question, the Wednesday Rebus was interested in?

'It bucketed down,' Colin said. 'Hardly any bugger went out that day, never mind those two.'

'They cancelled then?'

Oh yes, they cancelled. And no, not even Mr Jack had turned up. Not that day, and not since.

The lull was over. Members were coming in, either for a quick one before starting out or for a quick one before heading home. They came over to the little group, shook hands, swopped stories, and the group itself started to fragment, until only Rebus and Hector were left. The dentist laid a hand on Rebus's arm.

'One more thing, Inspector,' he said.

'Yes?'

'I hope you won't think I'm being unsubtle . . .'

'Yes?'

'But you really should get your teeth seen to.'

'So I've been told, sir,' Rebus said. 'So I've been told. Incidentally, I hope you won't think *I'm* being unsubtle . . .?'

'Yes, Inspector?'

Rebus leaned close to the man, the better to hiss into his ear. 'I'm going to try my damnedest to see you on a charge for obstruction.' He placed his empty glass on the bar.

'Cheers then,' said Barman Bill. He took the glass and rinsed it in the machine, then placed it on the plastic drip-mat. When he looked up, Hector was still standing where the policeman had left him, his sherry glass rigid in his hand.

'You told me on Friday,' Rebus said, 'that you were jettisoning what you didn't need.'

'Yes.'

'Then I take it you *did* feel you needed the alibi of your golf game?'

'What?'

'Your weekly round with your friend Ronald Steele.'

'What about it?'

'Funny isn't it? *I'm* making the statements and *you're* asking the questions. Should be the other way round.'

'Should it?'

Gregor Jack looked like a war casualty who could still hear and see the battle, no matter how far from the front he was dragged. The newsmen were still outside his gates, while Ian Urquhart and Helen Greig were still inside. The sounds of a printer doing its business came from the distant back office. Urquhart was ensconced in there with Helen. Another day, another press release.

'Do I need a solicitor?' Jack asked now, his eyes dark and sleepless.

'That's entirely up to you, sir. I just want to know why you've lied to us about this round of golf.'

Jack swallowed. There was an empty whisky bottle on the coffee table, and three empty coffee mugs. 'Friendship, Inspector,' he said, 'is . . . it's . . .'

'An excuse? You need more than excuses, sir. What *I* need right now are some facts.' He thought of Hector as he said the word. 'Facts,' he repeated.

But Jack was still mumbling something about friendship. Rebus rose awkwardly from his ill-fitting marshmallow-chair. He stood over the MP. MP? This wasn't an MP. This wasn't *the* Gregor Jack. Where was the confidence, the charisma? Where the voteworthy face and that clear, honest voice? He was like one of those sauces they make on cookery programmes – reduce and reduce and reduce . . .

Rebus reached down and grabbed him by his shoulders. He actually shook him. Jack looked up in surprise. Rebus's voice was cold and sharp like rain.

'Where were you that Wednesday?'

'I was . . . I . . . was . . . nowhere. Nowhere really. Everywhere.'

'Everywhere except where you were supposed to be.'

'I went for a drive.'

'Where?'

'Down the coast. I think I ended up in Eyemouth, one of those fishing villages, somewhere like that. It rained. I walked along the sea front. I walked a lot. Drove back inland. Everywhere and nowhere.' He began to sing. 'You're everywhere and nowhere, baby.' Rebus shook him again and he stopped.

'Did anyone see you? Did you speak to anyone?'

'I went into a pub . . . two pubs. One in Eyemouth, one somewhere else.'

'Why? Where was . . . Suey? What was he up to?'

'Suey.' Jack smiled at the name. 'Good old Suey. Friends, you see, Inspector. Where was he? He was where he always was – with some woman. I'm his cover. If anyone asks, we're out playing golf. And sometimes we are. But the rest of the time, I'm covering for him. Not that I mind. It's quite nice really, having that time to myself. I go off on my own, walking . . . thinking.'

'Who's the woman?'

'What? I don't know. I'm not even sure it's just the one . . .'

'You can't think of any candidates?'

'Who?' Jack blinked. 'You mean Liz? My Liz? No, Inspector, no.' He smiled briefly. 'No.'

'All right, what about Mrs Kinnoul?'

'Gowk?' Now he laughed. 'Gowk and Suey? Maybe when they were fifteen, Inspector, but not now. Have you seen Rab Kinnoul? He's like a mountain. Suey wouldn't dare.'

'Well, maybe Suey will be good enough to tell me.'

'You'll apologize, won't you? Tell him I *had* to tell you.'

'I'd be grateful,' Rebus said stonily, 'if you'd think back on that afternoon. Try to remember where you stopped, the names of the pubs, anyone who *might* remember seeing you. Write it all down.'

'Like a statement.'

'Just to help you remember. It often helps when you write things down.'

'That's true.'

'Meantime, I'm going to have to think about charging you with obstruction.'

'What?'

The door opened. It was Urquhart. He came in and closed it behind him. 'That's that done,' he said.

'Good,' Jack said casually. Urquhart, too, looked like he was just hanging on. His eyes were on Rebus, even when he was speaking to his employer.

'I told Helen to run off a hundred copies.'

'As many as that? Well, whatever you think, Ian.'

Now Urquhart looked towards Gregor Jack. He wants to shake him, too, Rebus thought. But he won't.

'You've got to be strong, Gregor. You've got to *look* strong.'

'You're right, Ian. Yes, look strong.'

Like wet tissue paper, Rebus thought. Like an infestation of woodworm. Like an old person's bones.

Ronald Steele was a hard man to catch. Rebus even went to his home, a bungalow on the edge of Morningside. No sign of life. Rebus went on trying the rest of the day. At the fourth ring of Steele's telephone, an answering machine came into play. At eight o'clock, he stopped trying. What he didn't want was Gregor Jack warning Steele that their story had come apart at its badly stitched seams. Given the means, he'd have kept Steele's answering machine busy all night. But instead his own telephone rang. He was in the Marchmont flat, slumped in his own chair, with nothing to eat or drink, and nothing to take his mind off the case.

He knew who it would be. It would be Patience. She would just be wondering if and when he intended making an appearance. She would just have been worried, that was all. They'd spent a rare weekend together: shopping on Saturday afternoon, a film at night. A drive to Cramond on Sunday, wine and backgammon on Sunday night. Rare . . . He picked up the receiver.

'Rebus.'

'Jesus, you're a hard man to catch.' It was a male voice. It was not Patience. It was Holmes.

'Hello, Brian.'

'I've been trying you for hours. Always engaged or else not answering. You should get an answering machine.'

'I've *got* an answering machine. I just sometimes forget to plug it in. What do you want anyway? Don't tell me, you're telephone-selling as a sideline? How's Nell?'

'As well as can be not expecting.'

'She's negative then?'

'I'm positive she is.'

'Maybe next time, eh?'

'Listen, thanks for the interest, but that's not why I'm calling. I thought you'd want to know, I had a very interesting chat with Mr Pond.'

A.k.a. Tampon, thought Rebus. 'Oh yes?' he said.

'You're not going to believe it . . .' said Brian Holmes. For once, he was right.

10
Brothel Creepers

The way Tom Pond explained it to Rebus, architects were either doomed to failure or else doomed to success. He had no doubt at all that he came into the latter category.

'I know architects my age, guys I went to college with, they've been on the dole for the past half dozen years. Or else they give up and go do something sensible like working on a building site or living on a kibbutz. Then there are some of us, for a time we can't put a foot wrong. This prize leads to that contract, and that contract gets noticed by an American corporation, and we start calling ourselves "international". Note, I say "for a time". It can all turn sour. You get in a rut, or the economic situation can't support your new ideas. I'll tell you, the best architectural designs are sitting locked away in drawers – nobody can afford to build the buildings, not yet anyway, maybe not ever. So I'm just enjoying my lucky break. That's all I'm doing.'

It was not *quite* all Tom Pond was doing. He was also crossing the Forth Road Bridge doing something in excess of one hundred miles an hour. Rebus daren't look at the speedo.

'After all,' Pond had explained, 'it's not every day I can go breaking the speed limit with a policeman in the car to explain it away if we get stopped.' And he laughed. Rebus didn't. Rebus didn't say much after they hit the ton.

Tom Pond owned a forty-grand Italian racing job that looked like a kit-car and sounded like a lawnmower. The last time Rebus had been sitting this close to ground level, he'd just slipped on some ice outside his flat.

'I've got three habits, Inspector: fast cars, fast women, and slow horses.' And he laughed again.

'If you don't slow down, son,' Rebus yelled above the engine's whine, 'I'm going to have to book you for speeding myself!'

Pond looked hurt, but eased back on the accelerator. And after all, he *was* doing them all a favour, wasn't he?

'Thank you,' Rebus conceded.

Holmes had told him he wouldn't believe it. Rebus was still trying. Pond had arrived back the previous day from the States, only to find a message waiting for him on his answering machine.

'It was Mrs Heggarty.'

'Mrs Heggarty being . . . ?'

'She looks after my cottage. I've got a cottage up near Kingussie. Mrs Heggarty goes in now and again to give it a clean and check everything's okay.'

'And this time everything *wasn't?*'

'That's right. At first, she said there'd been a break-in, but then I called her back and from what she said they'd used my spare key to get in. I keep a key under a rock beside the front door. Hadn't made any mess or anything, not really. But Mrs Heggarty knew somebody'd been there and it hadn't been me. Anyway, I happened to mention it to the detective sergeant . . .'

The detective sergeant whose geography was better than fair. Kingussie wasn't far from Deer Lodge. It certainly wasn't far from Duthil. Holmes had asked the obvious question.

'Would Mrs Jack have known about the key?'

'Maybe. Beggar knew about it. I suppose *everybody* knew about it, really.'

All of which Holmes had relayed to Rebus. Rebus had gone to see Pond, their conversation lasting just over half an hour, at the end of which he had announced a wish to see the cottage.

'Be my guest,' Pond had said. And so Rebus was trapped in this narrow metal box, travelling so fast at times that his

211

eyeballs were aching. It was well after midnight, but Pond seemed neither to notice nor to mind.

'I'm still in New York,' he said. 'Brain and body still disconnected. You know, this all sounds incredible, all this stuff about Gregor and Liz and her being found by Gowk. Just incredible.'

Pond had been in the United States for a month; already he was hooked. He was testing out the language, the intonation, even some of the mannerisms. Rebus studied him. Thick, wavy blond hair (dyed? highlighted?) atop a beefy face, the face of someone who had been good-looking in youth. He wasn't tall, but he *seemed* taller than he was. A trick of posture; yes, to a certain extent, but he also had that confidence, that aura Gregor Jack had once possessed. He was firing on all cylinders.

'Can this car take a corner or what? Say what you like about the Italians, they build a mean ice cream and a meaner car.'

Rebus gritted his lower intestine. He was determined to talk seriously with Pond. It was too good a chance to miss, the two of them trapped like this. He tried to talk without his teeth knocking each other out of his mouth.

'So, you've known Mr Jack since school?'

'I know, I know, it's hard to believe, isn't it? I look so much younger than him. But yes, we only lived three streets apart. I think Bilbo lived in the same street as Beggar. Sexton and Mack lived in the same street, too. I mean, the same street as one another, not the same as Beggar and Bilbo. Suey and Gowk lived a bit further away, other side of the school from the rest of us.'

'So what drew you all together?'

'I don't know. Funny, I've never really thought about it. I mean, we were all pretty clever, I suppose. Down a gear for this corner . . . and . . . *like shit off a goddamned shovel!*'

Rebus felt as though his seat was trying to push its way through his body.

'More like a motorbike than a car. What do you think, Inspector?'

'Do you keep in touch with Mack?' Rebus asked at last.

'Oh, you know about Mack? Well ... no, not really. Beggar was the catalyst. I think it was only because I kept in touch with him that I kept in touch with everybody else. But after Mack ... well, when he went into the nuthouse ... no, I don't keep in touch. I think Gowk does. You know, she was the cleverest of the lot of us, and look what happened to her.'

'What did happen to her?'

'She married that spunk-head and started shovelling Valium because it was the only way she could cope.'

'Is her problem common knowledge then?'

He shrugged. 'I only know because I've seen it happen to other people ... other times.'

'Have you tried talking to her?'

'It's her life, Inspector. I've got enough trouble keeping myself together.'

The Pack. What did a pack do when one of its number grew lame or sick? They left it to die, the fittest trotting along at the head ...

Pond seemed to sense Rebus's thoughts. 'Sorry if that sounds callous. I was never one for tea and sympathy.'

'Who was?'

'Sexton was always ready with a willing ear. But then she buggered off south. Suey, too, I suppose. You could talk to him. He never had any answers, mind, but he was a good listener.'

Rebus hoped he'd be as good a talker. There were more and more questions to be answered. He decided – how would an American phrase it? – yes, to throw Pond a few curve-balls.

'If Elizabeth Jack had a lover, who would be your guess?'

Pond actually slowed down a little. He thought for a moment. 'Me,' he said at last. 'After all, she'd be stupid to plump for anybody else, wouldn't she?' And he grinned again.

'Second choice?'

'Well, there were rumours ... there were *always* rumours.'

'Yes?'

213

'Jesus, you want me to list them? Okay, Barney Byars for a start. Do you know him?'

'I know him.'

'Well, Barney's all right I suppose. Bit screwed up about class, but otherwise he's fine. The two of them were pretty close for a while . . .'

'Who else?'

'Jamie Kilpatrick . . . Julian Kaymer . . . I think that fat bastard Kinnoul even tried his luck. Then she was supposed to have had a fling with that grocer's ex.'

'You mean Louise Patterson-Scott?'

'Can you imagine it? Story was, the morning after a party they were found together in bed. But so what?'

'Anyone else?'

'Probably hundreds.'

'You never . . . ?'

'Me?' Pond shrugged. 'We had a kiss and a cuddle a few times.' He smiled at the memory. 'It could have gone anywhere . . . but it didn't. The thing with Liz was . . . generosity.'

Pond nodded to himself, pleased that he had found the right word, the fitting epitaph.

Here lies Elizabeth Jack.
She gave.

'Can I use your telephone?' Rebus asked.

'Sure.'

He called Patience. He had tried twice before in the course of the evening – no reply. But there was a reply this time. This time, he got her out of bed.

'Where are you?' she asked.

'Heading north.'

'When will I see you?' Her voice had lost all emotion, all interest. Rebus wondered if it was merely a trick of the telephone.

'Tomorrow. Definitely tomorrow.'

'It can't keep on like this, John. Really, it can't.'

214

He sought for words which would reassure her while not embarrassing him in front of Pond. He sought too long.

'Bye, John.' And the receiver went dead.

They reached Kingussie well before dawn, having met little enough traffic and not a single patrol car. They had brought torches, though these weren't really necessary. The cottage was situated at the far corner of a village, a little off the main road but still receiving a good share of what street-lighting there was. Rebus was surprised to find that the 'cottage' was quite a modern bungalow, surrounded by a high hedge on all four sides, excepting the necessary gates which opened on to a short gravel drive leading up to the house itself.

'When Gregor and Liz got their place,' Pond explained, 'I thought what the hell, only I couldn't bear to rough it the way they do. I wanted something a bit more modern. Less charm, better amenities.'

'Nice neighbours?'

Pond shrugged. 'Hardly ever seen them. The place next door is a holiday home, too. Half the houses in the village are.' He shrugged again.

'What about Mrs Heggarty?'

'Lives the other side of the main drag.'

'So whoever's been living here . . . ?'

'They could have come and gone without anyone noticing, no doubt about that.'

Pond left his headlights on while he opened the front door of the house. Suddenly, hallway and porch were illuminated. Rebus, freed from the cage, was stretching and trying to stop his knees from folding in on him.

'Is that the stone?'

'That's the one,' Pond said. It was a huge pebble-shaped piece of pinkish rock. He lifted it, showing that the spare key was still there. 'Nice of them to leave it when they went. Come on, I'll show you around.'

'Just a second, Mr Pond. Could you try not to touch anything? We might want to check for fingerprints later on.'

Pond smiled. 'Sure, but my prints'll be everywhere anyway.'

'Of course, but all the same . . .'

'Besides, if Mrs Heggarty's tidied up after our "guests", the place'll be polished and tidied from ceiling to floor.'

Rebus's heart sank as he followed Pond into the cottage. There was certainly a smell of furniture polish, mingling with air-freshener. In the living room, not a cushion or an executive toy looked to be out of place.

'Looks the same as when I left it,' Pond said.

'You're sure?'

'Pretty sure. I'm not like Liz and her crew, Inspector. I don't go in for parties. I don't mind other people's, but the last thing I want to have to do is clean salmon mousse off the ceiling or explain to the village that the woman with her arse hanging out of a Bentley back window is actually an Hon.'

'You wouldn't be thinking of the Hon. Matilda Merriman?'

'The same. Christ, you know them all, don't you?'

'I've yet to meet the Hon. Matilda actually.'

'Take my advice: defer the moment. Life's too short.'

And the hours too long, thought Rebus. Today's hours had certainly been way too long. The kitchen was neat. Glasses sat sparkling on the draining board.

'Shouldn't think you'll get many prints off them, Inspector.'

'Mrs Heggarty's very thorough, isn't she?'

'Not always so thorough upstairs. Come on, let's see.'

Well, someone had been thorough. The beds in both bedrooms had been made. There were no cups or glasses on display, no newspapers or magazines or unfinished books. Pond made show of sniffing the air.

'No,' he said, 'it's no good, I can't even smell her perfume.'

'Whose?'

'Liz's. She always wore the same brand, I forget what it was. She always smelt beautiful. Beautiful. Do you think she was here?'

'Someone was here. And we think she was in this area.'

'But who was she with – that's what you're wondering?'

Rebus nodded.

'Well, it wasn't me, more's the pity. I was having to make do with call girls. And get this – they want to check your medical certificate before they start.'

'AIDS?'

'AIDS. Okay, finished up here? Beginning to look like a wasted journey, isn't it?'

'Maybe. There's still the bathroom . . .'

Pond pushed open the bathroom door and ushered Rebus inside. 'Ah-ha,' he said, 'looks like Mrs Heggarty was running out of time.' He nodded towards where a towel lay in a heap on the floor. 'Usually, that would go straight in the laundry.' The shower curtain had been pulled across the bath. Rebus drew it back. The bath was drained, but one or two long hairs were sticking to the enamel. Rebus was thinking: We can check those. A hair's enough for an ID. Then he noticed the two glasses, sitting together on a corner of the bath. He leaned over and sniffed. White wine. Just a trickle of it left in one glass.

Two glasses! For two people. Two people in the bath and enjoying a drink. 'Your telephone's downstairs, isn't it?'

'That's right.'

'Come on then. This room's out of bounds until further notice. And I'm about to become a forensic scientist's nightmare.'

Sure enough, the person Rebus ended up speaking to on the telephone did not sound pleased.

'We've been working our bums off on that car and that other cottage.'

'I appreciate that, but this could be just as important. It could be *more* important.' Rebus was standing in the small dining room. He couldn't quite tie up these furnishings to Pond's personality. But then he saw a framed photograph of a couple young and in love, captured some time in the 1950s. Then he understood: Pond's parents. The furniture here had once belonged to them. Pond had probably inherited it but decided it didn't go with his fast women/slow horses lifestyle. Perfect, though, for filling the spaces in his holiday home.

Pond himself, who had been sitting on a dining chair, rose to his feet. Rebus placed a hand over the receiver.

'Where are you going?'

'For a pee. Don't panic, I'll go out the back.'

'Just don't go upstairs, okay?'

'Fine.'

The voice on the telephone was still complaining. Rebus shivered. He was cold. No, he was tired. Body temperature dropping. 'Look,' he said, 'bugger off back to bed then, but be here first thing in the morning. I'll give you the address. And I *mean* first thing. All right?'

'You're a generous man, Inspector.'

'They'll put it on my gravestone: he gave.'

Pond slept, with Rebus's envious blessing, in the master bedroom, while Rebus himself kept vigil outside the bathroom door. Once bitten . . . He didn't want a repetition of the Deer Lodge 'break-in'. This evidence, if evidence it was, would stay intact. So he sat in the upstairs hallway, his back against the bathroom door, a blanket wrapped around him, and dozed. Then he slid down the door, so that he was lying in front of it on the carpet, curled into a foetus. He dreamed that he was drunk . . . that he was being driven around in a Bentley. The chauffeur was managing to drive and at the same time stick his backside out of the window. There was a party in the back of the Bentley. Holmes and Nell were there, copulating discreetly and hoping for a boy. Gill Templer was there, and attempting to undo Rebus's zip, but he didn't want Patience to catch them . . . Lauderdale seemed to be there, too. Watching, just watching. Someone opened the drinks cabinet, but it was full of books. Rebus picked one out and started to read it. It was the best book he'd ever read. He couldn't put it down. It had everything . . .

In the morning, when he awoke, stiff and cold, he couldn't recall a line or a word of the book. He rose and stretched, twisting himself back into human shape. Then he opened the bathroom door and stepped inside, and looked towards where the glasses should be.

The glasses were still there. Rebus, despite his aches, almost smiled.

He stood in the shower for a long time, letting the water trampoline on his head, his chest and his shoulders. Where was he? He was in the Oxford Terrace flat. He should be at work by now, but that could be explained away. He felt rough, but not as rough as he'd feared. Amazingly, he'd been able to sleep on the journey back, a journey taken at a more sedate pace than that of the previous night.

'Clutch trouble,' Pond had said, only twenty miles out of Kingussie. He'd pulled into the side of the road and had a look under the bonnet. There was a lot of engine under the bonnet. 'I wouldn't know where to start looking,' he'd admitted. The trouble with these fancy cars was that capable mechanics were few and far between. In fact, he had to take the car to London for every service. So they'd ambled, an early-morning amble, having left the cottage under the stewardship of a bemused Detective Sergeant Knox and two overworked forensics people.

And Rebus had slept. Not enough, admittedly, which was why he'd resisted the temptation to run a bath and had opted for the shower instead. Difficult to nod off in a shower; all too easy in a hot morning bath. And he had chosen Patience's flat over his own – an easy choice, since Oxford Terrace was the right side of Edinburgh after the drive. They'd had a hellish crossing of the Forth Bridge: commuter traffic crawling citywards. Sales reps in Astras gave the Italian car the once-over, and comforted themselves with the thought that its crew looked like crooks of some kind, pimps or moneylenders . . .

He turned off the shower and towelled himself dry, changed into some clean clothes, and began the process of becoming a human being again. Shaving, brushing his teeth, then a mug of fresh-brewed coffee. Lucky pleaded at a window, and Rebus let the cat in. He even tipped some food into a bowl. The cat looked up at him, full of suspicion. This wasn't the Rebus he knew.

'Just be thankful while it lasts.'

What day was it? It was Tuesday. Over a fortnight since the brothel raid, nearly two weeks since Alec Corbie heard the lay-by argument and saw either two or three cars. There had been progress, most of it thanks to Rebus himself. If only he could shake his superiors' minds free of William Glass . . .

There was a note on the mantelpiece, propped up against the clock: 'Why don't we try meeting some time? Dinner tonight, or else – Patience.' No kisses: always a bad sign. No crosses meant she was cross. She had every right to be. He really had to make up his mind one way or the other. Move in or move out. Stop using the place as a public amenity, somewhere to have a shower, a shave, a shit, and, on occasions, a shag. Was he any better than Liz Jack and her mysterious companion, making use of Tom Pond's cottage? Hell, in some ways he was worse. Dinner tonight, or else. Meaning, or else I lose Patience. He took the biro out of his pocket and turned the note over.

'If not dinner, then just desserts,' he wrote. Utterly ambiguous, of course, but it sounded clever. He added his name and a row of kisses.

Chris Kemp had his scoop. A front-page scoop at that. The young reporter had worked hard after the visit from John Rebus. He'd tracked down Gail Crawley, a photographer in tow. She hadn't exactly been forthcoming, but there was a photograph of her alongside a slightly blurred picture of a teenage girl: Gail Jack, aged fourteen or so. The story itself was riddled with get-out clauses, just in case it proved to be false. The reader was left more or less to make up his or her own mind. MP's Visit to Mystery Prostitute – His Secret Sister? But the photos were the clincher. They were definitely of the same person, same nose, same eyes and chin. Definitely. The photo of Gail Jack in her youth was a stroke of genius, and Rebus didn't doubt that the genius behind it was Ian Urquhart. How else could Kemp have found, and so quickly found, the photograph he needed? A call to Urquhart, explaining that the story was worth his cooperation. Either

Urquhart himself searched out the picture, or else he persuaded Gregor Jack to find it.

It was in the morning edition. By tomorrow, the other papers would have their own versions; they could hardly afford not to. Rebus, having recovered his car from outside Pond's flat, idling at traffic lights had seen the paper-seller's board: Brothel MP Exclusive. He'd crossed the lights, and parked by the roadside, then jogged back to the newspaper booth. Returned to the car and read the story through twice, admiring it as a piece of work. Then he'd started the car again and continued towards his destination. I should have bought two copies, he thought to himself. He won't have seen it yet . . .

The green Citroën BX was in its drive, the garage doors open behind it. As Rebus brought his own car to a halt, blocking the end of the driveway, the garage doors were being pulled to. Rebus got out of the car, the folded newspaper in one hand.

'Looks like I just caught you,' he called.

Ronald Steele turned from the garage. 'What?' He saw the car parked across his driveway. 'Look, would you mind? I'm in a – ' Then he recognised Rebus. 'Oh, it's Inspector . . .?'

'Rebus.'

'Rebus, yes. Rasputin's friend.'

Rebus turned his wrist towards Steele. 'Healing nicely,' he said.

'Look, Inspector . . .' Steele glanced at his wristwatch. 'Was it anything important? Only I'm meeting a customer and I've already overslept.'

'Nothing too important, sir,' Rebus said breezily. 'It's just that we've found out your alibi for the Wednesday Mrs Jack died is a pack of lies. Wondered if you'd anything to say to that?'

Steele's face, already long, grew longer. 'Oh.' He looked down at the toes of his well-scuffed shoes. 'I thought it was bound to come out.' He tried a smile. 'Not much you can keep hidden from a murder inquiry, eh?'

'Not much you *should* keep hidden, sir.'

'Do you want me to come down to the station?'

'Maybe later, sir. Just so we can get everything on record. But for the moment your living room would do.'

'Right.' Steele started to walk slowly back towards the bungalow.

'Nice area this,' commented Rebus.

'What? Oh, yes, yes it is.'

'Lived here long?' Rebus wasn't interested in Steele's answers. His only interest was in keeping the man talking. The more he talked, the less time he had in which to think, and the less time he had to think, the better the chances of him coming out with the truth.

'Three years. Before that I had a flat in the Grassmarket.'

'They used to hang people down there, did you know that?'

'Did they? Hard to imagine it these days.'

'Oh, I don't know . . .'

They were indoors now. Steele pointed to the hall phone. 'Do you mind if I call the customer? Make my apologies?'

'Whatever you like, sir. I'll wait in the living room, if that's all right.'

'Through there.'

'Fine.'

Rebus went into the room but left the door wide open. He heard Steele dialling. It was an old bakelite telephone, the kind with a little drawer in the bottom containing a notepad. People used to want rid of them; now they wanted them back, and were willing to pay. The conversation was short and innocent. An apology and a rescheduling of the meeting. Rebus opened his morning paper wide in front of him and made show of reading the inside pages. The receiver clattered back into its cradle.

'That's that,' said Steele, entering the room. Rebus read on for a moment, then lowered the paper and began to fold it.

'Good,' he said. Steele, as he had hoped, was staring at the paper.

'What's that about Gregor?' he said.

'Hm? Oh, you mean you haven't seen it yet?' Rebus

handed over the paper. Steele, still standing, devoured the story. 'What do you reckon, sir?'

He shrugged. 'Christ knows. I suppose it makes sense. I mean, none of us could think *what* Gregor was doing in a place like that. I can't think of a much better reason. The photos certainly look similar . . . I don't remember Gail at all. Well, I mean, she was always *around*, but I never paid much attention. She never mixed with us.' He folded the paper. 'So Gregor's off the hook then?'

Rebus shrugged. Steele made to hand the paper back. 'No, no, you can keep it if you like. Now, Mr Steele, about this non-existent golfing fixture . . .'

Steele sat down. It was a pleasant, book-lined room. In fact, it reminded Rebus strongly of another room, a room he'd been in recently . . .

'Gregor would do anything for his friends,' Steele said candidly, 'including the odd telling of a lie. We made up the golf game. Well, that's not strictly true. At first, there *was* a weekly game. But then I started seeing a . . . a lady. On Wednesdays. I explained it to Gregor. He didn't see why we shouldn't just go on telling everyone we were playing golf.' He looked up at Rebus for the first time. 'A jealous husband is involved, Inspector, and an alibi was always welcome.'

Rebus nodded. 'You're being very honest, Mr Steele.'

Steele shrugged. 'I don't want Gregor getting into trouble because of me.'

'And you were with this woman on the Wednesday afternoon in question? The afternoon Mrs Jack died?'

Steele nodded solemnly.

'And will she back you up?'

Steele smiled grimly. 'Not a hope in hell.'

'The husband again?'

'The husband,' Steele acknowledged.

'But he's bound to find out sooner or later, isn't he?' Rebus said. 'So many people seem to know already about you and Mrs Kinnoul.'

Steele twitched, as though a small electric shock had been administered to his shoulder blades. He stared down at the floor, willing it to become a pit he might jump into. Then he sat back.

'How did you . . . ?'

'A guess, Mr Steele.'

'A bloody inspired guess. But you say other people . . . ?'

'Other people are guessing too. You persuaded Mrs Kinnoul to take up an interest in rare books. It makes a good cover, after all, doesn't it? I mean, if you're ever found there with her. I even notice that she's modelled her library on your own room here.'

'It's not what you think, Inspector.'

'I don't think anything, sir.'

'Cathy just needs someone to listen to her. Rab never has time. The only time he has is for himself. Gowk was the cleverest of the lot of us.'

'Yes, so Mr Pond was telling me.'

'Tom? He's back from the States then?'

Rebus nodded. 'I was with him just this morning . . . at his cottage.'

Rebus waited for a reaction, but Steele's mind was still fixed on Cath Kinnoul. 'It breaks my heart to see her . . . to see what she's . . .'

'She's a friend,' Rebus stated.

'Yes, she is.'

'Well then, she's sure to back up your story; a friend in need and all that . . . ?'

Steele was shaking his head. 'You don't understand, Inspector. Rab Kinnoul is . . . he *can* be . . . a violent man. Mental violence and physical violence. He terrifies her.'

Rebus sighed. 'Then we've only your own word for your whereabouts?'

Steele shrugged. He looked as though he might cry – tears of frustration rather than anything else. He took a deep breath. 'You think I killed Liz?'

'Did you?'

Steele shook his head. 'No.'

'Well then, you've nothing to worry about, have you, sir?'

Steele managed that grim smile again. 'Not a worry in the world,' he said.

Rebus rose to his feet. 'That's the spirit, Mr Steele.' But Ronald Steele looked like there was just about enough spirit left in him to fill a teaspoon. 'All the same, you're not making it easy for yourself . . .'

'Have you spoken to Gregor?' Steele asked.

Rebus nodded.

'Does *he* know about Cathy and me?'

'I couldn't say.' They were both heading for the front door now. 'Would it make any difference if he did?'

'Christ knows. No, maybe not.'

The day was turning sunny. Rebus waited while Steele closed and double locked the door.

'Just one more thing . . . ?'

'Yes, Inspector?'

'Would you mind if I took a look in the boot of your car?'

'What?' Steele stared at Rebus, but saw that the policeman was not about to explain. He sighed. 'Why not?' he said.

Steele unlocked the boot and Rebus peered inside, peered at a pair of mud-crusted wellingtons. There was muck on the floor, too.

'Tell you what, sir,' said Rebus, closing the boot. 'Maybe it'd be best if you came down to the station just now. Sooner we get everything cleared up the better, eh?'

Steele stood up very straight. Two women were walking past, gossiping. 'Am I under arrest, Inspector?'

'I just want to make sure we get *your* side of things, Mr Steele. That's all.'

But Rebus was wondering: Were there *any* forensics people left spare? Or had he tied each and every one of them up already? If so, Steele's car might have to wait. If not, well, here was another little job for them. It really was turning into *Guinness Book of Records* stuff, wasn't it? How many forensic scientists can one detective squeeze into a case?

'What case?'

'I've just told you, sir.'

Lauderdale looked unimpressed. 'You haven't told me *anything* about the murder of Mrs Jack. You've told me about mysterious lovers, alibis for assignations, a whole barrel-load of mixed-up yuppies but not a blind thing about *murder*.' He pointed to the floor. 'I've got someone downstairs who swears he committed both murders.'

'Yes sir,' Rebus said calmly, 'and you've also got a psychiatrist who says Glass could just as easily admit the murders of Gandhi or Rudolf Hess.'

'How do you know that?'

'What?'

'About the psychiatric report?'

'Call it an inspired guess, sir.'

Lauderdale began to look a little dispirited. He licked his lips thoughtfully. 'All right,' he said at last. 'Go through it one more time for me.'

So Rebus went through it one more time. It was like a giant collage to him now: different textures but the same theme. But it was also like a kind of artist's trick: the closer he moved towards it, the further away it seemed. He was just finishing, and Lauderdale was still looking sceptical, when the telephone rang. Lauderdale picked it up, listened and sighed.

'It's for you,' he said, holding the receiver towards Rebus.

'Yes?' Rebus said.

'Woman for you,' explained the switchboard operator. 'Says it's urgent.'

'Put her through.' He waited till the connection was made. 'Rebus here,' he said.

He could hear background noise, announcements. A railway station. Then: 'About bleedin' time. I'm at Waverley. My train goes in forty-five minutes. Get here before it leaves and I'll tell you something.' The line went dead. Short and sour, but intriguing for all that. Rebus checked his watch.

'I've got to go to Waverley Station,' he told Lauderdale. 'Why don't you talk to Steele yourself meantime, sir? See what you make of him?'

'Thank you,' said Lauderdale. 'Maybe I will . . .'

*

She was sitting on a bench in the concourse, conspicuous in sunglasses which were supposed to disguise her identity.

'That bastard,' she said, 'putting the papers on to me like that.' She was talking of her brother, Gregor Jack. Rebus didn't say anything. 'One yesterday,' she went on, 'then this morning, half a dozen of the bastards. Picture plastered all over the front pages . . .'

'Maybe it wasn't your brother,' Rebus said.

'What? Who else could it be?' Behind the dark lenses, Rebus could still make out Gail Crawley's tired eyes. She was dressed as though in a hurry – tight jeans, high heels, baggy t-shirt. Her luggage seemed to consist of a large suitcase and two carrier bags. In one hand she clutched her ticket to London, in the other she held a cigarette.

'Maybe,' Rebus suggested, 'it was the person who knew who you were, the person who told Gregor where to find you.'

She shivered. 'That's what I wanted to tell you about. God knows why. I don't owe the bastard any favours . . .'

Nor do I, thought Rebus, yet I always seem to be doing them for him.

'What about a drink?' she suggested.

'Sure,' said Rebus. He picked up her suitcase, while she clip-clopped along carrying the bags. Her shoes made a lot of noise, and attracted glances from some of the men lolling about. Rebus was quite relieved to reach the safety of the bar, where he bought a half of export for himself and a Bacardi and Coke for her. They found a corner not too near the gaming machine or the frazzled loudspeaker of the jukebox.

'Cheers,' she said, trying to drink and inhale at much the same time. She spluttered and swore, then stubbed out the cigarette, only seconds later to light another.

'Good health,' said Rebus, sipping his own drink. 'So, what was it you wanted to get off your chest?'

She snorted. 'I like that: get off your chest.' This time she remembered to swallow her mouthful of rum before drawing on the cigarette. 'Only,' she said, 'what you were saying, about how somebody might have known who I was . . .'

'Yes?'

'Well, I remembered. It was a night a while back. Like, a couple of months. Six weeks ... something like that. I hadn't been up here long. Anyway, the usual trio of pissed punters comes in. Funny how they usually come in threes ...' She paused, snorted. 'If you'll pardon the expression.'

'So three men came to the brothel?'

'Just said so, didn't I? Anyway, one of them liked the look of me, so off we went upstairs. I told him my name was Gail. I can't see the point of all those stupid names everybody else uses – Candy and Mandy and Claudette and Tina and Suzy and Jasmine and Roberta. I'd just forget who I was supposed to be.'

Rebus glanced at his watch. A little over ten minutes left ... She seemed to understand.

'So, anyway, I asked him if *he* had a name. And he laughed. He said, "You mean you don't recognize the face?" I shook my head, and he said, "Of course, you're a Londoner, aren't you? Well hen," he said, "I'm weel kent up here." Something stupid like that. Then he says, "I'm Gregor Jack." Well, I just started laughing, don't ask me why. He *did* ask me why. So I said, "No you're not. *I know* Gregor Jack." That seemed to put him off his stroke. In the end, he buggered off back to his pals. All the usual winks and slaps on the back, and I didn't say anything ...'

'What did he look like?'

'Big. Like a Highlander. One of the other girls said she thought she *had* seen him on the telly ...'

Rab Kinnoul. Rebus described him briefly.

'Sounds about right,' she conceded.

'What about the men who were with him?'

'Didn't pay much attention. One of them was the shy type, tall and skinny like a beanpole. The other was fat and had on a leather jacket.'

'You didn't catch their names?'

'No.'

Well, it didn't matter. Rebus would bet she could pick them out from a line-up. Ronald Steele and Barney Byars. A night out on the town. Byars, Steele, and Rab Kinnoul. A curious little assembly, and another incendiary he could toss in Steele's direction.

'Finish your drink, Gail,' he said. 'Then let's get you on to that train.'

But on the way, he extracted an address from her, the same one she had given before, the one he'd had George Flight check on.

'That's where I'll be,' she said. She took a final look around her. The train was idling, filling with people. Rebus lifted her suitcase in through one of the doors. She was still staring up at the glass roof of the station. Then she lowered her gaze to Rebus. 'I should never have left London, should I? Maybe nothing would have happened if I'd stayed where I was.'

Rebus tilted his head slightly. 'You're not to blame, Gail.' But all the same, he couldn't help feeling that she had a point. *If* she'd stayed away from Edinburgh, *if* she hadn't come out with that "*I know* Gregor Jack" . . . who could say? She stepped up on to the train, then turned back towards him.

'If you see Gregor . . .' she began. But there wasn't anything else. She shrugged and turned away, carrying her case and her bags with her. Rebus, never one for emotional farewells where prostitutes were concerned, turned briskly on his heels and headed back towards his car.

'You've what?'

'I've let him go.'

'You've let Steele go?' Rebus couldn't believe it. He paced what there was of Lauderdale's floor. 'Why?'

Now Lauderdale smiled coldly. 'What was the charge, John? Be realistic, for Christ's sake.'

'Did you talk to him?'

'Yes.'

'And?'

'He seems very plausible.'

'In other words, you believe him?'

'I think I do, yes.'

'What about his car boot?'

'You mean the mud? He told you himself, John, Mrs Kinnoul and he go for walks. That hillside's hardly what you'd call paved. You need wellies, and wellies get muddy. It's their *purpose*.'

'He admitted he was seeing Cath Kinnoul?'

'He admitted nothing of the sort. He just said there was a "woman".'

'That's all he'd say when *I* brought him in. But he admitted it back in his house.'

'I think it's quite noble of him, trying to protect her.'

'Or could it be that he knows she couldn't back up his story anyway?'

'You mean it's a pack of lies?'

Rebus sighed. 'No, I think *I* believe it, too.'

'Well then.' Lauderdale sounded – for Lauderdale – genuinely gentle. 'Sit down, John. You've had a hard twenty-four hours.'

Rebus sat down. 'I've had a hard twenty-four years.'

Lauderdale smiled. 'Tea?'

'I think some of the Chief Superintendent's coffee would be a better idea.'

Lauderdale laughed. 'Kill or cure, certainly. Now look, you've just admitted yourself that you believe Steele's story – '

'Up to a point.'

Lauderdale accepted the clause. 'But still, the man wanted to leave. How the hell was I going to hold him?'

'On suspicion. We're allowed to hang on to suspects a bit longer than ninety minutes.'

'Thank you, Inspector, I'm aware of that.'

'So now he toddles back home and gives the boot of his car a damned good clean.'

'You need more than mucky wellies for a conviction, John.'

'You'd be surprised what forensics can do . . .'

'Ah, now that's another thing. I hear you've been getting up people's noses faster than a Vick's inhaler.'

'Anybody in particular?'

'*Everybody* in the field of forensic science, it seems. Stop hassling them, John.'

'Yes, sir.'

'Take a break. Just for the afternoon, say. What about the Professor's missing tomes?'

'Back with their owner.'

'Oh?' Lauderdale waited for elucidation.

'A turn-up for the books, sir,' Rebus said instead. He stood up. 'Well, if there's nothing else – '

The telephone rang. 'Hold on,' Lauderdale ordered. 'The way things have been going, that'll probably be for you.' He picked up the receiver. 'Lauderdale.' Then he listened. 'I'll be right down,' he said at last, before replacing the receiver. 'Well, well, well. Take a guess who's downstairs.'

'The Dundonald and Dysart Pipe Band?'

'Close. Jeanette Oliphant.'

Rebus frowned. 'I know the name . . .'

'She's Sir Hugh Ferrie's solicitor. And also, it seems, Mr Jack's. They're both down there with her.' Lauderdale had risen from his chair and was straightening his jacket. 'Let's see what they want, eh?'

Gregor Jack wanted to make a statement, a statement regarding his movements on the day his wife was murdered. But the prime mover was Sir Hugh Ferrie; that much was obvious from the start.

'I saw that piece in the paper this morning,' he explained. 'Phoned Gregor to ask if it was true. He says it was. I felt a sight better for knowing it, though I told him he's a bloody fool for not telling anyone sooner.' He turned to Gregor Jack. 'A bloody fool.'

They were seated around a table in one of the conference rooms – Lauderdale's idea. No doubt an interview room wasn't good enough for Sir Hugh Ferrie. Gregor Jack had been smartened up for the occasion: crisp suit, tidied hair, sparkling eyes. Seated, however, between Sir Hugh and Jeanette Oliphant, he was always going to come home third in the projection stakes.

'The point is,' said Jeanette Oliphant, 'Mr Jack told Sir Hugh about something else he'd been keeping secret, namely that his Wednesday round of golf was a concoction.'

'Bloody fool – '

'And,' Oliphant went on, a little more loudly, 'Sir Hugh contacted me. We feel that the sooner Mr Jack makes a statement regarding his genuine actions on the day in question, the less doubt there will be.' Jeanette Oliphant was in her mid-fifties, a tall, elegant, but stern-faced woman. Her mouth was a thin slash of lipstick, her eyes piercing, missing nothing. Her ears stuck out ever so slightly from her short permed hair, as though ready to catch any nuance or ambiguity, any wrong word or overlong pause.

Sir Hugh, on the other hand, was stocky and pugnacious, a man more used to speaking than listening. His hands lay flat against the table top, as though they were attempting to push *through* it.

'Let's get everything sorted out.' he said.

'If that's what Mr Jack wants,' Lauderdale said quietly.

'It's what he wants,' replied Ferrie.

The door opened. It was Detective Sergeant Brian Holmes, carrying a tray of cups. Rebus looked up at him, but Holmes refused to meet his eyes. Not normally a DS's job, playing waiter, but Rebus could just see Holmes waylaying the *real* tea-boy. He wanted to know what was going on. So, it seemed, did Chief Superintendent Watson, who came into the room behind him. Ferrie actually half rose from his chair.

'Ah, Chief Superintendent.' They shook hands. Watson glanced from Lauderdale to Rebus and back, but there was nothing they could tell him, not yet. Holmes, having laid the tray on the table, was lingering.

'Thank you, Sergeant,' said Lauderdale, dismissing him from the room. In the general mêlée, Rebus saw that Gregor Jack was looking at him, looking with his sparkling eyes and his little boy's smile. Here we are again, he was saying. Here we are again.

Watson decided to stay. Another cup would be needed, but then Rebus declined the offer of tea, so there was a cup for

Watson after all. It was obvious from his face that he would have preferred coffee, his own coffee. But he accepted the cup from Rebus with a nodded thanks. Then Gregor Jack spoke.

'After Inspector Rebus's last visit, I did some thinking. I was able to recall the names of some of the places I went to that Wednesday . . .' He reached into his jacket's inside pocket and drew out a piece of paper. 'I looked in on a bar in Eyemouth itself, but it was packed. I didn't stay. I *did* have a tomato juice at a hotel outside the town, but again the bar there was packed, so I can't be sure anyone will remember me. And I bought chewing gum at a newsagent's in Dunbar on the way down. Apart from that, I'm afraid it's pretty vague.' He handed the list to the Chief Superintendent. 'A walk along the front at Eyemouth . . . a stop in a lay-by just north of Berwick . . . there was another car in the lay-by, a rep or something, but he seemed more interested in his maps than he did in me . . . That's about it.'

Watson nodded, studying the list as though it contained exam questions. Then he handed it on to Lauderdale.

'It's certainly a start,' said Watson.

'The thing is, Chief Superintendent,' said Sir Hugh, 'the boy knows he's in trouble, but it seems to me the only trouble he's in stems from trying to help other people.'

Watson nodded thoughtfully. Rebus stood up. 'If you'll excuse me a moment . . .' And he made for the door, closing it behind him with a real sense of escape. He had no intention of returning. There might be a slap on the wrist later from Lauderdale or Watson – bad manners that, John – but no way could he sit in that stifling room with all those stifling people. Holmes was loitering at the far end of the corridor.

'What's up?' he asked when Rebus approached.

'Nothing to get excited about.'

'Oh.' Holmes looked deflated. 'Only we all thought . . .'

'You all thought he was coming in to confess? Quite the opposite, Brian.'

'Is Glass going to end up going down for both murders then?'

233

Rebus shrugged. 'Nothing would surprise me,' he said. Despite his morning shower, he felt grimy and unhealthy.

'Makes it nice and neat, doesn't it?'

'We're the police, Brian, we're not meant to be char ladies.'

'Sorry I spoke.'

Rebus sighed. 'Sorry, Brian. I didn't mean to dust you off.' They stared at one another for a second, then laughed. It wasn't much, but it was better than nothing. 'Right, I'm off to Queensferry.'

'Autograph-hunting?'

'Something like that.'

'Need a chauffeur?'

'Why not. Come on then.'

A snap decision, Rebus was later to think, which probably saved his life.

11
Old School Ties

They managed not to speak about work on the way out to Queensferry. Instead, they spoke about women.

'What about the four of us going out some night?' Brian Holmes suggested at one point.

'I'm not sure Patience and Nell would get on,' Rebus mused.

'What, different personalities, you mean?'

'No, similar personalities. That's the problem.'

Rebus was thinking of tonight's dinner with Patience. Of trying to take time off from the Jack case. Of not making a Jack-ass of himself. Of jacking it all in . . .

'It was only a thought,' said Holmes. 'That's all, only a thought.'

The rain was starting as they neared the Kinnoul house. The sky had been darkening for the duration of the drive, until now, it seemed, evening had come early. Rab Kinnoul's Land-Rover was parked outside the front door. Curiously, the door to the house was open. Rain bounced off the car bonnet, becoming heavier by the second.

'Better make a run for it,' said Rebus. They opened their doors and ran. Rebus, however, was on the right side for the house, while Holmes had to skirt around the car first. So Rebus was first up the steps, and first through the doorway and into the hall. He shook his hair free of water, then opened his eyes.

And saw the carving knife swooping down on him.

And heard the shriek behind it.

'Bastard!'

Then someone pushed him sideways. It was Holmes, flying through the doorway. The knife fell into space and kept falling floorwards. Cath Kinnoul fell after it, her weight propelling her. Holmes was on her in an instant, pulling her wrist round, twisting it up against her back. He had his knee firmly on her spine, just below the shoulder blades.

'Christ almighty!' gasped Rebus. 'Jesus Christ almighty.'

Holmes was examining the sprawled figure. 'She took a knock when she fell,' he said. 'She's out cold.' He prised the knife from her grasp and released her arm. It flopped on to the carpet. Holmes stood up. He seemed wonderfully calm, but his face was unnaturally pale. Rebus, meantime, was shaking like a sick mongrel. He rested against the hallway wall and closed his eyes for a moment, breathing deeply. There was a noise at the door.

'Who the – ?' Rab Kinnoul saw them, then looked down at the unconscious figure of his wife. 'Oh hell,' he said. He knelt down beside her, dripping rainwater on to her back, her head. He was drenched.

'She's all right, Mr Kinnoul,' Holmes stated. 'Knocked herself out, that's all.'

Kinnoul saw the knife Holmes was holding. 'She had that?' he said, his eyes opening wide. 'Dear God, Cathy.' He touched a trembling hand to her head. 'Cathy, Cathy.'

Rebus had recovered a little. He swallowed. 'She didn't get those bruises from falling though.' Yes, there were bruises on her arms, fresh-looking. Kinnoul nodded.

'We had a bit of a row,' he said. 'She went for me, so I . . . I was just trying to push her away. But she was hysterical. I decided to go for a walk until she calmed down.'

Rebus had been looking at Kinnoul's shoes. They were caked with mud. There were splashes, too, on his trousers. Go for a walk? In *that* rain? No, he'd run for it, pure and simple. He'd turned tail and run . . .

'Doesn't look as though she calmed down,' Rebus said matter of factly. Matter of factly, she had almost murdered him, mistaking him for her husband, or so incensed by then that any man – any victim – would do. 'Tell you what, Mr Kinnoul, I could do with a drink.'

'I'll see what there is,' said Kinnoul, rising to his feet.

Holmes phoned for the doctor. Cath Kinnoul was still unconscious. They'd left her lying in the hall, just to be on the safe side. It was best not to move fall victims anyway; and besides, this way they could keep an eye on her through the open door of the living room.

'She needs treatment,' Rebus said. He was sitting on the sofa, nursing a whisky and what were left of his nerves.

'What she needs,' Kinnoul said quietly, 'is to be away from me. We're useless together, Inspector, but then we're just as useless apart.' He was standing with his hands resting against the window sill, his head against the glass.

'What was the fight about?'

Kinnoul shook his head. 'It seems stupid now. They always start with something petty, and it just builds and builds . . .'

'And this time?'

Kinnoul turned from the window. 'The amount of time I'm spending away from home. She didn't believe there were any "projects". She thinks it's all just an excuse so I can get out of the house.'

'And is she right?'

'Partly, yes, I suppose. She's a shrewd one . . . a bit slow sometimes, but she gets there.'

'And what about evenings.'

'What about them?'

'You don't always spend *them* at home either, do you? Sometimes you have a night out with friends.'

'Do I?'

'Say, with Barney Byars . . . with Ronald Steele.'

Kinnoul stared at Rebus, appearing not to understand, then he snapped his fingers. 'Christ, you mean *that* night. Jesus, the night . . .' He shook his head. 'Who told you? Never mind, it must have been one or the other. What about it?'

'I just thought you made an unlikely trio.'

Kinnoul smiled. 'You're right there. I don't know Byars all

that well, hardly at all really. But that day he'd been in Edinburgh and he'd sewn up a deal ... a *big* deal. We bumped into each other at the Eyrie. I was in the bar having a drink, drowning my sorrows, and he was on his way up to the restaurant. Somehow I got roped in. Him and the firm he'd done the deal with. After a while ... well, it was good fun.'

'What about Steele?'

'Well ... Barney was planning on taking these guys to a brothel he knew about, but they weren't interested. They went their way, and Barney and me nipped into the Strawman for another drink. That's where we picked up Ronnie. He was a bit pissed, too. Something to do with the lady in his life ...' Kinnoul was thoughtful for a moment. 'Anyway, he's usually a bit of a boring fart, but that night he seemed all right.'

Rebus was wondering: Did Kinnoul know about Steele and Cathy? It didn't look like it, but then the man was an actor, a pro.

'And,' Kinnoul was saying, 'we all ended up going on to the ill-famed house.'

'Did you have a good time?'

Kinnoul seemed to think this an unusual question. 'I suppose so,' he said. 'I can't really remember too clearly.'

Oh, thought Rebus, you can remember clearly enough. You can remember, all right. But now Kinnoul was looking through the hallway at Cathy's still figure.

'You must think I'm a bit of a shite,' he said in a level tone. 'You're probably right. But, Christ ...' The actor had run out of words. He looked around the room, looked out of the window at what, weather willing, would have been the view, then looked towards the door again. He exhaled noisily, then shook his head.

'Did you tell the others what the prostitute told you?'

Now Kinnoul looked startled.

'I mean,' said Rebus, 'did you tell them what she said about Gregor Jack?'

'How the hell do you know about that?' Kinnoul fell onto one of the chairs.

'An inspired guess. Did you?'

'I suppose so.' He thought about it. 'Yes, definitely. Well, it was such a strange thing for her to say.'

'A strange thing for you to say, too, Mr Kinnoul.'

Kinnoul shrugged his huge shoulders. 'Just a laugh, Inspector. I was a bit pissed. I thought it would be funny to pretend to be Gregor. To be honest, I was a bit hurt that she didn't recognize Rab Kinnoul. Look at the photos on the wall. I've met all of them.' He was up on his feet again now, studying the pictures of himself, like he was in an art gallery and not seeing them for the thousandth, the ten thousandth time.

'Bob Wagner . . . Larry Hagman . . . I knew them all once.' The litany continued. 'Martin Scorsese . . . the top director, absolutely the top . . . John Hurt . . . Robbie Coltrane and Eric Idle . . .'

Holmes was motioning for Rebus to come into the hall. Cathy Kinnoul was coming round. Rab Kinnoul stood in front of his photographs, his mementoes, the list of names sloshing around in his mouth.

'Take it easy,' Holmes was telling Cathy Kinnoul. 'How do you feel?'

Her speech was slurred to incoherence.

'How many have you taken, Cathy?' Rebus asked. 'Tell us how many?'

She was trying to focus. 'I've checked all the rooms,' Holmes said. 'No sign of any empty bottles.'

'Well, she's taken something.'

'Maybe the doctor will know.'

'Yes, maybe.' Rebus leaned down close to Cathy Kinnoul, his mouth two inches from her ear. 'Gowk,' he said quietly, 'tell me about Suey.'

The names registered with her, but the question seemed not to.

'You and Suey,' Rebus went on. 'Have you been seeing Suey? Just the two of you, eh? Like the old days? Have you and Suey been seeing one another?'

She opened her mouth, paused, then closed it again, and slowly began to shake her head. She mumbled something.

'What was that, Gowk?'

Clearly this time: 'Rab mussn know.'

'He won't know, Gowk. Trust me, he won't know.'

She was sitting up now, holding her head in one hand while the other hand rested on the floor.

'So,' Rebus persisted, 'you and Suey have been seeing one another, eh? Gowk and Suey?'

She smiled drunkenly. 'Gow' an' Suey,' she said, enjoying the words. 'Gow' an' Suey.'

'Remember, Gowk, remember the day before you found the body? Remember that Wednesday, that Wednesday afternoon? Did Suey come and see you? Did he, Gowk? Did Suey pay a visit that Wednesday?'

'Wensay? Wensay?' She was shaking her head. 'Poor Lizzie ... poor, poor ...' Now she held her hand palm upwards. 'Gi' me th' knife,' she said. 'Rab'll never know. Gi' me th' knife.'

Rebus glanced at Holmes. 'We can't let you do that, Gowk. That would be murder.'

She nodded. 'Thas right, murder.' She said the final word very carefully, enunciating each letter, then repeated it. 'Cut off his head,' she said. 'An' they'll put me beside Mack.' She smiled again, the thought pleasing her. And all the time Rab Kinnoul's names were drifting from the other room ...

'... best, absolutely ... like to work with him again. Consummate professionalism ... and good old George Cole, too ... the old school ... yes, the old school ... the old school ...'

'Mack ...' Cathy Kinnoul was saying. 'Mack ... Suey ... Sexton ... Beggar ... Poor Beggar ...'

'The old school.'

Some school ties you just kept too long. Way after they should have been thrown out.

Rebus telephoned Barney Byars. The secretary put him through.

'Inspector,' came Byars' voice, all energy and business, 'I just can't shake you off, can I?'

'You're too easy to catch,' Rebus said.

Byars laughed. 'I've got to be,' he said, 'otherwise the clients can't catch me. I always like to make myself available. Now, what's your beef this time?'

'It's about an evening you spent not so long ago with Rab Kinnoul and Ronald Steele . . .'

Byars was able to substantiate the story in all but the most crucial details. Rebus explained about Kinnoul coming downstairs and repeating what Gail had said to him.

'I don't remember that,' Byars said. 'I was well on by then, mind. So well on I think I stumped up for the three of us.' He chuckled. 'Suey had his usual excuse of being flat broke, and Rab was carrying not more than ten bar by then.' Another chuckle. 'See, I always remember my sums, especially when it's money.'

'But you're sure you don't recall Mr Kinnoul telling you what the prostitute told him?'

'I'm not saying he *didn't* say it, mind, but no, I can't for the life of me remember it.'

Which made it Kinnoul's word against Byars' memory. The only thing for it was to talk to Steele again. Rebus could call in on the way to Patience's. It was a long way round for a shortcut, but it shouldn't take too long. Cathy Kinnoul was another problem. It didn't do to have knife-wielding pill-poppers running around at large. The family doctor, summoned by Holmes, had listened to their story and suggested that Mrs Kinnoul be admitted to a hospital on the outskirts of the city. Would there be any criminal charges . . .?

'Of course,' said Holmes testily. 'Attempted murder for starters.'

But Rebus was thinking. He was thinking of how badly Cath Kinnoul had been treated. Thinking, too, of all those obstruction charges he might be filing – Hector, Steele, Jack himself. And, most of all, thinking of Andrew Macmillan. He'd seen what 'special hospitals' did with the criminally insane. Cath Kinnoul would be treated anyway. So long as

241

she underwent treatment, what was the point of pressing a charge of attempted murder on her?

So he shook his head – to Brian Holmes' astonishment. No, no charges, not if she was admitted straight away. The doctor checked that the paperwork would be a mere formality, and Kinnoul, who had come back to something like his senses by this time, agreed to the whole thing.

'In that case,' said the doctor, 'she can be admitted today.'

Rebus made one more call. To Chief Inspector Lauderdale.

'Where the hell did you disappear to?'

'It's a long story, sir.'

'It usually is.'

'How did the meeting go?'

'It went. Listen, John, we're formally charging William Glass.'

'What?'

'The Dean Bridge victim had had intercourse just before she died. Forensics tell me the DNA-test matches our man Glass.' Lauderdale paused, but Rebus said nothing. 'Don't worry, John, we'll start with the Dean Bridge murder. But really, just between us ... do you think you're getting anywhere?'

'Really, sir, just between us ... I don't know.'

'Well, you'd better get a move on, otherwise I'm going to charge Glass with Mrs Jack, too. Ferrie and that solicitor are going to start asking awkward questions any minute now. It's on a knife edge, John, understand?'

'Yes, sir, oh yes, I understand all about knife edges, believe me ...'

Rebus didn't walk up to Ronald Steele's front door – not straight away. First, he stood in front of the garage and peered in through a crack between the two doors. Steele's Citroën was at home, which presumably meant the man himself was at home. Rebus went to the door and pushed the bell. He could hear it sounding in the hall. Halls: he could write a book on them. My night sleeping in a hallway; the day I was almost stabbed in a hallway ... He rang again. It was a loud and unpleasant bell, not the kind you could easily ignore.

So he rang one more time. Then he tried the door. It was locked. He walked on to the little strip of grass running in front of the bungalow and pressed his face against the living room window. The room was empty. Maybe he'd just popped out for a pint of milk ... Rebus tried the gate to the side of the garage, the gate giving access to the back garden. It, too, was locked. He walked back to the front gate and stood beside it, looking up and down the silent street. Then he checked his watch. He could give it five minutes, ten at most. The last thing he felt like was sitting down to dinner with Patience. But he didn't want to lose her either ... Quarter of an hour to get back to Oxford Terrace ... twenty minutes to be on the safe side. Yes, he could still be there by seven thirty. Time enough. *Well, you'd better get a move on.* Why bother? Why not give Glass his moment of infamy, his second – his *famous* – victim?

Why bother with anything? Not for the praise of a pat on the back; not for the rightness of it; maybe, then, from sheer stubbornness. Yes, that would just about fit the bill. Someone was coming ... His car was pointing the wrong way, but he could see in his rearview. Not a man but a woman. Nice legs. Carrying two carrier bags of shopping. She walked well but she was tired. It couldn't be ...? What the ...?

He rolled down his window. 'Hello, Gill.'

Gill Templer stopped, stared, smiled. 'You know, I thought I recognized that heap of junk.'

'Ssh! Cars have feelings, too.' He patted the steering wheel. She put down her bags.

'What are you doing here?'

He nodded towards Steele's house. 'Waiting to talk to someone who isn't going to show.'

'Trust you.'

'What about you?'

'Me? I *live* here. Well, next street on the right to be honest. You *knew* I'd moved.'

He shrugged. 'I didn't realize it was round here.'

She gave him an unconvinced smile.

'No, honest,' he said. 'But now I *am* here, can I give you a lift?'

She laughed. 'It's only a hundred yards.'

'Please yourself.'

She looked down at her bags. 'Oh, go on then.'

He opened the door for her and she put the bags down on the floor, squeezing her feet in beside them. Rebus started the car. It spluttered, wheezed, died. He tried again, choke full out. The car gasped, whinnied, then got the general idea.

'Like I said, heap of junk.'

'*That's* why it's behaving like this,' Rebus warned. 'Temperamental, like a thoroughbred horse.'

But the field of an egg-and-spoon race could probably have beaten them over the distance. Finally, they reached the house unscathed. Rebus looked out.

'Nice,' he said. It was a double-fronted affair with bay windows either side of the front door. There were three floors all told, with a small and steep garden dissected by the stone steps which led from gate to doorway.

'I haven't got the whole house, of course. Just the ground floor.'

'Nice all the same.'

'Thanks.' She pushed open the door and manoeuvred her bags out on to the pavement. She gestured towards them. 'Vegetable stir-fry. Interested?'

It took him a moment's eternity to decide. 'Thanks, Gill. I'm tied up tonight.'

She had the grace to look disappointed. 'Maybe another time then.'

'Yes,' said Rebus, as she pushed the passenger door shut. 'Maybe another time.'

The car crawled back along her road. If it gives out on me, he thought, I'll go back and take her up on her offer. It'll be a sign. But the car actually began to sound healthier as it passed Steele's bungalow. There was still no sign of life, so Rebus kept going. He was thinking of a set of weighing scales. On one side sat Gill Templer, on the other Dr Patience Aitken.

The scales rose and fell, while Rebus did some hard thinking. Christ, it was hard too. He wished he had more time, but the traffic lights were with him most of the way, and he was back at Patience's by half past.

'I don't believe it,' she said as he walked into the kitchen. 'I really don't believe you actually kept a date.' She was standing beside the microwave. Inside, something was cooking. Rebus pulled her to him and gave her a wet kiss on the lips.

'Patience,' he said, 'I think I love you.'

She pulled back from him a little, the better to look at him. 'And there's not a drop of alcohol in the man either. What a night for surprises. Well, I think I should tell you that I've had a *foul* day and as a result I'm in a *foul* mood ... that's why we're eating chicken.' She smiled and kissed him. '"I think I love you,"' she mimicked. 'You should have seen the look on your face when you said that. A picture of sheer puzzlement. You're not exactly the last of the red-hot romantics, are you, John Rebus?'

'So teach me,' said Rebus, kissing her again.

'I think,' said Patience ... 'I think we'll have that chicken cold.'

He was up early next morning. More unusually, he was up before Patience herself, who lay with a satisfied, debauched look on her sleeping face and with her hair wild around her on the pillow. He let Lucky in and gave him a bigger than normal bowl of food, then made tea and toast for himself and Patience.

'Pinch me, I must be dreaming,' she said when he woke her up. She gulped at the tea, then took a small bite from one buttered triangle. Rebus half refilled his own cup, drained it, and got up from the bed.

'Right,' he said, 'I'm off.'

'What?' She looked at her clock. 'Night shift is it this week?'

'It's morning, Patience. And I've a lot on today.' He bent over her to peck her forehead, but she pulled at his tie, tugging him further down so that she could give him a salty, crumbly kiss on the mouth.

'See you later?' she asked.

'Count on it.'

'It would be nice to be able to.' But he was already on his way. Lucky came into the room and leapt on to the bed. The cat was licking his lips.

'Me too, Lucky,' said Patience. 'Me too.'

He drove straight to Ronald Steele's bungalow. The traffic was heavy coming into town, but Rebus was heading out. It wasn't yet quite eight. He didn't take Steele for an early riser. This was a grim anniversary: two weeks to the day since Liz Jack was murdered. Time to get things straight.

Steele's car was still in its garage. Rebus went to the front door and pressed the bell, attempting a jaunty rhythm of rings – a friend, or the postman ... someone you'd want to open your door to.

'Come on, Suey, chop-chop.'

But there was no answer. He peered through the letter box. Nothing. He looked in through the living room window. Exactly as it had been yesterday evening. The curtains hadn't even been pulled shut. No sign of life.

'I hope you haven't done a runner,' Rebus muttered. Though maybe it would be better if he *had*. At least it would be an action of some kind, a sign of fear or of something to hide. He could ask the neighbours if they'd seen anything, but a wall separated Steele's bungalow from theirs. He decided against it. It might only serve to alert Steele to Rebus's interest, an interest strong enough to bring him here at breakfast time. Instead, he got back into the car and drove to Suey Books. A hundred-to-one shot this. As he'd suspected, the shop was barred and meshed and padlocked. Rasputin lay asleep in the window. Rebus made a fist and pounded it against the glass. The cat's head shot up and it let out a sharp, shocked yowl.

'Remember me?' said Rebus, grinning.

Traffic was slower now, treacle through the sieve of the

246

road system. He slipped down on to the Cowgate to avoid the worst of it. If Steele couldn't be found, there was only one thing for it. He'd have to change Farmer Watson's mind. What's more, he'd have to do it this morning, while the old boy was bristling with caffeine. Now there was a thought . . . what time did that deli just off Leith Walk open . . . ?

'Well thank you, John.'

Rebus shrugged. 'We drink enough of *your* coffee, sir. I just thought it was time someone else did the buying for a change.'

Watson opened the bag and sniffed. 'Mmm, freshly ground.' He started to tip the dark powder into his filter. The machine was already full of water. 'What kind did you say?'

'Breakfast blend, sir, I think. Robustica and Arabica . . . something like that. I'm not exactly an expert . . .'

But Watson waved the apology aside. He put the jug in position and flipped the switch. 'Takes a couple of minutes,' he said, sitting down behind his desk. 'Right, John.' He put his hands together in front of him. 'What can I do for you?'

'Well, sir, it's about Gregor Jack.'

'Yes . . . ?'

'You know how you told me we'd to help Mr Jack if possible? How you felt he'd perhaps been set up?' Watson merely nodded. 'Well, sir, I'm close to proving not only that he was, but *who* did it.'

'Oh? Go on.'

So Rebus told his story, the story of a chance meeting in a red-lit bedroom. And of three men. 'What I was wondering was . . . I know you said you couldn't divulge your source, sir . . . but was it one of them?'

Watson shook his head. 'Way off, I'm afraid, John. Mmm, do you smell that?' The room was filling with the aroma. How could Rebus *not* smell it?

'Yes, sir, very nice. So it wasn't – ?'

'It wasn't anyone who *knows* Gregor Jack. If pro – ' He stuttered to a halt. 'Can't wait for that coffee,' he said, rather too eagerly.

'You were about to say, sir?' But what? What? Providence? Provost? Prodigal? Problem?

Provost? No, no. Not provost. Protestant? Proprietor? A name or a title.

'Nothing, John, nothing. I wonder if I've any clean cups . . .?'

A name or a title. Professor. *Professor!*

'You weren't about to mention a professor then?'

Watson's lips were sealed. But Rebus was thinking fast now.

'Professor Costello, for instance. He's a friend of yours, isn't he, sir? He doesn't know Mr Jack then?'

Watson's ears were turning red. Got you, thought Rebus. Got you, got you, got you. That coffee was worth every last penny.

'Interesting though,' mused Rebus, 'that the Professor would know about a brothel.'

Watson slapped the desk. 'Enough.' His light morning mood had vanished. His whole face was red now, except for two small white patches, one on either cheek. 'All right,' he said. 'You might as well know, it *was* Professor Costello who told me.'

'And how did the Professor know?'

'He said . . . he *said* he had a *friend* who'd visited the place one night, and now felt ashamed. Of course,' Watson lowered his voice to a hiss, 'there isn't any *friend.* It's the old chap himself. He just can't bring himself to admit it. Well,' his voice rising again, 'we're all tempted some time, aren't we?' Rebus thought of Gill Templer last night. Yes, tempted indeed. 'So I promised the Professor I'd have the place closed down.'

Rebus was thoughtful. 'And did you let him know when Operation Creeper was set for?'

It was Watson's turn to be thoughtful. Then he nodded. 'But he's . . . he's a *professor* . . . of *divinity.* He wouldn't have been the one to tip off the papers. And he doesn't *know* Gregor bloody Jack.'

'But you told him? Date *and* time?'

'More or less.'

'Why? Why did he need to know?'

'His "friend" ... The "friend" needed to know so he could warn anyone he knew from going there.'

Rebus leapt to his feet. 'Jesus Christ, sir!' He paused. 'With respect. But don't you see? There *was* a friend. There *was* someone who needed to be warned. But not so they could stop their friends being caught ... so they could *ensure* Gregor Jack walked straight into the trap. As soon as they knew when we were going in, all they had to do was phone Jack and tell him his sister was there. They knew he couldn't *not* go and check it out for himself.' He tugged open the door.

'Where are you off to?'

'To see Professor Costello. Not that I need to, not really, but I want to hear him say the name, I want to hear it for myself. Enjoy your coffee, sir.'

But Watson didn't. It tasted like charred wood. Too bitter, too strong. For some time now he'd been wavering; now he made the decision. He'd stop drinking coffee altogether. It would be his penance. Just like Inspector John Rebus was his comforter ...

'Good morning, Inspector.'

'Morning, sir. Not disturbing you?'

Professor Costello waved his arm airily around the empty room. 'Not a student in Edinburgh's awake at this – to them – ungodly hour. Not the divinity students at any rate. No, Inspector, you're not disturbing me.'

'You got the books all right, sir?'

Costello pointed towards his glass-fronted bookshelves. 'Safe and sound. The officer who delivered them said something about them being found abandoned ...?'

'Something like that, sir.' Rebus glanced back at the door. 'You haven't had a proper lock fitted yet.'

'*Mea culpa,* Inspector. Fear not, one's on its way.'

'Only I wouldn't like you to lose your books again ...'

'Point taken, Inspector. Sit down, won't you? Coffee?' The hand this time was directed towards an evil-looking percolator sitting smoking on a hotplate in a corner of the room.

'No thanks, sir. Bit early for me.'

Costello bowed his head slightly. He slid into the comfortable leather chair behind his comfortable oaken desk. Rebus sat on one of the modern, spindly metal-framed chairs the other side of it. 'So, Inspector, social niceties dispensed with . . . what can I do for you?'

'You gave some information to Chief Superintendent Watson, sir.'

Costello pursed his lips. 'Confidential information, Inspector.'

'At one time perhaps, but it may help us with a murder inquiry.'

'Surely not!'

Rebus nodded. 'So you see, sir, that changes things slightly. We need to know who your "friend" was, the one who told you about the . . . er . . .'

'I believe the phrase is "hoor-hoose". Almost poetic, much nicer at any rate than "brothel".' Costello almost squirmed in his chair. 'My friend, Inspector, I did promise him . . .'

'Murder, sir. I'd advise against withholding information.'

'Oh yes, agreed, agreed. But one's conscience . . .'

'Was it Ronald Steele?'

Costello's eyes opened wide. 'Then you already know.'

'Just an inspired guess, sir. You're a frequent customer in his shop, aren't you?'

'Well, I do like to browse . . .'

'And you were in his shop when he told you.'

'That's right. It was a lunchtime. Vanessa, his assistant, she was on her break. She's a student here, actually. Lovely girl . . .'

If only you knew, thought Rebus.

'Anyway, yes, Ronald told me his little guilty secret. He'd been taken to this hoor-hoose one night by some friends. He really was *very* embarrassed about it all.'

'Was he?'

'Oh, terribly. He knew I knew Superintendent Watson, and he wondered if I could pass word on about the establishment.'

'So we could close it down?'

250

'Yes.'

'But he needed to know the night?'

'He was *desperate* to know. His friends, you see, the ones who'd taken him. He wanted to warn them off.'

'You know Mr Steele is a friend of Gregor Jack's?'

'Who?'

'The MP.'

'I'm sorry, the name doesn't ... Gregor Jack?' Costello frowned, shook his head. 'No.'

'He's been in all the newspapers.'

'Really?'

Rebus sighed. The real world, it seemed, stopped at the door to Costello's office. This was a lighter realm altogether. He was almost startled by the sudden electronic twittering of the high-tech telephone. Costello apologized and picked up the receiver.

'Yes? Speaking. Yes, he is. Wait one moment, please.' He held the receiver out towards Rebus. 'It's for you, Inspector,' Somehow, Rebus wasn't surprised ...

'Hello?'

'The Chief Superintendent said I'd find you there.' It was Lauderdale.

'Good morning to you too, sir.'

'Cut the crap, John. I'm just in and already a bit of the ceiling's fallen off and missed my head by inches. I'm not in the mood for it okay?'

'Understood, sir.'

'I'm only phoning because I thought you'd be interested.'

'Yes, sir?'

'Forensics didn't take long with those two glasses you found in Mr Pond's bathroom.'

Of course they didn't. They had all the match-up prints they needed, taken so as to eliminate people from Deer Lodge.

'Guess who they belong to?' Lauderdale asked.

'One set will be Mrs Jack, the other set Ronald Steele.'

There was silence on the other end of the telephone.

'Was I close?' asked Rebus.

'How the hell did you know?'

'What if I told you it was an inspired guess?'
'I'd tell you you're a liar. Get back here. We need to talk.'
'Right you are, sir. Just one more thing . . .?'
'What?'
'Mr Glass . . . is he still on for the double?'
The line went dead.

12
Escort Service

The way Rebus saw it . . .

Well, it didn't take too much brain activity once the name had been established. The way he saw it, Ronald Steele and Elizabeth Jack had been lovers, probably for some time. (Christ, Sir Hugh was going to *love* this when it came out.) Maybe nobody knew. Maybe everybody but Gregor Jack knew. Anyway, Liz Jack decided to head north, and Steele joined her whenever he could. (Deer Lodge and back every day? A superhuman effort. No wonder Steele looked ready to drop all the time . . .) Deer Lodge itself though was a tip, a heap. So they moved into Pond's cottage, only using Deer Lodge itself for fetching changes of clothes. Maybe Liz Jack had been fetching clean clothes when she'd stopped and bought the Sunday rags . . . and found out all about her husband's apparently naughty night.

Steele, though, had plans way above the occasional legover scenario. He wanted Liz. He *wanted* her to himself. The quiet ones always got intense about that sort of thing, didn't they? He'd been making anonymous calls maybe. And sending letters. Anything to throw a spanner in the works of the marriage, anything to unsettle Gregor. Maybe that's why Liz had headed north, to get away from it all. Steele saw his chance. He'd already been to the brothel, and he'd already discovered just who Gail Crawley was. (All it took was a halfway decent memory, and maybe a question or two asked of the likes of Cathy Kinnoul.) Ah, Cathy . . . Yes, maybe Steele *was* seeing her too. But Rebus doubted it was for

253

anything but conversation and counselling. There was that side to Steele, too.

Which didn't do anything to stop him trying to strip Gregor Jack, his lifelong friend, ally in his bookshop, all-round good guy, to strip him completely and utterly naked. The brothel plan was simple and knife-sharp. Find out the time of the planned raid . . . a call to Gregor Jack . . . and calls beforehand to the Docklands dirt-diggers.

The set-up. And Gregor Jack shed his first layer.

Did Steele try to keep it from Liz? Maybe, maybe not. He thought it would be the final screw in the marriage-coffin. It nearly was. But he couldn't be north with her all the time, telling her how great they could be together, what a shit Gregor was, et cetera, et cetera. And during the time she was alone, Liz Jack wavered, until finally she made up her mind not to leave Gregor but to leave Steele. Something like that. She was unpredictable after all. She was fire. And they argued. In his interview, he'd alluded to the argument itself: *She always accused me of not being enough fun . . . and I never had enough money either . . .* So they argued, and he stormed off, leaving her in the lay-by. Alec Corbie's blue car had been a green car, the green Citroën BX. Steele had sped off, only to return and continue the argument, an argument which became violent, violence which went a little too far . . .

The next bit was, to Rebus's mind, the cleverest, either that or the most fortuitous. Steele had to dump the body. The first thing to do was to get it away from the Highlands: there were too many clues up there to the fact that they'd spent time together. So he headed back towards Edinburgh with her in the boot. But what to do with her? Wait, there had been another killing, hadn't there? A body dumped in a river. He could make it look the same. Better still, he could send her body out to sea. So he headed for someplace he knew: the hill above the Kinnoul house. He'd walked up there with Cathy so many times. He knew the small road, a road never used. And he knew that even if the body *were* found, the first suspect would be the Dean Bridge killer. So, at some point, he gave her that blow to the head, the blow so like the one administered to the Dean Bridge victim.

And the beautiful irony was: his alibi for the afternoon was provided by Gregor Jack himself.

'And that's how you see it, is it?'

The meeting was in Watson's office: Watson, Lauderdale and Rebus. On the way in, Rebus had passed Brian Holmes.

'I hear there's a meeting in the Farmhouse.'

'You've got good hearing.'

'What's it about?'

'You mean you're not on the guest list, Brian?' Rebus winked. 'Too bad. I'll try to bring you a doggie-bag.'

'Big of you.'

Rebus turned. 'Look, Brian, the paint's hardly dry on your promotion as it is. Relax, take it easy. If you're looking for a quick road to Detective Inspector, go track down Lord Lucan. Meantime, I'm expected elsewhere, okay?'

'Okay.'

Too cocky by half, thought Rebus. But speaking of cocky, he was doing a bit of strutting himself, wasn't he? Sitting here in Watson's office, spouting forth, while Lauderdale looked worriedly towards his suddenly caffeine-free superior.

'And that's how you see it, is it?' The question was Watson's. Rebus merely shrugged.

'It sounds plausible,' said Lauderdale. Rebus raised half an eyebrow: having Lauderdale's support was a bit like locking yourself in with a starved alsatian . . .

'What about Mr Glass?' asked Watson.

'Well, sir,' said Lauderdale, shifting a little in his seat, 'psychiatric reports don't show him to be the most stable individual. He lives in a sort of fantasy world, you might say.'

'You mean he made it up?'

'Very probably.'

'Which brings us back to Mr Steele. I think we'd better have him in for a word, hadn't we. Did you say you brought him in yesterday, John?'

'That's right, sir. I thought we might give the boot of his

car a once-over. But Mr Lauderdale seemed convinced by Steele's story and let him go.'

The look on Lauderdale's face would remain long in Rebus's memory. Man bites alsatian.

'Is that so?' said Watson, also seeming to enjoy Lauderdale's discomfort.

'We'd no reason to hold him *then*, sir. It's only information received this morning which has allowed us – '

'All right, all right. So have we picked him up again?'

'He's not at home, sir,' said Rebus. 'I checked last night and then again this morning.'

Both men looked at him. Watson's look said: Very efficient. Lauderdale's look said: You bastard.

'Well,' said Watson, 'we'd better get a warrant out, hadn't we? I think there's quite enough that needs explaining by Mr Steele.'

'His car's still in its garage, sir. We could get forensics to take a look at it. Most probably he'll have cleaned it, but you never know . . .'

Forensics? They loved Rebus. He was their patron saint.

'Right you are, John,' said Watson. 'See to it, will you?' He turned to Lauderdale. 'Another cup of coffee? There's plenty in the pot, and you seem to be the only one drinking it . . .'

Strut, strut, strut. He was the little red rooster. He was the cock of the north. He'd felt it all along, of course: Ronald Steele. Suey, who had once tried to commit suicide when found by a girl masturbating in his hotel room.

'Bound to be a bit screwed up.' Who needed a psychology degree? What Rebus needed now was a combination of orienteering skills and old-fashioned man-hunting. His instincts told him that Steele would have headed south, leaving the car behind. (What use was it, after all? The police already had its description and licence number, and he'd known they were closing in. Or rather, he'd known *Rebus* was closing in.)

'Ain't nothing but a bloodhound,' he sang to himself. He'd just phoned the hospital where Cathy Kinnoul was now a patient. Early days, he'd been told, but she'd had a peaceful night. Rab Kinnoul, however, hadn't been near. Maybe this was understandable. It could be that she'd go for him with a broken water jug or try to strangle him with pyjama cord. All the same, Kinnoul was as shitty as the rest of them. Gregor Jack, too, risking all for a career in politics, a career he'd planned from birth, it seemed. Marrying Liz Ferrie not for herself but for her father. Completely unable to control her, so that he just stuffed her into a compartment, dusting her off for photo-shoots and the occasional public engagement. Yes, shitty. Only one person, to Rebus's mind, came out of this with anything like dignity intact, and that person was a burglar.

The forensics team had come up with a match for the prints on the microwave: Julian Kaymer. He'd swiped Jamie Kilpatrick's keys and driven to Deer Lodge in the dead of night, smashing the window to gain entry.

Why? To tidy away evidence of anything *too* scandalous. Which meant the cocaine-stained hand-mirror and two pairs of tights tied to a four-poster. Why? Simple: to protect what he could of a friend's reputation ... a dead friend's reputation. Pathetic, but noble, too, in a way. Stealing the microwave was outrageous really. PC Plod was supposed to put the whole thing down to kids, smashing their way into an empty house on the off-chance ... and making off not with the hi-fi (always a favourite), but with the microwave. He'd driven off with it, then thrown it away, only to have it found by the magpie himself, Alec Corbie.

Yes, Steele would be in London by now. His shop operated in the sphere of cash. There would have been some hidden somewhere; perhaps quite a lot. He might be on a flight out of Heathrow or Gatwick, a train to the coast and the boat over to France.

'Trains and boats and planes ...'

'Somebody sounds happy.' It was Brian Holmes, standing in the doorway to Rebus's office. Rebus was seated at his desk, feet resting on the desk itself, hands behind his head.

'Mind if I come in, or do we need to reserve tickets to touch your hem?'

'You leave my hem out of this. Sit down.' Holmes was halfway to the chair when he tripped over a gash in the linoleum. He put his hands out to save himself, and found himself sprawled on Rebus's desktop, an inch from one of the shoes.

'Yes,' said Rebus, 'you may kiss them.'

Holmes managed something between a smile and a grimace. 'This place really should be condemned.' He slumped into the chair.

'Mind out for the shoogly leg,' warned Rebus. 'Any progress on Steele?'

'Not much.' Holmes paused. 'None at all, really. Why didn't he take his car?'

'We know it too well, remember? I thought *you* were responsible for putting together that list? Everybody in the world's car make, colour and registration number. Oh no, I forgot, you delegated the work to a detective constable.'

'What was it for anyway?' Rebus stared at him. 'Seriously. I'm just a *sergeant*, as you'll recall. Nobody tells me anything. Lauderdale was vaguer even than usual.'

'Mrs Jack's BMW was parked in a lay-by,' explained Rebus.

'That much I knew.'

'So was another car. An eye witness said it might be blue. It wasn't, it was green.'

'That reminds me,' said Holmes, 'I meant to ask you: what was she waiting around for?'

'Who?'

'Mrs Jack. At that lay-by, what was she hanging around there for?' While Rebus considered this, Holmes thought of another question. 'What about *Mr* Jack's car?'

Rebus sighed. 'What about it?'

'Well, I didn't get a good look at it that night you dragged me out there . . . I mean, it was in the garage, and there were lights to the front and back of the house, but not to the side. But you did say to have a snoop. The side door to the garage was open, so I wandered in. Too dark really, and I couldn't find the light switch . . .'

'Jesus Christ, Brian, get on with it!'

'Well, I was only going to ask: what about the car in Jack's garage? It was blue. At least, I *think* it was blue.'

This time, Rebus rubbed his temples. 'It's white,' he explained, slowly. 'It's a white Saab.'

But Holmes was shaking his head. 'Blue,' he said. 'It could never have been white, it was blue. And it was an Escort, *definitely* an Escort.'

Rebus stopped rubbing his temples. 'What?'

'There was some stuff on the passenger seat, too. I peered in through the side window. All that bumpf they give you with hire cars. That sort of thing. Yes, the more I think back on it, the clearer it comes. A blue Ford Escort. And whatever else was in that garage, there certainly wasn't room to swing a Saab . . .'

No rooster now, no strutting cock, no bloodhound. But rather cowed, sheepish, with his tail between his legs . . . Rebus took Holmes and his story to Watson first, and Watson called for Lauderdale.

'I thought,' Lauderdale said to Rebus, 'you told us Mr Jack's car was *white?*'

'It *is* white, sir.'

'You're sure it was a hire car?' Watson asked Holmes. Holmes thought again before nodding. This was serious. He was where he wanted to be, in the thick of things, but he was realizing, too, that here one mistake – one slightest error – could send him to limbo.

'We can check,' said Rebus.

'How?'

'Phone Gregor Jack's house and ask.'

'And warn him off?'

'We don't have to talk to *Jack.* Ian Urquhart or Helen Greig would know.'

'They could still tip him off.'

'Maybe. Of course, there's another possibility. The car Brian saw could have been Urquhart's or even Miss Greig's.'

'Miss Greig doesn't drive,' said Holmes. 'And Urquhart's car's nothing like the one I saw. Remember, they've all been checked.'

'Well, whatever,' said Watson, 'let's tread carefully, eh? Get on to the hire firms first.'

'What about Steele?' Rebus asked.

'Until we know what we're dealing with, we still want to talk to him.'

'Agreed,' said Lauderdale. He seemed aware that Watson was back in control, at least for now.

'Well,' said Watson, 'what are you all waiting for? Jump to it!'

They jumped.

There weren't that many hire firms in Edinburgh, and the third call brought a result. Yes, Mr Jack had hired a car for a few days. Yes, a blue Ford Escort. Did he give any reason for the hire? Yes, his own car was going in for a service.

And, thought Rebus, he needed a change of cars so he could escape the attentions of the press. Christ, hadn't Rebus put the idea into his head himself? Your car's out there ... being photographed ... everyone'll know what it looks like. So Jack had hired another car for a few days, just to help him get around incognito.

Rebus stared at the office wall. Stupid, stupid, stupid. He would have banged his head against the wall if he could have been sure it wouldn't fall down ...

It had been a devil of a job, the man from the hire firm said. The client had wanted his car-phone transferred from his own car to the hire car.

Of course: how else could Liz Jack have contacted him? He had been on the move all day, hadn't he?

Had the hire car been cleaned since its return? Naturally, a full valet service. What about the boot? The boot? The boot, had it been cleaned too? A bit of a wipe maybe ... Where was the car now? On hire again, a London business-man. A forty-eight-hour hire only, and due back by six

260

o'clock. It was now a quarter to five. Two CID men would be waiting to drive it from the car-hire offices to the police pound. Were there any forensics people available at Fettes HQ . . . ?

Stupid, stupid, stupid. Not the same car returning to the lay-by, but another car. Holmes had asked the question: what had Liz Jack been waiting for? She'd been waiting for her husband. She must have telephoned him from the box in the lay-by. She'd just had the argument with Steele. Too upset to drive herself home maybe. So he'd told her to wait there and he'd pick her up. He had a free afternoon anyway. He'd pick her up in the blue Escort. But when he'd arrived there had been another argument. About what? It could have been anything. What would it take to smash the ice that was Gregor Jack? The original newspaper story? The police finding evidence of his wife's lifestyle? Shame and embarrassment? The thought of further public scrutiny, of losing his precious constituency?

There was enough there to be going on with.

'Okay,' said Lauderdale, 'so we've got the car. Let's see if Jack's at home.' He turned to Rebus. 'You phone, John.'

Rebus phoned. Helen Greig answered.

'Hello, Miss Greig. It's Inspector Rebus.'

'He's not here,' she blurted out. 'I haven't seen him all day, or yesterday come to that.'

'But he's not in London?'

'We don't know where he is. He was with you yesterday morning, wasn't he?'

'He came into the station, yes.'

'Ian's going up the wall.'

'What about the Saab?'

'It's not here either. Hold on . . .' She placed her hand over the mouthpiece, but not very effectively. 'It's that Inspector Rebus,' he heard her say. Then a frantic hiss: 'Don't tell him anything!' And Helen again: 'Too late, Ian.' Followed by a sort of snarl. She removed her hand.

'Miss Greig,' said Rebus, 'how has Gregor seemed?'

261

'Same as you might expect of a man whose wife's been murdered.'

'And how's that?'

'Depressed. He's been sitting around in the living room, just staring into space, not saying much. Like he was thinking. Funny, the only time I got a conversation out of him was when he asked me about last year's holiday.'

'The one you went on with your mum?'

'Yes.'

'Remind me, where did you go again?'

'Down the coast,' she said. 'Eyemouth, round there.'

Yes, of course. Jack had uttered the name of the first town that had come to mind. Then he'd pumped Helen for details so he could prop up his rickety story . . .

He put down the receiver.

'Well?' asked Watson.

'His car's gone, and Gregor Jack with it. All that stuff he told us about Eyemouth . . . eye *wash* more like . . . he got it all from his secretary. She went there on holiday last year.'

The room was stuffy, the late afternoon outside preparing itself for thunder. Watson spoke first.

'What a mess.'

'Yes,' said Lauderdale.

Holmes nodded. He was a relieved man; more than that, inwardly he was rejoicing: the hire car had turned out to be fact. He'd proved his worth.

'What now?'

'I'm just thinking,' said Rebus, 'about that lay-by. Liz Jack has an argument with Steele. She tells him she's going back to her husband. Steele buggers off. What's the next he hears of her?'

'That she's dead,' answered Holmes.

Rebus nodded. Throwing all those books around the shop in his grief and his anger . . . 'Not only dead, but murdered. And the *last* he saw of her, she was waiting for Gregor.'

'So,' said Watson, 'he must know Jack did it? Is that what you're suggesting?'

'You think,' Lauderdale said, 'Steele's run off to *protect* Gregor Jack?'

'I don't think anything of the sort,' said Rebus. 'But *if* Gregor Jack is the murderer, then Ronald Steele has known for some time that he is. Why hasn't he done anything? Think about it: how could he come to the police? He was in way too deep himself. It would mean explaining everything, and explaining it would make him if anything a bigger suspect than Gregor Jack himself!'

'So what *would* he do?'

Rebus shrugged. 'He might try persuading Jack to come forward.'

'But that would mean admitting to Jack that – '

'Exactly, that *he* was Elizabeth Jack's lover. What would you do in Jack's position?'

Holmes dared to supply the answer. 'I'd kill him. I'd kill Ronald Steele.'

Rebus sat all that evening in Patience's living room, an arm around her as they both watched a video. A romantic comedy; only there wasn't much romance and precious little comedy. You knew from reel one that the secretary would go off with the bucktoothed student and not with her bloodsucking boss. But you kept on watching anyway. Not that he was taking much of it in. He was thinking about Gregor Jack, about the person he'd seemed to be and the person he really was. You peeled away layer after layer, stripped the man to the bone and beyond ... and never found the truth. Strip Jack Naked: a card game, also known as Beggar my Neighbour. Patience was a card game, too. He stroked her neck, her hair, her forehead.

'That's nice.'

Patience was a game easily won.

The film rolled past him. Another foil had entered the picture, a big-hearted con man. Rebus had yet to meet a con man in real life who was anything but the most predatory shark. What was the phrase? – they'd steal your false teeth and drink the water out of the glass. Well, maybe *this* con man was in with a chance. The secretary was interested, but she was loyal to her boss too, and *he* was doing everything short of whipping his sausage out and slapping it on her desk . . .

'A penny for them.'

'They're not worth it, Patience.' They'd find Steele, they'd find Jack. Why couldn't he relax? He kept thinking of a set of clothes and a note, left on a beach. Stonehouse. Lucan had done it, hadn't he, disappeared without trace? It wasn't easy, but all the same . . .

The next thing he knew, Patience was shaking him by the shoulder.

'Wake up, John. Time for bed.'

He'd been asleep for an hour. 'The con man or the student?' he asked.

'Neither,' she said. 'The boss changed his ways and gave her a partnership in the firm. Now come on, partner . . .' She held her hands out to help him up on to his feet. 'After all, tomorrow *is* another day . . .'

Another day, another dolour. Thursday. Two weeks since they'd found Elizabeth Jack's body. Now all they could do was wait . . . and hope no more bodies turned up. Rebus picked up his office phone. It was Lauderdale.

'The Chief Super's bitten the bullet,' he told Rebus. 'We're holding a press conference, putting out wanteds on both of them, Steele and Jack.'

'Does Sir Hugh know yet?'

'I wouldn't want to be the one who tells him. He marches in here with his son-in-law, not knowing the bugger killed his daughter? No, I wouldn't want to be the one who tells him.'

'Am I supposed to be there?'

'Of course, and bring Holmes, too. After all, *he's* the one who spotted the car . . .'

The line went dead. Rebus stared at the receiver. Alsatian bites man after all . . .

*

Spotted it *and* told Nell about it all last night. Repeating the story, adding missed details, hardly able to sit down. Until she'd screeched at him to stop or else she'd go off her head. That calmed him down a little, but not much.

'You see, Nell, if they'd told me earlier, if they'd let me in on the whole story of the car colours, of *why* they were needed, well, we'd have nailed him all the sooner, wouldn't we? I don't want to, but really I blame John. It was him who . . .'

'I thought you said it was Lauderdale who gave you the job in the first place?'

'Yes, true, but even so John should have – '

'Shut up! For God's sake, just shut up!'

'Mind you, you're right, Laud – '

'*Shut up!*'

He shut up.

And now here he was at the press conference, and there was Inspector Gill Templer, who had such a rapport with the press, handing out sheets of paper – the official release – and generally making sure that everyone knew what was going on. And Rebus, of course, looking the same as ever. Which was to say, tired and suspicious. Watson and Lauderdale hadn't made their entrance yet, but would do so soon.

'Well, Brian,' said Rebus quietly, 'reckon they'll promote you to Inspector for this?'

'No.'

'What then? You look like a kid who's about to get the school prize.'

'Come on, be fair. We all know you did most of the work.'

'Yes, but *you* stopped me haring after the wrong man.'

'So?'

'So now I owe you a favour.' Rebus grinned. 'I *hate* owing favours.'

'Ladies and gentlemen,' came Gill Templer's voice, 'if you'll find yourselves a seat we can start . . .'

A moment later Watson and Lauderdale entered the room. Watson was first to speak.

'I think you all know why we've called this conference.' He

paused. 'We're looking for two men we think may be able to help us with a certain inquiry, a murder inquiry. The names are Ronald Adam Steele and Gregor Gordon Jack . . .'

The local evening paper had it in by its lunchtime edition. The radio stations were broadcasting the names in their hourly news slots. The early evening TV news carried the story. The usual questions were being asked, to which the usual 'no comment's were being appended. But the phone call itself came only at half past six. The call was from Dr Frank Forster.

'I'd have known sooner, Inspector, only we don't like to let the patients listen to the news. It just upsets them. It's only when I was getting ready to go home that I turned on the radio in my office . . .'

Rebus was tired. Rebus was terribly, terribly tired. 'What is it, Dr Forster?'

'It's your man Jack, Gregor Jack. He was here this afternoon. He was visiting Andrew Macmillan.'

13
Hot-Head

It was nine that evening when Rebus reached Duthil Hospital. Andrew Macmillan was sitting in Forster's office, arms folded, waiting.

'Hello again,' he said.

'Hello, Mr Macmillan.'

There were five of them: two 'nurses', Dr Forster, Macmillan and Rebus. The nurses stood behind Macmillan's chair, their bodies less than two inches from his.

'We've sedated him,' Forster had explained to Rebus. 'He may not be as talkative as usual, but he should stay calm. I heard about what happened last time . . .'

'Nothing happened last time, Dr Forster. He just wanted to have a normal conversation. What's wrong with that?'

Macmillan looked on the verge of sleep. His eyes were heavy-lidded, his smile fixed. He unfolded his arms and rested the hands delicately on his knees, reminding Rebus at that moment of Mrs Corbie . . .

'Inspector Rebus wants to ask you about Mr Jack,' explained Forster.

'That's right,' said Rebus, resting against the edge of the desk. There was a chair for him, but he was stiff after the drive. 'I was wondering why he visited. It's unusual after all, isn't it?'

'It's a first,' corrected Macmillan. 'They should put up a plaque. When I saw him come in, I thought he must be here to open an extension or something. But no, he just walked right up to me . . .' His hands were moving now, carving air, his eyes held by the movements they made. 'Walked right up to *me*, and he said . . . he said, "Hello, Mack." Just like that. Like we'd seen one another the day before, like we saw one another *every* day.'

'What did you talk about?'

'Old friends. Yes, old friends . . . old friend*ships*. We'd always be friends, he told me. We couldn't *not* be friends. We went back *all the way*. Yes, all the way back . . . All of us. Suey and Gowk, Beggar and me, Bilbo, Tampon, Sexton Blake . . . Friends are important, that's what he said. I told him about Gowk, about how she visited sometimes . . . about the money she gives this place . . . He didn't know about any of that. He was interested. He works too hard though, you can see that. He doesn't look healthy any more. Not enough sunlight. Have you ever seen the House of Commons? Hardly any windows. They work away in there like moles . . .'

'Did he say anything else?'

'I asked him why he never answered my letters. Do you know what he said? He said he *never even received them!* He said he'd take it up with the post office, but I know who it is.' He turned to Forster. 'It's you, Dr Forster. You're not letting out any of my mail. You're steaming off the stamps and using them for yourself! Well, be warned, Gregor Jack MP knows all about it now. Something'll be done now.' He remembered something and turned quickly to Rebus. 'Did you touch the earth for me?'

Rebus nodded. 'I touched the earth for you.'

Macmillan nodded too, satisfied. 'How did it feel, Inspector?'

'It felt fine. Funny, it's something I've always taken for granted – '

'Never take *anything* for granted, Inspector,' said Macmillan. He was calming a little. All the same, you could see him fighting against the soporifics in his bloodstream, fighting for the right to get angry, to get . . . to get mad. 'I asked him about Liz,' he said. 'He told me she's the same as ever. But I didn't believe *that*. I'm sure their marriage is in trouble. In-com-pat-ible. My wife and I were just the same . . .' His voice trailed off. He swallowed, laid his hands flat against his knees again and studied them. 'Liz was never one of The Pack. He should have married Gowk, only Kinnoul got to her first.' He looked up. 'Now *there's* a man who needs treatment. If Gowk knew what she was about, she'd have him see a psychiatrist. All those roles he's played . . . bound to have an effect, aren't they? I'll tell Gowk next time I see her. I haven't seen her for a while . . .'

Rebus shifted his weight a little. 'Did Beggar say anything else, Mack? Anything about where he was headed or why he was here?'

Macmillan shook his head. Then he sniggered. 'Headed, did you say? *Headed?*' He chuckled to himself for a few moments, then stopped as abruptly as he'd started. 'He just wanted to let me know we were friends.' He laughed quietly. 'As if I needed reminding. And one other thing. Guess what he wanted to know? Guess what he asked? After all these years . . .'

'What?'

'He wanted to know what I'd done with her head.'

Rebus swallowed. Forster was licking his lips. 'And what did you tell him, Mack?'

'I told him the truth. I told him I couldn't remember.' He brought the palms of his hands together as if in prayer and touched the fingertips to his lips. Then he closed his eyes. The eyes were still closed when he spoke. 'Is it true about Suey?'

'What about him, Mack?'

'That he's emigrated, that he might not be coming back?'

'Is that what Beggar told you?'

Macmillan nodded, opening his eyes to gaze at Rebus. 'He said Suey might not be coming back . . .'

The nurses had taken Macmillan back to his ward, and Forster was putting on his coat, getting ready to lock up and see Rebus out to the car park, when the telephone rang.

'At this time of night?'

'It might be for me,' said Rebus. He picked up the receiver. 'Hello?'

It was DS Knox from Dufftown. 'Inspector Rebus? I did as you said and had someone stake out Deer Lodge.'

'And?'

'A white Saab drove in through the gateway not ten minutes ago.'

There were two cars parked by the side of the road. One of them was blocking the entrance to Deer Lodge's long driveway. Rebus got out of his own car. DS Knox introduced him to Detective Constable Wright and Constable Moffat.

'We've already met,' Rebus said, shaking Moffat's hand.

'Oh yes,' said Knox. 'How could I forget, you've been keeping us so busy? So, what do you think, sir?'

Rebus thought it was cold. Cold and wet. It wasn't raining now, but any minute it might be on again. 'You've called for reinforcements?'

Knox nodded. 'As many as can be mustered.'

'Well, we could wait it out till they arrive.'

'Yes?'

Rebus was sizing Knox up. He didn't seem the kind of man who enjoyed waiting. 'Or,' he said, 'we could go in, three of us, one standing guard on the gate. After all, he's either got a corpse or a hostage in there. If Steele's alive, the sooner we go in, the better chance he's got.'

'So what are we waiting for?'

Rebus looked to DC Wright and Constable Moffat, who nodded approval of the plan.

'It's a long walk up to the house, mind,' Knox was saying.

'But if we take a car, he's bound to hear it.'

'We can take one up so far and walk the rest,' suggested Moffat. 'That way the exit road's good and blocked. I wouldn't fancy wandering up that bloody road in the dark only to have him come racing towards me in that car of his.'

'Okay, agreed, we'll take a car.' Rebus turned to DC Wright. 'You stay on the gate, son. Moffat here knows the layout of the house.' Wright looked snubbed, but Moffat perked up at the news. 'Right,' said Rebus, 'let's go.'

*

They took Knox's car, leaving Moffat's parked across the entrance. Knox had taken one look at Rebus's heap and then shaken his head.

'Best take mine, eh?'

He drove slowly, Rebus in the front beside him, Moffat in the back. The car had a nice quiet engine, but all the same ... all around was silence. Any noise would travel. Rebus actually began to pray for a sudden storm, thunder and rain, for anything that would give them sound-cover.

'I enjoyed that book,' said Moffat, his head just behind Rebus's.

'What book?'

'*Fish Out of Water.*'

'Christ, I'd forgotten all about it.'

'Cracking story,' said Moffat.

'How much further?' asked Knox. 'I can't remember.'

'There's a bend to the left then another to the right,' said Moffat. 'We better stop after the second one. It's only another couple of hundred yards.'

They parked, opening the doors and leaving them open. Knox produced two large rubber torches from the glove compartment. 'I was a cub scout,' he explained. 'Be prepared and all that.' He handed one torch to Rebus and kept the other. 'Moffat here eats his carrots, he doesn't need one. Right, what's the plan now?'

'Let's see how things look at the house, then I'll tell you.'

'Fair enough.'

They set off in a line. After about fifty yards, Rebus turned off his torch. It was no longer necessary: all the lights in and around the lodge seemed to be burning. They stopped just before the clearing, peering through what cover there was. The Saab was parked outside the front door. Its boot was open. Rebus turned to Moffat.

'Remember, there's a back door? Circle around and cover it.'

'Right.' The constable moved off the road and into the forest, disappearing from sight.

271

'Meantime, let's check the car first, then take a look through the windows.'

Knox nodded. They left their cover and crept forwards. The boot itself was empty. Nothing on the car's back seat either. Lights were on in the living room and the front bedroom, but there was no sign of anyone. Knox pointed with his torch towards the door. He tried the handle. The door opened a crack. He pushed it a little further. The hall was empty. They waited a moment, listening. There was a sudden eruption of noise, drums and guitar chords. Knox jumped back. Rebus rested a calming hand on his shoulder, then retreated to look again through the living room window. The stereo. He could see its LEDs pulsing. The cassette player, probably on automatic replay. A tape had been winding back while they'd approached the house. Now it was playing.

Early Stones. 'Paint It Black'. Rebus nodded. 'He's in there,' he said to himself. *My secret vice, Inspector.* One of many. At any rate, it meant he might not have heard the car's approach, and now the music was on again he might not even hear them entering the house.

So they entered. Moffat was covering the kitchen, so Rebus headed directly upstairs, Knox behind him. There was fine white powder on the wooden banister, leftovers from the dusting the house had been given by forensics. Up the stairs . . . and on to the landing. What was that smell? *What was that smell?*

'Petrol,' whispered Knox.

Yes, petrol. The bedroom door was closed. The music seemed louder up here than downstairs. Thump-thump-thump of drum and bass. Clashing guitar and sitar. And those cheesegrater vocals.

Petrol.

Rebus leaned back and kicked in the door. It swung open and stayed open. Rebus took in the scene. Gregor Jack standing there, and against the wall a bound and gagged figure, its face puffy, forehead bloody. Ronald Steele. Gagged? No, not exactly a gag. Scraps of paper seemed to fill his mouth, scraps torn from the Sunday papers on the bed, all the stories which had started with his plotting. Well, Jack had made him eat his words.

Petrol.

The can lay empty on its side. The room was reeking. Steele looked to have been drenched in the stuff, or was it just sweat? And Gregor Jack standing there, his face at first full of mischief, but then turning, turning, softening, softening into shame. Shame and guilt. Guilt at being caught.

All of this Rebus took in in a second. But it took less time than that for Jack to strike the match and drop it.

The carpet caught immediately, and then Jack was flying forwards, knocking Rebus off balance, powering past Knox, heading for the stairs. The flames were moving too fast. Too fast to do anything. Rebus grabbed Steele by his feet and started to drag him towards the door. Dragging him of necessity *through* the fire itself. If Steele *was* soaked in petrol . . . Well, no time to think about that. But it was sweat, that was all. The fire licked at him, but it didn't suddenly engulf the body.

Out into the hallway. Knox was already pounding down the stairs, following Jack. The bedroom was an inferno now, the bed like a kind of pyre in the centre of it. Rebus went back and glanced in. The mounted cow's head above the bed had caught and was crackling. He grabbed the door handle and dragged the door shut, thanking God he hadn't kicked it off its hinges in the first place . . .

It was a struggle, but he managed to haul Steele to his feet. Blood was caked on the face, and one eye had swollen shut. The other eye had tears in it. Paper was spilling from his mouth as he tried to speak. Rebus made a perfunctory attempt at loosening the knots. It was baler twine, and tight as tight could be. Christ, his head was hurting. He couldn't think why. He hefted the taller man on to his shoulder and started down the stairs.

At some point, Steele disgorged the paper from his mouth. His first words were: 'Your hair's on fire!'

So it was, at the nape of the neck. Rebus patted his head with his free hand. The back of his head was crispy, like

273

strands of breakfast cereal. And something else: it was hurting like blazes.

They were at the bottom of the stairs now. Rebus dumped Steele on to the floor then straightened up. There was a tidal sound in his ears, and his eyes fogged over for a moment. His heart was thumping in sympathy with the rock music. 'I'll get a knife from the kitchen,' he said. Entering the kitchen, he saw that the back door was wide open. There were noises from outside, shouts, but indistinct. Then a figure stumbled into view. It was Moffat. He was holding both hands to his nose, covering the nose like a protective mask. Blood was pouring down his wrists and chin. He lifted the mask away to speak.

'The bastard butted me!' Flecks of blood flew from his mouth and his nostrils. 'Butted me!' You could tell he thought it wasn't fair play.

'You'll live,' said Rebus.

'The sergeant's gone after him.'

Rebus pointed to the hall behind him. 'Steele's in there. Find a knife and cut him loose, then both of you get out.' He pushed past Moffat and out of the back door. Light from the kitchen flooded the immediate scene, but beyond that was darkness. He'd dropped his torch up in the bedroom, and now cursed the fact. Then, eyes adjusting to the changing light, he ran across the small clearing and into the forest beyond.

More haste, less speed. He moved carefully past trunks and bushes and saplings. Briars tugged at him, but they were a minor nuisance. His main worry was that he didn't know where he was heading. The ground was sloping upwards, that much he could tell. As long as he kept moving upwards with it, he wouldn't be chasing his own tail. His foot caught on something and he fell against a tree. The breath left him. His shirt was wringing wet, his eyes stinging from a mixture of recent smoke and present sweat. He paused. He listened.

'Jack! Don't be stupid! Jack!'

It was Knox. Up ahead. A good distance ahead, but not impossible. Rebus took a deep breath and started walking.

Miraculously, he came out of the forest and into a larger clearing. The slope seemed steeper here, the ground sprawling with bracken and gorse and other low spiky plants. He caught a sudden flash of light: Knox's torch. Way over to the right of him and slightly uphill. Rebus began jogging, lifting his legs high to avoid the worst of the undergrowth. All the same, something kept tearing at his trouser-legs and his ankles. Stinging and scratching. Then there were patches of short grass, areas where quicker progress was possible – or would have been possible if he'd been fitter and younger. Ahead of him, the torch moved in a circle. The meaning was clear: Knox had lost his quarry. Instead of continuing to head for the beam of light, Rebus swung away from it. If it were possible for only two men to fan out, then that's what Rebus was trying to ensure they did, widening the arc of the search.

He came to the top of the rise, and the ground levelled out. He got the feeling that in daytime it would make a bleak picture. There was nothing here but stunted wilderness, hardly fit for the hardiest sheep. Way ahead a shadow rose into the sky, some hill-range or other. The wind, which had dried his shirt but chilled him to the marrow, now dropped. Jesus, his head was hurting. Like sunburn but a hundred times worse. He stared up at the sky. The outlines of the clouds were visible. The weather was clearing. A sound had replaced the whistling of the wind in his ears.

The sound of running water.

It grew louder as he moved forwards. He had lost Knox's torchlight now, and was conscious of being alone; conscious, too, that if he strayed too far, he might not find his way back. A route wrongly taken could leave him heading towards nothing but hill and forest. He glanced back. The line of trees was still just about visible, though the house lights beyond were not.

'Jack! Jack!' Knox's voice seemed miles away. Rebus decided that he would skirt round towards it. If Gregor Jack was out there, let him freeze to death. The rescue services would find him tomorrow . . .

The running water was much closer now, and the ground beneath his feet was becoming rockier, the vegetation sparse. The water was somewhere below him. He stopped again. The shapes and shades in front of him . . . they didn't make sense. It was as if the land were folding in on itself. Just then, a huge chunk of cloud moved away from the moon, the large, nearly full moon. There was light now, and Rebus saw that he was standing not four feet from a sheer drop of five or six yards, a drop into a dark, twisting river. There was a noise to his right. He turned his head towards it. A figure was staggering forwards, bent over nearly double from exhaustion, its arms swinging loose and almost touching the ground. An ape, he thought at first. He looks just like an ape.

Gregor Jack was panting hoarsely, almost moaning from effort. He wasn't watching where he was going; all he knew was that he had to keep moving.

'Gregor.'

The figure wheezed, the head jerking up. It came to a stop. Gregor Jack rose to his full height, arching his head to the sky. He lifted his tired arms and rested his hands on his waist, for all the world like a runner at the end of his race. One hand went instinctively to his hair, tidying it back into place. Then he bent forwards and put his hands on his knees, and the hair flopped forwards again. But his breathing was becoming steadier. Eventually he straightened up again. Rebus saw that he was smiling, showing his perfect teeth. He began shaking his head and chuckling. Rebus had heard the sound before from people who'd lost: lost everything from their freedom to a big bet or a game of five-a-side. They were laughing at circumstance.

Gregor's laughter collapsed into a cough. He slapped at his chest, then looked at Rebus and smiled again.

Then sprang.

Rebus's instinct was to dodge, but Jack was moving away from him. And both of them knew precisely where he was headed. As his foot touched the last inch of earth, he leapt out into the air, jumping feet first. A couple of seconds later came the sound of his body hitting the water. Rebus toed his way to the edge of the rock and looked down, but the cloud was closing in again overhead. The moonlight was lost. There was nothing to see.

Making their way back to Deer Lodge, there was no need for Knox's torch. The flames lit up the surrounding countryside. Glowing ash landed on the trees as they made their way through the woods. Rebus ran his fingers over the back of his head. The skin was stinging. But he got the feeling shock might have set in: the pain wasn't quite so bad as before. His ankles stung too – thistles, probably. He'd run through what had turned out to be a field full of them. There was no one near the house. Moffat and Steele were waiting by Knox's car.

'How good a swimmer is he?' Rebus asked Steele.

'Beggar?' Steele was massaging his untethered arms. 'Can't swim a stroke. We all learned at school, but his mum used to give him a note excusing him.'

'Why?'

Steele shrugged. 'She was scared he'd catch verrucas. How's the head, Inspector?'

'I won't need a haircut for a while.'

'What about Jack?' Moffat asked.

'He won't be needing one either.'

They searched for Gregor Jack's body the following morning. Not that Rebus was there to participate. He was in hospital and feeling dirty and unshaven – except for his head.

'If you have a problem with baldness,' one senior doctor told him, 'you could always wear a toupee till it grows back. Or a hat. Your scalp will be sensitive, too, so try to keep out of the sun.'

'Sun? What sun?'

But there was sun, during his time off work there was plenty of it. He stayed indoors, stayed underground, reading book after book, emerging for brief forays to the Royal Infirmary to have his dressings changed.

'I could do that for you,' Patience had told him.

'Never mix business and pleasure,' was Rebus's enigmatic response. In fact, there was a nurse up at the infirmary who had taken a shine to him, and he to her . . . Ach, it wouldn't go anywhere; it was just a bit of flirting. He wouldn't hurt Patience for the world.

Holmes visited, always with a dozen cans of something gassy. 'Hiya, baldie,' was the perennial greeting, even when the skinhead had become a suedehead, the suedehead longer still.

'What's the news?' asked Rebus.

Apart from the fact that Gregor Jack's body had still not been recovered, the big news was that the Farmer was off the booze after having been 'visited by the Lord' at some revivalist Baptist meeting.

'It's communion wine only from now on,' said Holmes. 'Mind you – ' pointing to Rebus's head, 'for a while there I thought maybe *you* were going to go Buddhist on us.'

'I might yet,' said Rebus. 'I might yet.'

The media clung to the Jack story, clung to the idea that he might still be alive. Rebus wondered about that, too. More, he still wondered why Jack had killed Elizabeth. Ronald Steele could shed no light on the problem. Apparently, Jack had spoken hardly a word to him all the time he'd held him captive . . . Well, that was Steele's story. Whatever *had* been said, it wasn't going any further.

All of which left Rebus with scenarios, with guesswork. He played out the scene time after time in his head – Jack arriving at the lay-by, and arguing with Elizabeth. Maybe she'd told him she wanted a divorce. Maybe the argument was over the brothel story. Or maybe there'd been something else. All Steele would say was that when he'd left her, she'd been waiting for her husband.

'I thought about hanging around and confronting him . . .'

'But?'

Steele shrugged. 'Cowardice. It's not doing something "wrong" that's the problem, Inspector, it's getting caught. Wouldn't you agree?'

'But if you *had* stayed . . .?'

Steele nodded. 'I know. Maybe Liz would have told Gregor to bugger off and have stuck with me instead. Maybe they'd both still be alive.'

If Steele hadn't fled from the lay-by ... *if* Gail Jack hadn't come north in the first place ... What then? Rebus was in no doubt: it would have worked out some other way, not necessarily any less painful a way. Fire and ice and skeletons in the closet. He wished he could have met Elizabeth Jack, just once, even though he had the feeling they wouldn't have got on ...

There was one more news story. It started as another rumour, but the rumour turned out to be a leak, and the leak was followed by notification: Great London Road was to undergo a programme of repair and refurbishment.

Which means, thought Rebus, I move in with Patience. To all intents, he already had.

'You don't have to sell your flat,' she told him. 'You could always rent it.'

'Rent it?'

'To students. Your street's half full of them as it is.' This was true. You saw the migration in the morning, down towards The Meadows carrying their satchels and ring-binders and supermarket carriers; back in the late afternoon (or late night) laden with books and ideas. The notion appealed. If he rented out his flat, he could pay Patience something towards living here with her.

'You're on,' he said.

He was back at work one full day when Great London Road Police Station caught fire. The building was razed to the ground.

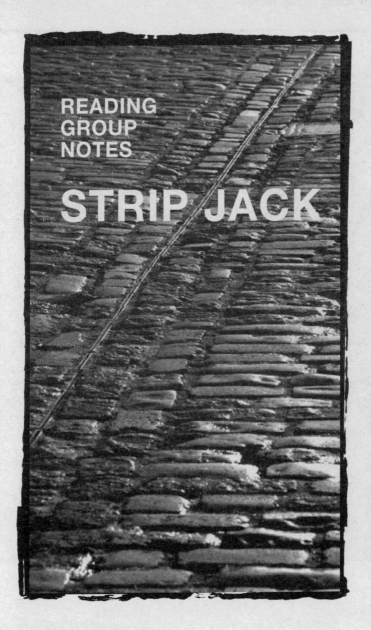

READING
GROUP
NOTES

STRIP JACK

© Rankin

ABOUT IAN RANKIN

Ian Rankin, OBE, writes a huge proportion of all the crime novels sold in the UK and has won numerous prizes, including in 2005 the Crime Writers' Association Diamond Dagger. His work is available in over 30 languages, home sales of his books exceed one million copies a year, and several of the novels based around the character of Detective Inspector Rebus – his name meaning 'enigmatic puzzle' – have been successfully transferred to television.

Introduction to DI John Rebus

The first novels to feature Rebus, a flawed but resolutely humane detective, were not an overnight sensation, and success took time to arrive. But the wait became a period that allowed Ian Rankin to come of age as a writer, and to develop Rebus into a thoroughly believable, flesh-and-blood character straddling both industrial and post-industrial Scotland; a gritty yet perceptive man coping with his own demons. As Rebus struggled to keep his relationship with daughter Sammy alive following his divorce, and to cope with the imprisonment of brother Michael, while all the time trying to strike a blow for morality against a fearsome array of sinners (some justified and some not), readers began to respond in their droves. Fans admired Ian Rankin's re-creation of a picture-postcard Edinburgh with a vicious tooth-and-claw underbelly just a heartbeat away, his believable but at the same time complex plots and, best of all, Rebus as a conflicted man trying always to solve the unsolvable, and to do the right thing.

As the series progressed, Ian Rankin refused to shy away from contentious issues such as corruption in high places, paedophilia and illegal immigration, combining his unique seal of tight plotting with a bleak realism, leavened with brooding humour.

In Rebus the reader is presented with a rich and constantly evolving portrait of a complex and troubled man, irrevocably tinged with the sense of being an outsider and, potentially, unable to escape being a 'justified sinner' himself. Rebus's life is intricately related to his Scottish environs too, enriched by Ian Rankin's attentive depiction of locations, and careful regard to Rebus's favourite music, watering holes and books, as well as his often fraught relationships with colleagues and family. And so, alongside Rebus, the reader is taken on an often painful, sometimes hellish journey to the depths of human nature, always rooted in the minutiae of a very recognisable Scottish life.

The Oxford Bar – Rebus and many of the characters who
appear in the novels are regulars of the Ox – as is Ian Rankin
himself. The pub is now
synonymous with the Rebus
novels to the extent that one of
the regular medical examiners
called in to assist with
investigations is named after
the pub's owner, John Gates.

Edinburgh plays an important role throughout the Rebus
novels; a character itself, as brooding and as volatile as
Rebus. The Edinburgh depicted in the novels is far short of

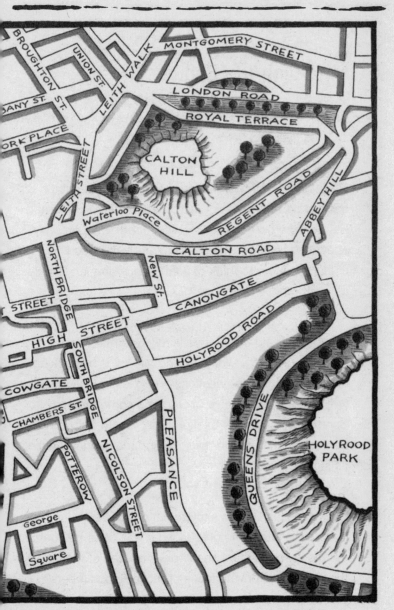

the beautiful city that tourists in their thousands flood to
visit. Hidden behind the historic buildings and elegant
façades is the world that Rebus inhabits.

For general discussion regarding the Rebus series

How does Ian Rankin reveal himself as an author interested in using fiction to 'tell the truths the real world can't'?

———

There are similarities between the lives of the author and his protagonist – for instance, both Ian Rankin and Rebus were born in Fife, lost their mothers at an early age, have children with physical problems – so is it useful therefore to think of John Rebus and Ian Rankin as each other's alter egos?

———

Could it be said that Rebus is trying to make sense in a general way of the world around him, or is he seeking answers to the 'big questions'? And is it relevant therefore that he is a believer in God and comes from a Scottish Presbyterian background? Would Rebus see confession in both the religious and the criminal sense as similar in any way?

———

How does Ian Rankin explore notions of Edinburgh as a character in its own right? In what way does he contrast the glossy public and seedy private faces of the city with the public and private faces of those Rebus meets?

How does Ian Rankin use musical sources – the Elvis references in *The Black Book*, for instance, or the Rolling Stones allusions in *Let It Bleed* – as a means of character development through the series? What does Rebus's own taste in music and books say about him as a person?

———

What do you think about Rebus as a character? If you have read several or more novels from the series, discuss how his character is developed.

———

If Rebus has a problem with notions of 'pecking order' and the idea of authority generally, what does it say about him that he chose careers in hierarchical institutions such as the Army and then the police?

———

How does Rebus relate to women: as lovers, flirtations, family members and colleagues?

———

Do the flashes of gallows humour as often shown by the pathologists but sometimes also in Rebus's own comments increase or dissipate narrative tension? Does Rebus use black comedy for the same reasons the pathologists do?

———

Do Rebus's personal vulnerabilities make him understanding of the frailties of others?

How does the characterisation of Rebus compare to other
long-standing popular detectives from British authors
such as Holmes, Poirot, Morse or Dalgleish? And are
there more similarities or differences between them?

STRIP JACK

Operation Creeper doesn't quite pan out as planned. When Rebus and his colleagues raid the brothel that's masquerading as a respectable Georgian house in Edinburgh's New Town, inside they find Gregor Jack, a popular Independent MP, and outside an unexpected and overexcited pack of national newspaper journalists baying for blood. Rebus, already conflicted about the raid, feels sorry for the charismatic Jack (who hasn't given in to temptation, after all? And, anyway, aren't there worse forms of prostitution than whoring?). But when Jack's wife Elizabeth disappears only to turn up soggy and very dead, Rebus has to confront the possibility that perhaps he's been taken in once again by a winsome public image and a firm handshake, not to mention a mutual love of whisky.

Despite the efforts of the new Chief Inspector to distract him with what appears to be a spurious case of theft, and the deepening of his own personal relationship with Dr Patience Aitken, Rebus believes that to get to the root of the scandal that is unfurling in the constituency of North and South Esk, he must endeavour to discover just who it is that wants to humiliate Jack and, more importantly, why.

But the relationships between Liz Jack, part of the influential Ferrie family, her cronies and her husband aren't quite as anticipated, and soon Rebus discovers that Liz and her posh pals – the Pack, the 'spokes on a bicycle wheel' – enjoyed life in a very fast lane, one where old allegiances can count for more than the paper ties of a marriage licence.

In one of Ian Rankin's most carefully plotted novels to date, an intricate story unfolds where chance meetings, faded dreams, broken alibis, secret liaisons and embarrassing moments from the past combine to lead back inevitably to unbreakable school ties, a language of friendship that Rebus must work hard to grasp.

Discussion points for *Strip Jack*

Ian Rankin calls *Strip Jack* one of his most Scottish works – what is the evidence for this?

Ian Rankin says that with *Strip Jack* his 'long apprentice-ship' as a writer of detective fiction was nearing its end. Is this an overly harsh comment?

'An Establishment establishment' is how Rebus describes the brothel. Discuss the implications of this.

How many different types of politics are dealt with in *Strip Jack*?

How does Ian Rankin subvert a well-known quotation from Jane Austen?

Is Chief Inspector Lauderdale really oblivious to Rebus's attempts at irony over the Case of the Lifted Literature, or is it more the case that Lauderdale is winding Rebus up? In any event, who comes out on top?

Consider the way in which Ian Rankin weaves together the serious murder case with the trivial-seeming book-theft case.

What does Rebus's evening with Brian Holmes and Nell say about his own attitudes to socialising?

Bearing in mind Rebus's sometimes fraught relationship with brother Michael, does he identify with Gregor's response to his own embarrassingly behaved sibling? How sympathetic is Rebus to Gregor's desire to distance himself from his past?

Rebus doesn't seem to have kept in touch with many of his old friends; is this why he finds the bonds and the motivations that govern this group of tightly knit friends to be simultaneously perplexing and fascinating?

There's more forensic evidence presented in *Strip Jack* than in previous Rebus books; how does Ian Rankin approach this?

Ian Rankin's use of Scottish slang is taken to a new level. Does this cause a problem for readers unacquainted with the idiom?

Is it necessity or merely symbolic that *Strip Jack* ends with a fire that burns down the fictitious Great London Road Police Station?

All Orion/Phoenix titles are available at your local bookshop or from the following address:

Mail Order Department
Littlehampton Book Services
FREEPOST BR535
Worthing, West Sussex, BN13 3BR
telephone 01903 828503, *facsimile* 01903 828802
e-mail MailOrders@lbsltd.co.uk
(Please ensure that you include full postal address details)

Payment can be made either by credit/debit card (Visa, Mastercard, Access and Switch accepted) or by sending a £ Sterling cheque or postal order made payable to *Littlehampton Book Services*.
DO NOT SEND CASH OR CURRENCY

Please add the following to cover postage and packing

UK and BFPO:
£1.50 for the first book, and 50p for each additional book to a maximum of £3.50

Overseas and Eire:
£2.50 for the first book plus £1.00 for the second book and 50p for each additional book ordered

---

BLOCK CAPITALS PLEASE

name of cardholder ....

address of cardholder ....

....

postcode ....

delivery address
(if different from cardholder)

....

....

postcode ....

☐ I enclose my remittance for £.......................................

☐ please debit my Mastercard/Visa/Access/Switch (delete as appropriate)

card number ☐☐☐☐☐☐☐☐☐☐☐☐☐☐☐☐☐☐

expiry date ☐☐☐☐   Switch issue no. ☐☐

signature ....

prices and availability are subject to change without notice